This story is a work of fiction inspired by a true event. Apart from historical fact, the names, characters and incidents portrayed in it, are the work of the author's imagination.

SAMMY

D1826223

First edition. 2019.

Copyright © 2019 Vince Gledhill.

Cover photograph: Bolton Town Hall by Vince Gledhill

Ebook Edition © February 2019 ISBN: 9781386018933
Print Edition © March 2019 ISBN: 9781090387080

CONTENTS

NIGHT DEMONS

SAMMY Kiteland was 14 when he decided he should kill his father. It would be a kindness, he told himself.

The old man suffered such terrible torments from the night demons, and there was no other way to defeat them. At least, none that the boy could think of.

But how to do it? That was the question.

Sammy trawled his memory for a solution; eventually, it took him back four years to an autumn day in 1904.

He had just booted an inflated pig's bladder down the back-lane outside his home in the Lancashire village of Darcy Lever, and was about to score the winning goal in this one-man match, when a wavering voice called his name.

Old Gladys Thompson leaned heavily on her backyard gate looking through tear-filled eyes at the boy with the bladder ball.

"Sammy, can you help me, please?" she said, dabbing wet cheeks with a damp handkerchief.

The boy belted the bladder into his own backyard before crossing the lane to stand in front of the old lady.

Sammy had never seen Mrs Thompson looking so upset. He was far more used to seeing her smiley face; the one she wore when she handed him some of the crunchy cinder toffee she usually made on Wednesday afternoons.

"Are you all right, Mrs Thompson? What's the matter? Why are you crying?"

The old woman took a deep breath, held it, then let the words tumble out.

"It's Judy. She's in so much pain. She needs to go to Billy Ackroyd, at number five. I want her to be put out of her misery, but I just can't do it. Would you take her for me?"

Sammy peered over Mrs Thompson's gate and saw a miserable mongrel sprawled at her feet. A frayed piece of washing line was looped around the dog's neck and the old lady bent stiffly to pick up the other end.

"She's sixteen, which is a really big age for a dog and she's had enough. She has lumps and sores all over and cries all the time. I can't abide hearing her suffer so much any longer. Please take her to Billy. It would be a kindness to me and to her."

She handed her end of the washing line to Sammy and shuffled back across the yard into her scullery. Once inside, she slammed the door shut without looking back.

Billy Ackroyd was the street's shoe man. Not a cordwainer, because he didn't make new shoes, and not a cobbler, because he couldn't make fancy alterations or complicated repairs. He could shove a shoe, or a clog, onto his cast-iron last and hammer in hobnails, or a set of Blakey segs, but that was the limit of this man's footwear skills.

Sammy could hear the sound of Mr Ackroyd's thin-shafted hammer as he approached number five. Judy followed him, whimpering pathetically with each painful step.

The yard gate swung open when Sammy tentatively pushed at it. He saw Mr Ackroyd in the middle of his backyard, sitting on a low stool. On the ground in front of him was a three-legged last with a work boot perched upside down on the largest of the legs. He seemed unaware of Sammy as he hammered curving lines of hobnails into the work boot's thick leather sole.

Sammy was fascinated by the speed and rhythm of Mr Ackroyd as he worked. In one smooth movement a nail was plucked from pursed lips, positioned on the sole and whacked home with a single strike.

Sammy approached him, stopped, and waited to be noticed. Judy gratefully lay down beside the last.

Mr Ackroyd's hammer froze mid-stroke and his grey eyes took in the boy with the mangy mutt at a glance. He did not speak.

"Mrs Thompson wants to know if you can put her dog out of its misery," Sammy told him.

He stared into Mr Ackroyd's pallid eyes, waiting for an answer. But none came. Instead, the shoe man's attention turned back to his last and Sammy heard *tap, tap, tap.*

Sammy's gaze never left the man's face as he waited for a response, but no response came, just *tap, tap, tap.*

Then, as two more nails were plucked from the shoeman's lips his grey eyes lifted from the last and stared over Sammy's right shoulder.

Sammy turned and saw that Mr Ackroyd was staring at his open yard gate. Thinking that meant the answer was "No" and he was being told to leave, Sammy turned towards the gate.

Tap, tap, pop.

Sammy tugged at the washing line, for Judy to get up and follow him. But the dog didn't move. Sammy looked back at the prone animal and saw a neat, hammer-sized hole in her skull. A tiny ring of blood gathered around it.

Sammy held onto the washing line, not sure what to do next. Should he drag the dead dog back to Mrs Thompson so that she could see he had done as she asked? He was uncertain and felt shaken as he looked at the reddened ball end of the hammer.

"Leave it be, lad," said Mr Ackroyd. "I'll sort out the rest with her at number ten."

Sammy dropped his end of the washing line and walked back into the street. From the yard behind him he could once again hear *tap, tap, tap.*

That same sound haunted him as he twitched and muttered in troubled sleep during the week that had followed.

But he was not the only one in his house to have bad dreams. Night demons were regular visitors to his home, and it was usually Sammy's father that the terrors came to torment.

Things had been different when Sammy was small. His memories of that time were of endless, hot summer days spent helping Dad dig in his allotment garden.

For a long time, young Sammy had been sure that gardening must be a really fun thing to do, because Dad laughed so much while he was doing it.

He laughed as he told Sammy that potatoes had eyes and they would "see" him through the winter. He also told his young son that every potato could be eaten twice- and he wasn't joking about that.

"Just cut off a potato peeling with the 'eyes' on it and

plant that in the ground," he said. "That way you can eat the rest of the potato and still get another one when the peeling in the ground grows into a new plant."

"Where's the eye, Dad?" young Sammy wanted to know.

His father pointed a grubby finger at a tiny, white shoot on the potato skin and said: "It's that bit there, Son." His wide walrus moustache twitched upwards as he grinned.

By the time Sammy was fourteen he could barely remember what that grin looked like. It had gone to Africa with his father, but he didn't bring it back. Sometimes, Sammy thought his father hadn't come back either, at least, not his real father. The man who returned, did look like his Dad, although he was much browner than Sammy remembered. He was also much more miserable.

Then one day the brown and miserable Dad threw a handful of shiny medals attached to coloured ribbons onto his allotment bonfire. Some papers and a photograph followed them. As the picture curled up in the flames Sammy just had time to see his father's face on it. He was standing in a line with other grim-faced men. All of them wore army uniforms.

Smoke from the bonfire must have gotten into the old man's eyes, because they were wet and bloodshot.

Sammy saw those eyes fill with water again one day when he came home from school after talking to other boys whose fathers had been soldiers.

When Sammy asked, "Did you fight in the Boer War, Dad?" he saw tears flood the old man's eyes. He blinked hard, but gave no reply. Young Sammy never did get an answer to that or any other question about the years his father had been in Africa.

What he did hear was Dad shouting at the demons who tormented him after he had gone to sleep.

Then there was the day at the allotment when some green wood burning on a rubbish fire cracked as loud as a rifle shot and Sammy heard a scream. Well, it wasn't really a scream; it was more of a squeal. The sort of squeal an allotment pig makes when the butchering knife is pulled across its throat.

Sammy spun to look in the direction of the squeal and saw his father spreadeagled among his cabbages, wild-eyed.

"Dad? *Dad!*" he shouted.

"Cover, take cover," his father yelled back. "Get down. Get down, Son."

After a few moments the wild look in his eyes dissolved and the old man shook his head as if to clear something from it.

"Sorry, Son, sorry. I had a bad turn there, I think it might have been a bit of my old trouble. You know, jungle fever, or something."

Sammy wondered about this "jungle fever" and whether it was brought on by the "jungle juice" his dad liked to drink. The two did seem to go together.

On some nights his father came home shouting and swearing, as if he wasn't Dad anymore, and Sammy's mother used to say: "He's been on the jungle juice again."

Sammy's father worked as a carter in those days. He had been a coal miner, but around the time he burned his army stuff on the bonfire he also refused to go back underground, saying he felt buried alive.

At night, in those unhappy times, Sammy and his big

sister, Cilla, would hold on to each other in the darkness of the bedroom that they shared, while the grown-ups shouted at each other downstairs.

It always seemed to be the same argument - how little he earned, how much she spent, food on the table, clothes for the kids, his drinking, her nagging. It seemed to go on forever, or at least until Sammy and Cilla fell asleep still holding each other tight.

Then, there came a time when Dad wasn't around anymore.

"Has he joined the army again?" Sammy asked his mother.

"No," she replied. "He can't be here anymore. He's alright; he just has to live away from us for a bit."

But Sammy's dad never came back to that family home.

The next time that Sammy saw his father was at the allotment gardens. The old man was in the shed he had made many years ago out of old doors and window frames.

He looked up sharply when Sammy pulled open the shed door, then his eyes softened when he saw who it was.

"Hello Son."

Sammy noticed that blankets and a sheet lay in a corner. They were folded and stacked in a neat pile. A small primus stove stood on top of a wooden crate, along with a metal pan and a tin cup.

"Is this where you live now, Dad?" Sammy asked, puzzled.

"Just temporary, Son. I need to get a bit of money together and then I'll rent somewhere proper. I'll be fine, you'll see."

"Can't you come back home?"

"No Son, I can't do that. I've got to stay away, but you can come here and see me whenever you like."

Three months later, on Sammy's 14th birthday, his mother's exhausted heart stopped beating, and she gave up her hold on life.

Sammy and Cilla had to move into the shabby lodgings their dad had managed to find in a cellar at Clap Row, and that became their new family home for the next two years.

During the move to his new home Sammy found a tiny brass box among his mother's few possessions. It had a handle on the lid and a hinged hasp that was meant to be secured with a tiny padlock. But the box had no padlock, so he opened it.

Inside, he saw some buttons, needles and a spool of black thread. There was also a folded newspaper cutting. When he unfolded the cutting Sammy saw that it was from the Bolton Evening News of three months ago.

The headline to the article was *Husband's drinking habits*, and the story that followed it said:

> *Mr Horridge appeared for*
> *Hannah Kiteland, of May Street,*
> *Darcy Lever, who summoned her*
> *husband, Harold Kiteland, on*
> *the grounds that he is a habitual*
> *drunkard.*
>
> *Complainant, who had been*
> *married 18 years, stated that her*
> *husband had gone on the spree for*
> *several weeks this year and neg-*
> *lected his work.*

*She told the Bench that, except
for a few weeks sickness, he could
have followed his employment.*

*When he was intoxicated he
had to be followed up the stairs
when he went to bed for fear he
would fall down.*

*The Bench granted a separation
order with an allowance of 5 s per
week, complainant to have cus-
tody of their two children.*

"Well Son, are you happy now?" was the response Sammy got when he showed his father the cutting. "She had me kicked out because I wasn't making enough money to satisfy her.

"I put a roof over that woman's head for twenty years and what did I get from her? I'll tell you what I got. I got dragged up in front of the Bench, that's what. Put in the papers. Kicked out of my house. Made a laughing-stock. That's what I got from her."

His walrus moustache, now grey, trembled as he spoke. The look in his eyes was the same one that Sammy saw on the day the old man lay among his allotment cabbages, wild-eyed and squealing.

"I get shouted at. I get shot at. I get tracked and trapped. I get Montjuich.* I get dead pals, good pals, dead, and... and..."

He choked on the rest of his words and tears raced down his cheeks to disappear behind his moustache. He collapsed into a rickety wooden chair and put his head in his hands, his shoulders heaving.

That's when Sammy thought back to the day when he was ten years old and witnessed the mercy of Mr

Ackroyd's hammer. It quickly ended the misery and suffering of Mrs Thompson's dog, Judy, and it would be a merciful end to Dad's torment. Those night demons who tortured him so cruelly would be silenced forever. A swift blow, then the peace of oblivion.

That thought lodged in Sammy's mind for the two years that followed. But so did a memory, and the two fought a long, bitter battle.

The memory was of the Dad who laughed so much in the old days, who showed Sammy how to plant potatoes, who swung him by an arm and a leg in huge circles when he was a tot and wanted to fly.

For as long as thought and memory battled, Sammy hesitated, waiting for a winner - and the night demons carried on gnawing at the old man's hopes and happiness.

Until the day arrived when hope and happiness were all gone and only the empty shell of a tormented old soldier remained.

And on that day the shell walked away from everything that had once been so important to Private Harold Kiteland.

It left his family, his home, his possessions, everything - on the day of his daughter's wedding.

Montjuich - a type of malaria combined with too much sun.

SONG IN THE SMOG

RUSTY iron wheels on a battered old baby carriage rattle over the cobblestones. Liver spots fleck the aged hands that grip the carriage handle, and each hand has a pattern of blue lines threaded just under the skin.

The lines form no discernible image or letters, but they do tell a story. The story written into the flesh of these hands is one of black chaos, blind panic and the breath of death. Yet the sleeves they emerge from belong to the frocked coat of an evangelist preacher.

Reverend Jacob Popplewell leans forward and peers into the baby carriage with a smile on his creased face.

"Nearly there Adeline, nearly there now," he croons affectionately.

The carriage wheels stop clunking on the lumpy highway and Rev Popplewell squints into the coal-fuelled smog around him.

It is a summer Saturday in the Year of Our Lord 1910 and the old man with the pram stares across Victoria Square towards Bolton Town Hall. All around him people are walking, talking, buying, selling, planning, dreaming, laughing, crying - and starving.

One of the starving sits on the Town Hall's ornate entrance steps. He is thin, pallid, dressed in coarse, shabby, stained clothes and at this moment is thinking of just how lucky he is.

Today's the day, old lad, the day you set away, Sammy Kiteland thinks to himself. *I've got nothing, I owe nothing and there's nothing to keep me here. Free. That's me. I'm free.*

He lifts his head, looks across the square and, through the veil of smog, makes out the figure of an aged preacher pushing a pram towards the centre of the square, but doesn't give him a thought.

"You can go anywhere, Sammy," he whispers. "anywhere at all; north, south, east, west, but today, Sammy, today you go."

In bustling Victoria Square other eyes turn towards the man with the clattering pram. Some people stare out of curiosity, others in recognition, as he moves towards his destination.

In the middle of the square Rev Popplewell stops and leans over the carriage. Tenderly he reaches into it and brings out a boxwood crate with the words 'Fentiman's Ginger Beer' stencilled on one side. He places the crate on the ground beside the pram and lifts its lid.

From inside it he takes another box. This box is made from cherry wood and has metal attachments. They include a black turntable on the top and a brass handle attached to one side.

The old man turns back to the baby carriage and brings out the rest of the machine - a huge brass horn attached to a sound reproducer.

He places the horn on the ground beside the body of the device, then flips the boxwood crate upside down and puts it back inside the baby carriage. The body of the music machine is lifted onto the crate in the pram before the horn and reproducer are fastened to it.

From a waistcoat pocket he pulls out a tiny tin box. The lettering on the box is almost worn away, but the words 'Songster Needles' are just visible.

Rev Popplewell opens the needle box and takes out a brand new steel stylus, which he attaches to the horn's sound reproducer. After securing it with a milled screw, he gently turns the brass winding handle on the side of the turntable, counting each turn in case he over-tensions the sensitive spring inside the music machine.

Next, he takes a square sleeve of white paper from the pram. On the sleeve is a drawing of a phonograph standing on a tall cabinet. Printed beside the drawing are the words 'The Gramophone and Typewriter Company'.

Rev Popplewell slides his fingers into the sleeve with care, and so he should, because the record inside it cost him a week's wages. But, handled correctly, it can earn so much more.

Printed on the other side of the paper sleeve is the message: 'Gramophone record by Madame Adelini Patti singing Casta Diva from Bellini's two-act opera Norma'.

Casta Diva is the old man's favourite song and one of only 17 recorded by the singer towards the end of an illustrious career that earned her acclaim at home and abroad from admirers, who included Queen Victoria.

Young Sammy raises his head as Patti's soprano voice soars from the brass horn. Some people in the square stop or turn to listen while others keep walking, knowing what is coming next. The old man by the pram gestures at people around him to come closer.

The sound from the horn is a shadow of the singer's pure vocal mastery. But it still has the power to elate the cleric.

Those people not enticed by the music are offered a new and intriguing entertainment as Rev Popplewell's hands rise high in the air where they dart and flicker at first, then, as the music swells, they drift and swoop.

Patti's song tells the story of Norma, a Druid high priestess, who falls in love with a faithless Roman, and as the drama unfolds, Rev Popplewell's elbows jerk, his wrists twist and his fingers spin, while the growing crowd around him watches with deepening fascination.

The old man appears not to notice his audience, only the singer and the song. But the people now surrounding him can hear a new layer of sound. Low and tuneless it shadows the voice emerging from the gramophone's brass horn. That sound is from the evangelist's own vocal chords.

His rumbling drone can't be called singing, but it develops a magnetic resonance of its own, and Rev Popplewell looks lost in the beauty of Patti's voice and the drama of Norma's story.

The man's actions and mannerisms catch and hold the eyes of his audience as much as the compelling sounds from the gramophone catch and hold their ears.

Sammy watches the preacher but makes no move to join the crowd that has built up around Rev Popplewell. He has been here before and he knows what will follow when the music stops.

The Popplewell name has a long association with generosity and devotional charity in the Darcy Lever district of Bolton where Sammy grew up. Whether the

Popplewell who is now being watched by Sammy and the crowd around him is related at all to those benefactors of old, Sammy does not know. But what he does know for sure is that, even today, the name this man uses is a byword for care and concern in Bolton.

In the town's Darcy Lever suburb alone needy people have received an annual dole of clothing and bread from a fund set up by the Popplewell family more than 70 years ago.

The spinning record reaches its dramatic last notes as Rev Popplewell's hands soar skyward once again before plunging down at the instant the music stops.

He remains motionless, head bowed, using the hypnotic click of the still-spinning record to strengthen his grip on the surrounding crowd.

The silence of the crowd changes subtly into self-conscious discomfort as everyone waits for somebody else to make the first move.

Rev Popplewell locks his gaze on the cobblestones at his feet, because he doesn't need to see what is happening to know when to strike.

A young couple are first to crack. She tugs his arm wanting him to take the first step away. His need to please her overcomes his reluctance, and he turns.

Rev Popplewell has his moment, and he strikes.

"You!"

He jabs a finger towards the couple who freeze and flush.

"And you!"

The preacher's finger finds a new target.

"And you!"

It jabs again and Rev Popplewell spreads his arms wide.

"All of you. All of you can help. You can help to wipe the tears from the cheeks of a child. Will you do that? Will you help me show the children of this great town that you care about them, that you want them to smile again?"

Some around him slowly nod their heads as others shuffle.

"Put your hand in your pocket, or your purse now. Can you find a penny? Can you live without it? There are children around you now who can't. Of course, you could take that penny and give it to the nearest unfortunate and it might buy him a bun. That will feed his stomach, but what about his soul - *what about his soul*?"

He speaks the last phrase quietly because the wily preacher knows his audience will move closer if he drops his voice. The listeners, who are also watching him, see the next word taking shape on his lips. But Rev Popplewell does not say the word. The hesitation hardens his grip on them. His eyes sweep the crowd before he voices the word that is sitting on his lips. The word is "You".

"You can feed his soul. You can help me show this wonderful town's forgotten children that somebody cares about them - and I will tell you how."

Sammy is too far away to hear what the preacher is telling those now crowded around him, but he doesn't need to, he has heard it before.

"Tell them about the train, Reverend," he says. "That'll get their hands in their pockets."

Rev Popplewell tells the crowd gathered around him: "Exactly one week from today I will walk through this very square to the railway station where a train will be waiting. That train will be waiting to take every single orphan who wants to join us, on a journey to Blackpool. There, at the seaside, in the sunshine, they will find friends, they will find laughter, they will have food and fun - and they will learn that their town, that YOU, care about them.

"We will use every penny you give now to buy their food and drink for that day. The generosity of the railway company has already provided their transport for the day.

"Just imagine what a fantastic adventure it will be for them. How much do you think a day at the seaside will mean to these poor children who have nothing, not even the love of a parent?

"Some of them have never seen the sea, never played with sand, never known the smell of salt air, never listened to the cry of the gulls. So, how much do you think will that mean to them, and could it change the way they see their world? Will it change them - change them for the better?

"At the least they will come back knowing there is more to life than mills and pits, coal and smoke. They will know God's good world has more to offer them than muck and misery. With their hearts and souls full of the memories and happiness provided by your generosity right now, who knows what dreams and ambitions might be inspired in them and, in time, what better citizens they might become.

"God bless you all for your kind hearts and generous donations."

Rev Popplewell removes the hat from his bald head and pushes it towards the couple who were first to turn away from him. Watched by the rest of the crowd, they scramble for a handful of coppers which they drop quickly into the outstretched hat. Others follow rapidly.

As the crowd disperses, Rev Popplewell carefully inserts the record back into its folder before disconnecting the phonograph's horn and soundbox. He switches the turntable motor back on to allow its power spring to lose what tension remains in it.

The old man picks up his hat and counts the day's takings. He whispers: "One penny, two, thruppence ha'penny, five," until he reaches the final total, when he says: "Five shillings, fourpence and one little Meg. Bless you my children."

From the Town Hall steps 50 yards away, the skinny young man in coarse clothes and wooden work clogs, watches Rev Popplewell attentively and says out loud: "Five shillings, fourpence and one little Meg. Bless you my children."

The preacher tips his takings into a leather drawstring purse with the 'Little Meg' farthing going in last.

Rev Popplewell pushes the baby carriage towards the town hall. Ahead of him are its wide entrance steps, guarded on either side by two stone lions. Sitting on the stone steps between the lions is a young man with a look on his face impassive as the carved creatures either side of him.

The old man smiles and the young man smiles back. They are close enough now to hear each other, and the young man speaks first.

"If you can spare a penny from that purse of yours, Reverend, I'll tell you exactly how much you've got in it, just by the weight of the coins."

Intrigued, Rev Popplewell moves closer.

"You might be able to tell me the weight, my boy,

but not the value. There are all kinds of coins in my purse. Five farthings might weigh the same as a penny, but their value is different."

"All the same, I can do it, sir," Sammy insists.

"Do you know who I am?" the old man asks.

"Oh yes sir, there's few people in Bolton as don't know you and what you do," the young man replies. "You're Reverend Popplewell and you take orphans to the seaside."

The old man smiles.

"That's right - I take them away from the smoke and noise of this place for a day of sea air and sunshine, with the help of the good folk of Bolton."

The young man's face clouds for a moment.

"Good folk? Aye, that's the trick - finding them good folk."

"Are you an orphan?" the older man asks.

"Nearly," says Sammy. "Mother died two years ago and last week Dad left."

The preacher looks puzzled. "What do you mean 'left', where did he go?"

"Don't know, don't care."

Sammy sees a puzzled expression on the old man's face and decides to tell him more.

"We were all at my sister's wedding do; just a little do in Mrs Dolan's house. Her lad married my sister Cilla. Everybody was just talking and laughing and nobody saw Dad go. He was just there one minute and gone the next.

"A bit later I walked back home to the lodge we had in Clap Row, and our room in the cellar was locked up. We never locked our door, but it was locked this time, so I banged on it and shouted for Dad. But a stranger opened the door.

"He said 'What's all this banging about?' So I said 'I live here and I want to be in. Where's Dad?'

"The man just laughed at me and said 'No you don't live here. I brokered a deal with the man who had this place. This room and everything in it is mine now, not that there's much. But we made a bargain and shook on it so that's that' and he shut the door in my face. I couldn't even get the work clothes I'd left on my bed. He got the lot.

"I went back to Cilla and asked if I could lodge with her. But she is just living-in with Mrs Dolan and there's only one little bedroom for Cilla and her man.

"She told me to try Auntie Ida, our mother's sister, so I went around to her place. Ida offered to let me lodge with her, if I paid some rent, but I didn't have a ha'penny. I'm just an apprentice at the foundry, and there's not much money in that."

Rev Popplewell nods sympathetically and asks: "What do you do at the foundry?"

"I'm an iron moulder in the fly shop. I mostly make the iron shafts for the flying shuttles in weaving machines, but there's no money in it. I get four shillings a week; four bob for 52 hours work that's all. I didn't tell Ida that of course. I said I'd give her my rent at the end of the week. Then, when payday came around, I skedaddled. I had to leave my best clothes behind so she wouldn't guess I wasn't coming back. She's probably sold them by now, so I reckon we are even."

"Where have you been living since then?"

"I found an empty barn, near Hunger Hill and for the past week I have been sleeping there."

Rev Popplewell looks troubled. "What have you

done for food?"

Sam unwraps a piece of cloth lying on the steps beside him to reveal an old stone ginger beer bottle with the image of an Alsatian on the neck. Alongside the bottle is half a loaf.

"I've been buying a penny loaf every other day and filling the bottle with water from one of the street standpipes. But this morning one of the farmer's lads found me in the barn. He was a decent enough sort. He let me get my loaf and my water from where I had hidden them before he booted me out.

"So here I am. I have nothing, I'm making next to nothing at the foundry, and I've nobody to stay here for. So the way I look at it I am a free man. I can go north, south, east or west. I have a strong body and I'm not frightened of hard work, when I can find it, so it's just a matter of deciding which way to point these clogs on my feet and then I'm off to better things."

The old man considers this young man's plight for a moment. The voice of his instinct says he should do his Christian best to help the lad. But Poor Law rules and parish help are not the answer here. Not for this young man.

Rev Popplewell shakes his head slowly and says: "All I have in this purse belongs to the orphans, and I'll not spend a penny of what is theirs by right. But I can point you in the direction of money if you are interested?"

"I don't take handouts, so if you're going to tell me to go on the parish, or to the workhouse, then forget it," Sammy tells him.

"No," Rev Popplewell smiles. "I can see they are not right for you. What I have in mind is a job with prospects and a chance to earn good money. But it isn't around here."

Sammy's grim expression gives way to a look of curiosity.

"I might be interested, but I pay my way in this world, so if you give me your information, I'll give you some information in return."

"Fair exchange being no robbery?" Rev Popplewell smiles. "Fine, give me your information and I'll give you mine."

Sammy narrows his eyes for dramatic effect and says: "I needn't weigh your purse to tell how much is in it. I can tell you that there is exactly five shillings and fourpence in it."

Rev Popplewell's eyebrows rise and he opens his mouth to speak. But, before he can say anything, Sammy adds: "Oh, and I almost forgot your Little Meg."

The preacher's open mouth snaps shut and the words he was about to utter freeze on his lips.

Sammy continues: "And I'll tell you something else for free. You haven't always been a reverend. You've known real hard graft, you used to be a coal miner, and you've been hurt in the pits."

The older man swallows and gives the boy a look of puzzled admiration.

"You are right on all counts young man. That is, indeed, the exact amount of money in my purse and I did work for many years as a coal miner, but that was a long time ago and not in these parts. How do you know all that? Can you read my mind?

Sammy laughs and tells him: "No sir, I can't read your mind, but I can read your lips and your hands."

Rev Popplewell is still perplexed.

Sammy respects what the old man does for Bolton's

orphans and chooses to be open with him.

"Foundries and mills are noisy places to work in," he explains. "You soon learn to listen with your eyes instead of your ears.

"These aren't any good in places like that," he says, jabbing a finger into each ear and silently mouthing the last three words "places like that."

Realization dawns on Rev Popplewell.

Sammy goes on: "When you were totting up your money across the square, I read your lips and you told me how much you had. Then, as you were pushing your old baby carriage towards me, your hands told me the rest. You have a pitman's tattoos on them."

Rev Popplewell looks at the blue marks embedded under the skin on the back of his hands and a flash of memory takes him back 30 years to a time when he was working as a shotfirer in a coal mine. Part of his job involved ramming packs of gunpowder, known as a shot, into a hole in the coal face before detonating them.

Pitman Popplewell was trained and experienced, but even that was not enough on his last day underground. He had fed three tubes of newspaper filled with blasting powder down a four-foot deep hole he had hand-drilled into the coal face.

As usual, he rammed the tubes into the hole with a metal rod before attaching the detonator. He pushed the rod into the hole once, twice and then a third time. The first and second blows made a 'thump' sound. But, as the rod travelled down the drill hole for a third time, he heard 'click'.

Popplewell never worked out which it was, but either experience or instinct saved him.

Something foreign in the hole, had made that 'click',

something that scraped a spark into existence in a space it shared with the packs of explosive.

The world around Popplewell erupted in the same instant that he slapped his hands over his eyes. The ram rod clipped his right ear as it shot out of the hole, and he felt the breath of death kiss his cheek as it shot past. The ramrod speared into the darkness behind him as the wall of coal it came from disintegrated into rubble and black dust.

Moments later, workmates who had been waiting in safety for the shotfirer to do his job, dragged him, unconscious and bleeding, from the chaos of coal and stone. Popplewell saved his eyes, but his hands were lacerated and ingrained with coal dust.

In time, his skin healed, but the coal grains trapped in Popplewell's scarred flesh formed a pattern of blue marks just below the surface - his pitman's tattoos.

That experience changed Popplewell's life. He refused to go back down the mine saying he had seen the light in the darkness underground. God had given him the rest of his life on the day of that explosion, so he decided, there and then, to give the rest of his days to God.

Rev Popplewell smiles at Sammy and says: "Well, my boy, I have to admit that you are undeniably observant. You will go far and, if you want my advice, you will go north."

"Why is that sir?" It is Sammy's turn to be curious now.

"Because an old mining friend of mine told me last week that, right now, new shafts are being sunk in the middle of the Northumberland coalfield and it will take more than 150 years to dig out all the coal there. A young lad like you, determined, hard-working and bright, could make something of himself by getting in at the start of a new enterprise like that.

"There will be work, there will be money, but more important for you, there will be opportunities, all kinds of opportunities, for somebody with ambition and determination to make the most of the life God has given them."

"How far is it from here to Northumberland?"

"About 200 miles, you could be there inside three weeks, even if you had to walk all the way."

Sammy thinks. He thinks about the foundry, his dad, the orphans, the workhouse, and the chance of a new start with nobody and nothing holding him back.

"I reckon I'll do just that Reverend, thanks."

When Sammy reaches the bottom of the Town Hall steps he turns towards an old Roman road heading north and a signpost that says *Chorley*.

SAMMYSHINE

IT'S so quiet in Chorley's Co-op Store on this sizzling summer day. Even the bluebottles aren't buzzing. Some hang, glum and glued, from the uncoiled strip of flypaper dangling from an unlit gaslight. Others bake and twitch listlessly in the shop window.

Saul Henderson leans on his spotless counter and tries to remember the words of that new song he'd heard in the pub last night. How did it go again?

If you were the only girl in the world, and I was the only...

"MISTER!!" The yell comes from the street outside. It is urgent, angry, tremulous, and meant for him.

Maisie Potts explodes into the store, all tousled locks and cherry cheeks; a three-foot, five-year-old fireball, dressed in her older sister's hand-me-downs.

The pinafore frock she wears has plenty of space to spare. It flaps and snaps like a flag in a storm. Her sister's shoes, three sizes too big for Masie's feet, make a 'tok, tok' sound as she clatters over the store's wooden floor.

"Slow down duck, what's the matter?" says Saul, suppressing a grin. But this is no laughing matter for Maisie. Tears trickle over her flushed cheeks and she fights to get the words out.

"Mum says... Mum says..." Beaten for the words she wants, Maisie shoves a piece of crumpled paper onto the counter.

Saul recognises it immediately. It is the page torn from last year's diary that the tot had proudly presented to him not half an hour ago. On a page dated 4th August 1909 is a pencilled shopping list.

He reads out: "Half a pound of butter, two pounds of strong flour, a small loaf and a pound of starch. What's wrong Maisie? I gave you all that."

Still too choked to speak, the youngster bangs a paper bag onto the counter. Inside it is the solid block of starch, and now Saul understands. The Co-op sells starch in two forms, either as a solid block or as a powder. Mothers often use powdered starch as a cheap alternative to talc on babies' bottoms, and Maisie has a newborn brother.

In the same instant Maisie recovers her composure enough to pass on a furious message from her sleep-deprived mother.

"That's no good," she yells indignantly, pointing at the block of starch. "Mum says that's no damned good. She wants the stuff for the bairn's arse!"

Saul struggles to keep a straight face since he knows Maisie has delivered her Scottish mother's message verbatim.

"Don't worry Maisie, I'll put it right for you. Here, have a stick of liquorice root to chew on while I sort this out."

The girl accepts the offered dry stick with as much grace as she can muster and pokes it into her mouth. There is nothing to taste at first. That will come later when she has crushed the root between her teeth and mixed a good slug of saliva with its fibrous inner strands to release their oil and flavour.

Saul takes his time weighing the powdered starch

into the steel bowl of the scales on his counter. He wants to give Maisie time to compose herself before she carries the bag of powder back home, in case she has an accident on the way and earns another tongue-lashing from her exhausted mother.

Saul tips the starch powder into a brown paper bag and then puts that into a second bag as an extra precaution. He hands the doubled bag to Maisie, who remembers her manners and says "Thank you". Although, with her mouth full of spit-soaked liquorice root, it sounds more as if Maisie is saying "Amph-oo".

Clutching the bag to her chest, Maisie leaves the shop and turns right. The street she walks along is empty except for a tired-looking young man coming slowly towards her. He is wearing worn work trousers, a collarless cotton shirt and an old fustian jacket. Hanging diagonally across his body is a cotton sling which bulges with something that little Maisie can not identify.

As they pass each other, Sammy Kiteland smiles and nods at the girl with the stick in her mouth, then looks at the Co-op store ahead of him.

The store has been there for more years than Sammy has been alive and looks like so many other Co-ops born in the middle of the last century. That was a boom time for the Co-operative movement, as the working classes discovered that, through mutual collaboration, they could set up their own farms, shops, banks and even cotton mills.

The Co-op Sammy is looking at is a food and hardware store. On the pavement outside it an old bike, with a battered basket attached to its handlebars, leans against a gas lamp-post.

The store's recessed entrance door is flanked on each side by angled display widows. In one window, ranks of pots, pans, crockery, and laundering equipment are on show. Behind them are eye-catching enamel advertisement signs. On one sign a brilliant white image of a spade is set against a midnight blue background with a message in white lettering declaring 'If you want the BEST SPADE of all ask for a Broad Acre'. Another sign, in the same shade of blue, urges 'Use Royal Standard Lamp Oil', while one more tells shoppers they can trust nightlight tapers produced by the Co-operative Wholesale Society's soap and candle works at Irlam, Leeds.

In the other display window are dummy cardboard boxes, tins and bags promoting polish, washing powder, black lead and wax. Beside them is a display of sugar and flour bags alongside fake cakes and a line of milk bottles painted white on the inside. The sight of so much fake food sets Sammy's stomach rumbling for real and an idea forms in his head.

Saul is still smiling after the dressing down delivered by little Maisie when he hears the shop doorbell and looks up to see a figure silhouetted in the store doorway. As the figure approaches the counter, Saul sees it is a young man - a hungry-looking young man - in soiled and sorry clothing.

"What can I get for you?" he asks in a tone pitched between friendly and wary.

"I want some Sammyshine," the young man replies.

"Sammyshine? Er? Are you sure that's the right name? I don't think we stock Sammyshine, what exactly is it?"

"Only the best metal polish money can buy," Sammy tells him. "Better than Brasso, and that takes some doing. But it is new, so maybe the Co-op hasn't heard about it yet."

"Maybe," Saul says, with a hint of doubt in his voice.

"That's a shame, mister, because I think I saw some in that little shop down the road. Never mind, I'll go back and get some there. Thanks."

Sammy is walking back through the sun-filled doorway when Saul calls after him: "Is it really that good?" He glances up at a shelf full of unsold tins of Brasso.

Sammy appears to think for a moment, then says: "Don't take my word for it, try it for yourself. I've got to come back up this way, so I'll call in with it and you can try some of mine."

"Well, that is very civil of you, young man and, if you do bring some back, I'll give you a penny loaf in exchange. You look as if you could do with some grub."

Sammy smiles: "It's a deal. I'll be back in half an hour."

Around the corner from the store is a long terrace of redbrick homes. Across the back lane behind them is a row of outhouses containing lavatories and coal sheds. An elderly man emerges from one of the ash midden closets adjusting the canvas belt that holds up his aged khaki trousers.

Sammy approaches him and says: "'Scuse me, mister, I'm bursting, can I use your lavvy?"

"Aye son, help yer sen, but 'old yer nose," the old man grins.

Inside the outhouse Sammy sees what he hoped would be there - a candle. It stands in a solid puddle of wax inside an old WD&HO Wills tobacco tin.

"Perfect," Sammy mutters as he prises the candle from its bed of wax. He puts the candle back on the floor and pockets the wax-filled tobacco tin.

Back outside, he sees that the street is now empty and goes into the next outhouse. In this one and the next two there are sheets torn from newspapers hanging from nails in their doors, but nothing else. Sammy's search has more success in in the next lavatory. He finds a paraffin lamp, put there to provide light and a modicum of warmth for poor souls in need of relief on bitter winter nights. Sammy lifts the paraffin lamp and shakes it. The slopping sound from inside says he is in luck. He unscrews the cap from the base and tips a little of the liquid into the tobacco tin before replacing the cap and putting the lamp back where he found it.

He warms and works the wax and paraffin with his thumbs as he goes back into the street, and the mixture turns into a light paste.

"Nearly there," says Sammy.

His last port of call is a dustbin standing outside one of the street's coal houses. He lifts the dustbin lid and finds what he is looking for – a thick layer of fine white ash on top of coal cinders. He scoops out a handful of the ash and rubs it between his hands over a sheet of newspaper from one of the middens. The finer dust falls onto the newspaper and he keeps the coarser grains in his hands until he has what he needs, then he throws the coarse grains away.

Sammy carefully rolls the newspaper into a funnel and pours the fine ash from it into the tobacco tin. Slowly, he works the wet and dry ingredients together into a firm paste. He adds a scrap more ash and carries on working the mixture until it has the consistency of soft shoe polish.

"Perfect," he says again and heads back up the street

towards the Co-op store.

Shopkeeper Saul has been busy since Sammy left. From the back storeroom he fished out an old Eccles Co. miners' safety lamp. It has lain there for years and its once brightly burnished brass casing is now black.

"There you go," he says when Sammy walks back into the shop. "Try it out on this. Let's see just how shiny Sammyshine can get it."

Saul hands the boy a piece of Hessian cloth which Sammy dips into the open tin in his other hand. After putting down the tin he takes up the miner's lamp and rubs it with the cloth. The grainy paste abrades the dirt from the surface of the lamp and, as he continues to rub, a brassy shine begins to emerge.

"Well," says Saul, taking the safety lamp from Sammy's outstretched hand. "I can't deny it. That stuff of yours has certainly put a real shine on that old lamp. I've learnt something new today, so here is your penny loaf. Now tell me where can I buy this Sammyshine?"

Sammy tears off a piece of crust and pops it straight into his mouth, chewing slowly.

"Actually, you can't buy it," he says.

Saul looks puzzled.

"I wanted you to see that it does the job before I told you, but you can't buy this because I have just made it."

"You made it?"

"Yes."

"Just now?"

"Yes."

"Well, I'll be blowed! Who taught you how to make that?"

"My dad showed me when I was little, and his dad showed him. The powder I use is just gritty enough to wear off the stubborn marks and stains, and it gets finer as you use it, fetching up the shine. It's a mix of powder, wax and paraffin, but the paraffin and wax are just there to stop the powder from blowing away. It's just common sense if you think it through."

"I'll grant you that son," says Saul. "But thinking like that could make you rich, *should* make you rich, so why are you wandering around looking like a ragamuffin?"

Sammy pauses a moment before answering: "I got set free."

Saul looks puzzled and asks: "Set free? What do you mean?"

Sammy's face clouds.

"I came home one day and Dad had buggered off. He'd sold everything that was in our lodgings and I was locked out. I had nothing, no money, no food and just the clothes I stood up in. I tried to struggle on, but it wasn't working and I was in big trouble.

"I thought I might seek help from the Guardians and went to the Town Hall. But I couldn't make myself go in. I'm young and fit and I can think, so I sat on the Town Hall steps trying to puzzle things out and decide what I could do. That's when I met Rev Popplewell, and he gave me an idea, which put me on the road here.

He shrugs his shoulders and continues: "I suppose I could have stayed where I was and tried to make extra money with Sammyshine, but that would be the old me. I want a fresh start, a clean sheet, a new me. Rev Popplewell suggested going up to Northumberland, because there's lots of jobs up there and ways to make the new me, so that is where I am headed."

Saul looks at him thoughtfully.

"Tell you what lad; I have a score of empty tins in the

back, as well as a bin full of ashes and plenty of paraffin and wax. I reckon I can sell Sammyshine for sixpence a tin, so what if I take twopence and you have the other fourpence? That would put seven shillings and eight pence clear profit into your pocket. How about that?"

Sammy sticks out his mucky hand.

"Two weeks' pay for two hours' work? It's a deal, but I'm still going north."

ROSE WITH THORNS

"MAISIEEEE!!!"

Rose is not in a good mood.

"Maisie Potts! Where are you?"

Maisie Potts stays still and silent. Maybe her older sister won't find her. Here in the scullery pantry it feels so cold, but she can put up with that for a while until Rose calms down. There's no light and not much space, so maybe Big Sister won't think of looking in here.

But Rose was also once little and in trouble, so of course she thinks of looking in her old hiding place.

"Get out here right now," she snaps. "No, wait a minute. Take off my good shoes first, and then come out, Madam."

Rose is just a blur as Maisie looks at her through tear-filled eyes.

"But Rose."

"But me no buts, our Maisie, I have told you before about playing in my shoes. They'll be yours one day, but NOT YET! I need those shoes and I need them now."

"But Mum sent me to the Co-op. She was shouting and everything and I couldn't find my clogs - and the bairn needed starch for his arse."

Rose's mouth opens, but no words come out. She

has felt the sharp end of their mother's tongue often enough to recognise Maisie's dilemma.

"Just come out of the pantry and let me get my shoes Maisie. I don't have time for this, I'm late already."

"Are you going to break some more windows, Rose?"

"No I'm not going to break more windows, Maisie. I haven't broken any at all, so I can't break more. I just said I would like to break the town hall windows, not that I had broken any."

Maisie tries to look disappointed, hoping it might get her back into her sister's good books.

"Well then, if you do break some windows, can I come and watch?" she says, still trying to ingratiate herself.

"No," Rose tells her. "You're too little to understand, but one day you will. It's not about making a public spectacle of myself, it's about standing up for what's right. I just want people to understand that my opinion matters, that I matter, that every woman matters."

"But you're not a woman Rose, you're a girl. Grand-dad used to say you had to marry before you could be a real woman, and you're not married, you're not even seventeen."

Rose shakes her head in exasperation.

"That old dinosaur has been dead for five years, but his stupid ideas are still alive and kicking. I give up. Just get out of my way and let me have my shoes, I need to pick up a parcel at the railway station and it will be there by now."

Maisie steps aside, still trying to work out why Rose would even try to say she is a woman when anybody can see that she's a girl - and a very pretty one, with those green eyes and that red hair.

Sammy notices the red hair first. He is filling the last of the old tins with Sammyshine in the back office of the Co-op when he looks up and sees the silhouette of a girl in the doorway. The sun streams through a mass of red hair around the girl's head, making it look like a halo on fire.

Saul speaks from behind the counter where he has been stacking some of the tins on a display shelf.

"Hello Rose, don't tell me you've come to complain as well. I've already had my ear bashed by your Maisie."

"No Mr Henderson, I've just come to ask if you can put one of these posters up in your shop. It's advertising a rally in London. I've just picked them up from the railway station. You'll soon see them all over town, but I came here first so that the Co-op can be ahead of the others. The rally isn't until next month, so it's giving people plenty of warning."

Saul takes the green poster and reads the message, in white lettering, on it.

VOTES FOR WOMEN

WOMEN'S SOCIAL AND POLITICAL UNION,

4, Clements Inn.

A DEPUTATION OF WOMEN
WILL ARRIVE IN
PARLIAMENT SQUARE

At 8 o'clock,
on
TUESDAY, AUGUST 22.

TO LOVERS OF FAIR PLAY! WOMEN
VERSUS THE GOVERNMENT!

Will you come and Umpire?

Read 'VOTES FOR WOMEN,' Weekly, One Penny,
from all Newsagents and Bookstalls.

He scratches his head and eventually says: "Mmm? I'm not sure. I don't really agree with all this suffragette stuff. I'm not even sure about the suffragists, although at least they don't go in for all the violence."

Rose replies calmly, much to her own surprise, and says: "Suffragists might want the vote. But it is the Suffragettes who will get it, and they will get it with the help of rallies like this and men like you, who believe in the Co-op's principles of fairness and equity."

Saul shakes his head and sighs. "Suffragettes, Suffragists, they're all the same Rose. They all just want to put women into trousers when it should be the men who are wearing them. It's not about equality; it's about going against the natural order of things, as far as I can see."

Rose's nails dig into the bundle of posters in her hands and her green eyes flash. She opens her mouth to unleash the tirade that has built up in her. But Sammy speaks before she can.

"I've finished all the Sammyshine, Mr Henderson; if I can have that seven shillings and eight pence I'll be on my way."

He holds out his hand and smiles, first at the shop-keeper and then at the girl.

Saul can see that he has overstepped the mark with young Rose and grabs the lifeline Sammy has thrown to him.

"Oh, yes, I'll get it from the cash box, just a minute."

As Saul turns to open a drawer in the counter, Sammy looks at Rose and keeps smiling. He doesn't actually know how to take the grin off his face, this girl is so nice to look at. He does his best to commit what his eyes are seeing to memory. Her skin is so fine it seems almost translucent. He is sure that, as she blinks, he can see green pupils showing through her, oh so, delicate eyelids. The expression on her face is one of barely contained fury, yet she looks as if a breeze could blow her away.

"Sorry," he says and hopes it is the last time he ever needs to say that particular word to this exceptional young woman. "I don't mean to interrupt," he lies. "But I might be able to help you."

"How?" she snaps at the scruff who has just appeared from the back office. "And why?"

"I have a plan," says Sammy, as he tries hard to think of one, "and you will like it."

Rose stares at him, unconvinced.

"But it might be better if we discuss it outside - out of earshot." He twitches his head towards Saul, who is closing the cash drawer. "Just give me a minute and I'll see you outside. I'm sure I can put this right for you."

He moves to take her elbow, but she jerks it away, as if she has been stung, and strides for the door.

Saul keeps his voice low as he reaches Sammy and says: "Proper little madam that one. Nobbut a lass, but she thinks she knows it all. That's education for you. Fills their heads full of stuff they don't understand and sets them against the rest of us."

"Listen Mr Henderson, I think I can sort this out, just leave it with me," Sammy says, holding out his hand to Saul.

The shopkeeper gives him the coins, with a wry grin.

"Aye well, good luck with that."

Rose stops outside the shop and wonders about what just happened. Why didn't she give that self-satisfied Saul Henderson a piece of her mind? How come she still has all the leaflets tucked under her arm? But most of all, what was it about that scruffy lad that persuaded her to leave like that, just because he asked?

He can't be that much older than she is, but there was something about his face. What was it? A lived-in look? Yes. A sincerity? Yes. Something to do with trust? Yes. It is all of those and maybe more, but she doesn't have time to think further because he comes out the shop and stands alongside her.

"It is a good plan," Sammy says, "a very good one, in fact. But we need to keep quiet about it, so let's make sure nobody can hear us."

He moves to take her elbow then thinks better of it and instead, points down the street to a grassed area with a bench seat.

When they reach it, Sammy looks around the street to check that they are alone and points to the terrace of homes on the other side of the road.

"I'll still have to be careful in case there are any lip-reading mill workers watching from those windows."

He cups his hands and closes in on her ear. She feels the light touch of his fingers on her cheeks and he feels the warmth as those cheeks flush. Then she feels the brush of his breath on her ear as he whispers, and Sammy smells the wonderful, fresh-washed scent of that red hair.

As he whispers his plan into her ear, Sammy sees Rose's cheek being stretched by a smile. He has not yet seen the smile on those delicate lips, but he knows it is going to be wonderful when he does see it.

Sammy lowers his cupped hands and stands back as she turns towards him with the reward he wants. He is dazzled by that smile, just as he expected.

"That is absolutely fantastic," she says. "When can we start?"

"Tomorrow," he tells her. "I'll need to find some lodgings for tonight so why don't we meet back here to-morrow morning at around ten?."

"Great. I'll see you then."

She half turns away, then looks back at him.

"Oh, I've just thought, I don't even know your name, what is it?"

"Smiley," he answers. "Er, I mean Sammy."

The next morning, at the Chorley branch office of

the Bolton Evening News, reporter Alan Robson's fingers stab at the keys on his new Swift Record typewriter, and the noise the machine makes tells him he is typing on three layers of thin copy paper with two sheets of worn carbon paper sandwiched between them, to make duplicates of the top sheet.

If he had just one sheet in the machine, the sound would be 'click, click' as he hit the keys. If there were two sheets with a carbon between them, it would go 'clack, clack'. But with three sheets and two carbons, the sound is 'thuck, thuck', and today his machine is definitely saying 'thuck, thuck'.

The top layer of copy paper will find its way to one of the newspaper's sub editors who will check for errors, add instructions for the compositors and give the story a headline.

The first carbon copy is for Alan's news editor, who will read it then skewer the story on a spike, along with the rest of the stories his reporters file that day. If there are any problems or queries, then the news editor can easily retrieve the copy from his spike.

The second carbon copy will be stuck onto another spike on a shelf in Alan Robson's office, where he can refer to it if necessary.

That office is only just big enough to accommodate an ancient roll-top desk and a chair which is squeezed between the desk and a thin partition wall. Piled up against the other side of the partition are back copies of the Bolton Evening News. Each chest-high pile contains one year's editions of the broadsheet newspaper and there are five stacks, all in date order.

It looks chaotic, but Alan knows that if he wants to refer to a story from 24th March five years ago, he has only to go 15 inches down in the first pile to find it.

Opposite the wall of newspapers is a door leading to the circulation office. When today's papers arrive, still smelling of fresh ink, this is where they will be sorted for Chorley's newsagents and newspaper sellers. This is also where yesterday's unsold newspapers are tied into bundles ready to be hurled onto the delivery van after today's editions have been unloaded.

Balding, gap-toothed and ever-grinning Jim Wood, circulation manager at the branch office, sticks his head through the doorway to the editorial office and yells: "Alan, you've got company."

Alan thuck thucks to the end of the sentence before he says: "Coming."

Some people say Alan is a man of few words. But Alan likes to think he just makes every word count and, wherever possible, punch above its weight, so "Coming" does the job for him this time.

Alan rises slowly from his chair. In an office as cramped as this one he knows from painful experiences of bumped elbows, shins and toes, that it is unwise to move too quickly.

Once through the doorway and into the circulation office he sees two young people on the other side of the counter. One is a young man who looks as if he is straight from work at a factory or mill. The other is a pale girl with red hair and emerald eyes. The girl speaks first.

"We have a story for you, Mr Robson."

"Straight to the point, I like that. What can I do for you young lady?"

Sammy puts a restraining hand on Rose's arm, fearing she will go to the nub of the matter when he would rather engage the reporter's curiosity first.

"Do you know Rev Popplewell?" he asks.

"Yes I do, but there is more than one. Do you mean Rev Popplewell from the Queen Street Mission, or...?"

"We mean the Rev Popplewell who takes the children to Blackpool every year," Sammy interrupts.

"Ah, that one. Yes, I've written one or two stories about him. Nice chap; he used to be a coal miner way back, did you know that?"

"Yes, he did tell me. The thing is, I need to get these to him before he goes to Blackpool next week."

Sammy takes the green posters from Rose and puts them face up on the counter.

The reporter looks at the posters and then back at Sammy.

"That's as might be, but where is there a story for me in this?"

"Because every one of the children on the train is an orphan and your newspaper is going to help them say 'Thank you' to the people of Bolton who put their hands in their pockets to pay for that trip to Blackpool."

Alan pulls a pad of paper from one pocket and a pencil stub from the other.

"Tell me more."

When that day's bundles of unsold newspapers reach the Evening News head office in Mealhouse Lane, Bolton, delivery driver Bob Charlton also hands over a package addressed to the news editor.

Half an hour later the package reaches the cluttered desk of news editor, Tom Brownlee. He opens a letter accompanying the package and sees it is from his Chorley district man, Alan Robson.

As he reads the letter, Brownlee smiles the smile of a news editor just guaranteed a good story, and hands the package to the office junior.

"Get over to Victoria Square and find Rev Popplewell. Give him this package," he barks.

Brownlee always barks. It comes with the job. The junior tries to take the package, but Brownlee tightens his grip on it and tells him: "If you can't see Popplewell you'll certainly hear that damned music machine of his, just follow the noise."

Later that afternoon Rev Popplewell returns home and carefully pulls the old perambulator over his front doorstep into the hallway beyond. The baby carriage and its music machine remain just inside his front door while he lifts out the mysterious package that was handed to him by the boy from the newspaper.

He carries it into his kitchen, unfastens the string around the package and unfolds the paper to reveal a bundle of printed sheets advertising a meeting in London. On top of the sheets is an envelope which bears his name. He opens it and finds a typewritten message inside.

Dear Rev Popplewell. I am Sammy. You met me the other day in Victoria Square. You might remember that I told you how much money you had collected that day, including your Little Meg. I have an idea that might help you raise more money for next year's Blackpool trip. It involves these posters and talking to a reporter from the Evening News.

As Rev Popplewell reads on, his eyebrows lift and a smile creases his old face.

"Pencils," he says. "I need pencils."

A few days later, chattering children fill the carriages of the Blackpool-bound train in Bolton Railway Station. Each of them carries several sheets of green paper with a printed advertisement about a meeting in London on one side and on the other is a message written in pencil.

The platform guard waves his flag, blows his whistle and the carriages jolt. The youngsters in the carriages chatter and laugh excitedly as they follow their instructions from Rev Popplewell and his helpers. With varying degrees of success they begin to fold the posters in the way they were shown, and then wait.

The train picks up speed as it clanks and rattles through Bolton town centre and still the children wait.

Engine driver Bill Gilbert has been making this run for 15 years and never tires of it. The sound of the engine, the smell of coal and oil, the rattle and sway of this marvellous machine, he loves them all. So, when he leans out of his cab window and squints into the buffeting wind, there is a smile on his face.

He could have waited longer, but Bill Gilbert is a man of habit and he always leans out of his cab window at this point in the journey. He is looking for a trackside sign and when he sees it he reaches for the cord overhead. Then, as the single word on the sign 'WHISTLE' comes clearly into focus, he yanks the cord twice.

At the sound of the double toot from the train whistle an adult in each of the carriages grabs the strap of leather below the carriage window, pulls it up briefly, and then lets it go. Windows along the length of the train drop open in unison and from them emerges a shower of paper darts.

Some of the sky fliers nose dive onto the track to be caught in the down-draught from this speeding train, or a later one. Others take flight, spiralling up and away from the carriages and the laughing youngsters inside them.

At each whistle point on the journey more showers of flying darts emerge to twist and flicker against the clear blue summer sky as they soar over bridges, viaducts and crossings.

Below one bridge is Mary Haslam, Poor Law guardian and leader of the Women's Movement in Bolton. She picks up the piece of green paper that has just landed at her feet and unfolds it to read about a meeting that she is already aware of and has been doing her best to publicise.

She turns the sheet over and sees words pencilled in a childish scrawl.

The words say: "We *have no mother. We have no father. But we have the people of Bolton. Thank you for our trip to the seaside. Your orphans.*"

More sky fliers are released as the train continues its journey through Bolton and other towns along the Calder Valley track before travelling through Preston and reaching Blackpool.

Rev Popplewell leans from one of the open windows smelling the steam and watching the green countryside rush past. He tries to work out which position will face him northwards, and when he does, he says: "Thank you Sammy" and he wipes some grit from his wet eye.

PITMAN

ROSE and Sammy composed their letter to Rev Popplewell just before walking into the newspaper office, but it had been a struggle.

Rose, who is never lost for words when she has to speak, feels intimidated by committing her thoughts to paper. Writing lacks the spontaneity of speech, and leaves no room for tone or emotion, as far as she is concerned. Sammy, on the other hand, is far more comfortable taking his time to consider and weigh each word so that it expresses exactly what he wants to say. As a result, he is happier writing than speaking.

His problem is that his handwriting is so scrappy. Sometimes his words slope right, sometimes left and they wander aimlessly across the page. He had tried throughout his school years to write neatly, but it was just beyond him and, eventually, he abandoned all hope for his spidery scrawl.

So when the reporter said he really liked their idea of sending 'thank you' messages flying from the Bolton to Blackpool train, Sammy plucked up the courage to ask for more help.

"Do you use one of those typewriter machines?" he asked.

"Yes I do, and it is quite a new one," the reporter told him.

"I want to tell Rev Popplewell about the plan, but he

might not be able to read my awful writing, could you type it out for me?"

"Of course. What is it you want to say?"

Sammy told him and, as he spoke, the reporter's hand skimmed over the notepad in front of him, making loops and swirls that Sammy had never seen before. Then, when Sammy stopped speaking, Alan Robson's hand stopped writing.

"Have you written all that down already?" Sammy asked in surprise.

"Oh yes. I've written it down in shorthand and if you wait here, I'll just go into the back office and type out the letter for you."

As he left, Sammy turned to Rose.

"Did you see that? I didn't know anybody could write as fast as that - and it looked to be pretty neat too. I wish I could write in shorthand like that; it must come in useful at times."

"You should ask him about it," she replied. "There might be somebody here who teaches shorthand."

"Oh, no, no, I couldn't take on something like that. I'm not stopping here. I'm just passing through. I'm going north."

The look on Rose's face puzzled Sammy, but a lot of things this girl said and did puzzled him, so he thought no more about it.

The reporter came back with a brown envelope which had Rev Popplewell's name typed on it.

"The letter is inside, just as you dictated it to me," he said.

"Thanks a lot, could you put it into the package that will go with your delivery man?"

"I can and I will. The package and your letter will go

back to my head office with yesterday's unsold newspapers this afternoon," the reporter answered.

"One more thing," Sammy began. "That shorthand stuff, is it hard to learn?"

"Not really. Learning it is easy enough, the real secret to shorthand is to practice, practice, practice. The type of shorthand that I write is called Pitman's Shorthand, which is quite straightforward. Isaac Pitman himself said that if you practice one or two hours a day for three months anybody should be able to write at 60 words a minute and manage 130 words a minute in a year. But, as I said, you must keep using it or you will lose it."

Sammy's eyebrows rose in disbelief as the reporter continued.

"The other thing to know is that you can only write really fast shorthand when you stop thinking in longhand. Shorthand is not about writing letters, it is a way of writing sounds. When Pitman invented this system, he called it 'Stenographic Soundhand' because each symbol represents a sound. Later, he changed the name for his system to 'Phonography' and later still it became known as shorthand."

The reporter could see that Sammy was genuinely interested.

He went on: "Because you are only writing the sound of a word you don't have to worry about spelling or words with double letters or special rules like always putting 'i' before 'e' except after 'c'. All of that makes shorthand easy to learn in the first place and very fast to write when you practice it a lot. I can manage 120 words a minute and I'm slower than a lot of reporters."

"Even 120 words a minute is amazing," said Sammy.

"Where did you learn to write as fast as that?"

The reporter laughed and told him: "I built up my speed with Pitman's shorthand down a coal mine."

Sammy gave him a dubious look, so Alan Robson explained: "I used to work at one of the pits around here, but it wasn't for me and I couldn't wait to get out. I like writing so I thought I would try to find a way of making a living from it. Newspapers were the obvious way to go, but I needed to be able to write shorthand at a decent speed, so I set out to teach myself.

"I got a book called The Phonographic Reporter, by Isaac Pitman when it was first published seventeen years ago. Half of it is advice about how to be a reporter, but the other half is about how to use the strokes, curves, hooks and ticks that make up his shorthand.

"I taught myself those symbols then used a piece of chalk to scribble them on bits of coal and stone as they went by on the conveyor belt at the pit. Soon I could write them faster than the speed of the stuff going past me, so I got the lad controlling the belt to speed it up, and I kept writing faster until I could match the belt machine's top speed.

"After that I went to Miners Union meetings and wrote whatever was said. That went well until some of the officials thought I was spying for the boss and kicked up a fuss. I told them to stuff their union and went looking for a job in newspapers. It was easier than I thought. The editor of the Bolton Evening News was impressed with my shorthand and even more impressed by what I had told the Miners Union bullies."

Sammy nodded all the way through the reporter's story, but said nothing.

"I'll tell you what, if you are so interested in shorthand, you can have my book. I have learnt all that I need from it now, and maybe it is time to pass it on. Hang on a minute."

He disappeared into his back office and emerged a moment later with a small, well-thumbed book that had the title *The Phonographic Reporter* in gold lettering on the front and *Pitman's Shorthand Phonography* in black lettering below it. The cover may have been green at one point, but it had been handled so much it now looked the colour of mud.

Sammy wanted it, but he took it reluctantly.

"I don't take charity Mr Robson, so how much do you want for it?"

"This is not charity, this is payment for a good, exclusive, story. You've earned that book, so good luck and remember to use it or you'll lose it."

"He's right," said Rose. "You've earned it. Now come on, let's go." She took Sammy's arm and when she tugged, he didn't resist.

Back out in the street Sammy stuffed the little book into his coat pocket and said: "I suppose I'd better get going."

"I thought you might be staying longer?" Rose replied, trying hard to sound matter of fact. She liked this boy, but didn't want to give him any wrong ideas. "Don't you want to stay around for a few days and see our story in the newspaper?"

"Not really, I'm not bothered about newspaper stories. I just wanted to solve your problem - and I did. That's what matters to me."

Rose looked into his eyes and saw honesty in them, which was a new experience for her. The boys she had met so far were never interested in being honest, only in winning, whether that was at school, on the sports field, or with their arms around her waist. They only wanted to win.

"You're a funny sort, Sammy Kiteland," Rose eventually said. "Why are you here? Why are you doing this?"

Sammy intended to tell her the same story he has told everybody else - the dad who abandoned him, the sister he lost, the apprenticeship he dumped. But new words come out of his mouth; words he had not expected to say. This girl with green eyes was so full of honest dreams, hopes and passions that Sammy wanted to be honest too. Honest with himself as well as her.

"Doors," he told her.

A puzzled look crossed Rose's face. "Doors? What do you mean?"

Sammy looked steadily into those emerald eyes and said: "While I was sitting on Bolton Town Hall steps the other day I realised that so many doors in life were open to me right at that moment in time. Doors to the south, the north, the east, the west; doors to a new way of working, to a new way of living, to new friends, new experiences, new everything.

"If I don't go through a door I will never know what there might be for me on the other side of it. But once I do go through that door, it will close behind me and never open again. As I get older, there will be fewer doors open to me, until, eventually, there's just one last door to go through.

"Right now, I am young and this is the time for me to go through as many doors as I can. That's what has brought me here, and that's why I have to go through the door taking me away from here. Does that make sense to you, because it does to me?"

Rose nods, but a frown creases her forehead as she answers: "Yes it does, it does make sense, in a way. But what I don't understand is why so many of those doors are already closed to me just because I am a woman."

THE ELEPHANT ON THE ROAD

THE ELEPHANT on the road between Chorley and Blackburn takes no notice of Sammy, but Sammy pays a lot of attention to the elephant.

At first, Sammy thought he was looking at a strange lump on the crest of the road rising ahead of him. Now, he can see that it is moving and getting bigger.

As it approaches the crest of the road, he can also see it has eyes - and ears, which flap lazily. Huge legs lumber into view and a snaking trunk explores the air ahead of them.

Sammy wonders whether he should run, hide or stand his ground. But since there is nowhere he can run to or hide in, he opts to face down the grey giant.

The elephant opts to ignore Sammy and trundles past him filling the air in its wake with the smell of earth and dung.

Sammy wonders whether he should notify some authority about this strange encounter, but who can he tell? He left Chorley and flame-haired Rose two hours ago and it will be two hours more before he reaches Blackburn. Besides which, who would believe him?

The elephant continues its solitary stroll towards Chorley as Sammy watches its huge hindquarters sway away from him. He turns back to the road ahead and continues walking towards its crest, but just before he reaches the top of the road he stops and looks back, still not believing this strange encounter. The impassive creature is still lumbering alone along the empty highway.

Only when he reaches the crest of the road to Blackburn and looks down the slope on the other side is the mystery solved. Sammy sees ahead of him a long line of trucks, trailers and wheeled cages. Most of them are coated in red and yellow paint and some have gaudy green lettering making equally gaudy claims.

One trailer brags *Gerda The Great*, another *Ninth Wonder of the World* and one more announces *Gerry Dixon's Three-Ring Circus*.

Leading this procession is a huge wagon covered in exotic painted images. The florid display shows trapeze artists flying over a lion and a tiger, flanked on one side by laughing clowns and on the other by an elephant looking remarkably like the one that has just strolled past Sammy. Words beside the images proudly boast that Gerry Dixon's three-ring circus was founded in 1882 and is currently on its 30th nationwide tour.

Sammy knows what to do now. He runs towards the lead wagon waving his hands and shouting "Stop!"

The wagon driver, a man in a blue braided uniform and peaked cap, yanks hard on the reins and the four plodding shire horses pulling the trailer gratefully lumber to a halt.

"Mister," shouts Sammy, "one of your animals has escaped."

The man looks concerned and leans from his seat to look back along the convoy.

"What? Which one?" he shouts.

"Your elephant," says Sammy. "It's got away. It's down the road, but a long way down."

The worried look falls away from the man's face and he laughs loudly.

"Oh, you mean Sally. Don't worry about her. She doesn't like to walk with the rest of us. The lions and tigers are too loud for her, so she walks ahead of us for the peace and quiet."

Dubiously, Sammy asks: "How does she know when to stop?"

"We've been along this road lots of times and she knows it as well as I do. Over this hill there's a bend by the river. She will go there for a drink while she waits for us, so there's nothing for you to get concerned about.   Anyway, young man, what are you doing out here in the middle of nowhere? Where are you going?"

"Northumberland eventually, but my next stopping place is Blackburn."

"Northumberland!" the man laughs again. "That is a devil of a hike you are on. Tell you what, we've just come from Blackburn and you've still got five miles to go to get there, would you like a lift?"

"Well, yes, but aren't you going the wrong way?"

The man in the peaked cap laughs again.

"*I* am, but the shit cart isn't. Go to the back of this line and ask for Willy the Shit and he will give you a lift."

The convoy begins to move again and Sammy walks against the flow of traffic until he comes to the last in line. A glum-faced man sits at the front of an empty farm cart.

"Are you Willy the Shit?" asks Sammy.

The man's glum face gives way to a menacing grimace.

"No!" He spits the word out. "I am certainly not Willy the Shit. I am Gwilym Davies, and before you ask your next question, yes, I am Welsh. I was born in that joke of a village in Anglesey.

"Which village?" Sammy asks. "And why is it a joke?"

"Because some clown thought it was funny to give it the longest train station name in the world and renamed it Llanfairpwllgwyngyllgogerychwyrndrobwllllantysiliogogogoch. But half a century later nobody is laughing any more, especially me. So don't ask where I am from and don't call me Willy the Shit. I am Mr Davies to you - and to the rest of that ignorant bunch of clowns up front."

"Sorry Mr Davies, the man at the front of the convoy told me I should see you about a lift to Blackburn."

"Oh he did, did he? Well, nobody gets a free lift from me, so you'll have to work for your ride. How are you at shovelling? There should be a cartload to be picked up from the road by now."

Sammy answers by hauling himself onto the cart's bench seat beside the grim Welshman, who turns it away from the rest of the convoy and heads northward towards Blackburn.

A cart load of horse manure will fetch a good price from the gardeners of Blackburn and Gwilym Davies, from the Anglesey village with the unpronounceable name, is soon shovelling his smelly, but profitable, crop into the cart, with the help of his new recruit.

Between collections 'Gwilym the Glum' tells Sammy his sad tale. Nobody likes him and he's had nothing but bad luck for the whole of his days. People either talk as if he is not there or cross the street to avoid him. Even the circus folk shun him, he mournfully admits.

"If they don't like you and you don't like them, then why stay with the circus," Sammy asks.

"Because I want to be a clown, I want to make people laugh," he says sadly.

Sammy wants to laugh right now, but doesn't.

"Have you asked the clowns about joining them? Is there some kind of apprenticeship that you can do?"

"Don't talk to me about that miserable lot. All I get from them is 'You've got to be born to it', or 'You can't use this clown face, or that clown face, it's been our family's face for hundreds of years'. Miserable - the lot of them."

"Can't you make up your own face - a Gwilym face?"

"I have, and I showed it to them. I had a photograph taken just to show them."

He leans back over the bench seat and reaches into a canvas bag behind him. Gwilym fishes out a photograph and pushes it into Sammy's hands.

The image that Sammy looks at is sepia-toned and stark. Gwilym has a tousled wig perched on his bald head and the right side of his face is covered in white makeup. Black makeup covers the left side, giving him the appearance of a face split down the middle. There is no huge grin, like the clowns painted on the sides of the circus wagons, nor any painted tears as used on some sad clown faces. Gwilym's clown face is disturbingly expressionless.

"That ignorant lot back there just didn't get it. Was I supposed to be happy or sad, they said. I tried to explain that one side of my face represents the bland fragility of life and the other side represents the dark emptiness of death. I wasn't a funny clown or a sad clown, I was a morbid clown and people should laugh at me while they can because all too soon their laughter will be gone.

"But that lot in the circus just didn't get it, they'd rather call me Willy the Shit and have a good laugh at my expense."

Gwilym still looks glum three hours later as he stuffs the last of the Blackburn gardeners' cash into his money belt.

"I will get back to the shitmakers before dark if I get a move on," he tells Sammy. "I've got to clean up the other half of the road to Chorley and deliver it to my usual customers there. Some gardeners at Chorley allotments pay good money for elephant shit. They're convinced it makes their leeks grow bigger. What a bunch of clowns."

He nearly smiles, but only nearly.

"Where are you going now, Sammy? Have you got a lodge for the night?" Gwilym asks.

"No, I'll have to see what I can get. I don't have much cash, so I might just try to find somewhere dry to doss down for free."

Gwilym thinks for a moment, then says: "This place is called Feniscowles. It's at the southern end of Blackburn, and, if you want my advice you should follow that road over there."

He points to a terrace of Victorian houses.

"At the end of that road you will come to a wood with a stream running through it. That stream bends around an old mansion, abandoned at least twenty years ago. You might find a shed or a barn there where you can doss for the night."

"I'll do that Mr Davies, thanks for the tip."

Sammy gives him an appreciative smile and gets a dour grimace in return. The cart trundles back to the circus convoy as Sammy walks onto Victoria Road where a finger post points him towards the hamlet of Pleasington.

Just before he reaches the hamlet, Sammy comes across a set of cast iron gates flanked on each side by a gatehouse. All have seen better days. The ornate gates are heavily rusted, the gatehouses are neglected and empty.

An iron fence fixed to the gatehouses by rusting bolts is no obstacle to a fit teenager and Sammy scrambles over it easily. On the other side of the fence is a long driveway leading through overgrown woodland.

When Sammy is half way along the drive, the mansion comes into view. Its massive front entrance door is dwarfed by the sheer scale of this once-magnificent dwelling. Sammy counts thirteen windows facing him and can see at least half a dozen more on the side wall. The River Darwen loops around the back of the mansion which is overlooked by a wooded hillside.

When he gets closer, Sammy sees that the mansion is as neglected as its gatehouses. Curled flakes of paint stand proud of neglected doors and rotting window frames only just manage to keep filth-covered window panes in place.

Sammy cups his hands, peers through curtains of dirt on both sides of one window, and can just make out a staircase with empty shelves beside it. He pushes at the door but it is either firmly locked or rooted in place by age and deterioration.

At the back of the building he finds what he is looking for, a block stone outbuilding that may once have been stables. A door in the building yields to his push and he is just able to squeeze through the gap he has created. The light inside is low, but he is able to see that his guess is right. These were indeed once stables where the horses each had their own stall with head-height troughs for food and water.

Sammy finds one stall where the ceiling above is it still intact.

"This will do nicely," he says to no-one in particular.

"No, it won't," a voice answers back.

PITCH THE FORK

HARRY Rushforth watches the startled young man jump and stare in his direction, but Harry is in the darkest corner of the stable's third stall and remains out of sight.

"No, this stall won't do for you, because it's already taken," he says, standing up.

Sammy's eyes catch a movement in the dark and he sees a smiling man emerge from the third stall.

"It's all right young 'un, there's room for one more in these stables. You can have your choice of the other stalls, but this one is mine."

Sammy relaxes, but only a little. The face he can now make out in the half-light looks more like it belongs to a fox than a man. It has a sharp nose and glittering eyes that dart everywhere; the lips are thin and the ears are long. The face also has a familiar weathered-leather look; the same sun-beaten tone that Sammy's dad had when he came back from Africa.

"I thought the place was empty," says Sammy apologetically. "I'm just looking for somewhere dry to doss down for the night. I'll keep on looking if it's a problem."

"No, no, no, lad. Sit yersel' down. I'm happy to have a bit of company for the night. Where are you headed?"

"I'm on my way to Blackburn, what about you?"

"Preston for me. That's in the opposite direction

from here. What's the attraction in Blackburn?"

"None at all. I'm going north and Blackburn is just the next stop on the way. I'll maybe stay there for a day or two and see if I can make some money for grub. I'm running low and getting hungry."

Sammy unhitches the sling he is carrying and lays it on the ground. It looks full but, as he puts it down, Harry Rushforth can see that most of the bulk is made up of crumpled newspapers. As well as the papers, Harry can see an old bottle and a small book with a green poster sticking from it. On the poster he observes the words "Votes For Women".

"Oh ho," Harry grins. "A suffragette boy, are you?"

"No." Sammy visibly reddens. "Well, yes, in a way. I met somebody in Chorley who gave me that poster. She had some interesting ideas and was very... um... she looked... well... we... we did some work together and this is a kind of reminder of that."

"Say no more son, I get the picture. We've all been there, at least, all of us who were once young lads."

Sammy turns to stuff the crumpled newspapers back into the sling and folds it into a pillow.

Harry looks at him quizzically. "Can you pitch the fork?" he asks.

Sammy is puzzled. "Pitch the what?"

"Ah, I can see that you've not been on the road for long. You've got to know how to pitch the fork, if you're going to eat. I'll show you how to do that tomorrow. It will soon be black dark and I don't want to light a fire here in case it brings any unwelcome visitors, so I'm going to turn in now. You should do the same."

Sammy takes a drink of water from his stone bottle, to wash down his last crust of dry bread, before tucking the book and poster under his sling pillow and waiting for the last of the day's light to drift out of the stables.

Sammy wakes up the next morning with a question in his ears.

"Is that the Bible you sleep on?"

Sammy's eyes are shut, but he can still see that it is daylight from the pink glow through his closed eyelids. His right arm flops to one side, but the left one is missing, or at least, that's how it feels to him. Then he realises that he must have lain on the arm for so long it has gone numb.

He rolls onto his back and waits for the inevitable. Warmth flows along his left arm, deceptively pleasant at first. Then comes the pins and needles. A tickle which turns into red-hot prickles from fingertip to shoulder, and then the agony of cramp grips the whole arm.

Harry Rushforth looks at Sammy's screwed-up face, watches him feverishly rubbing his dead arm back to life, and asks his question again: "I said is that the Bible you sleep on? Because if you're using it to keep the night demons away, it certainly seems to work. You slept like you were dead."

Sammy shakes his head and opens his sticky eyes. His mouth feels just as sticky and needs a couple of attempts to get it working properly.

"No, it's a phonographic reporter book."

"A phono what?"

"It's a book for learning shorthand. A reporter gave me it because I did him a favour, and I think it might come in useful to me."

Harry looks unconvinced: "Are you pitching the fork to me?"

"No, it's true, look for yourself." He throws the book to Harry, who flicks through its pages and throws it back.

"Gobbledegook, it's just lines and squiggles. I think you *are* pitching the fork, lad."

Sammy is losing patience.

"I'm not pitching the fork - whatever that means. What does it mean anyway?"

Harry smiles and says: "It's what's going to get you your breakfast today. Pitching the fork is what people on the road do to convince other folk that they're not tramps; just journeymen between jobs.

"Do it right and you wind up with free drinks, if you pitch your fork in a pub, or food if you pitch your fork in a grocery shop. Yesterday I pitched the fork at Blackburn Butchery and wound up with this."

He pulls a brown paper package from his sack and opens it. Sammy sees four slices of bacon, two sausages, a slab of black pudding and some chunks of fatty mutton.

"I told a good tale for that lot and I had an extra trick up my sleeve," says Harry.

"What trick was that?" Sammy asks.

"I gave him the secret sign."

"What sign?"

"Can't tell you, it wouldn't be a secret then, but that special sign told the slaughter man that I was somebody he was obliged to help, and he did. Anyway, I'm hungry and I can't cook here, so how about a little walk?"

Sammy nods and gathers together his few belonging before following Harry out of the stables.

As they re-join the road that brought Sammy to his

lodge for the night, Harry says: "It's not a long walk from here; just through these woods and down beside a stream. The water's clean so we can get a drink, and there is a place where I can make a little fire."

Minutes later, he has done just that and the mutton is first into a battered pan that Harry lodges among burning twigs and branches.

The meat puts a pool of melted fat on the floor of the pan and Harry carefully places the bacon, sausages and black pudding into it.

The sizzling mix soon has Sammy's mouth-watering and, once the meat is cooked, Harry shares the meal equally between them. Neither speaks as they munch their way through the grub. Only when it is all gone does Harry say: "You could go north through Preston rather than Blackburn, it won't take any longer and we'd be company for each other."

Sammy thinks. He thinks of how comfortable his stomach feels with some hot food inside it, and he thinks of how much this man seems to know about the ways of the road.

"Yes, that sounds like a good idea," he tells Harry. "And maybe I can talk you into parting with the secret of the sign, on the way."

"We'll see about that, but there is another secret just up the road, and I *can* tell you about this one."

The road ahead descends slightly and gives them a clear view across moorland towards Preston, which is only eight miles away. As they walk along an unmade path, lined with untended blackthorn hedging, Harry suddenly veers left into the undergrowth. Sammy follows and finds Harry standing in a patch of tall grass and wildflowers.

Harry pulls the grass apart and teases from it one cluster of withering stems that Sammy recognises.

"Isn't that a potato plant?" he asks.

"Certainly is. Here, give me a hand."

Harry reaches into the sack he was carrying and fishes from it a small gardening fork, which he passes to Sammy before pulling a trowel out of the bag for himself.

"Come on, let's see what we can find here," Harry says, as he loosens the soil at the base of the brown stems. They dig deep and ease the plant from its bed. Once it is free, Harry hauls the plant out of the soil.

Potatoes and soil rain down as Harry shakes it vigorously. Sammy counts at least eight tubers, all as big as his fist, in the loose soil at his feet.

"Won't you get into trouble for taking the farmer's potatoes?" he asks.

"Not at all," Harry laughs. "They aren't his potatoes, they are mine. I planted seed potatoes in different places along this road three months ago and now I am collecting my crop."

Sammy says: "Do you do that wherever you go?"

"Yes I do and not just potatoes. I have carrots, turnips, beetroot, onions, leeks all over the place. If I can't collect them for whatever reason they'll go to seed and the next year, there will be all the more for me."

"Doesn't your stuff get pinched?"

"You've got to know it is here in the first place to be able to spot it, and so what, if some does get pinched? I've got plenty more like this and it hasn't cost me a penny to plant them."

Sammy thinks for a moment.

"Well then, let me ask you this. Can you eat one of

those potatoes and still grow more from it?"

Harry senses a trick question coming. "Maybe, but I'm not sure how."

"Well you can, and I will tell you how, if you show me that secret sign you talked about. That's fair, isn't it?"

"Mmm? All right, you've got a deal," says Harry.

Sammy thinks Harry has agreed to his offer far too easily, but a promise is a promise, so he shares his secret.

"My dad showed me this one when I was little. You can peel off the piece of potato with the eyes and eat the rest of it."

Harry nods.

"Then you can plant that peeling and eat the potatoes that grow from it, so the same potato feeds you twice over."

Harry smiles and says: "I see. Clever man, your dad."

"Now, show me that sign," Sammy tells him.

Harry raises his right hand and puts his thumb across his palm. Then he folds his two middle fingers over it, leaving his little finger and index finger sticking up to make the shape of a pitchfork.

"That is the sign, but you won't be able to use it for forty or fifty years."

"Why is that?"

"Because it is a sign used by people who have had a lifetime of working with farm beasts."

His hand is still held up with the two fingers extending from it and now Sammy sees an animal's head with a pair of horns rather than a pitchfork.

Harry explains: "It's a hard life working out in the open with the beasts and it takes its toll on those men.

They usually wind up with the rheumatics or 'arthur-itis', but they still need to work until they drop, if they want to eat. So they often end their days doing casual or low paid work.

"If an old cowman on hard times finds himself in a butcher's shop or a slaughterhouse, he will use this sign to show the young men working there that he is one of their own. When they see the sign, and his weathered old face, they know this is a man who has spent a life-time working outdoors. That's when they will slip him a better cut than usual or more meat than he has asked for, because they know that the day will come when they too will be an old man with an empty stomach and aching muscles."

Harry waits for a response from Sammy, but gets none. He assumes that the young man is trying to im-agine being old and finding it as difficult as Harry did when he was 16.

He gives up waiting and pulls something wrapped in an oiled cloth from his sack to make space for the freshly dug potatoes.

"What's that?" says Sammy, interrupting his own train of thought.

"What's what?"

"What's that thing in the cloth."

"Aha, you've discovered another one of my secrets. You know how I get my food and drink, but this is how I get my fun."

Harry pulls away the oiled cloth covering the object on the ground and Sammy sees it is a trumpet, probably made from brass, but too dulled by time and use to tell.

"I can bring a shine back to that," says Sammy. "I have just the thing."

Harry watches him take a piece of crumpled newspaper from his sling and unfold it. Inside the paper is an old Co-op shoe polish tin. Sammy removes the lid and dips the newspaper into the tin before rubbing the paper against the trumpet's horn. After a few strokes Harry can see that the brass is indeed beginning to shine, so he stays silent and watches.

Gradually, with fresh newsprint, more dips into the tin, and a good deal of rubbing, the instrument is gleaming and Sammy hands it to Harry.

"Well, well, Sammy, you've certainly earned your breakfast, thank you. What is that stuff you are using?"

"It's just something I made. I call it Sammyshine."

Harry's eyebrows rise and he says: "You should be in business, not tramping the roads."

Sammy opens his mouth to respond, but before he can, Harry lifts the trumpet to his lips and gives a blast on it. A family of squawking crows flaps from a tree overhead. Harry's own version of Purcell's Trumpet Tune and Air follows them into the sky.

When the tune finishes, Sammy says: "That was really good, Harry, where did you learn to play like that?"

"In the Army; I was a bugler first, then I learned to play the trumpet. It's what kept me sane through all the hell in Africa."

Sammy's eyebrows rise. "*You* were in the Boer War?"

"Oh, yes, I was in the First Loyal North Lancashire Regiment."

Sammy says: "I think my dad was in that regiment too. He went away when I was five and came back a couple of years later looking like you, all brown and with lots of wrinkles."

"You *think* he was in my regiment? Don't you know? Didn't he ever tell you about it?"

"No, I asked him once if he had fought in the Boer War, but he wouldn't answer, and all of his Army things got burned up when he threw them on his allotment fire."

"Not good, not good at all," says Harry. "I've met too many like your dad. They shut the war inside their heads and keep on fighting it in there alone. That never ends well. All too often it winds up with a trip to the loony bin. Where is your dad now?"

"I don't know, and I don't care. I tried to go back to our lodging after my sister's wedding and found somebody else there. Dad had sold him everything in the house, including my stuff. I've been wandering ever since and Dad could be dead for all I know or care."

"That is rough, very rough. But I still don't think he deserves so much hate from his son. Your dad would have seen and heard some awful things, I know that I did. He will have lost some close friends and been forced to take a long hard look into his own soul. Something like that can scramble your brain so much that you can't tell right from wrong, or good from bad. I know, I've been there.

He takes a deep breath before adding: "I was one of the poor sods who thought we had taken Spion Kop just by killing a few Boers. But when the mist lifted from that damned hill there was higher ground on three sides of our position and they were full of Botha's blokes. There was nearly a thousand English soldiers up there with nowhere to hide and just twenty picks and twentyone shovels between us to dig some sort of shelter in hard rock. Talk about Hell, now that *was* Hell.

Generals killed, nobody knowing what to do, shells dropping around us, and then there was the hand to hand stuff.

Harry holds out his hands, palms up, and looks at them.

"You might just see dirt on these. But I see blood on them. You've seen them hold a trowel, but I've seen them hold a bayonet, and shove it into somebody."

He looks up at Sammy.

"And while these hands were shoving that bayonet in, I was looking into a stranger's eyes. Take it from me, the pain in his gut was nothing compared to the pain in his eyes. When he knew it was all over for him. All he had learned, all he had worked for, all the friends he'd made, the women he'd loved, the children who needed him, all lost in the shove of an enemy's bayonet. That's the real pain and it's a pain that doesn't die.

"He dies, but his pain doesn't. It just gets passed over to the one pushing the bayonet - the last person to look at his face, the last person to look into his eyes.

"You don't feel that pain at first, because you're so pleased it isn't you lying there with empty eyes on the sky. No, it's later, when the battle is over, when you are exhausted and try to shut your own eyes and get some sleep. That's when it comes for you, and it keeps on coming for you whenever you shut your eyes. That's why we shout in the night. Our guard is down, you see, and we are alone with our thoughts and memories of what we have seen and done. Look at this."

He reaches into his sack and pulls out a wallet which he opens and extracts a newspaper cutting.

"Don't just take my word for it. That reporter fellow, Winston Churchill, was there, running messages between us and General Buller. Read what he said."

Sammy looks down at the cutting and reads Churchill's eyewitness account of Spion Kop.

> *Corpses lay here and there. Many of the wounds were of a horrible nature. The splinters and fragments of the shells had torn and mutilated them. The shallow trenches were choked with dead and wounded.*

It is a lot for Sammy to take in, and as he hands back the cutting he says: "Harry, I don't want to talk about it just now. I think we should just get going."

He walks across the verge back to the road and strides towards Preston. Harry quickly returns the cutting to his wallet and stuffs the shining trumpet back into his sack before following Sammy.

They reach the outskirts of Preston with not much more being said, but as they near the town centre Harry speaks up.

"Sammy, do me a favour and we'll both have a bed for the night?"

"What do you want me to do?"

"I'm going down to the docks. I can usually make good money playing down there. Sailors coming home can be a sentimental lot. If I pick the right tunes and catch them on their way back from the pub, they can be even more sentimental, to the point of being downright careless with their cash. It would help a lot if you could collect the money for me and keep a watch on it."

"Yes, of course I will, Harry. It's the least I can do after what you've already done for me."

"Thanks. In that case, we'll both have a comfortable bed tonight."

When they reach the Albert Edward Dock Harry points to the vast man-made waterway and says, with delight: "Just look at that. I bet you've never seen anything like it before. It's a thousand yards long, two hundred yards wide, and filled with ships from across the Empire. There is no single dock bigger anywhere else in in the country. Coal, cattle, cotton, clay, wheat from America, bananas from Africa, they are all coming ashore here."

Sammy gazes around, taking in all the sights, sounds and smells of this exotic and seemingly chaotic place.

Colourful posters advertising day trips to Blackpool, North Wales and the Isle of Man are stuck to many walls. Sammy wonders what life would be like if he had enough money to stop working and just spend time and money on indulgences.

Harry interrupts Sammy's musing.

"See what I mean, about this place?" he says. "We can't go wrong here. There's workers, hawkers, sailors, visitors, and all with money to spend on a few minutes' distraction."

Four hours later Sammy picks up the cap that Harry had left in his care. It is now full of coins and he wishes that he really could tell the value of the cash in the cap just by its weight, as he had told Rev Popplewell. But he can't, so Sammy and Harry retire to a nearby pub to sit in a quiet corner and count their earnings.

They eventually tot up the tidy sum of £1 12s 6d and as Harry pushes half of the coins across the table to Sammy, he says: "I can recommend a very nice lodging house just up Ashton Close. It's run by a lady called

Sally Burgham. She charges a shilling a night for comfortable beds and nice grub. For three pence more she'll stick your kit in her wash tub and run it through her mangle.

"Speaking of which, there's a public bathing house in Riversway along that street down there. It would be a kindness to Mrs Burgham if you called in there first.

"I'm going to wet my trumpeting tubes with some ale. Fancy a pint before your scrub down?"

"Not really. Dad put me off drink a long time ago."

"In that case, Sammy, I'll meet you in Ashton Close at around eight. You can't miss Sally's place, there's a sign outside with a bed on it. See you there."

Sammy watches Harry go, scoops up his sixteen shillings and threepence, and in the process takes a quick sniff under his arm.

Outside the pub he turns right and heads for the public baths.

THE
ENTERTAINERS

SMELLING of coal tar soap, Sammy stands outside the large house with the bed sign attached to its wall. He's been here for more than an hour and decides that's long enough to wait for Harry.

After walking along the curved pathway between front gate and front door he raps on a brass knocker in the shape of a clown's face.

Moments later the door slowly swings open and Sammy gazes down a long, dark, and apparently empty, passageway. Only when he lowers his gaze does he see that he is not alone.

In front of him is the smallest woman he has ever seen. She has long, black hair, a beautiful face, sharp blue eyes and short, very short, limbs.

"Looking for a bed, young man?"

"Er, yes. I'm supposed to meet Harry Rushforth here, but he hasn't turned up yet."

"Come on in. I bet that Harry is down at the Masons Arms hanging around with the theatricals?"

"I'm not sure where he went, he just said to meet him here. Are you Sally Burgham?"

"I am indeed and who are you?"

"Sammy, Sammy Kiteland."

"Kiteland? That's an unusual name, are you from around here?"

"My dad is from Halifax, in Yorkshire, originally, and I think the name is more common there. He once told me that there's a hill near Halifax that was famous for the number of birds that used to glide around it, red kites especially. Our family lived there, way back, and were known as the Kiteland folk at first, and then as the Kitelands."

"Well, well, you learn something new every day, don't you? Come on in."

She points a short finger down the passageway and in an off-guard moment Sammy thinks of the short-hand book in his sling. Then he has a flash of guilt and embarrassment at having such a thoughtless thought.

The landlady leads him into the parlour of her lodging house where a man, who looks to be in his 40s, is seated by the fireplace. He is reading a copy of a publication that Sammy has not heard of. The name displayed on the magazine simply says 'Variety'.

"I'll go and get a room ready for you," says the landlady. "Just make yourself comfortable here."

Sammy takes the seat on the other side of the fireplace and the man opposite lowers his magazine to look at Sammy. He says "Aye" and disappears back behind the publication.

Sammy opens his mouth to respond in similar vein to the typical northern greeting, but opts to say more.

"I've never seen that magazine before. Variety? Is that because it is about all sorts of things?"

"No, lad, it's about theatricals; show folk, singers, dancers, actors, dog acts, anything you might see at the variety theator."

From the last word spoken by this man Sammy can tell that he is from somewhere in North East England. Anyone else would have pronounced it 'theatre' and not ended the word with the distinctive glottal rolling 'r' used by some in that part of the country.

"Are you a theatrical?" Sammy enquires.

The man lowers the magazine and raises his voice.

"I'll have you know that you are looking at none other than The Great Doo-Fell. Entertainer, educator, morality tale teller, that's me."

"What does a morality tale teller do?" Sammy asks, and The Great Doo-Fell sees he has an audience.

"I shall tell you, my friend, I shall tell you indeed. Picture this scene; a young mother is in her humble abode cradling a fretting child. The child is hungry, and so is she.

"Her man comes home. Has he brought any food? Well, possibly. He does have something wrapped in paper, which he places on the table. Is it meat, is it fish? Even brawn, or tripe or sausage would do; anything for this starving wife and her starving mite.

"She reaches for the parcel and sees it contains the finest beef sausages. But then… WHACK! The man slams a stick on the table a whisker from her fingers.

"'They're are mine', he sneers. She protests, but to no avail. He begins to shout, she begins to cry. The more she cries the louder he shouts. Eventually he can contain his vile temper no longer. He strikes the defenceless woman with the stick. She screams in pain and in fear, but still shields her child lest any of the cruel blows fall on the howling baby.

"But help is at hand. A passing policeman hears her terrible cries and he bangs hard on the door. 'Police.

What's going on in there? Are you all right?' he shouts.

"The husband is out of control with rage by this time. He yanks the door open and without warning rains blows on the policeman who is caught off guard. The injured officer tries to draw his truncheon to defend himself, but he is too late. One wallop across his skull sends him sprawling on the floor, senseless.

"Her rescuer is helpless, the woman is helpless and her baby screams in distress. Her husband, puce with rage, lifts his stick one more time and then... and then..."

The Great Doo-Fell takes a slow, deep breath.

"And then... the crocodile eats all the sausages."

The Great Doo-Fell roars with laughter as Sammy stares stone-faced.

Behind Sammy there are more peals of laughter, from Harry, who has just arrived, and Sally Burgham, standing with him in the parlour doorway.

"Punch and Judy," says Harry, wiping the tears from his eyes. "He's a Punch and Judy man."

"And he's not The Great Doo-Fell, either," says the landlady. "He's Billy Duffell from Northumberland."

Billy Duffell, from Northumberland, nods because he can't speak for laughter.

Sammy is laughing too, now that he has got the joke, and he realises just how long it's been since he had a real belly laugh. *Too long, far too long*, he thinks.

Later, as they all eat together, Harry and Billy swap tales of entertaining and being on the road, while Sammy soaks up all he can about this strange world of which he knows so little.

"It's Blackpool next for me," says Billy. "I can always set up my show somewhere on the beach for a couple of weeks."

"Show!" Harry snorts. "You mean that one-man tent with a gaping hole at the top. There's more space in my Aunt Jessie's shift. In fact, if you had Jessie inside that little stripey tent of yours, you'd have to call it the Punch or Judy show, because there would only be enough room left for one of them."

"Ha, ha, very funny, Captain Blowhard, I hope your music is more original than your jokes," Billy replies, and with a wink to Sammy, he adds: "Did you hear that our Captain Blowhard here relieved Mafeking when he was over in Africa?"

Sammy shakes his head.

"Yes, the Boers surrounding Mafeking gave up and went home because they couldn't stand any more of his trumpeting. So did a herd of elephants because yhey could each only manage to plug one ear with their trunk."

Despite himself, Harry laughs, along with Sammy and their landlady.

"Ah, that is what I miss," she says, plucking a silk handkerchief from her sleeve and dabbing her eyes. "The backstage banter is better than anything the audiences hear."

"Were you in the theatre too?" Sammy asks.

"I was for a while. I got bitten by the acting bug when I was younger and a lot more naïve than I am now," she tells him. "It took a while for it to sink in that I was only being offered parts in pantomimes, and the reason why.

"I played along with it at first, because I loved the thrill of going on stage and thinking that made me special somehow, maybe even a bit exotic. But that wore off eventually and I decided to make my money from the theatre in a different way, by giving theatre folk the sort of lodge that I would like to have had when I was touring."

This intoxicating world of music, laughter and performance is a world away from the everyday struggles that have filled Sammy's life so far.

He feels now, for the first time since getting up from Bolton Town Hall steps, that he might actually be on the right road to his new future.

Later that night in the bedroom that Sammy and Harry share, Harry talks more about his dreams and ambitions, and Sammy allows himself to hope and dream too. He tells himself that his future life will be whatever he chooses to make of it. Whether the decisions he makes turn out to be good or bad ones, it will at least be *his* decisions that determine *his* life.

He is drifting off to sleep on that thought when Harry's voice, from the other bed, drags him back to wakefulness.

"By the way, I met a bloke in the Masons Arms who has an idea that might make you a bit of pocket money. But I'll tell you all about that tomorrow."

"Who's the bloke?" Sammy asks sleepily.

"He's called Wally. Wally The Wall-Eyed Hypnotist."

Harry has already left the bedroom when Sammy opens his eyes the next morning. He has to pull on his freshly laundered clothes and find the breakfast room before he can confirm what he thinks Harry said last night.

"Did you say something about a hypnotist last night, Harry, and has he got wall eyes?"

"Yes on both counts, Sammy. I met him in the pub yesterday and he said he needs somebody just like you."

"But I know nothing about hypnotism, why does he need somebody like me?"

"We'll see him later on and he'll explain everything then. But for now, just help yourself to Sally's fry-up breakfast from those tureens on the sideboard."

Before either of them can say any more, there is a bang from the direction of the front door and the sound of heavy footsteps in the passageway leading from it. A large woman bustles into the dining room, shouting: "Miss Burgham, Miss Burgham, have you seen this?"

She looks around the room, sees two male faces with surprised expressions staring back at her.

From the kitchen Sally Burgham shouts: "I'm in here, Mrs Black."

The two women meet over the kitchen stove and from the dining room it sounds as if they are both talking at the same time. Occasionally the odd word, or phrase surfaces from the stream of chatter.

"Well!" "Never!" "Shouldn't be allowed!" "Disgusting!"

Tea cups clink on saucers in the kitchen as the conversation flows, but, eventually, the words and the tea reduce to a trickle and the large lady says her farewells.

"That is one unhappy woman," Harry says, as Sally Burgham walks into the dining room carrying a tray with a single sheet of folded green paper on it.

"She has every right to be unhappy," the landlady replies frostily.

"Annie Black believes in votes for women - and so do I. So when somebody makes a mockery of our struggle it upsets us, and you should never upset a woman, not if you want to sleep at night."

"In that case, I pity the unlucky soul who has upset

you and your friend. What did they do?" Harry asks, sympathetically. He knows he is walking on thin ice and will be in deep trouble if he slips.

"This," she says, holding up a green poster that both Harry and Sammy recognise.

"This is meant to advertise an extremely important meeting. It should be in shop windows or stuck on lamp-posts or walls, but look at it. Somebody has turned it into a child's toy."

Harry can see that the poster is full of creases, but can't work out how they would turn the notice into a child's 'toy'.

Sammy explains: "It looks like it has been folded to turn it into a paper dart."

His landlady gives a snort of disgust.

"Exactly, and somebody has been throwing these from the train to Blackpool. Throwing them away, mark you. Not sharing the important information on them, but turning them into rubbish and throwing them away. It's just disgusting.

"Mrs Black is on her way to the Town Hall right now to tell the council what she thinks of the hooligans who did this. Then she will write to the newspapers and bring this up at the next meeting of the Women's League."

"So, everybody will be talking about this meeting, then?" Sammy says, and he thinks: *Well done Rev Popplewell, well done Alan Robson.*

Sally Burgham misses the irony of what Sammy has just said. She is on her high horse, galloping for the finishing line and neither of these men at her breakfast table dare stop her.

"It will happen," she says. "Mark my words. One day

women will have the vote and then this country will change, and change for the better."

Harry and Sammy nod and opt for diplomatic silence as their landlady pauses to see if either of them will dare to challenge her. When they don't, she scoops the breakfast dishes from the table and struts back to the kitchen with them.

Harry breaks the silence. "I think it's time for us to meet Wally."

Sammy agrees and they leave quietly after pushing the dining chairs neatly back under the table. Sammy puts the salt and pepper pots back onto their tray to avoid any further aggravation for their landlady.

Outside the lodging house Sammy asks: "Where to now?"

"That way, towards Fishergate," Harry answers.

Fishergate, a long, cobbled street, is bustling with traffic and people when they arrive. Harry takes Sammy's arm and pulls him across the road.

"Here it is."

Sammy looks at the red brick building ahead of him. Over its arched entrance he sees, in large golden letters, the name *Shelley Arms and Commercial Hotel.*

They walk into the entrance, passing the door to the public bar on the left and an office door on the right. At the end of the entrance corridor is a staircase and beside it is another door with the words *Smoking Room* etched on its glass panel.

Harry guides Sammy towards the door and Sammy opens it. Inside the room the walls are coloured nicotine brown and through clouds of blue smoke Sammy can see that men smoking cigarettes and pipes of all shapes and sizes occupy about half of the tables. Some of the customers have small cases by their tables. Sammy assumes that they must be commercial travellers.

One man is not smoking - yet. He has a once-white, now-yellow, clay pipe lying on the table in front of him. Harry walks towards the man who looks straight at him - with one eye. The other eye is aimed at Sammy, who guesses that this must be Wally.

Wally gestures towards the one other chair at his table and says: "Sit you down."

He is looking at Harry and Sammy at the same time and they both reach for the chair.

Harry says "Thanks" and Sammy drops his hand in confusion and some embarrassment. Harry and Wally both laugh.

"Sorry, son," says Wally "just my little joke. Grab that other chair and pull it over here."

Harry smiles and shakes his head, before saying: "Wally, this is the lad I was telling you about. He's on his way up north and needs to earn a bob or two to keep him going on the way. He's a reliable lad who knows what's what and when to stay shtum."

"Has he been here long?" Wally takes a long hard look at Sammy with his right eye.

"We got into town last night."

Wally smiles and looks at Harry with his left eye. "So nobody will know this face, that's good."

With his right eye still on Sammy, he asks: "What's your name?"

"Sammy, Sammy Kiteland. I'm from Bolton."

"Right, Sammy Kiteland from Bolton, have you ever been hypnotised?"

"No, never."

"Well, I'm going to hypnotise you now, just so you know I'm not faking, but I won't hypnotise you during my show. I need you on the stage keeping watch for me. The others will be hypnotised, but you won't. Your job is to be the eyes in the back of my head."

The smile leaves Wally's face as he adds: "There was trouble at the Theatre Royal here a couple of weeks ago. A bunch of ruffians tried to start a fight during one show by a mesmerist called Ahrensmeyer."

He picks up his pipe and points the stem at Sammy.

"I can handle heckling, but violence is another matter, I don't want to get involved in that, so I need someone to warn me if there is trouble brewing while I'm preoccupied with the volunteers on stage. Your job will be to tip me the wink at the first sign of trouble and I can have the safety curtain dropped pronto."

"I can do that, but what is the pay," Sammy replies, looking directly into Wally's right eye.

"There are two rates. If you come along tonight and just keep a watch, it will earn you one shilling and sixpence. But I could teach you how to hypnotise yourself, a very useful skill if you are feeling low, and in that case the pay is one shilling."

Sammy doesn't need to think about that offer.

"Teach me and pay me."

"Fine, you can have your first lesson here and now. I want you to relax, so take off that sling thing, and your jacket."

Sammy unhitches the sling and places it on the pub table. As he does so, it opens, revealing a stone bottle, a Pitman's shorthand book, a poster and crumpled pages of newsprint.

Wally reads the poster.

"So, you support the suffragettes do you?"

Sammy shrugs his shoulders.

"Not exactly, I don't know very much about it. I just met a girl and helped her to deliver these posters."

"Aha, and she was pretty, I guess?"

Sammy sees that the hypnotist has both eyes trained on him now and finds it strangely unsettling.

"Um, I suppose so. I never really... well, yes she was. She was very pretty."

He recalls flame hair in the sunshine, eyes of the deepest green and a heart-melting smile, until Wally interrupts his thoughts.

"Right, here is your first lesson. This is the simplest thing you can do in hypnotism and once you have practised with me a few times, you will be able to do it on your own.

It's called a hypnotic dream and all that will happen is you will relax and enjoy a pleasant memory for one minute. Then I will say three, two, one, wake up and you will be back with us, but you will feel relaxed and happy."

Sammy nods, but looks uncertain.

"First of all make yourself comfortable in that seat and I will move mine a little closer so that I don't have to shout to make myself heard."

Sammy looks around self-consciously, but the others in the room are engrossed in their own conversations and pay him no heed.

"First of all let's get rid of that furrow in your brow. Just relax the muscles in your forehead, and after that, the muscles in your cheeks and your jaw. Just let them all relax."

Sammy hadn't been aware of the tension in his face

until now. But it was definitely there because he can feel it slipping away as he eases his face muscles.

"That's good. Now for your shoulders. Let those muscles relax and allow your shoulders to droop, then your arms, all the way down to your fingertips, all relaxing.

"Take a deep breath and let it out slowly, relaeasing the tension in your body as you do so. Then think about your leg muscles and relax them completely."

Sammy can't believe how much tension there had been in his body and how loose it now feels.

"Now to relax your mind," says Wally. "Let your eyelids drop and concentrate on my voice. The rest of the noise in this room is just that - noise, and it is of no interest to you. Just listen to my voice and enjoy following it into your dream."

Sammy knows that he is in a pub with lots of people around him, but has no interest in the other conversations going on. It is all just a babble.

"Think of a time when you were happy, really happy," says the only voice that he can hear clearly.

Sammy is enjoying this sense of wellbeing, and the sound of this voice giving him permission to switch off, even for just a minute.

He searches for a happy memory and decides that it will be way back in time. Back to the days when the sun shone and his dad's walrus moustache seemed like a big black grin that spread across his whole face as they walked down to the allotment gardens.

In his mind's eye, Sammy can see the allotments exactly as they were. The cobbled-together greenhouses, the rickety sheds, the rows of potatoes, carrots, onions, leeks, they are all there.

Sammy is standing in Dad's garden and looks down at a row of leeks. The vegetables are fat and in the brilliant summer sun their leaves are a deep, rich, green, while their bodies are dazzling white. He bends forward to examine them, but suddenly they change.

Now he is looking at sheets of green paper with bright white writing on them.

The words he reads say:

VOTES FOR WOMEN
WOMEN'S SOCIAL AND POLITICAL UNION,
4, Clements Inn.
A DEPUTATION OF WOMEN
WILL ARRIVE IN
PARLIAMENT SQUARE....

Sammy looks up from the poster, straight into a face that he thought he would never see again - Rose.

She smiles that smile he will never forget and speaks. Sammy isn't sure whether he is hearing Rose, or just reading her lips. What he does know is that she is repeating the last words she said as they went their separate ways in Chorley.

"We are in a world that is changing," she had told him. "I don't know how it will have changed by the time I am an old woman, but I do know that it will be different and it will be different because of me and people like me handing out posters and convincing men that women's opinions matter as much as theirs."

The smile seems to fade from that lovely face and more words follow.

"I hope that you will be also be a different man, Sammy. Not the kind of man who would laugh at a defenceless woman being battered and threatened, will you?"

"But it wasn't real," Sammy wants to tell her. "It was just puppets, just Punch and Judy, just a children's show."

Rose's lips are moving again. "Just a children's show? Where children are shown that cruelty does not matter, or even worse, that it is funny. Funny to whack a doll because it cannot feel? Funny to whack a dog because it is an animal and can't feel pain the way we do? Funny to whack a woman because she doesn't have the strength of a man?

"It's not funny, Sammy, and it's not right, because teaching children to laugh at cruelty hurts us all and we feel every single blow. Three blows, two blows and one ... wake up, Sammy."

The noise in the bar seems to rush in as Sammy opens his eyes.

"How do you feel, Sammy?" Harry leans forward with a look of concern on his face.

"I feel fine, but that wasn't what I expected."

Wally asks: "What was your dream about?"

"I felt nice at first. I went back to when I was four years old and helping Dad on his allotment. But then I saw the girl I told you about and she wanted to tell me something that was important to her."

"No lad," says Wally. "It wasn't important to her. It was important to you. Everything you saw was put there by your mind. You may have hidden it from yourself, but these are your thoughts and you'd do well to think about why you had them. You might be trying to tell yourself something."

Sammy nods as he considers what he was trying to tell himself.

Wally continues: "Hypnosis gives you permission to be completely honest with yourself and that will make a better man of you, so use it to your advantage. We can talk more about it when you come to the Theatre Royal tonight. In the meantime, I am thirsty for a laugh, so watch this."

Wally The Wall-Eyed Hypnotist walks to the centre of the bar which has a man serving at one end and a woman serving at the other. They both look at Wally and he looks back.

"A pint of your finest ale, thank you."

He is served with two pints, one from each of them.

MESMERISED

"I JUST love being a girl," says Kathleen Houlihan. "Because I never know what I will say next."

The other girls smile tolerantly at their bright-eyed friend. They are used to her erratic ways, and they love her for them.

"What do you mean, Kath?" asks Mary, feeding her friend the line she is waiting for.

"Well…" Kathleen smiles indulgently. "If somebody says 'I like your hair Kath', I might say 'thanks love', or 'did you not like it the old way', or 'bitch!' or a dozen other things. The point is, I don't know what I'll say until I have said it, and I love that."

Mary says "Oh." She knows what Kath means, but is so pleased that she doesn't think the same way. Mary also feels a bit sorry for the boys who always seem to be hanging around Kath. They are only boys after all, which means that they can never outflank her flighty friend, since she constantly outflanks herself.

Two boys are already eyeing Kathleen and her three friends as they all wait in the queue outside Preston's Theatre Royal. They are also doing the usual boy stuff to grab the girls' attention.

"Hypnotist?" The taller youth says more loudly than he needs to. "More like trickster."

"Yes, you showed that last one," says the other boy, who is carrying a paper bag. "What was his name again?"

"Ahrensmeyer," answers his pal. "What kind of name is that anyway, Ahrensmeyer? Should have called himself Mr Trickster. Those chains he got out of had been cut nearly all the way through and those people he got up on stage were just his stooges. What a fraud, and this one will be no better, will he girls?"

Kathleen's eyes flash in his direction. "And what do you know about hypnotism, Billy Price?"

"More than you, Kathleen Houlihan, that's for sure. I didn't see *you* here two weeks ago."

"Maybe I was avoiding you and your crowd, Billy. This girl has got her standards, you know."

The queue moves towards the theatre's entrance door, and as Billy Price reaches it he shouts back: "Just watch and learn, Kath. Once you're inside, watch and learn."

Sammy listens to the exchange as he waits behind Kathleen and her friends. A few minutes earlier he had been sent to join the queue by Walter Finch, otherwise known as Wally The Wall-Eyed Hypnotist.

Just before being sent outside, Sammy had stood with Wally behind drawn curtains on the theatre stage.

"Look through that peephole in the curtains," Wally had told him. "See the front rows? When you are up here on stage, with the other volunteers, I want you to keep an eye on those rows in particular. If there are any troublemakers in here tonight, that is where they will sit. If they sit any further back, the theatre staff, or the police, will get to them before they can reach the stage. After the trouble they had here two weeks ago, there'll be a couple of bobbies at the back of the stalls, so all we have to worry about is the three front rows."

Sammy looked through the hole in the curtain at the empty theatre stalls, then back at Wally, whose hand was stretched towards him.

"Here is your ticket. Go out through the stage door and come in by the main entrance with the rest of the audience. Find yourself a seat on the end of one of the middle rows and wait for me to ask for volunteers."

Sammy took the ticket and, as he turned to leave, Wally put a restraining hand on his arm and told him: "While you are waiting for the show to start, remember what I told you this morning about how to find the right kind of volunteers."

Sammy walked to the stage door and then around the outside of the theatre to join the queue at the front, just as it began to move. Ahead of him he saw a bunch of laughing girls and in front of them two unsmiling young men. One of the young men was holding a paper bag. The other shouted to the girls behind them.

"Once you're inside, watch and learn," he'd said.

In the foyer Sammy hands his ticket to an attendant and finds a midway row with an empty aisle seat. From here he has a good view of the front stalls and sees the sullen-faced youths already seated in the second row. In the row behind them are the girls, talking, giggling and fidgeting.

Wally had told Sammy to watch for people in the audience who seemed up for a laugh.

Any of those, Sammy thinks.

Wally had also said to look for anyone who was dressed more smartly than the average audience member, someone who looked as if they wanted to be noticed. That fellow in the fourth row would do. He looked as if he was wearing in his Sunday best, his hair was slicked back, moustache manicured. Then there were the timid ones he had been told to look for. They were harder to spot, but that nervous-looking woman two seats along from Sammy might be what Wally wants. She is on her own and apparently engrossed in the programme on her lap. But she is not reading. Her head is tilted forward over the programme, but her eyes are locked on the stage.

A sudden fanfare blasts from the orchestra pit, startling the staring woman. Then the Master of Cere-monies, wearing an immaculate evening suit and bow tie, strides onto the stage from the wings.

"Ladies and gentlemen, welcome to another night of entertainment and astonishment at your one and only Theatre Royal." He opens his arms expansively and continues: "For your delectation tonight we have the amazing harpist Lityka, vocal comedienne Miss Marie Terry, hilarious comedy duo Piero and Anita and renowned ventriloquist, Gillan. But topping the bill is the amazing, the astounding, the hypnotising, the one and only, Wall-Eyed Wally."

The stage curtains bulge, twitch and part as Wally steps through them to the accompaniment of cheers and laughter from his audience. But he acknowledges neither.

He stands rigid until the noise abates. One of his eyes is aimed squarely at the stall seats to his right and the other is trained on the seats in the centre.

The auditorium falls silent and still he does not move.

When every eye in the theatre is locked on one of his, a smile begins to spread across Wally's face and his right eye slides inward towards his nose until it is perfectly in line with his left eye. Then, just as slowly, the left eye begins to drift away from the right and keeps going until it is looking at the far left of the auditorium.

Only then does Wally speak.

"My doctor says I have perfect vision in each of my eyes. But they will never make a pair."

The audience laughs in unison and Wally knows the ice is broken. Now he can begin his real work.

"Every one of you out there raise your right arm now," he orders. "Keep it up, keep it straight, while I count to ten." He counts to ten.

"Now, some of you will find that your arm is frozen and you can not bring it down."

Billy Price sniggers and drops his arm, quickly followed by his pal. Across the theatre other arms drift down, but the majority stay in the air.

"Very good, you are doing wonderfully well," says Wally. "Now, all of you people with your arms in the air must stand up."

Sammy follows Wally's instructions to the letter and stands up. But not everyone with their arms in the air gets to their feet. Some of those who stay seated also drop their arms.

Sammy sees that three of the four girls in the third row are standing with their arms raised, despite Billy and his pal jeering at them.

"I will need some helpers so I want you to leave your seats and come to the front to stand beside me," Wally continues in a calm voice.

A few begin to move, but others self-consciously lower their arms and sit back on their seats.

Sammy walks, with about 20 other members of the audience, to the front of the auditorium where Wally smiles at them.

"Thank you my friends. I need your further help to get ready for the main part of the night and we will do that backstage while the rest of tonight's audience is being entertained by the other acts.

"Those of you here who would rather listen to the lovely Lityka and the other entertainers on stage to-night are welcome to return to your seats with my thanks. The others should walk through that door to the left of the stage.

Sammy and about half of the group head for the door as Wally disappears behind the curtain. They all meet in a small rehearsal room backstage where Wally thanks them for volunteering and says they will all be refunded the cost of their tickets.

He tells them that they are all going to enjoy a pleasant hypnotic dream to relax them before going on stage with him. Wally tells them all to close their eyes and takes them through the same process he showed Sammy at the Shelley Arms.

Once the others have shut their eyes, Wally signals to Sammy that he does not want him to take part in the hypnotic dream, and Sammy watches the others instead. So does the hypnotist, who is looking for any signs of distress or abreactions in the dreamers.

There are none and after Wally has said "three, two, one, wake up" he is happy to go on to the next part of the process. He starts with Sammy, who knows what he must do next.

Wally stands behind Sammy and says: "Close your eyes and lean back against my hands."

He places his hands between Sammy's shoulders then gently withdraws them and Sammy tilts back.

Wally uses his foot to position a chair behind Sammy and says: "Sit down." Sammy sits and waits, as he has been told to do, while Wally repeats the procedure with the other volunteers.

At the end of that process six of the ten volunteers have done exactly the same as Sammy. The others lost confidence and their knees buckled when they thought they were falling and that Wally wouldn't catch them.

Wally now knows he has six volunteers who trust him, will go along with his suggestions, and don't mind being the centre of attention on stage.

After the interval, the curtain goes up and the volunteers are all standing by chairs allocated to them.

Wally repeats the falling backwards hypnosis routine with the six volunteers, and Sammy, before guiding each of them to a chair where they sit with their eyes shut.

He turns his attention to Sammy first and says: "Stand up."

Sammy stands.

In a commanding voice Wally tells him: "Sammy, you are now a spy for Lord Baden Powell. There may be Boers in this place and your job is to find them and report back to me."

Sammy salutes, then walks to the front of the stage, where he is not blinded by the footlights, and pretends to scan the audience with a pair of binoculars. In reality, he is reading lips while Wally focuses his attention on the other volunteers and assigns tasks to them.

Sammy concentrates, as he had been told to do, on the front rows and watches the scowling face of Billy Price and his pal in particular. Price leans towards the boy next to him and whispers.

"This is a rotten show. I think it deserves some rotten eggs," are the words that Sammy reads on Billy's lips.

The other boy responds: "Funny you should say that. In this here paper bag I just happen to have…" and they share a knowing grin.

Wally is talking to Kathleen Houlihan now. He tells her: "You are the famous film star Mary Pickford. You are so beautiful that this theatre is filled with people just here to look at you because you are just so-o-o-o pretty."

Kathleen makes exaggerated preening gestures and slinks across the stage soaking up the imagined admiration of adoring fans.

Sammy lowers his imaginary binoculars and points into the centre of the stalls as if he has spotted something. He turns and makes an exaggerated display of whispering in Wally's ear. What he actually whispers is: "Those two lads in the centre of row two have some eggs in that paper bag and I'm pretty sure they are going to throw them."

"Are they, by gum? Leave them to me, I know what to do," Wally whispers back.

Sammy returns to his task of scouring the audience with his 'binoculars' as Wally turns his attention to the well-dressed man on stage who is awaiting his assignment.

"Fine sir," says Wally. "You are the best turned out person here tonight. You are indeed the Cock of the North. But, someone is ruffling your feathers and you can't have that. Someone has stolen all the eggs from your lady's nest and you must get them back."

The well-dressed man springs up from his chair,

glowers at the audience and scrapes his feet on the stage.

Wally looks at Sammy and says: "Baden Powell's spy, can you spot the stolen eggs?"

Sammy peers towards the second row and jabs a finger towards Billy Price and his pal.

'Cock of the North' squawks angrily and jumps from the stage. Other people in Billy's row rapidly stand up to let the squawking man run past them. Billy shakes his head and holds out his hands, just as his petrified pal pushes the paper bag into them.

There is a collision, there is a cracking, and there is a gasp that is echoed across the front rows as the reek of rotten eggs reaches them.

Theatre manager Henry Ginn is primed and ready for this. At his signal a stage hand rings down the safety curtain, two policemen waiting at the back of the theatre rush to the front rows and the pit orchestra strikes up 'God Save the King'.

The audience stands to attention giving the two policemen arriving at either side of row two a clear run to the struggling figures in the middle.

"Scuse me sir," PC Tom Wilkes says as he barges past the well-dressed man.

The well-dressed man says "Cluck."

Billy Price and his pal are grabbed and roughly bundled into the aisle.

"Get off, get off me," Billy shouts and tries to struggle free. The calming hand of the officer of the law makes loud contact with the side of Billy's head and he struggles no more.

Behind the safety curtain Wally has told his volunteers to return to their seats and to the hypnotic dream they had enjoyed earlier. He looks at Sammy and with a flick of his head tells him to bring back the well-dressed rooster.

The theatre manager is waiting in the foyer when the policemen and their charges arrive.

"Just a minute," he says and the ejection of the two troublemakers is paused briefly.

"Everybody," Henry Ginn says to his front of house staff in the foyer. "Look at these two and remember their faces. They are barred. Thank you officers, now you can throw them out."

A few minutes later Kathleen Houlihan has re-joined her three friends on the street outside the theatre. They all have the same question for her, but Mary asks it first.

"What was it like being hypnotised, how do you feel?"

Kathleen pauses, thinks, and answers: "I just love being a girl."

"Yes, we know," says Mary. "And it's because you never know what you are going to say next."

"No," Kathleen shakes her head. "I love being a girl because I am so-o-o-o pretty."

MOONS BRIDGE

BUNIONS are high on the agenda the next morning when Sammy and Harry talk over breakfast.

"You will get them if you don't put proper shoes on your feet," says Harry. "Those clogs won't do you any good at all."

Sammy looks down at the wood-soled clogs he's had on his feet since leaving Bolton.

"There is plenty of wear left in them and they've done me no harm yet," he tells his new friend.

"They are fine for clogging around a factory or walking home in, but not for the distance that you plan to go. If you are lucky, they will just hurt like hell. If you're not, you will wind up with bunions, and, take it from me, bunions are a different level of pain."

Sammy shrugs. "But what can I do, I don't have enough money to buy proper boots, these will just have to do for now."

"You are walking to Garstang next, aren't you?" Harry persists. "That is around twelve miles, which is no problem for a young lad like you. Lancaster is about the same distance beyond that. But once you leave Lancaster you are getting into hill and mountain territory on the edge of Lakeland, and that's a very different kettle of fish. Up there, towns are few and far between and the walking is heavy. One way or another, you will be crippled before you get to Northumberland."

"I know, Harry, but I will just have to do the best I can and be careful. I'll try to walk on grass with my clogs off, and if I find a stream I'll soak my feet to keep them cool. That will keep the bunions away. As for mountains, I don't plan to climb any. What I will do is talk to the locals and ask them about the easiest routes to take."

"Oh, you can speak sheep, can you?" Harry asks with a straight face.

"What do you mean?"

"You've got to realise that once you are up in the likes of Cumberland and Northumberland there are more sheep than people, so you must be able to speak sheep if you want to talk to the locals," Harry says, smiling.

"Well then, when I do meet the occasional human being I'll make sure I'm not sheepish and pump them for all the information I can," Sammy smiles back.

Harry shakes his head and tells him: "Do me a favour, walk on grass and in water as far as Lancaster, but when you get there go to my cousin Winnie Wilding. She runs her dad's shoe shop and might help you as a favour to me."

Sammy's feet feel fine, but just to keep Harry happy, he agrees to find the shoe shop and commits its address to his young, sharp memory.

He knows he can make the walk to Garstang by lunchtime, but takes longer. It's a warm summer day and Sammy decides that he will take a few breaks on route. Although he won't admit it, Sammy has taken seriously Harry's warning about looking after his feet.

Some of his stops will be for food breaks, but he also has other stops in mind. At least one will be to practise the hypnotic technique for resting mind and body that Wally taught him. Part of the technique involves switching attention to something other than any present problem.

Sammy reckons that spending time reading the shorthand book and practising some of its contents should be enough of a distraction for him. With that in mind he takes a lump of charcoal from a kitchen scuttle in Sally Burgham's boarding house.

An hour later, outside their lodgings, Sammy and Harry shake hands.

"Good luck Sammy, it has been an interesting few days," says the older man. "Nice to have met you and good luck with the rest of the walk - the rest of your life."

"Where are you going next, Harry?"

"Talking to Billy Duffell the other night has got me thinking about Blackpool. It will be busy at this time of the year and there should be plenty of scope on the beach and around the tower for a man and a trumpet."

"Won't you ever settle down and stay in one place, Harry?"

"Can't see that, Sammy. In Africa I got used to looking for the far horizon, and since I've been back, I just can't stop. I'm at my happiest when I am walking to that horizon."

Sammy can't see the appeal in never having a destination to aim for, or arrive at, but he doesn't say so. He just waves and turns away to head, not for the horizon, but north east along Ashford Road.

As he walks out of Preston he reaches a long, winding country road by the name of Sandy Lane, and settles into a leisurely stroll to outfox the threat of bunions.

Hedges and fields drift by and eventually it feels as if one foot is overtaking the other almost of its own accord. The sling slaps against his waist in rhythm with each step.

The only sound is from a skylark. The bird is too high overhead to see, but too loud to ignore, and since he can't ignore it, Sammy decides to use the bird's song. It becomes a distraction, something that his mind can work on and play with. At first, he tries to detect the pattern in its trills and warbles, but they are too fast and too complex. He decides, instead, to commit the soaring sounds of that song, to memory because soon he will be hundreds of feet underground, where there is no warm sun, blue sky, or birdsong.

That is when the gloom settles on Sammy. The sun is still shining, the scent of fresh grass fills his nostrils, the birdsong still inhabits his ears, but he imagines being in that dark place. He thinks about the blue scars on Rev Popplewell's hands and how they got there. He wonders what went through the preacher's mind when he was trapped underground. What must it feel like to be buried alive, unable to move legs or arms, feeling coal dust fill his mouth and nose, tasting a sleck of coal and saliva?

His guard is down and the Trojan thought plants a seed of doubt in Sammy's mind. Will that be his future? Is that what he is walking towards? Has he made the right decision?

Without realising it Sammy has stopped walking and become motionless as if he really is pinned down underground. But in that moment of doubt, another thought defeats the Trojan. It is beaten by a memory from Bolton Town Hall steps, where Sammy sat and told himself he could go north, south, east or west.

Sammy tells himself that whichever direction he took after walking down those steps, if death wanted him, then death would find him. Whether he is on a battlefield or desert island, in a shipyard or coal mine, is not important. What is important are the days of his life and how he lives each one, until the moment of that last breath, whenever and wherever he takes it.

Slowly and deliberately, Sammy registers all the smells around him and deposits them in his bank of memories, along with the soaring sound of the skylark and everything else that his five senses can detect on this warm summer day.

The skylark's song ends and the bird drops to the ground to vanish among the green vegetation. It is time to move on. But within half an hour Sammy has stopped again.

As he walks over Moons Bridge, a tiny, stone-built crossing above the Lancaster Canal, he stops to look down. The land at the side of the canal is flat and grassed, and just right for a lunch and anti-bunion break.

Seated beside the canal Sammy removes his clogs and unhitches his sling. He takes out the stone bottle of water, a penny loaf and some cheese he'd bought in Preston. He also has a few early wild raspberries he'd picked from a hedge near the entrance to Sandy Lane. The last item he takes from the sling is a piece of damp newspaper, which he unfolds to reveal the po-tato peelings he offered to dispose of for landlady Sally Burgham.

Each piece of peel has two 'eyes' and he separates two peelings from the rest to bury in a patch of soft soil between the canal bridge and a blackthorn hedge.

"I doubt if I'll be back this way, but maybe Harry will, or somebody like him, so here is a nice surprise for you, whoever you are," he says under his breath.

Back at the canal side Sammy rinses his hands and sticks his feet into the water before tearing off a piece bread to eat with some cheese and settle his rumbling stomach.

After the meal he shelters in the shadow of the canal bridge and dozes for an hour before waking to the sound of a cart rattling overhead. The cart stops and he hears footsteps nearby. A carter carrying a canvas bag walks to the canal side and fills it with water. He looks up and sees Sammy.

"Aye lad," he says, with a nod. "I'm just gettin' watter for 'oss. Are you on the road?"

"Yes, I am, I'm on my way to Garstang."

"Garstang, y' don't say? Would tha like a lift?"

"Well, yes, thanks?"

"It's nowt for nowt, mind. There's summat y' can do for me on t' way."

"What's that?"

"I'll be stopping for a pint at Wheatsheaf. Can you mind the 'oss while I'm inside?"

"Yes, I'll do that for you."

Of course, the carter sinks more than a pint at the Wheatsheaf Inn, but Sammy doesn't mind. He takes the piece of charcoal from his sling and breaks off a fragment. With it he copies symbols from the shorthand book onto whitewashed stones outside the pub.

As he writes, he realises that almost all the basic shorthand symbols are either a straight line or a curved line. The straight lines are easy. Some are vertical, others horizontal, and the rest are at a 45-degree angle, leaning forward or back.

The curved lines are trickier to remember until he works out that if he can draw a circle, he can draw any of them. He draws a circle and then intersects it with a vertical line followed by a horizontal line, splitting the circle into four quarters. The outside curve of each quarter matches four of the eight curved shorthand shapes. The other curves are the shape made by the top, bottom and two sides of the circle.

He draws them a few times, then tries putting some curves together to make simple words.

Sammy thinks this shorthand stuff is all too easy until it he realises just how many words can be made from the simple shapes he has drawn. The shape he made for the word liar could also represent leer, lore, lair and lure. The shape for shell could also be shall, shale and shoal.

Clearly it is time to go back to the book for more answers, but before Sammy can turn a single page he sees a man weaving out of the Wheatsheaf. The man takes two steps forward and one back before steadying himself by grabbing a rail and looking around with a glassy gaze. Sammy waves his shorthand book at the man and shouts: "Over here."

The carter stares at him, confused at first, then smiles in recognition and walks unsteadily towards his cart.

He hauls himself deftly enough into the driver's seat, but holds out the reins to Sammy.

"Do me a favour, lad. Just take these. The 'oss knows the way home and I need to sleep this off."

Sammy climbs onto the bench seat beside the driver

and flicks the reins. The horse plods off at its own pace and along a route it knows by heart.

The carter is already snoring, and the horse has taken command of the journey, so Sammy flicks open his book to unravel the further mysteries of Pitman's shorthand.

When they reach Garstang, the carter is still asleep and Sammy has discovered that dots and dashes in different positions on Pitman's straight and curved lines represent different vowel sounds.

The horse comes to a halt outside a cottage with a rope fence. Beyond the rope is a tiny garden crammed with vegetables.

The carter wakes on cue and takes the reins from Sammy's hand.

"Thanks son, are you headed for anywhere special?"

"No, just somewhere to put my head down for the night, are there any lodging houses nearby?"

"You'll be lucky. There's hardly any around here, but you could try London."

"London? We're a long way off London."

"No, no, lad. That's just what we call her in these parts. It's where she's from, so that's what we call 'er. Not sure what 'er real name is. She's always just been 'London' to us. Just go down to Barnacre Cottages on the old Drover's Road and you'll see 'er place no trouble.

"It's called the Fourpenny Coffin."

THE FOURPENNY COFFIN

THE COTTAGES are all so tiny that Sammy wonders if he has come to the right place. But, just as the carter had told him, there it is, third along the lane from the Drover's Road. It looks like all the other cottages except for a wooden nameplate attached to its gable end wall, with the words 'Fourpenny Coffin' scorched onto its surface by some sort of branding implement.

The front door of the cottage is double hung, like a stable door, and the top half is open. Draped over the closed lower half are the folded arms and ample bosom of a woman with a clay pipe in her mouth.

Her eyes twinkle as she asks: "Looking for a lodge?"

"Er, yes," Sammy answers and quickly adds "depending on the price."

"Oh, I'm sure we can come to an accommodation," she winks. "How about sixpence a night, with a bowl of broth thrown in?"

"Is it not fourpence?" Sammy asks, looking at the little coffin.

The woman at the door almost loses her pipe when a wheezing laugh erupts from deep in that ample chest and turns into a hacking cough.

She shoves a hand inside her floral pinafore and, from somewhere within, hauls out a wrinkled handkerchief to wipe her eyes. "No son," she says, although to Sammy her unfamiliar accent makes the words sound like "Now san".

This must be the woman they call London, he guesses.

"That's just my name for the place, my little joke, you understand?" But she can tell from the look on Sammy's face that he doesn't understand, and further explanation is needed.

"I used to work for the Sally Army in London, in the Burne Street Hostel for the homeless. It has rows of wooden boxes each the size of a coffin and the homeless sleep in them for fourpence a night, so they are called fourpenny coffins. Do you get it now, young man?"

Sammy doesn't get it and doesn't smile at this lady's odd idea of what is funny.

"It can't be very comfortable to spend the night lying in a coffin?" he asks.

The woman clamps the pipe between her nicotine-stained teeth. She is no longer smiling either.

"Take it from me, the fourpenny coffin was the best of the choices at that hostel. Every one of them came with a canvas sheet that the sleepers could pull over themselves. If they couldn't afford fourpence, they could have a penny sit up instead. For that they could sit on a bench all night, but they weren't allowed to sleep. If they wanted sleep they had to pay another penny for a lean over."

"A lean over? What's that?"

"See that rope?" She says, pointing at a coiled washing line hanging from a nail in a door.

Sammy nods, but remains puzzled.

"A lean over is when we would stretch a rope like that in front of a bench so that people sitting on the bench could lean forward over it for the night.

"I call my place the Fourpenny Coffin to show that, compared to the hostel option, sixpence is a good deal for a proper bed and a bit of grub."

She is grinning again. Sammy grins back because he now gets the joke.

"My dad used to talk about being so tired that he could sleep on a washing line. Now that I know what he meant, sixpence for a proper bed and a bite to eat does sound like a fair deal."

Sixpence also sounds very fair to Lizzie Fowler, better known in Garstang as 'London'. Sammy is her only lodger for the night, so she fusses around him rather more than she would do normally.

"Is this room all right? It has two beds and you're my only lodger tonight, so you can have your choice. There's a basin and a jug of water over there and I'll fetch you a new piece of coal tar soap. I've got a loaf baking in the fire oven. It'll be nice and fresh for you to have with your broth. Have you travelled far? You look as if you have. Do you have much further to go?"

For some strange reason Sammy thinks of his dad on an African battlefield with shots and shrapnel peppering the ground all around him, just like this woman's questions.

Sammy decides he needs an evasive manoeuvre.

"Where is the lavatory?" he asks.

Sammy puts his sling on the bedroom floor and is heading for the door before she answers: "To your right, in the yard."

As he shuts the lavatory door Sammy sighs and relishes the moment of silence. He also decides that he'd better check how much money he has left. There is a hole in each of his trouser pockets, so Sammy has his coins wrapped in two pieces of newspaper. Each piece is crumpled into a ball around the coins and the ball is bigger than the holes in his pockets.

Sammy takes the paper ball from his right pocket and unfolds it. He counts the money then carefully wraps it up again and stuffs the ball back where it came from. He does the same with the contents of his left pocket and discovers that all he has in the world is four shillings and ninepence. If Harry's cousin feels like being kind, he might just have enough money to buy a pair of second-hand boots, but they won't be very good quality and Sammy wonders whether he might be about to waste his precious coins.

He also wonders about this lady with all the questions and decides that attack is his best defence. She obviously enjoys talking and maybe the questions she asks are not because she is interested in his answers, but because she just needs to be talking. If that is the case then he needs to stop her questions by asking one of his own - and quickly.

"Mrs Fowler?" The lavatory door is still opening as Sammy speaks. "I can hear that you are not from Garstang, so what brought you here?"

She waves her new lodger back inside the cottage and points to a bleached white kitchen.

"Sit you down lad and I'll tell you. And, by the way, it's Miss Fowler, not Mrs, or, better still, just call me Lizzie."

Sammy sits at the table while Lizzie dips a ladle into

a cast-iron pot hanging from a soot-coated hook over the fire and scoops some of its bubbling contents into a large bowl. She fills another bowl with the steaming, thick mix for herself and pushes a breadboard, with a cob loaf on it, towards Sammy. He picks up a bread knife and hacks off a still-warm slice of the loaf to dunk in his broth.

"Eels," says his landlady. "To answer your question, eels brought me here."

Sammy has time for a questioning glance towards her, but nothing more.

"Pa was in eels. He had a stall at Billingsgate It was called Dick's Eels, but that wasn't his name. It was his dad's stall at first. He was the 'Dick' of 'Dick's Eels'. Grandpa got the business going and Pa took it over when the old man got too addled and doddery. I was Pa's only one, and he wanted to pass Dick's Eels on to me when his time came, so he taught me all he knew about running that stall."

"Did you want to run the eel stall?" Sammy wonders.

Lizzie shakes her head.

"I learnt the trade for his sake, but I hated it. Then one day Pa's heart attacked him and he dropped stone dead over the counter.

"Dick's Eels became mine, but my heart wasn't in it and having dozens of dead eyes staring up from the counter where Dad's dead eyes had stared down started to get to me. It wasn't too long before I sold the business, and I got a good price for it too.

"I made my money stretch even further by coming up north."

She doesn't give Sammy a chance to ask the next, and most obvious, question.

"Like I said, I'm not married and there has never been a man in my life. I think the smell of eels must have put them off. Mum died five years before dad and I was an only one so, when Pa was gone, I had nobody to please but myself.

"This place we are in now was going cheap as chips and is twice the size of what we had in London, so I bought it and here I am, a lodger lady."

Sammy finishes his broth, but wants her to keep talking about herself rather than peppering him with questions.

"I don't know much about eels Mrs Fowler, are they easy to catch?"

That rasping laugh bursts out again, along with a spray of broth droplets.

"Bless you son, there's nothing easier. You can find them anywhere, rivers, lakes, quarries and even canals, and you can catch them in all sorts of ways. One of the cheapest and easiest ways is blobbing."

"Blobbing? What's that?"

"Well, you don't need a fishing net, a fishing rod or a fishing hook, for a start. All you need is string, a piece of wool and a few worms."

Despite his pummelled eardrums Sammy starts to take an interest in what this lady is saying and asks: "How do you catch eels with just that?"

"First you take a darning needle and thread the wool through the eye. Then you use the needle to thread the worms onto the wool until you have a long line of them. Bundle the line into a ball and tie the ends of it to the string, then weight it with a piece of stone and Bob's your uncle, you've got yourself some eel fishing gear for free."

Sammy has another question.

"If the blob doesn't have a hook, then how do you catch the eel, won't it just let go of the bait when you try to pull it in."

Lizzie Fowler is expecting this one.

"That's the trick," she says. "You need to know a couple of things about eels. Number one is that they have curved teeth. Number two is they like to swim backwards."

Sammy is still baffled.

"When they bite on the bait with their curved teeth, you have to pull the blob up fast. Those curved teeth keep Mr Eel hooked on the wool in the blob. The other thing in your favour is that if an eel is in trouble, it instinctively swims backwards.

"They usually live in a hole underwater with their head sticking out and at the slightest sign of danger they swim backwards down the hole. So, you pulling the line up and Mr Eel swimming backwards usually means that he can't unhook himself and you can land him quick and easy.

"Freshwater eels like you catch in the rivers and canals are best for making into jellied eels."

Sammy sees Lizzie's twinkling eyes glaze over as the memories crowd in.

"I was practically weaned on eels and I've had them every way you can think of; smoked, roasted, grilled and jellied, with mash, in eel pie, as eel soup, and all of them delicious," she sighs.

"For a special treat Dad and me used to go to Michael Manze's shop in Tower Bridge Road for a double helping of eel pie mash and liquor - mmm."

For the first time since Sammy met Lizzie she is silent, lost in her reveries of taste and time.

But Sammy wants to keep her talking about herself, so he has another question.

"Is there much money in the eel trade? Do they cost much to buy?"

"The price jumps around depending on the supply," she tells him. "But at the auction we used to pay between sixteen and twenty shillings a barrel and that gave Dad a decent living."

"Are they difficult to cook?" Sammy is running out of questions, but by now it is almost dark enough for the cottage's candles to be lit.

"Bless you, no. It's as easy as pie," Lizzie laughs. "For jellied eels just chop them up and boil them in vinegar and water. Throw in nutmeg and lemon as well, if you like, and after that it's just a matter of letting it go cold and turn into jelly.

"For broth you just take a pound of eels and a quart of water, boil that up, throw in some pepper, parsley and onion, then Bob's your uncle, Fanny's your aunt."

Sammy has run out of eel questions so he switches track. "How did you get involved with the Salvation Army?"

"Oh, I've been in the Sally Army for as long as I can remember. I loved the Sunday School and singing all those rousing songs, 'All Things Bright and Beautiful' was my favourite, along with 'Onward Christian Soldiers'. Then, when I got older, I used to play the tambourine in our band, and later still I helped out at the Burne Street Hostel."

"You must have met some funny sorts there?"

Her face becomes more serious. "I met all sorts at Burne Street, but not a single one of them was funny.

Most were sad, some were damaged, and others were lost souls. We did what we could; fed them, kept them warm and safe for a little while, but at the end of the day we could only do so much.

"The soldiers were the worst, and we had lots of them. Some had damage that everybody could see and they, at least, got some sympathy out on the streets, for their missing arms and legs.

"But others were hurt in the head by what they had seen and done. They were the lost souls. Some just shook all the time and some couldn't bring themselves to say a word about the war when they were awake. But they said plenty about it when they were asleep, shouting and screaming."

Sammy asks: "Did any of them get better?"

"Some of them did, but not many. The ones that did were the ones who found a way to talk about what they had seen and done. That was a big part of what I used to do. I like to chatter on, you might have noticed, and that seemed to make it easier for them to talk back. Mind you, I didn't really want to hear what they had to say; some of it was awful, but I knew they needed to say it.

"One nice fellow from up this way told me some of the terrible stuff he'd seen and how he was still seeing it in his head.

"What was worst for him was that when he came back all his pals were telling him that he was a hero and wanted to know everything that had gone on in Africa. He just wanted to shut it all out of his mind, but he couldn't.

"Even when his little son wanted to know if he had been fighting the Boers, he couldn't bring himself to tell the lad about it. In the end, he had to get away from it all. He just left them and took to the road. That is how he ended up in Burne Street."

Sammy is paying full attention now, and he leans forward over the table.

"This man, did he have a walrus moustache?"

"A lot of them did," says Lizzie "but not this one. He was clean shaven and bald."

"Do you know his name?"

"Yes, I do, he went by the name of Hutchins, Frank Hutchins."

"Not Kiteland then?"

"No, not Kiteland, that's an odd name, I would remember if I'd heard that one before. Why do you ask?"

"Just in case he is somebody I know, but he isn't. It's getting late, Mrs Fowler, I think I'll take myself off to bed now. Thank you for the broth, it was delicious."

Upstairs, he uses one of the bedside matches to light a candle and climbs into a bed furthest from the window. He is not actually sleepy at all, so he pulls out his book of shorthand and spends an hour studying a list of alphabetically arranged grammalogues and marvelling at how each of the simple lines and ticks can represent a whole word.

But before reaching the end of the list, he puts down the book, snuffs out the candle and replays the hypnotic dream Wally had taught him as a way to escape the demands of today and prepare for the trials tomorrow will surely bring.

EELS AND TOES

GARSTANG is now eight miles behind Sammy. The walk, since he left talkative Londoner Lizzie Fowler earlier this morning, has been easy. Whenever there is soft grass to walk on Sammy slips out of his clogs, and whenever he encounters a stream, he soaks his feet.

The weather is not as hot as it has been on some days in the past week, but the lack of any breeze today still makes him feel sticky, so the cool water is a welcome relief.

He is enjoying that welcome relief right now as he sits on a rock dangling both feet in a clear stream. Sammy watches for river eels, but sees none. Eventually, he dips his cupped hands into the stream and brings a cold, refreshing drink to his lips before topping up the water bottle and resuming the walk to Lancaster.

There are buildings on the road ahead of him, but too few for this to be the town he is seeking. As he gets nearer to the buildings, a signpost tells him he has reached the village of Scotforth, two miles south of Lancaster. Ahead of him is a village pub and, as he gets closer, he can make out its name on a swingboard sign.

"Well, that's a coincidence," he says to no-one in particular.

The swingboard outside the pub tells him it is called 'The Boot and Shoe'.

Sammy stops and checks his money. He counts out four shillings five pence and shakes his head.

A decent pair of boots will set him back six shillings and even a pair of re-soled second hand boots will cost between four and five shillings. This is going to be a tight call, and he needs Harry's cousin to be in a generous frame of mind when he gets to Lancaster.

On the corner of Green Street and Bulk Road in Lancaster the sign over the shop doorway says 'John Wilding and Son, Boot, Shoe and Clog Maker', but that's a lie. John Wilding is no more, and neither is his son. They perished together on a beautiful summer day two years ago after John Wilding Junior decided to show off to some girls by diving from a bridge into a part of the River Lune that was not nearly as deep as he thought it was.

Stunned by the impact of hitting the river bed head-first he drifted face down in the current until he reached deeper, slower moving, water. That was where John Wilding Senior found his son after he calmed a group of screaming girls enough to understand what they were telling him.

Mr Wilding had tremendous upper body strength, after years of hammering at his cobbler's bench, but his legs were nowhere near as strong as his arms.

He ran along the river bank as fast as those legs could take him, but by the time he got close to his son the muscles in his calves and thighs felt as if they were on fire. Ignoring the pain he flung himself into the Lune fully clothed and thrashed through the deep, ice-cold water until his hand closed on his son's hair.

He kicked out hard to drag himself and his son back to the bankside, but spasms of cramp seized his shocked and chilled leg muscles. The pain was so sudden and so sharp that he gasped in agony and took in his first mouthful of water.

It was not his last.

When that final mouthful flowed gently into his lungs it remained there while his body rotated in river eddies alongside his dead son.

Two years later the shop sign still says 'John Wilding and Son' when what it should say is 'Winifred Wilding Boot, Shoe and Clog Maker'. John's daughter, Winnie, is as accomplished at the family craft as her show-off brother and maybe as much as her old-fashioned father.

Winnie had argued long and often that the business name should include 'daughter', but John Wilding Senior was a traditionalist and wouldn't budge; no matter how much his daughter complained that times were changing and how unfair it was for him to make her invisible when she did just as much work as either of the men in the business. But her protests fell on deaf ears and the shop sign stayed unchanged.

Today, John Senior and John Junior are two years dead, yet the sign that caused Winnie so much aggravation is still there. She just can't bring herself to change it because the sense of guilt and betrayal is just too powerful whenever she thinks of putting her own name in place of the two men she loved, and hated, so much.

Sammy arrives at the corner of Green Street, looks up and sees a shop sign that reads 'John Wilding and Son Boot, Shoe and Clog Makers'. Through the shop window, he sees a young woman with wide shoulders, muscled bare arms and hair cut as short as a boy's.

He walks into the shop quietly because he can see that she is deep in concentration as she shaves fine slivers from a block of sycamore wood on its way to being the sole of a clog. Sammy watches and marvels at her skill.

The three-foot long stock-knife shaping tool, which she holds with one hand, is huge and heavy, yet she works on the piece of wood in her other hand with delicate precision. The tool she is using is one of the strangest that Sammy has seen. It is an arched shaft of wrought iron with a nine-inch tempered blade at one end, and next to that is a large hook inserted into a cast-iron eye embedded in a big block of wood.

The hook and eye take the weight of the tool while the girl tugs and twists the shaft to alter the angle of the razor sharp carbon steel blade. She strokes the blade over the wood making deep and shallow curving cuts to coax a sole from the wood.

Sammy could happily watch this craftswoman at work all day, but he doesn't get the chance.

He hears "Waddyawant!" and looks away from the girl's hands to her face. That face is impassive and its eyes remain focused on the course of the blade as it skims fine curls from the wood.

"Um. I'm looking for Winnie Wilding."

"You've found her, now waddyawant."

"Harry Rushforth told me to come and see you. He is your cousin isn't he?"

The girl stops shaving the wood and unhooks the tool. She looks at Sammy with expressionless eyes.

"And why did Harry the Happy Wanderer tell you that?"

"Well, he thought you might help me. I'm doing a long walk and…"

"And he said you might get a pair of boots cheap

from me?" the girl finishes his sentence.

"Well, er..."

"The roof over Harry's head is free, but mine isn't, the sun that warms him is free, but I have to buy coal. Harry is a dreamer, but I can't afford to dream. So I hope you're not dreaming of getting a good pair of boots for nothing, just because you bumped into my drifter cousin."

Sammy decides that he needs to adopt a different approach. This girl may not have the good nature to which he hoped he could appeal.

"What I hoped to find here was some good advice. I am not an expert on shoes, boots and clogs and I need somebody who is."

He points to the scruffy clogs on his feet and asks: "Could I walk 150 miles in these if I went north from here?"

"Not in those. They're just yard clogs, and cobbler's dozen at that."

Sammy wonders if flattery might help.

"Well, you're the expert, which is why I have come to you, although, to be honest, I didn't understand any of what you've just said. What are yard clogs?"

"They're rough and ready clogs; the sort used for work and left outside in the yard."

"And cobbler's dozen?"

"A well-made clog should only have a dozen nails around the cortis."

"What's the cortis?" Sammy interrupts

"The back of the shoe. The part where the leather is attached to the heel. Anyway, as I was saying before you interrupted, the leather upper should be attached with a dozen nails, but if it is a poor fit at the back, then one more nail will have to be used to hide the poor work-manship. So a cobbler's dozen is thirteen nails, and that's a sure sign of a shoddy job."

"Oh, right; so you don't think these clogs will last my walk?"

"The clogs might, but your feet certainly won't. They're not even a good fit for those feet of yours."

"Harry was right then?"

"What did Harry say?"

"That I will wind up with bunions."

A faint smile flickers on her face and vanishes.

"It sounds as if 'Hopeless Harry' has picked up a bit of common sense during all of his drifting around. If he picks up any more, he might realise that working puts food on the plate, not walking, and only work will get the boots that you need."

Sammy can see that he is getting nowhere with this single-minded young woman. He is wasting time looking for generosity or sympathy, and his flattery fell on deaf ears, so maybe it is time to sell her an idea that fits with her view of the world.

"Can I ask why, in your opinion, boots are better than clogs for the sort of walk I'll be doing?"

She takes a deep breath and wonders whether giving this young man the answer he seeks is worth the effort. But it is a question she can answer easily and she enjoys showing off her knowledge of footwear, especially to a man, when so many men who know nothing think they know everything.

"A pair of clogs is cheaper than the average pair of leather boots and they are better than boots when it is wet underfoot and the soil is light, but when the soil is heavy and wet, you need a good pair of boots," she tells him. "The way you are planning to go will take you over all kinds of ground, light and heavy, therefore boots are best for you."

"And the best boots for me will be ones that will repel water and mud. Is that right?"

Winnie gestures towards some shelves and says: "That's right, and you will find them over there, along with their prices."

Sammy can feel an idea growing and decides to test it out.

"I know that boots and shoes are made from all kinds of animal skins, but are some more waterproof than others?"

"Yes," Winnie replies, beginning to lose patience.

"And are any skins completely waterproof?"

"Not completely waterproof, but the thicker the leather the longer it will hold back water. The problem with that is thick leather means uncomfortable shoes."

Sammy now knows where he is going with his germ of an idea.

"What if you could have shoes made from a thin skin that is totally waterproof?"

"Well, then you would be onto a real money-maker," Winnie tells him.

"If I give you a skin that is not just thin and waterproof, but won't cost you a penny, will you give me a pair of your boots?" Sammy asks.

Winnie's business brain processes that idea for a moment.

"If the skin is thin, waterproof and free, I *will* give you a pair of boots, but I'll choose which ones."

Sammy sticks out his hand and they shake on the deal.

He says: "I'll be back in a couple of days with the skin, so have the boots ready for then. Just one more thing, could you give me a length of string and some wool? Oh and have you got an old stitching needle I can borrow?"

Two days later Winnie thinks Sammy is looking tired as he ambles along Bulk Road towards her shop. She also thinks he is not her problem and turns back to the job in hand. One slip, one moment of lost concentration, and the half-carved wooden sole she is holding will be fit only for the fire.

The stock knife tool being used by Winnie bears the trade name *By Henry Carter*, and Winnie admires that.

"If you are proud of what you have done, you should be proud to put your name to it," she was fond of saying. But that was also why she was reluctant to put her own name to the clogs that she made. Although the footwear she crafted was far from being slapdash 'yard' clogs, she felt that nothing about her boots and clogs was special enough to boast the brand *By Winnie Wilding*.

She puts down the stock knife and the piece of wood she is carving, when Sammy enters the shop. Winnie looks at him expectantly.

He smiles, unhitches the sling from his left shoulder, and places it on the counter.

"There you are, as promised, skins ready for tanning and turning into shoes that are soft and waterproof."

Winnie watches Sammy open the sling and lift out something covered in damp newspaper. It has an odd smell, but she is used to that. Winnie is a regular visitor at her local tannery and is familiar with the overpowering odours that surround it. But this one is new.

"Is that eel skin?" she asks, turning up her nose.

"That's exactly what it is," Sammy tells her. "I caught them on Tuesday night down at the Lune. It took me all night, but I got a dozen of them. Tricky things, eels, they kept slithering back towards the river at first. Then I worked out that I could grip them if I threw a newspaper page over them first.

"I spent yesterday going around fishmongers until I found one that would skin them for me in return for keeping the flesh. I managed, eventually, and now you have a dozen eel skins ready for tanning and turning into shoes fit for a queen."

Winnie looks unconvinced.

"Any skin can be tanned, and the tannery I get my leather from is the best in town, but eels? Really?"

"Yes, really. Look, this skin is as waterproof as it comes and is so soft. Once those shoes are on display in your shop window all Lancaster will be talking about them - and talking about you. They could make the name Winnie Wilding famous in this town."

"But-" she begins, then stops and looks up at the top of the shop window where she can see John Wilding & Son in reversed lettering.

"*My* name? Famous?"

She looks at the eel skins again, then over to her Bradbury's shoemaking machine in a corner of the shop.

Sammy sees her expression change from disbelief to doubt and then to curiosity.

He presses home his advantage with: "Your tanner will make that skin usable and your skill will make it beautiful. Just imagine a pair of soft, shiny, waterproof ladies' shoes available from only one shop in the whole of Lancaster - your shop. You will be able to name your own price."

Curiosity gives way to credence.

"You might be right, but it will take a lot of hard work."

"And hard work is what you are good at."

She looks at Sammy and for the first time, doesn't notice his patched and worn clothing, or his rubbish yard clogs.

"What's your name?"

"Sammy, Sammy Kiteland."

"Well, Sammy Kiteland. You are not as stupid as you look."

"No, I'm not," he agrees.

She thinks for a moment, then tells him: "Listen, I know I said I would give you some boots if you could come up with a skin that was waterproof, soft and free."

"Yes, you did."

"Well, you've kept your side of the deal, so I will keep mine, but this idea of yours might not work out, for whatever reason, so you wouldn't expect me to give you one of my best pairs of boots, would you?"

"What are you saying?"

"I have a pair of boots that are second-hand, but I have re-soled and rebuilt them so they look like new, and they are your size. You can have those."

Sammy smiles: "That sounds fine to me, I'll take them, thanks."

Winnie hesitates briefly, then adds: "There is something else, Sammy. I wasn't going to mention this, but it might matter to you. Those boots used to be army boots. After the Boer War the Government had a lot of old kit to get rid of and the cheapest boots they sold off were ones that came back from the front when their owners didn't. You will be walking in a dead man's boots."

"No," says Sammy. "I will be walking in a brave man's boots. Why on earth would that bother me?"

When he pulls them on, the 'dead man's' boots feel like fireside slippers to Sammy's feet after so many miles inside yard clogs.

"Here," says Winnie, and she puts a large, round tin in his hand.

"What is it?" Sammy asks, hoping it isn't Sammy-shine.

"It is something I make that will help to keep the water out of your new boots. It is a combination of mutton fat and beeswax. If you rub that regularly along the seams of the boots water will never get in through the stitching."

Sammy is about to put the tin and his old clogs into his sling when he catches a whiff of eel, and says: "I think I'll just go down to the Lune and give this sling a good wash before I do anything else."

Winnie thinks that is a very good idea and nods.

After rinsing the sling thoroughly in the waters of the Lune Sammy spreads it over a nearby bush to dry off in the sun, then sits down for a lunch of cheese, carrot and bread. As Sammy chews, his thoughts turn to the next stage of his walk, which will cover the 14 miles between where he is now and Kirkby Lonsdale.

He can't afford another night at a lodging house. But Sammy is confident that, if he pushes himself, he should be able to make it to Kirkby Lonsdale before the end of this long summer day. If he doesn't get there before dark, then he will just have to bed down for the night under a bush somewhere.

Back at the fishmonger's shop, Sammy collects the possessions he had left there while he delivered the eel skins to Winnie Wilding. Into the sling he puts his water bottle and some old newspapers, donated by the fish shop owner, along with two carrots, the remains of his bread and some broken biscuits.

The sling also has a new aroma. It no longer smells of eel skins. Now, it smells of mutton fat and bees wax after Sammy used all of Winnie's waterproofing mixture to coat the sling. He hopes that the waterproofing will protect the sling's contents if it rains.

As Sammy leaves Lancaster, he makes a serious mistake. He walks past a baker's shop. The smell from the shop wafts out of the open doorway and suddenly he is taken hostage by the aroma of baked bread and cakes. The smell is mouth-watering and irresistible.

He asks the woman behind the shop counter: "How much are those cheese scones?"

"Usually a penny each, but those have been there since yesterday, so it's two a penny."

"I'll take them."

Back on the road to Kirkby Lonsdale Sammy stuffs one of the scones into his sling. He has already munched through the other one.

The path out of Lancaster follows the twists of the River Lune until it reaches a bridge which takes him over the river and into the village of Halton.

At the entrance to the village there are two roads, one called High Road, and the other called Low Road. With a full stomach and comfortable feet Sammy is in a cheerful mood and he starts singing an old Scottish ditty.

"Oh, you tak' the high road and I'll tak' the low road..."

He started the ditty as he walked into Halton and now discovers that it is so small he is striding out of the village and into open countryside before he has even reached the last verse.

There are trees on either side of this road to Kirkby Lonsdale. Just past them he turns a bend in the road and can see that the route ahead runs through miles of gently undulating moorland. The late afternoon sun is bright and the sky cloudless.

This will be easy, Sammy thinks. *Just another dozen miles and I'm home and dry.*

SIMPLE

SAMMY is not home and he is not dry. The storm came out of nowhere.

About an hour ago the wind changed direction and picked up strength. Dark clouds appeared first over the hilltops behind him and now they fill the sky overhead.

There's not a scrap of shelter here on the moors and when the rain falls, it is in an unremitting downpour of fat drops that each burst and spray on contact with Sammy.

His fustian jacket is overwhelmed at the outset of the deluge, the shirt below it soaked in moments and saturated trousers cling to his legs. But the newly waterproofed sling does its job and repels the storm rain with ease.

Just wish it was big enough to shelter under, Sammy thinks.

Only his feet stay dry, inside the 'dead man' boots.

"Thanks for that at least, Winnie," Sammy mutters. "I could have done with an eel skin suit as well."

He struggles on, hoping to come across a bush or tree to shelter under, but sees nothing. Sammy repeatedly wipes his waterlogged eyes and eventually he thinks he may have rubbed them too much because he can't even see the rain in the surrounding gloom. Then he realises that he has plodded his way through sodden dusk and into the blackness of drowned night.

With no moon to light his way or distant town lights to aim for he knows that he is in real trouble. Sammy must now rely on the feel of the road under his feet. If he feels it rise to the right or left, he knows that he is straying from the path and adjusts his direction, but it is a painfully slow process.

Up here on the moors there is no room for error and Sammy is acutely aware that if he falls and injures himself in these unforgiving conditions, with no-one else around, he could quickly be in a life-threatening situation.

Half an hour later, cold, saturated and miserable, Sammy blinks hard. Are his eyes deceiving him or is that a flicker of light in the distance to his right? He changes direction and heads towards the flicker feeling the road beneath his feet slope downwards.

After 15 minutes the speck of light is no brighter or bigger. After 30 minutes it is still the same size and Sammy wonders if the light is moving away from him. Seconds later something solid thumps him in the chest.

Thrown off balance, Sammy stumbles and instinctively reaches out. His hand touches the dry stone wall that he has just walked into. He is winded, but relieved that it is just a dry stone wall, even if it is a very wet dry stone wall, because where there is a wall, there is often a -

He feels along the wall for a hundred paces and then his hands close on what he was hoping to find – a gate. A wire loop attaches the gate to a post and Sammy lifts it. He pushes the gate open and steps onto a footpath on the other side.

The path takes him towards the light, which, at last, seems to get brighter and bigger. The light takes the shape of a square and Sammy realises that it is a window. He heads towards it.

Johnny Miller is getting edgy.

"He should have been back by now, look at the time."

Johnny gets no response.

"He said he would only be a couple of hours, and that was nearly four hours ago."

Silence.

"He was only going to check the sheep over by the bothy. It shouldn't take him so long, even in this weather."

Nothing.

"I should have gone with him. I would have if it hadn't been for you.

"Listen! What's that? Must be him."

The look of hope in Johnny's face turns to puzzlement when he hears a knock at the cottage door.

"It's not him, he wouldn't knock. But who…?"

The question is left unanswered as he reaches the door and lifts the latch to pull it open.

Outside the cottage door is a young man who looks as if he has been for a swim fully clothed.

Sammy gratefully feels a gust of warmth from inside the shepherd's cottage and sees a young man with a worried look.

"Yes?" the young man says.

"Sorry to bother you, but the storm caught me out and I'm looking for somewhere to shelter until it passes. Maybe you could point me to a barn or something so I can dry off."

Johnny looks disappointed, but says "Er, yes, come in."

Sammy gratefully walks in and shrugs off his soaked coat to leave it in the doorway. Johnny waves him over to the blazing fire.

"Come over here and dry off. Fetch your coat as well."

Sammy picks up the coat, turns towards the fire and notices that there is someone else in the cottage. A boy of around 12 is sitting awkwardly on a wooden chair in front of the fire. Sammy smiles at him and the boy's face twitches in response, but he does not speak.

"I'm Johnny and that's my brother George," Sammy is told.

"Hello Johnny, I'm Sammy. Hello George."

"He won't answer you," says Johnny. "He's a bit simple in the head."

"Oh, I see." Sammy nods and notices that George's lips are moving. They twitch and form shapes, but there is nothing there for Sammy to hear, or lipread. He turns back to Johnny and thinks that he looks rather young to be a shepherd.

"Do you and George live here on your own?" he asks.

"No, this is our dad's place. Mother died having George, so it's just the three of us."

"I hope your dad's not out in that storm."

"He is, and I'm getting worried. He should have been back above an hour ago. I hope he has taken shelter in the bothy because he doesn't have any waterproofs with him. It was such a nice day earlier on, he didn't think he would need them. I would have gone up to the bothy with some waterproofs for him, but George can't be left on his own."

Sammy thinks for a moment, looks at George and then back at Johnny.

"I could keep a watch on George while you go up to the bothy, if you like. It'll take a while for me to dry out so I'm not going anywhere."

Johnny looks torn. "Well? That storm's not easing and Dad will be in a foul mood if he's stuck up there for the night. George has eaten, and he likes to just watch the fire, so there won't be anything to do other than keep an eye on him and throw the odd log onto the fire."

Sammy looks at George and asks: "Would it be all right with you if I sat here until Johnny comes back with your dad, George?"

George's bent left leg jerks straight, his shoulders twist and his cheek muscles briefly tug his lips into what might be a grin or a grimace.

"That's settled then," Johnny tells Sammy. "I'll be back in about an hour."

He disappears into another room and returns moments later, dressed for the weather and carrying a spare set of oilskins.

At the door he stops and looks back to see Sammy steaming gently in front of the blazing fire and George watching the dancing flames.

He shakes his head and walks out into the howling storm.

"Would you like a drink?" Sammy asks George.

He gets a sideways jerk of the head in answer.

"Something to eat?"

A similar jerk follows.

"Fine. But if you do want something just a... I mean, just let me know."

George looks at Sammy. The look is long and steady and Sammy sees something in it, but he is not sure what.

"If you don't want to eat or have a drink and you are happy just looking at the fire, George, I think I will do some work of my own."

George's head dips forward.

Sammy reaches for his rain-covered sling and pulls out a dry book. From the fireplace he picks up a charcoal fragment and writes on the sawn ends of a pile of logs at the fireside.

George watches as Sammy keeps referring back to the book and scribbling on the log pile.

He is practicing the shortform symbol for the word 'you', which looks like the letter n, when George makes a sound.

"Dat?"

Startled, Sammy says: "What?"

George sucks air noisily through his nose and, looking at the logs, says: "Dat?"

Sammy repeats the question: "Dat? Do you mean that? Do you mean what's that?"

George's head jerks forward.

"It's just something I'm learning to do; a kind of writing called Pitman's Shorthand. Can you write?"

George's head jerks once to the side and he tries to lift his right hand, but it shoots sideways and then downward as he struggles to bring it under control.

Sammy nods as he understands George's message.

"Yes, I can see why you can't write, but maybe you can read. Have you been shown how to do that?"

George's head jerks sideways.

"That's a shame, I always enjoyed reading at school and learnt such a lot from books, even story books. If you can write as well, then you can send messages and tell stories for yourself and for other people."

George fixes Sammy with one of his long stares.

"Emma Horey," he says.

"Who's that? Who's Emma Horey."

George twists his head, both ways this time.

"No? I'm sorry George, I don't understand what you mean. Are you telling me somebody's name when you say Emma Horey?"

George jerks his head again.

"It's not a name then, so what can it be? Are they words?"

George's head tilts forward.

"They are words, then. Let's take the first one, emma, what does that mean?"

George's right arm jerks out and he struggles to bring it under control. When he does, he slaps his hand against his chest.

"You," says Sammy, "It means you? I've got that, so what about the second word horey, what does that mean?"

George turns his gaze to the pile of logs and the charcoal scribbles on them.

"You mean words? Right, I've got that. So what do words make? A story?"

George's head tilts forward.

"Do you mean tell you a story?"

George's head jerks.

"No, not tell a story *to* you. Tell a story *for* you, tell *your* story, is that it? Emma Horey means 'tell my story' is that right?"

George's cheek muscles pull and his face twitches. It is definitely a grin this time.

Sammy claps his hands in delight. "Right, I've got it now. You want me to tell your story."

Then the grin slips from his face. "How on earth can I do that?"

George is still smiling crookedly and Sammy is looking serious when Johnny opens the cottage door and staggers in, pushed by a blast of rain and wind.

"We've got trouble," he says. "Dad has had a fall and done something to his ankle. He managed to hobble to the bothy, and he's holed up there waiting for me to fetch help. I'm going over to the Dalton's farm, just down the way, to see if I can borrow a cart or a trap and take him to see the doctor in Kirkby Lonsdale.

"I don't know how long it will take to get the doctor to sort Dad out, so it might be morning before we get back. Could you stay with George until then?"

"Of course," says Sammy.

"You can help yourself to some food and there is an easy chair over there if you want to doze. George can put himself to bed. He can manage that much on his own."

Sammy nods and tells him: "I'm quite happy to spend a horrible night like this in front of a warm fire, but what about you? It's so dark out there, will you be able to find your way?"

Johnny smiles and says: "I can find my way around these moors blindfolded. I know every tree, every bush, every blade of grass, every piece of sheep shit out there. Don't worry about me, just keep a watch on George, he can be very clumsy."

He turns back to the door and opens it.

"And as for that old misery in the bothy whingeing about me taking so long to come looking for him? Well, I'll make him eat his words. You can count on that," Johnny says, disappearing into the blackness.

George gives Sammy a long look and jerks his right hand up to his mouth.

"Are you hungry, George?"

The boy tilts his head forward.

"Where is the food?"

George makes himself speak rather than just pointing.

"Nnnn, nnn, mmm antree," he says.

"And tree?" Sammy ponders. "Um? Antree? Ah, got it! Pantry, is that it, pantry?

George smiles and lifts a wobbling hand towards a door behind Sammy.

There is a substantial amount of meat in the pantry, most of it mutton, and an uncut cob loaf. Sammy makes sandwiches for himself and George. He also fills a kettle and puts it onto a trivet which he swings over the fire to boil up water for a pot of tea.

After they have eaten, Sammy throws two more logs onto the dying fire and looks at George.

"Right then, let me think. How *am* I going to tell your story when it's so hard for me to understand what you are saying?"

George turns his face towards the fire as flames lick around the logs and considers the problem. Sammy does the same.

"If you'd been able to write, then not being able to speak wouldn't be such a problem. You could have just written what you want to say. But it takes years to learn to write and I certainly couldn't teach you overnight. There are so many letters to remember and you have to learn how to put them together into words. Then the words have got be built up to make sentences. You've got spelling to get right, grammar to get right. It's just so confusing when you first start.

"On the other hand, if you'd been able to read, but not write, I could have written a few key words for you to point at and we could have built up sentences that way. But since you haven't learned to read we can't do it that way either. What we need is something quick and simple that we both understand."

George still has his eyes on the fire and Sammy turns his gaze back to the blaze.

Flames dance, curl and flicker around the logs. Their sawn ends blacken and burn away. So do the marks that Sammy had scribbled on them with a piece of charcoal when he was first left with George.

As he stares at the burning logs Sammy notices how many of the twisting, leaping flames briefly take on the curving shape of some shorthand outlines. Here is a curl that looks like the shape for the sound of the letter 'L'. There is the sweep of a 'Sh' sound and this quick flicker mirrors the tick of the vowel sound 'Ah'.

Sammy sees whole words formed by the dancing shapes in the fireplace and an idea sparks to life in his mind.

"I've got it, George. I know what to do."

George takes his eyes away from the fire to stare expectantly at Sammy.

"I will teach you some shorthand words. I'll keep the shapes simple and easy to remember and there won't be many of them at first, but once you have got the hang of the few, we can add more. How about that?"

George pulls his crooked grin and dips his head forward three times.

"Are there any pens and paper in the cottage?"

George nods and shakes his head.

"Sorry, George, I asked two questions there, didn't I. Let me start again. Is there any paper in the cottage?"

George nods and looks towards a curtain at the far side of the room.

"But no pens. Is that what you're saying?"

George nods.

Sammy walks over to the curtain and pulls it back to stare into what is obviously the cottage's 'glory hole' where everything that might be needed, but probably never will be, is dumped.

Among the clutter of broom shanks, rusting buckets and a stepladder, Sammy sees a box full of scraps of wallpaper.

"Is this what you mean, George?"

George nods and Sammy carries it over to the fireside.

"Right. We have paper, but no pens, or pencils, I suppose?"

George jerks his head.

"Never mind, I have an idea. Is there any ink here?"

George pauses before responding, but eventually nods and looks straight at the 'glory hole'.

Sammy goes back and searches.

"I can't see any ink here George, are you sure?"

George nods and Sammy looks again.

"I can't see any ink, just a tub of something with no name on it."

He opens the tub lid, looks inside, and laughs.

"Ah. I see what you mean George. Bright boy. There's no ink, but this sheep dye will do nicely. I just need one more thing and that's a donation from you."

George stares at Sammy as he walks towards him with a pair of sheep shears that had also been in the 'glory hole'.

"I don't need much, so don't worry, you've got plenty of hair to spare."

He snips a lock of hair from the thick mane draped down the back of George's neck then ties it to a peg that he'd found beside the shears.

"There you go. We have everything we need. I'll just get some of these pieces of wallpaper and paint the shapes of the first six words I want you to learn."

He paints the shapes of the words *me, you, the, of, to*, and *go*, then, one at a time, he lifts each piece of wallpaper, shows the shape to George, and says the word it represents. Then he places all the pieces of wallpaper on the floor in front of George and says: "Can you remember *go*?"

The shorthand symbol is is a straight, thick, horizontal line and George looks straight at it.

"Now show me *the*."

George looks at the single dot which Isaac Pitman chose to represent that word.

Sammy sees a new look in George's eyes as they work through the other words. Excitement and understanding shine in those eyes. But so does something else. A new world is opening up for George.

After more practise Sammy says: "Now look at this" and draws a thick, black line leaning left with a tiny hook at the top.

"If you were writing this word in longhand, it would take eight separate letters, but in shorthand it is just one line with a hook on the top, and it is easy to remember this word because the word this shape represents is 'remember'. You won't forget that one, will you?"

A grin stretches George's face.

"Now try to make a sentence from the words you know."

George looks at Sammy, then down to the shape representing *you*, then *go*, then *to* and then he looks up and straight at the 'glory hole.'

"You want me to go to the 'glory hole', is that it?"

George nods and shakes his head.

"You don't actually want me to go there, you're just saying it for practise, is that right?"

George nods.

"See how easy it is for somebody as bright as you are George. We'll practise more with these words so you'll know the shapes really well. Then we will keep adding new words and do the same with those."

George tilts his head forward three times.

The dog cart bringing Jacob Miller and his son Johnny home the next morning trundles through the hamlet of Newton on its way to their cottage in the rolling moors ahead.

It has been a trying time for father and son. Both are tired and irritable in equal measure. Jacob's swollen ankle is painful, but at least he now knows it is not broken.

Johnny has had a miserable night of tramping for miles over sodden ground in a downpour, finding no-one at either of the two farms nearest to his dad's cottage, and scaring another neighbour by hammering on her door late at night to beg for some transport. Then, despite all his best efforts, he still got a flea in his ear from his ungrateful dad for taking so long about it.

It is afternoon now, and home is, at last, in sight. Johnny flicks the reins in his hands startling the dogcart pony, which jerks forward.

"Ow, take it easy lad," says his father, stroking his bandaged ankle. "I'm not bothered about getting home quick, I just want to get there in one piece."

Johnny doesn't respond, he just tugs the rein in his right hand gently and the pony turns from the road onto the track leading home.

When they arrive, Johnny jumps down from the dogcart. He holds out a supporting hand for his father, who takes it. The older man hobbles towards the cottage door, which Johnny reaches first and holds open for him. Johnny is still holding the door open when he hears his father's voice from inside.

"Oh good God! What's happened here?"

Johnny quickly moves inside, closing the door behind him.

The room inside the cottage looks totally different to the way it was when he left last night. George is there and so is the young man who came looking for shelter. But it seems as if scraps of wallpaper occupy every spare space around them.

"Hello Johnny." Sammy grins then holds his hand out to the red-faced man who came in first. "You must be Mr Miller. I'm Sammy, and I've been talking to your George all last night. Now he has something he wants to say to you."

"Say to me? He can't say anything to me, or anybody else for that matter, he's a cripple and a simpleton, and what is all this mess about?"

"This, Mr Miller, is not mess. This is your son's voice if you care to listen to it."

Sammy can feel anger rising in his chest, and not just on George's behalf.

He puts his hand on the shepherd's arm and looks

147

him in the face.

"My dad *could* speak to me, but wouldn't. George *can't* speak to you, but wants to, so why don't you sit down and listen to what he has to say?"

Jacob Miller is feeling tired, sore and belligerent. He does not appreciate being spoken to like this in his own home. But he does sit down

"And just how is he going to talk to me, Mr Whatsyourname? Through bits of wallpaper? You do know that he can't read, don't you?"

"Mr Miller," Sammy says, as calmly as he can manage. "George might not be able to write, but he can certainly read what is on these pieces of wallpaper and he *can* talk through them.

The old man shakes his head and opens his mouth, but before he can speak, Sammy puts a hand on his shoulder and points towards some of the shorthand outlines.

"Those symbols on the wallpaper are a kind of writing and George has learnt to read them. He just needs to look at each symbol and I will speak the word he is looking at. Go on George, what is your message to your dad?"

George directs his gaze towards one symbol and Sammy reads it out.

"I."

Then the next one.

"Am."

His eyes fix on the third.

"Not."

The fourth shape is more complex, consisting of a thick line shaped like a hump-back bridge. Below the left side of the hump is a small circle and rising from the right end is an upwardly curving line.

The circle represents the sound 'S', the hump signifies the sound 'MP' and the upward line is the sound of the letter 'L'.

It took a while for Sammy to work out the shorthand word that George wanted him to write, but eventually he understood and George learnt the shape quickly, because it is a word he knows very well.

He is looking at that fourth word now and Sammy voices it for him.

"Simple," he says.

Mr Miller's red face loses its colour as George's message to him sinks home.

"I AM NOT SIMPLE."

YAN TAN

GEORGE wakes the next morning and his arm spasms. He'd wanted to stretch it, but only made it jerk and thrash. That's just the way it is and always has been. While everybody else's arms and legs work the way they are meant to, George's have a mind of their own. Something inside his head is tangled so that when he thinks *pick up the spoon* his hand slaps the bowl instead. When he tries to tell his dad, or brother "I'll have a cup of tea, thanks" what comes out of his mouth sounds to him and everyone around him like a groan followed by a hiss.

He gave up trying to talk at a very early age. It just wasn't worth the effort, or the humiliation. Looking at things would get part of his message across, but it was easier to just let people guess what he wanted and pull a grin when they got it right or thrash around when they got it wrong.

Eventually, he had his dad and brother reasonably well trained so that most of the time they knew what he wanted with no need ask.

The fire was his real pleasure. What a world that was. It didn't just keep him warm; it kept him entertained too. The flames danced for him - and such a dance. Sometimes flames bobbed and twisted with showers of sparks and loud cracks. Other times the flames were slow and sensual, lazily entwining themselves around fire logs and each other.

Then there were the stories they told. Stories of blue flame birth, yellow flame life and red ember death.

Sometimes dragon breath filled the fireplace and George saw a magic forge where swords of wonder and beauty were hammered and shaped in its white heat.

Hours could pass as the stories the fire had to tell unfolded for trapped George. It was his favourite thing - until now.

Sammy had opened a window that George didn't even know was there. A window through which he could pass messages to his dad and brother - messages they could understand. Growl and hiss no longer hide his meaning; now he can 'talk' with his eyes, in a language that is clear and simple. The shapes on the paper have meanings that are easy to remember. All he has to do is look at them one at a time to tell Johnny or his dad what he wants to say.

"He's looking again. For goodness' sake, what does he want this time?" Johnny fakes annoyance and watches the direction of George's eyes. "What does that one mean?" he asks Sammy.

"Well, that symbol represents either brick or break," Sammy replies.

"He's looking at this one over here now, what's this one?"

"That one could be fist or fast. So, he either wants a brick in his fist, or he is asking for breakfast? My guess is that he wants breakfast."

"Mine too," Johnny grins. He holds a bowl in one hand and bread knife in the other as he looks at George. "Porridge or toast, brother?"

A twisted grin fills George's face and his eyes look at

the bowl.

"Porridge it is, then. Would you like some too, Sammy?"

"Definitely, it's a long time since I had porridge."

Johnny scoops two large helpings from a soot-blackened pot on the fireplace and, after adding milk, salt, and a spoonful of a lumpy mix from a jar, tips a third helping into a bowl for his brother.

As he spoon-feeds George, Johnny says to Sammy: "Dad has got to keep his feet up for the next two or three days so he has asked me to check our sheep. Do you fancy a walk later?"

"Yes, that would be good; I know nothing about sheep, so I might learn a thing or two."

"We'll go when Dad gets up and can keep a watch on George. When we find the sheep, I'll teach you how to count them."

Sammy is about to say he learnt to count at infant school, but there is a mischievous look on Johnny's face, so he just nods.

The sun is climbing through the morning sky later that morning as they walk across the moors.

"Thanks for putting the real words next to your symbols so that Dad and me can see what they mean," says Johnny.

"You're welcome." Sammy replies. "They're there to help me too. I am only just learning about this shorthand stuff myself. By the way, thanks for the porridge, it was the nicest I've ever tasted, what was in it?"

"I put honey in and a chopped up apple."

"Did your mother teach you to cook like that?"

"No. I was just little when she died having George. Dad's cooking is rubbish, so I had to teach myself."

Sammy nods, but says nothing.

White flecks speckle the distant moorland hill ahead of them and Sammy asks: "Are they your sheep?"

"That's most of them. The rest won't be too far away."

They walk in silence for a while, then Sammy asks: "Have you always lived in that cottage?"

"No, we moved there after mother died. Dad was a shepherd in Swaledale for a long time, but after mother died, he couldn't bear to be there, so we came over here.

An old lady called Molly Middleton used to have our cottage before us. Folks here say she was strange in the head. Never married and spent all her time on the hills with her sheep. That's where they found her one winter's day. Frozen solid on the moor."

"That's sad. Didn't she have any friends or family?"

"No family, no friends, she was all on her own, but apparently that's the way she wanted it. It is a shame though; you should always try to have friends."

"Did you make friends when you came here?"

"Not at first, but I did when I went to school. I got teased a lot over my Yorkshire words and Yorkshire ways, but there was no harm in it and I soon learnt to give as good as I got."

Sammy nods, but says nothing as they get close enough to see the sheep clearly.

"Right," Johnny points at the hillside. "Can you count the sheep here, Sammy?"

"Yes, no trouble, one, two, three, four, five…"

"No, no, that's not how you do it. I said I would teach you to count properly, and this is the way Dad taught me in Swaledale.

"Yan, tan, thether, mether, pip." He holds up five fingers.

"Aysa, saysa, acca, cotta, dick." He holds up the other five.

"Yannadick, tannadick, tetheradick, metheradick, bumfit." The first five fingers are extended for a second time.

"Yanabum tanabum tetherabum, metherabum, jiggit." The other five go up a second time and Johnny reaches into his left pocket, draws out a stone and transfers it to his right hand which puts it into his right pocket.

"That's what you do when you reach jiggit. When we get back to the cottage, I take all the stones out of my right pocket and that, times twenty, is how many sheep we have. All I have to do is remember the odd number of sheep I count after putting the last stone in my pocket."

Sammy is intrigued, but puzzled.

"Why don't you say one, two, three, like everybody else. Surely that would be simpler."

Now it is Johnny's turn to look puzzled.

After a moment's thought, he tells Sammy: "I don't know, and I've never thought to ask why. It's just always been done that way in Swaledale and you learn it from the cradle. One, two, is the way you count numbers at school, but yan, tan is the way you count sheep."

Sammy makes Johnny repeat his mantra a few more times before saying: "I think I have got it now."

He counts out the shepherd numbers and gets them all right. Johnny congratulates Sammy for his sharp memory, then his face becomes more serious.

"Sammy, what do you think of Dad?"

"What do you mean?" Sammy asks, trying to buy

himself time to think why Johnny is asking the question.

"I mean what kind of man do you think he is?"

"Well, he seems a decent enough sort. He's obviously had a hard time in the past, losing his wife, and having George the way he is, but he was pleasant enough last night once he got over the shock of George saying he wasn't simple. He's invited me to stay with you all for another night before I move on tomorrow."

Johnny shakes his head and says: "Take it from me, he *is* a changed man, and it's because of what *you* did.

"Dad has been miserable and grumpy for as long as I can remember. But last night, when he was learning to talk with George, he was smiling for the first time since God knows when. Then, at breakfast this morning, he took his porridge over to George's chair and sat there asking him questions. He's just never done that before; he *is* a different man, believe me."

"Well, you would know about that, Johnny, but I don't. I have only just met your dad, and he seems a decent sort to me."

"My point, Sammy, is that if he can change then maybe your dad can change too. I know you told me that he was a real swine to you and your sister, but I wonder if he could change too, given the right circumstances."

Sammy looks at Johnny, shakes his head, and tells him: "He's already done that. He *has* changed, but he changed the wrong way and changed for good, so I'd rather not talk about that man anymore. He is out of my life and that is the way I want it to stay. If you are finished with the counting, I think we should get back to the cottage. I made a promise to your brother and tonight is my last chance to keep it, because tomorrow I'll be back on the road to Kirkby Lonsdale."

"Well, if your mind is set, then that's that. But there is one thing I can do for you. I can get you off to a good start. How about making the first part of your journey by pony and trap? Remember the one I borrowed to fetch Dad from the bothy? Well, I got them from a lady called Calder and they need to be returned. Her place is on the road to Kirkby Lonsdale, and you'd be doing us a favour if you returned them to her tomorrow. It will also give you an easy start to your day."

"It certainly would Johnny, much obliged."

"Don't thank me just yet, Sammy. That Calder woman is a bit strange, so drop off her pony and the dogcart, but I wouldn't hang around if I was you."

This is the way to travel, Sammy thinks the next day on the road to Kirkby Lonsdale.

The pony is well behaved and the dog cart is well sprung. The bench seat on which he sits barely sways as the trap passes over ruts and rocks on the road to Kirkby Lonsdale.

If only the whole journey to Northumberland could be like this.

But all too soon he sees the yellow-painted gateway that Johnny Miller told him to look for. He passes through it onto a winding drive.

At the far end of the drive is a large house with a large, yellow door and a large brass knocker which he lifts and lets drop. The rap it makes echoes inside the building. As the echoes fade a voice from the other side of the door says: "Who's there? Is it you Damasius?"

"No, my name is Sammy, I'm returning the pony and trap that Johnny Miller, from the shepherd's cottage, borrowed."

"TRAP! It's a trap! Go away."

"No Miss Calder, it's not a trap, it's your *pony* and trap. I'm just returning it, would you like me to leave it here or take it around to the back of your house?"

A bolt slides back, followed by another, and the door opens slightly. Two deep-set eyes flicker nervously from the lined face of a woman with grey hair and a worried look.

"You are not Damasius then?"

"No, I'm not. Who is Damasius?"

"Damasius is the murdering monk, and he knows where I am. He is coming, He's coming for me."

"I don't think so, Miss Calder, but if you will just tell me where to take this pony, I'll be on my way."

She looks both ways and in two short steps is by his side.

"Come," she says and takes hold of the reins in his hand.

Sammy follows her to the back of the stone-built house and sees a large outbuilding.

"Pony goes here, carriage goes there."

Sammy is about to argue, but thinks better of it. He guides the pony into the outbuilding and it stops beside a wall with a bricked-up doorway. After the pony is unharnessed, it makes its own way to one of two empty stalls and begins drinking noisily from a water trough. Sammy closes the stall gate gently and leaves the building.

"Come, come." The woman waves imperiously towards the back door of the house and Sammy follows her.

"Thank you for returning my pony, you must have

tea."

"That's nice of you Miss Calder, but…"

"No buts. Tea. Black tea."

Sammy has never had black tea before, but guesses it will be easier to drink a quick cup of the beverage than argue about it with this strange lady.

One sip tells Sammy that this will not be a quick cup. It tastes like tarry rope and although the cup is tiny; it seems to be bottomless.

Sammy forces down a second mouthful and decides that he needs a tea break.

"You mentioned Damasius, who is this Damasius?" he asks.

"The murdering monk. Damasius Maczoch is his name, and we were lovers years back. We lived in Poland then, Warsaw it was. That was before I came over here and changed my name."

"You changed your name? Who were you before you changed it?"

"Hekmo Ostrowska, but over there everybody called me 'Beautiful Hekmo Ostrowska'. We lived in Warsaw with Damasius's brother, Wenzel. Poor Wenzel, Damasius killed him, killed his own brother."

Sammy is now feeling very uncomfortable about being in this big empty house with this very odd woman. He decides the break has gone on long enough. He needs to get back on the road as fast as he can.

The old woman puts a hand on his arm and leans towards Sammy, lowering her voice.

"I told Wenzel everything. I told him that Damasius had stolen the robe and crown from the statue of the Madonna at the Chapel of Notre Dame Grace in Czentochowato. He stole jewels too. They were in a casket at the foot of the statue.

"No-one suspected Damasius at first. He was a well-respected monk, after all. But, after two months of lies and evasion, people began to suspect, so we ran away to Warsaw, where Wenzel lived.

"But in Warsaw Damasius changed. He became convinced that we were being followed and that the monks would take their revenge. He gave me the jewels and other stuff and told me to hide them from him so that, if they caught him, he could truthfully tell the police, and the monks, that he had no idea where they were.

"He even wanted me to marry his brother to show that he couldn't be my lover.

"I refused, but I did tell Wenzel everything. Damasius was so angry when Wenzel confronted him. They argued terribly and Damasius killed poor Wenzel. I thought he would kill me too, so I ran away with the pearls and jewels and came here.

"That was years ago, but now Damasius has found me and he is coming to kill me too. He might be here today or tomorrow."

Sammy feeling scared now. What if the murderer does come today and finds him in this house with the woman who betrayed him?

"Miss Calder, that tea was delicious, but I just can't finish that last drop, do you mind if I leave the cup here on your table?"

He carefully puts the delicate bone china cup onto a kitchen table covered in a protective layer of pages from yesterday's Lancaster Evening News.

As he rests the cup on the paper a headline catches his eye.

It says:

MONASTERY MURDERER
MONK'S ALLEGED TERRIBLE CRIME'
Sammy reads on:

> *The Berlin police have requested their confreres in Warsaw to search for a monk named Damasius Maczoch who is accused of murder and robbery.*

The newspaper story tells in lurid detail a tale that mirrors exactly the one that the strange Miss Calder has just told him and Sammy gives a sigh of relief. It seems that his host is just an ordinary lunatic living out a lurid newspaper tale, and not the target for a murderous, avenging monk.

But then he sees a neighbouring story in the newspaper about a woman being committed to an asylum for sticking a kitchen knife into a total stranger for no apparent reason.

He looks around the kitchen and sees a grindstone knife sharpener with knife handles sticking from slots in it.

"Miss Calder, thanks very much for the tea, I'll just go out through the back door, and don't you worry; if I should come across Damasius out there, I'll tell him you moved away last month."

He doesn't hear her reply because it turns out that Winnie Wilding's boots are really good for running as well as walking.

SUSPICIONS

"NOW that does look suspicious," Police Constable Richard Leighton mutters to no-one in particular.

He has just watched a young man in dishevelled clothes, with a swag bag slung around his body, leap over a yellow gate and sprint down the road ahead of him.

PC Leighton pushes hard on the left pedal of his police-issue bicycle and reaches for his police-issue whistle.

Sammy stumbles as he hears the shrill blast behind him and turns to see an overweight policeman struggling to build up speed on a blue bike.

This two-wheeled officer-of-the-law is also shouting something.

"Hey you! Stop! Stop where you are!"

Sammy stops, much to the policeman's surprise. Given that this is a, probably, fit young lad who is some distance away, he had expected him to race off. But, instead, the lad has stopped and appears to be waiting. Grateful that he won't have to make a sprint pursuit, PC Leighton settles for a more dignified approach to this potential criminal.

Sammy says nothing when the policeman reaches him.

"Now then, if you don't mind me asking, just what are you up to young lad - and what have you got in that there bag?"

"Nothing officer, I'm just on my way to Kirkby Lonsdale."

"Jumping over gates and sprinting like Springheeled Jack?"

"Oh," says Sammy realising how suspicious he must have looked. "No, it's nothing like that. I have just returned a pony and trap to the lady who lives down that drive," he says, pointing towards the yellow gate. "Johnny Miller, from the shepherd's cottage up the road, borrowed them from her and asked me to return them on my way to Kirkby Lonsdale."

The officer says: "I know Jacob Miller well, and Johnny, as it happens. Shame about that older son of Jacob's, is he still bedbound?"

"He doesn't walk very well, but he's not bedbound," Sammy answers. "And George is Jacob's *younger* son."

"*I* know that lad, I'm just making sure *you* do and you're not spinning me a yarn. Anyway, what's in that swag bag wrapped around you?"

"Swag bag!" Sammy exclaims, with a laugh. "For one thing, there's no 'swag' in here, just these," he says, revealing the contents.

PC Leighton checks them off with mock formality. "One empty ginger beer bottle, a pair of old clogs, random pages from a newspaper, some wallpaper with scribbles on it and a book. Now then, what is this book all about?"

"It's a shorthand book that used to belong to a reporter, but he didn't want it anymore. I've been trying to learn shorthand since he gave me it."

"Is that so? Is it easy?"

"It is so far, but maybe it will get harder when I get to

the more complicated stuff."

"You might be right, but knowing even the easy stuff could still be useful. I could have done with learning shorthand when I was starting out. It's a just a pity that I'm closer to Miss Calder's age than yours."

"Do you know Miss Calder well?" Sammy asks.

"Everybody knows Miss Calder, that's why folk around here keep a watch out for her. We make sure that she isn't bothered by ne'er-do-wells or rag-amuffins."

"She's a strange woman, isn't she?"

"Not at all, at least, not for these parts. Everybody around here thinks somebody is trying to murder them."

PC Leighton leans forward and the serious look on his face relaxes into a knowing grin."

"You've definitely met Dotty then."

"Miss Calder, I met Miss Calder."

The policeman appears to be laughing at some private joke and Sammy waits patiently to be let in on it.

"Dorothy Calder," that's her name, but we call her Dotty. Dotty by name and Dotty by nature. She's harmless, but Dotty is obsessed with the idea that somebody is plotting to kill her. It's been an obsession with her for years and it began with a tragedy.

"She used to live here with her two brothers. Then one day they were both found dead in that stable at the back of the house, along with the family Labrador. The brothers were in their 40s and apparently fit and healthy. The dog was not much more than a pup either, but there they all were - dead, with no signs of injury or explanation for their demise."

"And that turned her mind, did it?" Sammy asks.

"That it did lad, that it did. Dotty loved both of her brothers and when they died like that, she just lost her reason. She was forever coming down to the station at Kirkby Lonsdale demanding that we should keep the investigation going."

"And did you?"

"Of course we did. But, as I said, they had no injuries and the post-mortem examination came up with nothing. The brothers hadn't been poisoned or had any kind of medical condition that would explain their deaths. They just stopped breathing.

The policeman shrugs his shoulders and continues: "We were left with three unexplained fatalities for a long time and it played on Dotty's mind something terrible. She just wouldn't let go of the idea that somehow they had been murdered. "Every time another murder was reported in the newspapers she would come to the police station and claim it was in some way connected to her brothers' deaths. It was sad, very sad; even more so when we did eventually find out what had killed them."

"You solved the murders?"

"Yes, we solved them, but they were not murders. It took a new recruit to crack the mystery. He was a bobby from over Halifax way who had worked in a coal mine before he joined the force.

"We gave him the usual briefing about the patch, including all the unresolved issues. He was a bright young officer and when we mentioned the Calder brothers to him he took a real interest in the case.

"He said he had a theory about it and asked if it was all right for him to go to the Calders' place. We said he could, but to be gentle with Dotty, and he was. When he came back he suggested that we have a mines expert check out the stables where the brothers died, and the expert's report made very interesting reading."

"What did it say?"

"The expert found that a barred door behind a cupboard, next to the horse stalls, led to an abandoned drift shaft. The shaft didn't go far and was abandoned long before reaching any coal, but there were other unused underground workings in the area and, over time, black damp had built up in those ones."

"What's black damp," asks Sammy.

"It's sometimes called stythe, and it is a mix of different pit gasses, but the one gas missing from the mix is oxygen. In certain atmospheric conditions stythe can rise to surface level, which is what must have happened at the Calders' place.

"When it comes to the surface normally it mixes with air and is safely blown away. But if it comes up inside a building it can be trapped indoors in shallow pools."

"Is that what happened in the stable?" Sammy wonders.

"Yes. The Calder brothers must have missed the warning signs that a pool of stythe was building up."

"What warning signs?"

"The first sign that anything was wrong would have been the odd dead mouse or rat. They might not have noticed that, but their dog probably did. Most likely the Labrador would have sniffed at the dead creature. In the process it would have inhaled the stythe and collapsed. That is what we think happened.

"When one of the brothers saw the dog lying there, he may have bent to pick it up and breathed in a lungful of stythe with the same result. The effect of stythe is pretty much instantaneous and the other Mr Calder would have collapsed as well, as soon as he tried to lift his brother.

"Black damp is tasteless, odourless and instantly fatal. It would have been as quick as snuffing out a candle."

"Did you explain that to Miss Calder?"

"We did, or we tried to, but by then she wasn't able to take it in. She was so sure that someone had murdered them, and still is to this day. She also thinks that she is next on the murderer's list, although the murderer changes depending on what she has read in that day's newspaper."

Sammy has a sudden thought.

"Hang on, I have just been in that stable, I could have been killed as well, surely?"

"No, lad. Once we discovered how they had died, we had the shaft sealed. Ian McDowell, one of the Calders' neighbours, came and bricked up the doorway. Ian's a good bricklayer and nothing can come up from that shaft now."

"That is good to know. But how come Miss Calder didn't die along with her brothers, she must have bent down to them when she went into the stable?"

"Luck, sheer luck. She was so shocked by what she saw that she didn't close the stable door behind her. The black damp must have drained away through the open doorway.

"Anyway, tell me this, young man, how is it you know Mr Miller and his boys. You're not local, are you?"

"Johnny took me in a couple of nights ago during that awful storm. That was the first time we'd met. I'm walking up to Northumberland to get a job in the pits there. I started out in Bolton a week ago."

"You've been a week on the road? Well then, I'll tell you what, since I'm feeling saddle sore, why don't we walk into Kirkby Lonsdale together and you can tell me all about this walk of yours?"

Sammy nods, pleased to have company for the two miles into town, and pleased to have a policeman with him - just in case there are any murderers on the road.

An hour later PC Laidler and Sammy Kiteland enter Kirkby Lonsdale.

"Well, here we are Sammy. Thanks for telling me your story, it's given me something new for my book," PC Leighton tells him.

"Are you writing a book?"

"Well, I'm writing a diary, I've been writing it since I joined the force.

"Everything I have done for the past 27 years is catalogued in that diary, so I can tell you with absolute accuracy that I've walked up one street 10,477 times, rendered first aid in one 121 cases, dealt with 132 quarrels between man and wife, received 15 black eyes, 13 kicks and six bites. I've also served under four chief constables, seven superintendents, 15 inspectors and 30 sergeants."

Sammy is impressed.

"Maybe I should keep a diary like yours," he tells the policeman. "When I get older I might forget about what I am doing now and that would be a shame. The trouble is I don't have a pencil or notepaper to write it all down, so I'll just have to rely on my memory."

PC Leighton leans forward and taps Sammy on the chest.

"An old headmaster of mine once gave me a good piece of advice and it has stayed with me ever since, so I'll pass it on to you. He told me that even a blunt pencil is still more reliable than a sharp memory, and after 27 years of taking statements and investigating crimes, take it from me, he was right. So this is what I am going to do for you."

He takes a pencil from his tunic breast pocket, snaps it in half and gives Sammy the end with the point.

"I'll just sharpen the other half when I get back to the station. You'll also need some of these."

PC Leighton pulls out his notebook and Sammy sees it is comprised of a thick wad of loose sheets held inside a stiff cover by a heavy clip. The officer opens the clip, removes some of the sheets and hands them to Sammy, telling him: "I've got plenty more of these in my office desk."

"Thanks a lot," Sammy says. "That means I can keep a promise I made to George Miller. He gave me a message which I wrote onto some old wallpaper, and now I can copy it out neatly, or as neatly as I can manage."

Sammy thinks for a moment then asks: "Will the records at your police station have the address of the Bolton Evening News' Chorley office?"

"I'm sure it will, and I'll tell you something else that it has. It's got a lost and found office, where on the third Sunday of every month we give clothes that have been unclaimed for a year to needy and deserving people in the parish. Guess what tomorrow is?"

"The third Sunday of June?"

"You've got it. Come back to the station tomorrow and I'll sort out a change of clothing for you."

"I'll do that, thanks a lot. Just one more thing, is

there anywhere In Kirkby Lonsdale that I can get a cheap lodge for the night? Even a ha'penny lean would do."

GEORGE

"PUT the kettle on, Jim, it's a slow news day and I need some fuel for my brain."

Alan Robson looks through the tiny window in his office onto the back yard of the Bolton Evening News' Chorley district office. It is sort of raining outside. Sort of mist, sort of drizzle, but mostly just sodden gloom.

A few minutes later Jim Wood puts a steaming mug onto Alan's desk with his right hand and dumps that day's post down beside it with his left.

Alan takes a sip from the mug and picks up the envelopes.

Two letters are from his head office. One, from the editor, announces the arrival of John Phillips, a replacement on the news desk for retiring news editor, Tom Brownlee. The other is from the new news editor.

"Quick off the mark, aren't you, Mr Phillips?" Alan says. "That does not bode well."

The letter from Alan's new boss reminds him that the country has been run by a hung Parliament since the January election and a conference to break the political deadlock has itself been stalemated for a month. Liberals, Tories, Labour and Irish Nationalists are all at each other's throats, the House of Lords is locked in a battle of will with the Commons over who ultimately runs the country. King Edward had been dead for just two months and King George V, crowned a month ago, is tentatively testing the boundaries of his influence as a ruler and unifier.

John Phillips' letter ends: "The current turmoil means that there are rich pickings out there for any reporter with ears and a willingness to use them. Stories will not come into the office looking for you. Get out onto the streets and talk to people, and remember that exclusives are a requirement of your job, not an option."

Alan snorts and throws the letter to one side before picking up an envelope with a Bolton postmark. He opens it to find a note from Rev Popplewell inside. The note begins with an expression of gratitude to Alan for the publicity the orphans' day out attracted, and adds that he has had many positive comments from people in Bolton and beyond, who picked up the 'thank you' fliers.

The fourth letter is in a police force envelope, but the sheets of notepaper inside it carry a message pencilled in spidery handwriting.

Alan threads his way through the scrappy scrawl and smiles.

"Thank you, young man, you've done it again," he says.

Alan tucks three sheets of copy paper, with two carbons between them, into his Swift typewriter and uses the carriage return lever to wind them into the correct position. When everything is in place, he begins to type out exactly what is on all but one sheet of notepaper. The one he does not copy is a cover note from Sammy. The note says:

Dear Mr Robson, the papers are
full of stories these days about

people who have one need or another. You write about orphans, the poor, the old, women's votes, equal pay for women and criminals who need to be punished. But what about people who can't talk or walk, people who can't go to school or work? You never write anything about them, so maybe it is time that you did. I met a boy yesterday who everybody thought was simple and dumb, but with the help of your shorthand book I got him to tell me his story and the rest of this note is what he told me he wanted you and all of your readers to know.

Yours faithfully,

Sammy Kiteland.

Alan puts Sammy's note to one side on his desk, picks up the other sheets and types the message on them. It begins "My name is George Miller".

My name is George Miller and I am not simple. People say I am, but I am not, I just can't talk or move like most of you.
Mother died when she had me and I got hurt too. Not my ears. I can hear when some people say I am a cripple. Not my head. I can think although some people say I am stupid. I can't move my legs and arms

*the way you can, but I can feel them
and I can feel it when people laugh
at me.*

*I need help to write this, but I don't
need help to think it. I am locked
inside my head that is all. I can't
say words, I can't write words. Dad
would not let me go to school. He
said other children are cruel and
would hurt me. But being locked in
my head hurts me more.*

*When you think a person is sim-
ple, think again, they might just be
locked in their own heads, like me,
and you might be the one that can
open the door that lets them out, as
a good friend has just done for me.*

*I am George Miller, please remem-
ber me, please remember the others
like me.*

Alan separates the typed copies of the message into three piles, one for the sub editors, one for the news desk and one for himself. He reads through what he has written and stabs his personal copy onto the spike. Then he types out the story that will accompany George's words in the newspaper.

When his story is completed, he puts it, along with George's words, into an internal mail envelope, hesitates for a moment, then reaches for his contacts book. Under the listing for the Press Association he finds its address at Wine Office Court in London and a telephone number.

"I will remember you George," he says. "I will remember you for a long time, and if I've got anything to do with it, so will a lot of other people."

While Alan is making his telephone call to London, PC Leighton is giving Sammy the once over.

"That is much better," he says.

Sammy is now wearing a clean jacket, unpatched trousers and a stain-free shirt. They were given to him yesterday after PC Leighton had foraged through the 'lost and found' collection at Kirkby Lonsdale Police Station.

Today Sammy has come to the station to give PC Leighton something in return.

"What's this?" the officer asks, as he removes the newspaper page covering the package that Sammy has just handed to him. "Your shorthand book? What's that for?"

"It's for your kindness and to help you write your book's next chapter."

PC Leighton still looks puzzled.

"It helped Alan Robson to get out of the pit and into his job on the newspaper. It has helped me to learn something new and interesting, and it has given George Miller a voice. I think it is your turn now. I know that it's too late to help with your police work, but you love to write and you'll be writing for a long time to come, so learning what is in here will be a useful tool for you to have."

"But I thought you said you were still learning short-hand," PC Leighton says.

"I've copied all the symbols I need from the book onto the notepaper you gave me. I don't need the book any more."

"Well, that's very generous of you Sammy, thanks."

As Sammy turns to leave, PC Leighton says: "Hang on a minute, just stay there."

Sammy waits at the front desk while PC Leighton walks through a door behind the counter. He returns from the back office moments later with a brown paper bag which he puts into Sammy's hands.

"I've just had a quick whip round and the lads in the station want you to have these to help you on your way."

Inside the bag Sammy sees an apple, two boiled eggs, a box of matches, a cheese sandwich, a bar of Fry's Five Boys milk chocolate, some coins and a small glass bottle with a maroon liquid inside.

"That bottle is mine," says PC Leighton. "It's rose-hip syrup. I usually keep it at the station and have a spoonful every day. It's my old gran's recipe. She always said it's good for keeping coughs and colds away and it has worked for me, so maybe it will help you too."

Back at the common lodging house where Sammy has spent the last two nights he repacks his sling before leaving. It is bulkier now since it contains his old clothes and as the goodwill gifts from PC Leighton and his fellow officers. He counts the coins from the paper bag. They add up to a shilling and twopence, which he stuffs into his new, hole-free trouser pockets.

Then, he heads out of Kirkby Lonsdale on the longest leg of his journey yet.

Sammy wants to reach Kirkby Stephen by the end of that day, but it won't be easy. The walk will be a 29-mile trudge through hills and valleys, mostly along old drovers' tracks, but also taking in an ancient Roman Road and part of a winding pathway through the Pennine Hills.

At his current walking speed that will take him at least ten hours if he takes no breaks. But Sammy doubts that he will manage the walk non-stop. If he has any breaks, or if the road underfoot is not good, it will take longer, and that means sleeping under the stars.

But on a warm summer day like this one, that's no hardship, he tells himself; and he has enough to eat - for the moment at least.

Sammy also has a list of written directions from PC Leighton that should get him safely to Kirkby Stephen. The list also indicates places where the road runs close to a stream.

Sammy feels confident enough to tempt fate. He whispers: "I'll not go hungry, I'll not go thirsty and I have some extra clothing if I have to stay out all night and it turns cold. What could go wrong?"

At the same moment, in Bolton, Sammy's sister, Cilla, is thinking *How much more can go wrong today?* She has just spilt a bucket of soapy water over the flagstone floor in her mother-in-law's scullery kitchen. She has already over-baked bread in the coal-fired oven and made a mess of chopping a block of wood into kindling. Cilla has yet to scrub the front doorstep with a pumice 'donkey' stone, and is dreading it.

She's sure she'll not manage to scrub the step completely grease free or stone it to exactly the right shade of white beloved by so many housewives across Bolton. No matter how hard she tried in the last three weeks, nothing she did was good enough for her sharp-eyed, sharp-tongued mother-in-law Margaret Dolan.

Cilla hadn't expected a honeymoon, but she had hoped for a honeymoon period after her wedding day. The memory of a nice cup of tea in bed and some warm words of love would have been enough for her before grey reality sucked the colour out of wedded bliss. But it seems even that was too much to hope for.

It had all started before the wedding day celebrations were even over, when her brother came back to the Dolans' house and announced that their dad had done a bunk after selling everything in their cellar lodgings at Clap Row.

She had never seen Sammy so angry, but it wasn't a red-faced, shouting anger. This was tight-lipped, cold fury. Their dad had crossed a line in her little brother's mind and there would be no stepping back over it.

When Sammy returned to the Dolans' place and asked Cilla if he could stay there that night, he was not begging for help or in despair. He was detached and calculating, weighing odds and options. But his big sister was not fooled. She could see the ice anger in his eyes, even if no-one else could.

Cilla is different to Sammy. He uses his sharp mind and memory to tackle problems head-on and build solutions to them. Cilla's approach is to starve problems to death. If anything upsets her, she refuses to let it intrude into her current thoughts, hoping that neglect will steal some of the problem's power to hurt, or upset her. Then she uses forgetfulness to weaken it more.

Sammy often teased his sister about her bad memory and she always countered by telling him: "What is the point of a good memory if it is full of bad things."

The day after Cilla's wedding, her brother came calling again to discuss their father's disappearance.

"He's dropped me right in it," Sammy said. "I put on my best for your wedding, so my work clothes were in the house when he sold everything that was there. It's just a good job today is Sunday or I'd be at the foundry dressed for a wedding. How stupid would I look?"

Cilla tried to reassure her little brother.

"Don't worry Sammy, something will turn up. I'll ask around and see what I can find. The rag and bone man usually comes around on Sundays and Mrs Dolan gets her 'donkey' stones from him. I'll see if he has anything that would do for work clothes."

"All right, but don't get anything that will make me look silly. I don't mind if it is old or patched as long as I don't look stupid in it. See if he has some cloth that I can fold into a sling as well so I can carry stuff in it."

"What sort of stuff?"

"Tools, grub, if I can find any, and a drink of water. It gets hot in that foundry."

"Oh yes, I see. I'll get you a bottle for your water as well, Mrs Dolan is always drinking fizzy pop, so there will be empties lying around."

"Thanks Cilla."

"Do you think he will come back?"

"Who?"

"Dad."

"Don't know. Don't care. I'm finished with that sod. He can just rot as far as I am concerned."

"I can understand that, Sammy, but don't get bitter about it, or you'll just wind up hurting yourself. Try to think of the good things we got from him before he went strange. You really enjoyed going down to the allotment with him when you were little, and he taught you a lot."

Sammy shakes his head, but she continues: "Remember how he used to make those paper darts for us and the hours we would spend flying them. When you got older, he showed you how to make Sammyshine and when you were twelve, he got you that job at the rope-works. You learnt how to tie some useful knots at that rope factory, didn't you? So don't just dwell on the bad things."

Sammy reluctantly nodded. He had to admit that he did learn a lot of knots in the year he was at the rope works, everything from an Alpine Butterfly to a Running Bowline. He would have stayed as well, but for the taunts of the women who worked there. They were a rough lot and some things they said to him made his ears burn.

Eventually he got his apprenticeship at the foundry. The men there were rough too, but they didn't make Sammy's ears burn with embarrassment.

Cilla wasn't finished yet.

"You must admit that at least we never starved. Dad saw to that. He worked as hard as he was able before he went funny in the head and Mother died.

"Besides which, you and me are grown up now, we can make our own way in life, with or without him, so he is the one who has lost out, not us. Just remember that, Sammy. We are young, we are fit and we have a lot of love still to give, so we will be fine. You and me, we *will* be fine."

A week later, she bumped into Will Richards, one of her brother's old school pals and Will said he had seen Sammy on the Chorley Road.

"He told me he was going to walk to Northumberland for work and asked if I wanted to go with him," Will told her.

"I said that I would happily go with him if it wasn't for my bunions. I've got them bad and would never make it. So he said that if I met you, I should say don't worry about him.

"He also said he won't be back in touch until he is rich."

FIVE BOYS

SAMMY has been walking on the road to Kirkby Stephen for five hours when Cilla's words come back to him and he says aloud: "Yes, I'm still young, still fit, not so sure about having lots of love to give, but I do have food, water and a bar of chocolate."

He looks ahead and sees that the road he is on snakes its way around the foot of heather-dressed hills. Behind him the road he has just walked along winds through open moorland as far back as the horizon, and that's when it hits him. He is alone, really alone.

Ever since leaving Bolton, Sammy has never travelled far without encountering other people, including red-haired Rose, shopkeeper Saul, Alan the reporter, Harry the wanderer, Wally the hypnotist, the Miller family, Dotty Carter and PC Leighton.

Only now, for the first time since setting out on this journey, does he feel alone. Yet he's not lonely. All around him is a vast, beautiful landscape of hills, valleys and a huge sky and, because he is on his own, all of it is there for him and no-one else.

A few days ago it was the warmest day of the year so far, and, right now, everything around him is thriving and growing. In the sky, on the ground, or under that gurgling stream he hears nearby, life is everywhere - so how could he feel lonely?

Maybe Cilla was right. Dad might have done him a favour by bunking off like that. If he hadn't been locked out of Clap Row he could still be at work. Melting, pouring and casting white hot iron in the foundry; mouthing banter with the other lippy apprentices that none of them can hear, but all can see; gulping bottle after bottle of standpipe water to replace all that sweat generated by the searing heat and sheer hard graft of earning his four shillings a week. But, instead, he is feeling the glow of the sun on his face, listening to the chatter of birds in the sky and the rustle of small things scurrying away from his feet.

Sammy stops, without noticing that he has stopped. He thinks for a moment about the foundry and how far away it is. He thinks about the clean air filling his lungs, the smell of heather filling his nostrils and the hopes for the future that now fill his head.

"Thanks Dad," he says out loud. "But you're still an old sod."

Sammy feels exhilarated - and hungry. It's more than five hours since he last ate, so he walks down a grassy bank leading to a stream, sits down and opens his sling.

After eating the cheese sandwich and one of the hard-boiled eggs, Sammy leaves the rest of his donated spread for later in the day - except for the chocolate.

It's been quite a while since Sammy tasted chocolate, and he is feeling so good on this sunny summer day he decides to end his lunch with a treat. He pulls the bar of Fry's Five Boy chocolate from his sling and looks at the five photographs on the wrapper for the one that matches his own mood. He chooses the final image of a smiling boy and unwraps the bar to find the chocolate version of that image. The boy is meant to be smiling because he realises that he is eating a piece of Fry's chocolate. But there are four other images impressed into the chocolate bar, and none of them shows that same look of satisfaction on the boy's face. In the fourth image the boy looks happy because he has received some, although he does not yet know it is Fry's. In the third he has an expression of expectation, but no chocolate. In the second he has been promised chocolate to pacify him and the first image shows why he needs to be pacified. In that image the boy is tearful and distressed because he has no chocolate at all.

Five-year-old Lindsay Poulton was certainly distressed when he posed for the photograph that is first of the five, but not because he wanted a Fry's Five Boy bar. Earlier attempts to get him to cry for the pose had come to nothing and the photographers, his father and his uncle, needed an ingenious solution.

Lindsay's grandfather came up with that solution. He was also a photographer and knew that among all the chemicals his son used to coat sheets of glass with a light sensitive layer, was a bottle of ammonia.

He soaked a cloth in ammonia and draped it around little Lindsay's neck. Within a few breaths chemically-induced tears poured down the youngster's cheeks and the Quaker makers of Fry's Chocolate had the last of the images they needed to tell their sweet treat story.

Sammy tucks the rest of the chocolate bar into his sling and turns to go back up the embankment he had walked down a few minutes earlier. But he stops.

Looking at him from the top of the embankment is another face and, like the first one on his chocolate bar wrapper, this face also has real tears running down its cheeks and an expression of genuine distress.

The owner of the face is a man of about 30 years.

"You're thin," he says to Sammy. "Thank God."

Surprised, Sammy says nothing and the distressed man speaks again.

"Help me," he says. "Please help me, it's my little boy. He's vanished."

Sammy hooks the sling over his head and begins to walk up the river embankment, but by then the man is already by his side, holding his arm.

"He's been missing for hours and he's only six."

The man tugs at Sammy's arm pulling him towards the top of the embankment. When they reach the top, Sammy sees a Wolseley automobile on the grassed path.

"Get in, get in," he urges, and Sammy climbs into the yellow and chrome vehicle.

The man frantically cranks its starting handle, and the engine roars into life. After storing the handle, he climbs into the driver's seat, beside Sammy, and accelerates towards the nearby road.

"What do you mean when you say he has vanished?" Sammy asks.

"He was playing. One minute he was there, playing with his ball while we got the picnic ready; next minute he was gone. There is a hollow in the ground with a hole at the bottom of it and he might have fallen into that. I stuck my head into the hole, but I couldn't see anything. I shouted his name, but there wasn't a sound. This is a wild place, could a wild thing have taken him?"

Sammy thinks about the beautiful hills and valleys, crystal clear streams, sweet-smelling moorland and wonders how anyone could think of this as a 'wild place'.

"I'm sure that your boy would have shouted if anything wild had tried to take him. Did you go into the hole in the ground?"

"No, I tried, but I couldn't. The hole is too narrow. My wife and some friends who came with us also tried, but none of us is thin enough to fit through that hole. We tried everything we could think of, but nothing worked. That's when I began to drive around looking for somebody who might be able to go into the hole and see if he is there. Would you do it? Would you do that for me?"

"I will if I can. Just how deep is this hole?"

"It's hard to say. I think I can see the bottom. It looks to be about eight feet down and sloping."

The drive takes about 15 minutes and during that time the man introduces himself as Charles Ransome. He tells Sammy that he is a commercial traveller from Manchester on holiday in with his wife, son, and two friends.

They had gone to the coast where, at first, the boy had enjoyed himself. But after four days of sand and sea he became bored, so Mr Ransome hired the automobile from a local garage to take everybody on a picnic in the countryside.

He turns the vehicle off the road and onto a grassy track. On the ground ahead of them Sammy can see a white sheet with picnic items scattered over it. Beside the sheet two women are holding each other and, a short distance away, a man stands with his back to them.

They all turn to face the automobile when they hear it approaching.

"Have you seen him?" Mr Ransome shouts as he jumps from the driver's seat. They all shake their heads and his shoulders slump.

He turns to Sammy and points.

"The hole is over that way."

Sammy makes no move to follow Mr Ransome and, instead, asks: "If I can get through that hole how will I get back? Do you have a tow rope in your motor?"

"I'm not sure," Mr Ransome replies. "The man at the garage said it has a box with spares and stuff, so there might be a tow rope."

They check the box and find a length of rope inside. Sammy carries it to the picnic cloth and lays it on the ground.

"It's over here," says the anxious father. "We need to hurry."

"And I need to get back out of that hole so I am putting knots in this rope to give me something that my hands and feet can grip," Sammy explains.

Minutes later they are at the edge of a depression in the ground and Sammy can see the hole at its base. He lies at the entrance to the hole and peers inside, waiting for his eyes to adjust to the darkness. Eventually, he can make out the shapes of smooth boulders below and reckons that Mr Ransome's estimate of an eight-foot drop is about right.

He secures one end of the rope to a limestone rock embedded in the ground and throws the rest into the hole. Sammy takes off his jacket and hands it to Mr Ransome's friend before positioning himself at the edge of the hole.

As he eases himself into the opening, he discovers just how narrow it is. His hips touch both sides of it at the same time. Sammy briefly wonders whether his shoulders are as narrow as his hips and soon discovers that they are. Knot by knot his hands work their way along the rope as he inches his way down the rock slope. The bottom of the hole is wider than the top and when he reaches it Sammy finds he has room to stretch out his arms in any direction.

"Can you see him?" Mr Ransome shouts from above.

Sammy's eyes quickly adjust to the gloom and he looks around.

"No, he's not here."

"Then where…?" Mr Ransome says.

"Hang on. There is something. It's not him, it's another hole. The rock slopes into another hole and it is bigger than the one I've just come down. I can't see into it. It's very dark, but if I can find a stone, I can see how deep it is."

Sammy bends and picks up a stone at his feet. He throws it onto the sloping rock and it skips twice before disappearing into the darkness. A second later Sammy hears another click as it hits bottom.

"It's not too deep, but it is deeper than this one. It's wider too, so it should be easier to get into."

"Please look. I need to know," the boy's father shouts back.

Sammy ties a larger rock to the end of the rope and feeds it into the hole until he feels it go slack and believes he has found the bottom.

He lies face down on the smooth rock and wriggles into the hole feet first. The slope becomes steeper and eventually the rope alone is taking his weight. It is pitch dark, but he descends only a couple more rope knots before his feet touch the bottom.

But this bottom is not rock. It is soft. He keeps a tight grip on the rope with one hand while sliding the other hand down his leg until it reaches his boot.

And under the boot he feels...

...clothing!

Sammy's heart thuds as he finds a new foothold, this time on solid rock. He reaches forward in total darkness and feels a small leg. The figure is lying on its side and does not respond to his touch. His hand travels along the side of the figure until he can feel a neck.

Such a cold neck, and with no pulse in it.

Above the neck is a thick tousle of hair and Sammy runs his fingers through it.

"Sorry lad," he says, "So sorry."

From far above, Sammy hears another voice. It is the poor boy's soon-to-be-devastated father.

"Can you see him?"

"No, I can't see him," Sammy answers truthfully. "It's totally black down here, just give me a minute while I make a light."

Sammy feels in his trouser pocket for the box of matches he had removed from his sling before going underground. Once he has the matchbox, he opens its inner tray slightly and removes two lucifers. He runs a finger along the edge of the box feeling for the striking surface, then rubs the friction sticks along it. The sudden flare as they burst ablaze blinds him for a moment and he lifts the matches above his field of vision.

He turns his gaze towards the body - and drops the matches in shock.

They go out instantly and in the pitch darkness an after image is left on his retina. The image floating in the darkess surrounding Sammy seems to be the face of

Morbid the clown, also known as Gwilym Davies, and sometimes Willy the Shit.

The sharp intake of breath which accompanied that image is still in Sammy's lungs, held there unintentionally, because he forgets to breathe out. He only releases it when he decides what to do next. He must look again, but this time he must be prepared for what he will see.

Sammy takes out three matchsticks. He plans to strike each in turn to give him the time he needs to verify what he thinks he saw.

His hand is shaking and at the first attempt the match head slips along the sandpaper strike surface without igniting.

He tries again.

The match flares into life and he lifts it high.

The face he sees in the flickering light is not Morbid the clown. It is a young boy lying on his side - a young boy with no heartbeat to keep the blood pumping around his small body and tinge his face with its normal healthy pink hue.

Gravity has made the blood all drain into the lower half of his lifeless body. As a consequence half of the boy's face, from his right ear to his nose, is a deep purple colour and the half from his nose to his left ear is death white, exactly as Gwilym had painted his own face for the monochrome photograph he showed to Sammy.

The match burns down to Sammy's fingers before he notices, and he throws it away. He doesn't strike a second match. Death is bad enough, but to make it grotesque as well? That is just plain cruel, and he doesn't want to see that clown mask of a face again.

"Is he there? Can you see him?"

It is the boy's father again, but he seems further

away this time. Sammy wants to be far away as well to do what he must do next.

"He is here, Mr Ransome, but it's not good news."

"Not good?"

There is a catch in the man's voice because he thinks he already knows the answer to his next question.

"How bad is it?"

"It's the worst," Sammy says, as gently as he can. "I'm going to tie the rope around him and help you bring him up."

From above Sammy can hear muffled voices and a scream. He feels for the rope because he doesn't need light for what must be done now. He threads the rope under the boy's arms and ties the end in a figure eight follow-through knot to make it secure, but easy to un-hitch when it is no longer needed.

Once that job is done Sammy reaches as far up the rope as he can, then grips hard as he lifts his feet off the ground and finds purchase for them on a knot in the rope. Pushing with his feet and gripping with his hands he inches his way up the rope until he has reached the top of the rocky slope. After hesitating to catch his breath he shouts towards the opening above: "Mr Ransome, are you there?"

The voice that comes back is thick with grief.

"Yes."

"Can you pull on the rope at your end and I will guide your boy up from here?"

"Yes."

Sammy's knot does its job and holds the boy securely as the rope tenses and the child rises, first rotating slowly in the empty blackness, then sliding up the rock slope towards the light.

When the boy's body reaches the top of the slope Sammy notices, with gratitude, that gravity has drained the young lad's blood away from his face and into his lower limbs where it is concealed inside his scuffed and muddied trousers. Sammy presumes that somewhere in the mass of thick hair above that white face there is a bruise where an unforgiving rock cracked open the youngster's skull.

For a moment, he thinks of climbing up the rope and helping the others to haul the boy back to the surface, but changes his mind.

Sammy would rather not be there when Mr and Mrs Ransome see the frail, broken corpse that was once their beloved son.

Instead, he will wait here in the quiet half-light, buffered from the cries and screams until they subside, and somebody remembers to untie the rope from the boy and feed it back down to him.

WHACKFORD'S TALE

IT TAKES a while, but they do eventually remember to send the rope back down to Sammy and he scrambles up to surface level.

By then, the dead boy is in the automobile, wrapped in the white picnic sheet and held in the arms of his weeping mother. Mrs Ransome's friend, also in tears, is on the back seat beside her.

"Sammy, you've done so much for us. I don't know how to thank you," says Mr Ransome, eyes red, face puffed with shock and grief. "I can't think straight just now, but I might think of something, so where can I get in touch with you?"

"There's no need, Mr Ransome, I only wish I could have brought good news out of that black place. As for getting in touch, well, you can't. I don't have an address. I'll have one when I get to Northumberland and find a job, but I have nowhere just yet."

Mr Ransome rubs his chin in thought.

"I must find a police station to report this and the nearest one will be at Kirkby Stephen, which is four miles away. There's only room in the automobile for the five of us, but there is a running board, so you could stand on that, if you don't mind?"

Sammy does mind. If the motor hits a rut or takes a sharp bend too fast, he might be thrown off that running board.

"Thanks Mr Ransome, but I'll just walk. It is only four miles and I can do that in just over an hour."

"Well, if you're certain then there's just one other thing. I'm sure that the police will want to ask you about this as well as us, Sammy, so would you call at the police station as soon as you get there?"

"I'll do that Mr Ransome, don't worry. I will make myself known. You might even still be there when I arrive."

"In that case I will see you in Kirkby Stephen. Goodbye for now."

"Goodbye Mr Ransome."

Sammy watches the automobile follow the grassy track back to the main road until it is out of sight before he picks up his sling and stuffs the box of matches back into it.

His hand touches the remains of the bar of Five Boys chocolate and he looks at the face on the wrapper with ammonia-fuelled tears flowing down its cheeks. Sammy opens the pack, snaps off the chocolate version of the same face and puts it into his mouth.

"Not bitter," he says, looking towards the limestone shake hole he has just climbed from. "Not nearly bitter enough," and he spits the chocolate out.

There is no sign of the Ransome's automobile when Sammy gets to the police station at Kirkby Stephen. But there is a smile for him when he announces his name at the reception desk.

"Ah, Mr Kiteland, I've heard a lot about you lately," says the man behind the desk.

Police Sergeant Harry Burns sees the worried look on Sammy's face and speaks quickly to put him at ease.

"Don't worry lad, it's all good stuff. First, we get a call from PC Leighton in Kirkby Lonsdale asking us to watch for a young man who seems to have made a good impression on him. Then a gentleman from Manchester comes in and says this same young man has done a very brave thing to help his family in tragic circumstances. You got his little boy out of a shake hole, at some risk to yourself. Is that not so?"

Sammy shrugs his shoulders. He can't find the right words to talk about what he did and what he saw."

The policeman sees his struggle and tries to help.

"Well, young Mr Kiteland, you can start by telling me something about yourself. Where are you from and where are you going?"

"I used to live in Bolton, but I am making my way up to Northumberland for work."

"That's good to hear. I'm not too fond of itinerant travellers. Layabouts and ne'er-do-wells is what I calls them, but journeymen looking for honest work? Well, that's another matter."

Sammy relaxes, but only a little.

"Do you get many itinerants around these parts?" he asks.

"We've got one in the cells right now; a dozy drunk. He was brought in last night fast asleep and is still snoring yet. But he's in for one hell of a shock when he wakes up and finds out who brought him in."

"Who brought him in?"

"Whackford."

"Whackford?"

"Yes, Whackford." A wry smile flickers on the sergeant's face.

"Tough as they come, is old Whackford. Hard as nails is Whackford. He even has his shoes nailed to his feet, does Whackford."

"*Nailed* to his feet?" Sammy exclaims.

"Certainly does. But that's normal for a horse."

"Whackford's a horse?"

"Yes."

"And he arrested a drunk?"

"I didn't say he arrested a drunk, I said he brought a drunk in. We did the arresting."

Sammy looks very confused, so Sgt Burns enlightens him.

"Whackford used to be a police horse, but he was retired last year and put out to grass behind the Groglin Castle Hotel on South Road. You'd have passed it on the way here.

"As far as we can tell, Mr Dozy Drunk came out of the hotel after a heavy session last night and decided that he couldn't be bothered to walk home, so he opened the field gate and climbed onto the horse.

"The last time that Whackford had anybody on his back was when he was working, and he did exactly what he was trained to do, he walked straight back to the police station here.

"Mr Dozy Drunk was fast asleep when he arrived, so we just pulled him off Whackford's back and threw him in a cell to sleep it off."

Sammy nods, but still looks puzzled.

"Whackford is a funny name for a horse, how did he get it?"

"That's down to the Chief Constable. About ten years ago the chief decided that we should name all our police horses after characters in Charles Dickens' books. It wouldn't have been right to call any of our horse's Little Nell, or Nancy, or Oliver. They're just not hard enough. But Whackford, well, that sounds right for a police horse, don't you think?. You wouldn't go up against a Whackford, would you?"

Sammy shakes his head.

Sgt Burn's years of experience in this kind of situation has taught him that witness statements are easier to extract, and usually more accurate, when the person giving the statement relaxes and can see past the police uniform to the man inside it.

Sammy's face has, at last, lost its worried expression and Sgt Burns thinks he has successfully negotiated the preliminary part of the interview process. So he gently steers the conversation in the direction that it must now go.

"Anyway, young man, that's enough chitchat. I do have work to do. I need to take a statement from you about this unfortunate lad you found in the shake hole. It shouldn't take too long. I just need you to tell me exactly what you saw, and what you did, so I can make out a report for the coroner."

Sammy nods and follows the policeman into an office where he sees a table, two chairs and an unlit coal fire.

The statement process is straightforward and Sammy describes everything that happened, except for the part about Morbid the clown.

"Just sign your name at the bottom here and we are all done" says Sgt Burns, pushing the handwritten statement towards Sammy, along with an inked pen.

"Now then, I have just one more thing to do and that

is to give you this."

Sgt Burns hands an envelope to Sammy, who opens it.

The envelope contains a letter written in carefully crafted, but shaky script.

Dear Sammy, I have had a lot to think about in the past few hours. My life has changed forever, and you had an honourable part to play in a dreadful situation. Today is a blur and my mind is still spinning, which became obvious as I tried to explain the sequence of events as lucidly as I could to the police. I hope your statement will fill any of the gaps left by mine.

We may never meet again, but please know that I am eternally grateful for what you did for us and tried to do for our little boy.

Yours ever

Charles Ransome

PS I know that you still have a long way to walk, so maybe some good food and a comfortable bed for the night will help you on your way. Please call at the White Lion Hotel in Market Street and make yourself known to the manageress. I have told her I will cover the cost of your stay there tonight and any expense that you incur.

"Do you know what this letter says?" Sammy asks the policeman.

"No, but I can guess. I've seen other people in his position. He seemed keen to leave before you arrived and I can understand why. His life has been ripped apart and any time he sees you, or thinks about you, will bring back all the pain of today. But he also knows if you had not been there when you were things would have been far worse. So his feelings about you will always be in conflict. If I was you, I would take whatever he has offered and never try to contact him."

Sammy is not sure he agrees with the policeman's analysis, but he nods and stands up to leave.

"Where exactly is the White Lion Hotel?" he asks.

"I'll show you in a minute, but first I have to wake up sleeping beauty in the cell and give him the standard bowl of porridge we serve up to all of our guests."

Nobody argues with Mary Little, nobody at all. Everyone in Kirkby Stephen knows that as a fact of life, because she has told them so, or at least all the drunks, rowdies and troublemakers who come into her bar at the White Lion Hotel. They are Mary Little's lambs when they are in Mary Little's bar because she won't tolerate any nonsense from them. When Mary shouts **"Best of order!"** then best of order is what she gets – every time.

As Sammy walks into the White Lion Hotel, the pulse of conversation from the bar is throbbing gently, with an occasional flutter of laughter.

The door to the bar is open and the woman behind the counter spots him. She lifts a folding flap at the end of the counter and opens the half-door beneath it. Sammy walks towards her and they meet in the barroom doorway.

"Are you wanting a room, or a drink? Because if it is hard liquor you are after, then you look too young," Mary Little tells him.

At 16, Sammy is just old enough to be served spirits, and it has been legal for him to drink beer for the past three years, but he doesn't feel like pushing his luck.

"I'm after a room, and I was told to mention the name of Mr Ransome."

"Mr Ransome, yes, yes, he was here a couple of hours ago. Are you Mr Kiteland?"

Sammy can't work out whether it is steel or humour he can see in those candid eyes.

"Yes, that's me. I'm Sammy Kiteland."

"The arrangements have been made, come to the reception desk and I will get you a room key."

At the desk she unhitches a key from a row of brass hooks on the wall behind it.

"Number nine, that's your room, it's straight up those stairs."

She points to a staircase with a turn half-way up. Just above the turn is a huge landscape scene which has been painted directly onto the wall plaster.

"That's an impressive painting," says Sammy. "Is it a local scene?"

"Yes, it's the view of the moors and hills from Great Musgrave, near here. A chap who stayed with us a couple of years ago did it. He travels around the country painting pub walls like this and taking payment in beer, food and accommodation."

Sammy looks again at the painting and says: "I might

go that way tomorrow, I'm on my way north and I think that's north of here. Am I right?"

"Well, you'll go past Great Musgrave, but the road you want to be on is the one going to Barnard Castle, and the best way to reach it is through Stainbridge."

"Is it an easy walk to Stainbridge? I'm trying to find the easiest route because I've got a long way to go."

"Being worn out is the least of your worries. They're a funny lot over that way, too inclined to take matters into their own hands if someone upsets them.

She lowers her voice and says, confidentially: "Their vicar was tarred and tied to a gate by some of them last year, just because he walked a young teacher back to her lodgings at night. Farm boys, they were, all eight of them. The papers were full of it at the time. Didn't you read about it?"

"No, I didn't. They tarred a vicar for just walking a schoolteacher home?"

"Well, she is blonde and very pretty, by all accounts, and the lads were in their twenties, so the green-eyed monster probably had something to do with it."

She sniffs disapprovingly and continues: "The tale they told the magistrates was that the vicar, who is married, walked through woods with his arm around the girl's waist. But that didn't wash with the Bench, and each of the lads was fined £5. So you watch out if you walk over Stainbridge way."

"I certainly will."

Mary Little glances over Sammy's shoulder briefly before looking back at him.

"Speaking of vicars has got me thinking about the man in the room next to yours. He's a priest and I wonder if you have seen him in the town. His clothes and dog collar were on a chair in his room when I went to tidy up earlier today. But his bed has not been slept in. He went out last night in his travelling clothes and it looks as if he did not come back."

"If he wasn't wearing his dog collar how would I know him?"

"You wouldn't have any trouble recognising this man. He is Irish, has jet black hair, a very red face and is built like a brick shithouse. I suppose he could take care of himself in a fight, but you never know."

"No, I've not seen anyone like that, but I will keep a lookout for him. What's his name?"

"Brown, Father Homer Brown."

Sammy turns towards the staircase and says: "Right now, all that I want to fight with is a bar of soap and a bowl of warm water."

"I'll get somebody to bring a bowl up in about ten minutes," Mary Little answers.

When the warm water arrives, as promised, Sammy quickly sheds his clothes and gets scrubbing.

An hour later, as he leaves his room to go downstairs for dinner, he pauses and thinks of priests, vicars and rough, tough farm hands. He closes his door and resolves to have nothing to do with attractive blondes.

"But if she's a redhead and wants to talk about women's rights. Well…?" he whispers with a smile, before locking the bedroom door.

In the dining room there is just one other guest. He is tall, red-faced, has jet black hair, and is wearing a dog collar. He also has a glass of water by his right hand.

"Good evening to you," says the man as he lifts the glass towards Sammy and takes a drink from it.

"Good evening," Sammy smiles in return.

"My name is Homer Brown. I think we may be the only diners tonight so, if you would like a helping of conversation along with your meal, then do join me."

Sammy doesn't feel like a night of religious chitchat, but he sits down opposite the priest hoping to get this man to talk about himself rather than his calling.

"I take it that since you're staying in a hotel you mustn't be local to this parish, Fr Brown?" he asks.

"No, my church is in Bishop Auckland. I have come over here to track down a miracle. I intended to stay with Father O'Neil at St Peter's, just down the road, but when I got here two days ago, I found that he is sick with scarlet fever and it wasn't safe for me to stay there."

"Miracle? What kind of miracle are you trying to track down?"

"I'm on my way to Preston to find a man called Dumb."

"Dumb? What kind of name is Dumb?"

"A very accurate one, since he has never uttered a word for the last four years. Nobody seems to know his real name and, since he is without speech, the good people of Preston have taken to calling him Dumb, or Dummy."

Sammy thinks of Harry Rushforth and his skill at 'pitching the fork'. This man could be just spinning him a yarn, but Sammy decides to take him on trust - for the time being.

"What is the miracle that makes him so special?"

"According to what we have been told, Mr Dumb has been unable to speak for at least eight years, ever since he came back from the war in South Africa.

"He lodged in Chapel Street, Blackburn and hawked wire from door to door around the town for a good few years. But then one of his neighbours got to hear about a cripple in Preston being cured by drinking water from St Winifred's Well at Holywell in Wales.

"Mr Dumb's neighbour visited the well and brought back a flask of water from it, along with instructions about how he should drink it.

"He followed the instructions to the letter and, miraculously, was able to speak again. The first words he'd spoken in eight years were when he asked the neighbour: 'How do you like me now, Kate?'

"Mr Dumb, who, I believe is really a man by the name of Kelly, and a Roman Catholic, then fell to his knees and gave thanks to the Lord in a clear and fluent voice. Soon after that he announced that he was going back to Cumberland, where he was born, to speak to his mother for the first time in eight years.

"My problem is that he told his story to a reporter from the Daily Post in Blackburn and then left without saying exactly where in Cumberland his mother lives. I am trying to trace him by calling at churches, monasteries and convents in the area in case anyone knows of this man or his family."

"Any luck so far?"

"Well…" The priest stretches out his last word and seems grateful when a waitress comes in to take their orders.

When she leaves, Sammy looks at the priest and waits for him to finish that sentence.

"Well…" he repeats. "… sort of."

Sammy's eyes still have a question in them, so the priest continues.

"I met some Kerry men, and it's always lucky for a priest to meet a Kerry man. They are open, generous, funny and true believers. At least, that's my opinion."

Brushing the matter of belief to one side, Sammy asks: "But could they tell you anything about the miracle man?"

"Well, no, but they took a long time to tell me they knew nothing, and they were very nice about it."

"How did you come to meet these men from Kerry?"

"Ah, well now, that is a story, if you have the time?"

"I have plenty of time and no plans to go anywhere for the rest of tonight."

"After I found out that I could not stay at St Peter's, as I had planned, I booked myself a room here at the White Lion and then went for a walk around the town.

"I met the Kerry men in South Road and got chatting. They had come over for the hay hirings last month and are making decent money, around £8 a month, so they were in good fettle. I wasn't wearing my clerical clothes, so they did not know that I was a priest at first and took me for another hired hand.

"We were inside a pub on the South Road before I could explain who I was and tell them about my mission. Well, that was it. When they knew I was a priest, they wouldn't hear of me paying my way. They said it was bad luck to ask a priest to pay for anything, and the rounds kept coming. The stories and the jokes came thick and fast and without really noticing it I'd had more than a monk can drink.

"The last thing I remember clearly was telling them the old joke about Ireland being called the Emerald Isle because nobody walks on the grass there since we are far too busy walking on the grass in other countries. They roared and laughed at that one - and got another round in.

"I have a vague recollection of them saying they would get me back into town and being taken outside. I thought they must have arranged a cab for me, but instead, they brought a horse from behind the pub and hoisted me onto its bare back. They said the horse knew its way to the town centre and I should jump off when I saw the White Lion Hotel."

Sammy smiles in understanding and says: "But on the way back you fell asleep?"

"That's right. I was coming to that bit. I fell asleep and you'll never guess where I ended up?"

"I think I can," says Sammy. "You woke up in a tiny room with a locked door."

"Yes, I did. I woke up in a cell at the police station. But how did you know that?"

"I know more than that. I can tell you that you were woken up this afternoon by a policeman called Sgt Harry Burns who brought you a bowl of porridge for lunch."

Fr Brown gives Sammy a puzzled look but says nothing.

Sammy likes this priest, not for his pious ways, but for his human flaws, so he explains: "I was at the police station earlier today, when you were still asleep. Sgt Burns told me that a retired police horse had come back to its old stables with somebody asleep on its back. But he didn't know who you were at the time - or that you were a priest."

"Well, he does now and, bless him, he saw the funny side of what happened and isn't taking things any further. All I had to do was make him a promise that I would stay away from the Groglin Castle Hotel and those Kerry men, which I am more than happy to do after experiencing their idea of hospitality."

HELLFIRE

"HAVE you seen this?"

Mary Little angrily slaps the newspaper onto the un-used breakfast cutlery in front of Sammy.

"After all that I said to you last night about that vicar at Stainbridge, it turns out that there *was* something going on between him and that hussy school-teacher after all."

Sammy picks up that day's copy of the Yorkshire Post and Leeds Intelligencer and reads a long-winded article headlined *Stainbridge Clerical Scandal.* In a col-umn-and-a-half of tiny text the article carries a near verbatim report from a session of the Chancery Court of York, which had been asked to investigate the behav-iour of the vicar of St John's Church in Stainbridge.

The Chancery Court became involved after a com-mission set up by the Bishop of Carlisle, found there was enough evidence to warrant a deeper examination of the vicar's behaviour leading up to the assault last September. At the Chancery Court hearing it was said that the vicar's wife had left him and later returned to the vicarage to smash its windows because of her suspicions about her husband and the young school-teacher. She'd been told people had seen him with his arm around the woman's waist, kissing her and spend-ing time with her in his church, in the vicarage and in a local pub. But after four hours of deliberation the court ruled that the charge had been brought under the wrong Clergy Disciplinary Act and threw the case out.

After reading the article Sammy puts the paper down and tries to calm this angry lady with a gentle tease.

"Well, Mrs Little, according to this, the case against the vicar was thrown out, doesn't that mean he is innocent?"

The landlady doesn't appreciate his joke.

"**INNOCENT**? Hah! Innocent, my foot. Why did his wife leave him? Why did the Bishop ask the Chancery Court to investigate him? I know it was wrong for those lads to attack him last year, but I see now why they did it. He is a disgrace to the cloth and should be kicked out of St John's."

A voice from behind her says: "I think God should be the judge of that, don't you Mrs Little?"

It is the voice of Fr Brown, who has been listening in silence from the dining room doorway.

"We are all made in *His* image, Mrs Little, but we are also human, with the weaknesses and frailties that go with human nature. *He* is in no hurry to judge us, so neither should we rush to judgement."

"That's your opinion, Father, not mine," says Mary Little, with a sniff as she snatches up her newspaper and struts out of the room.

"Oh dear," Fr Brown turns to Sammy. "I think I have upset her."

"Still, you can see why everybody is so well-behaved in her bar when she is there, Father," Sammy replies. "Maybe they could do with somebody like Mrs Little in the Groglin Castle hotel, eh?"

The priest looks sharply at Sammy and sees a twinkle in his eyes.

"You may be right, Sammy," Fr Brown sighs. "But just remember that you are still a young man with a long way to go and a lot of mistakes of your own to make on the way, just like everybody else."

"Fair enough, Father, I can't argue with that. What are your plans for today?"

"I have decided to go to Penrith by train. It will take just over an hour, so I will have plenty of time to find somewhere to stay and begin my enquiries about Mr Dumb, or should I say Mr Kelly? What about you? Where are you going next?"

"Next for me will be Stainbridge, but I am only passing through. I plan to make it to Barnard Castle by the end of the day and then go on to Bishop Auckland."

"Ah, Bishop Auckland, that's where I call home these days, and it is what I call a really nice town. It has deep roots in the devotional way of life. Bishop Pudsey set up a hunting lodge there almost eight hundred years ago, and that was turned into a castle by Bishop Bek. Ever since then the castle has been the Bishop of Durham's Palace. So, if it is good enough for all those Bishops of Durham, it is good enough for me. How are you going to get to Barnard Castle?"

"By walking, it's the only transport I can afford. I'm only here in this hotel because somebody else is paying for it. Right now I have exactly two shillings and sixpence in my pocket, and that has got to get me up to Northumberland."

"Mm? That won't get you far, will it?"

"No, but I can turn my hand to anything, so I expect to work my way up there."

"Well, if you can turn your hand to anything, then

let me make a suggestion that you might find helpful. When you get to Barnard Castle, or any other town, for that matter, call at its churches and ask for the sexton. Tell him you are a journeyman fosser and ask if he has any work to be done. You won't make much, but it may keep the wolf from the door."

Sammy is not sure whether to look pleased or just grateful, so instead, he opts for honesty.

"What is a fosser?"

"You'll find out," says Fr Brown, getting up to leave. "But for now, just know that it is well within your capabilities, it is honest work and will earn you some cash."

Sammy suspects that the priest has just paid him back for his joke about Groglin Castle Hotel, but he will have to wait to find out.

The road to Stainbridge takes Sammy through a rugged landscape made to look even more challenging by gloomy clouds building up from the west. On the far side of hills to his left it appears to be raining already, and he hopes that the heavy clouds will have shed all their tears climbing over the hills before they reach him.

Earlier that day, before parting company with Mrs Little and Fr Brown, Sammy had enjoyed a hearty, and free, breakfast, thanks to Mr Ransome's generosity. He had also pushed a bread bun and a couple of apples from a fruit bowl into his sling. Mrs Little gave him a chunk of Wensleydale cheese, to show that she didn't hold a grudge.

Half way along his journey to Barnard Castle Sammy walks into Stainbridge. Fifty years earlier this had been a thriving, if small, pit village, but now the heapstead pit wheel is still. The pit's promise of rich reserves turned out to be a false hope. There was coal enough in the early days and half a dozen streets had been built for the miners and their families. The strictly utilitarian street names included First Row, Second Row, Cross Row and Middle Row.

A pub, a Co-op store, a church, a chapel and a school all followed, and for a while Stainbridge and its people had money enough to feed and clothe themselves. But 15 years ago the coal seam got narrower and men had to lie on their sides to hack at the thinning harvest underground. Eventually the seam petered out, and the pit closed.

Today, five years later, Sammy walks into this sad, sullen and exhausted ex-pit town at the same time as black clouds arrive overhead. Unhappily for him, they still have tears left to shed.

He sees a noticeboard and the peeling lettering on it tells him he is outside St John's Church. Sammy decides that its arched entrance might be a good place to shelter from the rain.

After reaching the archway he tries the recessed church door and is surprised to find it locked. Then he remembers the article in this morning's Yorkshire Post and Leeds Examiner. Maybe locking the door is a sensible precaution in case any of the parishioners want to discuss the story with the vicar who inspired it.

Sammy decides to just shelter in the church entrance and wait for the rain to pass.

Two hours later he is still there, and the rain is only just easing. Then, as suddenly as it came, the rain stops and Sammy is aware of an emptiness. This place could be a ghost town. Not a soul walks its streets, not a breath of wind rustles leaves on the graveyard trees and even the steady drum of rain on the porch roof has stopped. Now, only the occasional slap of a fat droplet on the flagstones at his feet, breaks the silence.

For the past two hours Sammy has gazed from the arched entrance across the home of the dead. Gravestones, withering flowers, weeds and carved names of the departed are all he has seen, and now that the rain has stopped, there is just a hollow stillness.

And yet?

Was that movement over to the left of the graveyard?

Sammy can see no-one, but as he looks to the left, he glimpses another movement, this time to the right. He looks that way, but again sees nothing. Then, over to the left once more, something shifts, and this time he sees it - whatever *it* is. Something he can't explain twists and curls from a layer of loose soil over a fresh grave.

Sammy tells himself that he does not believe in ghosts, but what he is looking at is definitely a wraith. It corkscrews upwards and hovers over the new grave. Around it more wraiths now leave the soil and become partners in a macabre dance as they find release from this place of death.

Across the whole graveyard white, twisting shapes lift from the ground - and drift menacingly towards Sammy.

That is when the smell reaches him, the smell of wet dog and burning wood.

Burning? It can't be burning, Sammy thinks. *The whole place is soaking wet. And this is a graveyard, not a crematorium.*

Unless?

He calls up a memory from his schooldays. Didn't his classmates terrify each other with tales about a man bursting out of Hell still ablaze?

"Hellfire Jack!" Sammy shouts, without being aware of it.

He is also unaware of running, until the church is well behind him. Five minutes later Stainbridge is also behind Sammy, and as his pace slows to a brisk walk, he realises that he has entered and left Stainbridge without seeing a single living soul.

It is getting dark and Sammy is still four miles short of his goal. The guide post he is passing says the tiny village of stone-built dwellings just ahead is called Bowes.

As he walks into Bowes, he notices a long building divided into separate homes. Its stone walls are clearly visible on the nearest half of the building, but the other half is covered by ivy.

Something else catches Sammy's attention. The daylight is fading, but he can just make out the writing on a 'For Sale' sign attached to the building. What he reads takes him straight back to his schooldays and Miss Grey, his old English teacher. Miss Grey had a passion for the works of Charles Dickens and for reading aloud huge chunks of his tales to her large class of fidgeting pupils.

Nicholas Nickleby was one of her favourite tales, possibly because its hero is sent to a school in Yorkshire as assistant to a bullying, one-eyed thug of a headmaster, and eventually turns on him.

Sammy can hear Miss Gray's clear, sharp voice now as he looks down at the signboard in front of him. It says FOR SALE 3 DOTHEBOYS HALL.

He smiles and wonders who on earth would be daft enough to call their home after that dreadful Dickens creation.

The road ahead of him goes past an old coaching inn called The Ancient Unicorn. Sammy turns and walks through the pub door. He doesn't have enough money for a room, but hopes he might negotiate an arrangement with the owner, even the chance to sit on a chair while the night passes.

The owner laughs when the young stranger asks if he can have 'a ha'penny lean', but leads him to the pub's gloomy stockroom.

He opens the door and shouts down a staircase leading to the cellar: "Gentlemen, you've got company tonight" and waves Sammy towards the stairs.

"You can stay here for the night, but since my stockroom is at the top of these stairs, I will lock this door shortly. If you need the facilities during the night, there is a drayman's door in the cellar and you can use that to get to the lavatory in the yard."

Sammy goes down the staircase into a room with a single, guttering gas light on a wall, and sees a thick rope covered in towels with half a dozen chairs on either side of it. He also sees a man sitting on one of the chairs and another leaning on a beer barrel.

"Come on down, laddie," says the seated man in a soft Scottish accent. "We'll no' bite, unless we get hungry enough."

The standing man laughs. "That's no way to greet our fellow boarder, Craig. Show some hospitality and give him that seat you've just warmed up."

"Get lost ya southern softie. I'm no' pampering him and I'm no' pampering you. Do your own arse warming if the seats are too cold."

Sammy interrupts before the argument can go any further.

"Don't worry about me, I can warm up my own seat, thank you very much. My name is Sammy, by the way."

"This is Craig and I am William, but you can call me Bill," says the standing man. "I take it that if you are here for a ha'penny lean, then you must be on the road. Which way are you walking?"

"North. I'm heading up to Northumberland to get work in the coalfield."

"Well, that's a good plan for somebody young and fit like you, but it wouldn't suit oldies like us," says Craig. "I'm a joiner and Bill here is a brickie. We were the best journeymen in our day, but that's a good while back. Nowadays we do whatever we can, jobbing about for baccy and booze."

"There can't be much work about if you're having a ha'penny lean instead of a bed in a lodging house," Sammy says.

"Oh, there's plenty of work about, but Craig's knees are shot, and there's only so much that a joiner can do without kneeling down. And I've got the brickie's curse."

"What's the brickie's curse?"

Bill rolls up the left sleeve of his shirt and shows Sammy a fleshy lump lying in the crook of his arm.

"What's that?" Sammy asks.

"That, young man, is my bicep. Years and years of lifting bricks and that's what happens. The muscle that used to hold my bicep in place got so stretched that the bicep dropped further and further down and now I can nip it in the crook of my arm. I can still lift, mind you.

But it hurts - a lot."

"What are the two of you doing in Bowes?"

"Just a little job up the road. There's a house for sale and the estate agent wants a couple of new doors fitted and some tiling done in the kitchen."

"Not 3 Dotheboys Hall, is it?"

"That's the one," says Bill.

"What kind of name is that anyway, Dotheboys Hall?"

Craig answers: "That place was originally a school called Bowes Academy, but once Dickens did his hatchet job on it, nobody called it that anymore. Everybody began to call it Dotheboys Hall, and the name stuck."

Bill butts in: "Just beside Dotheboys is St Giles Church and if you go in there, you'll see a gravestone for William Shaw, who died in 1850. He used to be the one-eyed headmaster of the academy and Dickens based Whackford Squeers on him, although he said he didn't. Another gravestone has the name George Ashton Taylor on it. He was the one that Dickens turned into the character Smike in the book. That churchyard is full of old ghosts."

"Not just the churchyard," says Craig. "This pub is said to be haunted as well, by the ghost of a twelve-year-old boy, and these very cellars are said to be his favourite haunt."

Sammy looks from Bill to Craig and says: "Thanks for that. I did wonder if I'd be able to get to sleep and now I know for sure I'll be awake all night, what with ghosts all around and a washing line for my bed."

Craig turns down the gaslight and chairs scrape as they settle down for the night. Sammy leans forward onto the rope and thinks *Hellfire Jack in the morning, Dotheboys in the afternoon and now Smike, Squeers and ghost boy at night. I bet these two snore like troopers.*

Sammy does fall asleep, but when he wakes the next morning he wishes that he hadn't. His back aches, his neck has a painful crick in it, his arms are locked and his legs are numb.

"Ow, ow, ow" he says as the numbness fades and cramp sets in.

"Ow, ow, ow," Bill answers.

"Ow, ow, bloody ow," adds Craig. "It gets no easier, does it?. The quicker we get paid for this job, the quicker we can find a lodge with feather pillows, soft mattresses and clean sheets."

"Shut up Craig, or I might have to kill you," says Bill, who yelps when he stretches his lumpy left arm too far.

Craig tries to rub the agony out of his knees and says: "Kill me please, just kill me now."

Their morning ritual of whinge and whine goes on for another 10 minutes before they acknowledge Sammy.

"How far are you going this morning, laddie?" Craig asks.

"I had expected to reach Barnard Castle yesterday, but that rain storm held me up, so that's where I am going first. Then I'll go straight on to Bishop Auckland. I might be able to find some cash work there to tide me over. After Bishop Auckland I will head for Durham."

"Good luck with that," says Bill. "If things had been different we might have been able to put a bit of labouring work your way at Dotheboys Hall, but we've not been paid a penny yet for what we have already done, so you're best off looking for something in Barney."

"Barney?"

"Yes, that's what they call Barnard Castle in these parts, Barney. Anyway, have a look there, or Bishop Auckland. You'll find something, I'm sure. Have you got any food with you?"

"Yes, I've got half a bread bun, an apple and some cheese and a few coppers to buy more on the way."

"Good. That will keep you going," says Bill. "And speaking of going it's time we got going down the road to finish our work. Did you pay the landlord on the way in, Sammy?"

"Yes, I did."

"Good, then all we have to do is open up the drayman's door and get on the road."

The two men pick up their tool bags from under their seats and head for the cellar door. Sammy follows and closes it behind him before heading east along the main street towards 'Barney'.

The walk is better than he expected. The weather has cheered up, the road is easy, he is fit and his young muscles soon unlock. There are few distractions on the open country road and he does the four-mile walk to Barnard Castle in a little over an hour. It is another 14 miles to Bishop Auckland and Sammy reckons he can make it there by teatime even if he buys some victuals in 'Barney' and has a break to eat them on route.

He has two shillings and fivepence ha'penny left and as he makes his way through Barnard Castle; he spends two-and-a-half pence on a loaf of bread, three and a half pence on a quarter pound of butter, three pence on two hard-boiled eggs and three pence on four slices of cooked ham, leaving him with one shilling and six-pence.

He opens his sling to stock it with the food and fills his bottle from a standpipe in the middle of a street of houses before also packing that into the sling and striding out for the road out of 'Barney' and, he hopes, towards some cash.

TALKING TO
THE DEAD

SAMMY can't help thinking of Beauty and the Beast as he strides along the road to Bishop Auckland.

He thinks that a century ago this landscape would have been 'Beauty' with its unspoilt moorland, patchwork fields, cottages and self-reliant communities. Then, along came the 'Beast' of industrialisation, with its quarries, pits, spoil heaps, rail tracks and people - thousands of them - who needed homes, shops, churches, middens and hostelries.

On his way to Bishop Auckland Sammy walks first into West Auckland where he passes brickworks, stone works, quarries, working coal mines, exhausted coal mines, gas plants, coke works, and a landscape punctured with dozens of used and unused air shafts, dug to let working men breathe hundreds of feet underground.

He's close to one of the air shaft outlets when he hears shouting. Men's voices; agitated voices, but Sammy can't tell what the voices are shouting or where they are coming from.

He walks towards the shaft outlet and as he does so, the direction of the sound changes, although the urgency in the voices does not. The sounds now seem to come from behind a terrace of miners' houses to the right of the shaft.

Sammy reaches the end of the terrace and walks around it to the back of the homes, where he sees a field and the answer to the puzzle of this noise. A crowd of men line one edge of the field watching 22 others play a game of football.

Sammy smiles at himself for suspecting the worst and is about to turn away when he spots a poster with some intriguing words painted on it. The poster is attached by drawing pins to a rickety pailing fence around the field and the words on it say World Champions V Scarborough - Pre-Season Friendly. But some joker has used a handful of mud to smear a question mark after that word 'Friendly'.

Sammy walks to the fence where two men draw deeply on the hand-rolled cigarettes between their lips.

"Who's the team playing Scarborough?"

One man unplugs his fag and shoots a straight jet of smoke through pursed lips while he considers the young man who has just asked such a daft question.

"Who's playing? Who's playing? Where have you been hiding? It's only famous West Auckland, Champions of the World, against the Northern League's second finest side.

"Sorry," Sammy shrugs his shoulders. "I don't know about West Auckland and I certainly didn't know they are World Champions."

"Not from around here, are you son?" asks the other smoker.

"No, I've walked here from Bolton."

"Walked! You've walked from Bolton?"

Sammy nods.

"Well, that would explain it. That and the fact that the Press, and pretty much everybody else, has ignored the fact that West Auckland FC won the World Football Tournament in Italy last year."

Sammy looks doubtful.

"Oh yes they did. The newspapers ignored it, even the local ones, but these lads, our lads, went to Turin to represent England against football teams from Italy, Switzerland and Germany and came back with the Sir Thomas Lipton Winner's Trophy."

Sammy is not sure whether these men are joking.

"Did they?"

"Oh yes, and they'll go back again next year to defend it, so keep a watch out and see if it gets into the papers this time. If they win again, then they will keep the trophy for good."

Sammy looks towards the playing field just in time to see one of the West Auckland players hook the legs from under a Scarborough forward in a clear foul that sparks loud protests and appeals to the referee.

"That was a dirty tackle. I thought this was this supposed to be a friendly?" Sammy says with a pained look on his face.

The man sucks hard on his cigarette, turning its tip from red, through yellow to white and watches it turn back to red, before answering through the fag fog now enveloping his face.

"They call him 'Dirty' Hogg, but Charlie is just hard, that's all. They are all hard, rock hard. That's how they beat those foreigners last year."

"Who did they play against in Italy?"

"They beat Germany 2 - 0 in the semi-final, then the

Swiss team in the final by the same score."

"But how come they went over there at all. West Auckland is just a little village team isn't it?"

"Yes, most of these lads work at West Auckland pit, but that's why they are so good. They are physically hard, yes, but more than that, they are a team, a proper team."

"What do you mean by that?"

"When you go down that hole in the ground you don't come back out because of what you do. You come out because of what everybody else does. What they do keeps you alive and what you do keeps them alive. So you've got to know each other inside out, and that means strengths, weaknesses, good moods and bad, because your life depends on it."

His friend nods and says: "You need to know who has a quick temper and who burns slow, who had a heavy night on the beer last night and whose daughter you tried to tap up, when you shouldn't have.

"A pit is a place full of accidents just waiting to happen. So, if you upset somebody, you may well have an accident. They won't make it happen, they'll just warn you a fraction too late."

The other smoker points towards the players.

"These men know each other inside out, at work and on the field. They know who will do what before they do it. As well as that they are fit as fiddles and hard as nails.

"Those foreigners, with all their fancy kickabout stuff, didn't stand a chance. 'Dirty' Hogg, 'Tot' Gubbins, 'Ticer' Thomas, and the other lads went through them like a hot knife goes through butter, and they'll do the same next year. Come on ref! That was never offside."

The two men had been looking at Sammy as they spoke, yet still didn't miss a kick of the ball.

Sammy wonders whether they too are miners who share the same team instincts as the men on the pitch and, whether some day, he will also be part of such a tight-knit 'team' underground.

Stanley Pearson gazes down the long, carpeted aisle between two blocks of empty pews at St John's Church, in Bishop Auckland. He is motionless and silent. Anyone seeing him now might think the sexton is deep in worshipful contemplation. But Stanley is adrift on his own soundless sea of calm. It's why he became sexton at this church.

Of course, he wants people to think he is committed completely to his faith, the church, the parishioners, the vicar and Parochial Church Council. But what he really prays for is solitude and silence, and not the complaints, the comments and the continuous chatter which, as sexton, is the cross he must bear.

Once in a while Stanley does get his own way and has days like today, when the church is empty and he can sit here at the back, with St John's huge oak doors shut tight to block out the street sounds beyond them.

The lack of interruptions gives him a chance to meditate and, for some of this quiet time, ponder the problems of the day and what he should do about them. Which is a big help since, as sexton of St John's, he has a huge responsibility for the living and the dead, as well as those on the edge, like Arthur Wright.

Arthur should have retired years ago, but he won't admit it. His eyesight is rubbish, and his hearing is no better, so he can't see when he is getting things wrong, and can't hear when Stanley tells him he has got something wrong.

What to do? What to do? The sexton thinks to himself. He thinks it because he doesn't even like the sound of his own voice.

I can't just order him to give up. I need an excuse. One that will make him think it is his own idea.. But what excuse would work with Arthur?

"Excuse me?"

Sammy's voice is barely a whisper, but to Stanley Pearson it rips apart his beloved silence.

"What? Who are you? What do you want?" the sexton tries to keep his own voice low, but only manages to make it sound menacing.

"I'm looking for the sexton."

"Well, you have found him. What is it you want?"

Sammy tries to say exactly what Fr Brown told him.

"I'm a journeyman fosser on my way to Northumberland, but I need to find a some paid work to keep me going. A priest told me to ask church sextons and you are the third one I have tried since I got here this afternoon. The others just said 'no' and if you can't help either, I'll not bother you anymore."

"A fosser?" The harsh tone in Stanley's voice melts because he believes his silent prayer has been answered.

"Well, well. A fosser? A young fosser, with good eyes?"

Sammy nods.

"And good hearing?"

Sammy nods again.

"Then, yes, young man, I believe I *can* help you, and you can help me. Just come to the graveyard."

The graveyard appears to be empty, but Sammy and

Stanley Pearson can hear a voice.

"That's right. Just a bit more. Over there. I'll soon have it. Nice job, nice job. You've got a good 'un here missus, you'll be snug as a bug down here."

Sammy and the sexton are standing at the edge of a deep hole before they can see Arthur Wright at the bottom. A small wooden barrel is in the hole beside him. A length of rope emerging from its bung hole.

"Arthur." Stanley shouts as loudly as he can and grimaces because his ears always hurt when he shouts.

"Come out. I need a word."

The old man in the grave hole looks first at the sexton, then at Sammy, then at the barrel. He steps onto the stool and from that onto the barrel which brings him close enough to surface level to heave himself out. He brings the end of the rope with him and lays that on the pile of fresh earth he has just dug up.

"Arthur." Stanley Pearson chooses his words carefully. "This young man needs your help."

Arthur Wright looks at Sammy curiously, wondering what help an old codger like him can give a youngster like the one in front of him.

The sexton explains: "This lad is just passing through Bishop Auckland, but he's short of cash. He's hoping to learn about being a fosser to help him pick up work on his way north. Would you mind showing him the ropes as a favour to me?"

Stanley whispers to Sammy: "Do me a favour and pretend that you know nothing about fossing. Talk as if Arthur is doing you a favour and use your eyes and ears to keep him on the right track. Last week he filled in one grave before the coffin had been put into it."

"Pretend I know nothing about fossing?" Sammy

nods, with a serious expression on his face. "Yes, I think I can do that."

In the hut where Arthur stores his grave digging tools he talks with passion about the craft that he loves so much.

"This here is the template frame. Made it myself I did. Seven feet by two feet exactly. I puts the template on the grass and cuts around it with my sod cutter, then I uses the digger spade to go six foot down. Always six foot down, so there's enough room to stack two more coffins on top of the first one. That way there's room for two parents and a child. See that big box over there, the one with canvas beside it? That's where I throws the soil. It keeps things tidy and when the funeral is taking place I covers the soil over with the canvas until the family has gone."

"How long have you been a fosser, Arthur?" Sammy yells.

"Since I were a young 'un about 60 year ago. The pay isn't great, but I've never been out of work."

Arthur laughs at the joke he has told more times than he has picked up a shovel.

A question occurs to Sammy, but he is embarrassed to ask it.

"Arthur, um, have you ever seen a ghost in the grave-yard?"

"No son. I've seen my share of spirits. The bottled kind. It gets awful cold down there in the winter. But I've not seen any ghosts. Have you?"

"Well, I don't know. I might have."

"Might have? What does that mean? You've either seen one or you haven't. There's nothing in-between."

Sammy hesitates for a moment, before continuing: "I was in a graveyard at Stainbridge yesterday and something funny happened. It was all quiet, there wasn't another soul around and something rose out of the graves. Just one at first. It was white, I could see through it and it moved, twisting and turning like it didn't know where it wanted to be and then there was more of them. The whole graveyard was full of weird shapes all moving and mixing."

Arthur nods and says: "And was there a smell, like wet dog and charcoal?"

Surprised, Sammy says: "Yes, that's it. That's the smell. It clung to me until I had run out of the graveyard and down the street."

"And had it been raining?"

"Yes, it had. Do you know what I saw? I need to know."

"I do, son, I do. We get that a lot around here and I'll admit it looks spooky, but it has nothing to do with ghosts."

"What is it?"

"Spontaneous cremation."

"What?"

"Some calls it spontaneous combustion, but I calls it spontaneous cremation, and it is a terrible thing. Those poor souls in the ground are there because they wanted to lie in peace beside their dearest departed. If they'd wanted to be cremated, they would have asked to go to the crematorium."

"But how does it happen?"

"It's down to pits and time. In the old days coal waste was dumped anywhere and sometimes it was used to fill excavation holes, then covered with topsoil. Over the years, the buried waste gets forgotten about and the land is used for other things, including graveyards.

"The problem is that the buried waste has coal in it and as pressure increases on that old coal increases, it gets hotter. That rarely matters because coal can't make fire without oxygen.

"But what happens when you dig six feet down? I'll tell you what happens. What happens is this, you open up that hot waste to oxygen, and when you do that it smoulders. Not straight away, but slow.

"Then, when you put a wooden coffin into that smouldering ground, you can guess what will happen next. Eventually, that wood will also burn and you wind up with a graveyard that looks normal on top, but is incinerating everything below the surface.

"What you saw the other day was steam. It's what you get when rain falls on hot ground filled with slowly burning coffins, and the folk inside them was being cremated.

"You didn't see ghosts. You saw worse than that for those unhappy souls in the ground. No rest in peace for them."

CHALLENGING WOMEN

SAMMY is happy, Stanley Pearson is happy and Arthur Wright is happy.

Arthur has somebody who seems to be interested in hearing him talk about digging grave holes, Stanley believes he has an experienced fosser who will take an apprentice's pay, and Sammy has got a cash-in-hand deal that earns him ninepence for every grave he digs and threepence for every one he backfills.

Arthur tells Sammy that he averages two or three graves a day. The digging takes a morning to finish, leaving Sammy time in the afternoon to find other paid work. Best of all, Arthur says Sammy can bunk down in the graveyard tool shed for free, as long as he tells no-one and keeps a watch on the equipment in it.

When they go back to the grave that Arthur had started to dig, Sammy sees why Mr Pearson was so pleased to recruit him. One end of the hole appears to be the regulation six feet deep, but the other end is barely five feet, and most of the soil thrown out of the pit has missed the wooden box meant to contain it.

"I can tidy up here, Arthur, if you like," Sammy says, lowering the stool and barrel into the hole before jumping in.

"Aye lad. It's all but done, but you can tidy up, that's right. A bit of tidying up does no harm that's what I say. You can't be too tidy, no, that's for sure. Do you want my shovel? It's here somewhere. I've just put it down. Good shovel that. I've had it for years. Never let me down. Cost me one shilling three pence, but it was worth it. It's always worth spending extra to get the right tool for the job, even one and thruppence, that's for sure. I remember one time..."

"Could you throw it down here Arthur?" Sammy says from the bottom of the gravehole.

"What? Oh yes. Here it is. Good shovel that, be careful not to damage it. Cost me one and thruppence that did. I remember one time..."

"Arthur, could you get me your measuring stick, I think I saw it in the shed?"

"What? Oh, aye, that I will, lad that I will."

The spade slides easily into the soft earth and, as he digs, Sammy can tell exactly how far away the old fosser is, just by the sound of his voice - which never stops.

By the time Arthur finds the measuring stick and returns to the graveside, Sammy is out of the levelled hole and standing beside the wooden box, which is now full of the loose earth that Arthur had scattered around it.

Arthur opens his mouth to tell Sammy what a useful tool the yard-long measuring stick is, when something at the entrance to the churchyard distracts him.

Sammy has already heard the clatter of hooves and is looking towards the churchyard gate when two horse-drawn cabs come into view. Both have women cabbies.

"Well, that's something you don't see often," he says,

too quietly for Arthur to hear.

From the first cab Kate Johnson sees old Arthur Wright with a young man standing beside him. She stops close to them and notices that the young man is holding a gravediggers' shovel.

"Hello Arthur, have you got yourself a helper?" she shouts.

"Yes, I'm teaching him the ropes," Arthur replies.

Kate climbs down from her seat as the second cab pulls up behind her. A younger woman dismounts from that one. Elsie Brooks pulls a woollen cap from her head and a hank of long black hair tumbles to her shoulders.

She gives Sammy a challenging look.

"Now then, mister, what are you gaping at? Haven't you seen a cabbie before?"

Sammy shakes his head.

"Not a woman cabbie. Women are usually in the back seat."

Elsie is smiling, but with clenched teeth.

"Well, you'd better get used to it. We aren't in the back seat any more. Times are changing for women and for men."

Sammy holds out his hands defensively.

"Sorry, no offence meant. I'm not saying that women driving cabs is a bad thing, just unusual, which, you must admit, it is?"

Elsie's jaw muscles give, but only a little.

"Agreed, it is unusual today, but it won't be unusual tomorrow. The time is coming when women will not just drive horse cabs, but motor ones too, and they'll make them, and they'll repair them too. Mark my words."

Sammy thinks he is on the edge of a tirade, so he tries

to defuse the situation.

"You're right I know, but you're wrong if you think it's just women who think that way. Plenty of us men are on your side too. Just last week I was helping a women's rights supporter to publicise a big rally in London."

Sammy's peace offering doesn't have its intended effect. Somehow, he has touched a raw nerve in this woman.

"Rally! Don't talk to me about rallies, or protests, or smashing windows, or all that votes for women rubbish," says Elsie. "Talk, it's all just talk, and where does talk get you? Nowhere, that's where it gets you. Change will happen when people *do* things differently, not when they *talk* about doing things differently."

Sammy glances at Arthur and Kate for support. Arthur seems to have switched off his chatter mode and switched on his deafness mode, while Kate is rolling her eyes skyward. Elsie is a dear friend of hers, but Kate has heard all of this before, many times.

Elsie follows the direction of Sammy's gaze, sees her friend's rolling eyes and applies the brake to her ire.

"Oh dear," she sighs apologetically. "Kate is going to say that I'm supposed to be riding my cab, not my high horse, and maybe she's right. I didn't mean to lecture you, but I feel strongly that it is the world of work we need to change, not the world of politics. That's my opinion and I am sticking to it."

Despite his blunder Sammy still wants to know more, and to stick up for a certain girl with red hair and green eyes.

"Surely it is politicians who make the laws that we live by and any change has got to start with getting them to think differently about women's rights," he says.

"And just how do you change the way those people see their world?" she replies acidly.

"They've spent years getting a certain kind of education and years only mixing with people who think the same way as they do. How are they going to unlearn all that? Far better for me, and women like me, to make our mark in the world of work; to operate machines, learn to drive, and to stand alongside men in shops, offices and factories, so that there is nothing odd in seeing us away from the kitchen and the nursery. That is the change I want to see; change that will make a difference for me now, and not when I am an old woman. What is the point in wasting time and energy yelling at those who don't have the brains or the will to hear what I am saying?"

Sammy shakes his head: "You're being harsh on the politicians. They're not all brainless and the ones that can think, can change. I changed last week."

"How?"

"I started the week thinking Punch and Judy is just a harmless children's show. But I don't think that any more. Somebody said something, and it made me see Punch and Judy in a new way."

"What way was that?"

"Well, they meant it to be a joke at my expense, but it got me thinking that Punch and Judy is all about a horrible man beating up a woman and anybody who tries to stop him. Getting us to laugh at him makes it seem as if that is a normal way for a man to go on, and it's not, is it?"

Now it is Elsie's turn to look perplexed.

"Punch and Judy? What on earth are you on about?"

"Right, you two, that's enough," Kate interrupts. "I think we'll call that one a draw and we'll all get back to work. Elsie and me only called in here to see whether the grave is ready for Albert Woodridge. We are due to drive two of the mourning coaches tomorrow."

"Mourning coaches?" Sammy says before he can stop himself. "You drive coaches as well?"

Elsie is about to snap back at this young man for his incredulity, but opts instead for a more subtle revenge.

"Yes, we do drive the mourning coaches. We learned to drive them when Kate challenged me to find a new way of making money and I said we should both become coach drivers."

Sammy looks impressed, so she springs her trap.

"Once a month we challenge each other to come up with a new money-making idea and the one that is the most profitable wins. This month's challenge is to make money from nothing. Do you think you can do better than us?"

"Well, I..."

"Good. Here are the rules. In exactly 24 hours the three of us will have each come up with an idea that cost nothing to implement, but will make money. Kate and me have to be back here at midday tomorrow with the mourners. Once we have delivered them to the church, we will meet up at Arthur's hut and compare our ideas, and our profits. Is that a deal?"

"Well, I..."

"Good, we'll see you back here then."

Sammy's mouth is still open as the two cabs leave the church drive.

Arthur resumes the position he was in when Kate

and Elsie first came through the church gates and speaks as if neither the cabs nor their sparky drivers had been there. He holds the yardstick towards Sammy.

"Grand little helper this is. I've had it 30 years, and it's as good as it ever was."

Elsie Brooks admires her mother. But she doesn't like her.

Kate Johnson loved her mother back in the old days. But that was before the stranger moved into her mother's body.

Sammy doesn't think about his mother anymore. It hurt too much, so he gave up. Thinking of her felt too much like pushing needles into his skin.

Back in Preston, Wally The Wall-Eyed Hypnotist had told Sammy of hypnotists who push needles through their flesh and appear to feel no pain. That made Sammy wonder if there might be a way to think of his mother without it hurting, so he asked Wally for more information. But Wally said it took years of training and, anyway, the pain was still there for those who put needles into their flesh, they just trained themselves to experience the sensation as something different, like heat or sound, rather than pain and injury.

So Sammy tried his sister Cilla's tactic instead and tucked memories of his mother away in a far corner of his mind where they could lie until they faded away.

Elsie doesn't want to forget her mother, she just wishes that Victoria Brooks was not such an embarrassment to her.

There is a lot to admire about Victoria. She is outspoken and self-assured about her rights, as a woman, as a member of society and as a defender of the downtrodden. She shouts, she marches, she breaks glass and even once tried, unsuccessfully, to knock a policeman's helmet from his head. She has also lectured Elsie interminably about her inalienable right to elect and be elected. The lectures lasted through breakfast, lunch, tea, dinner and supper, all of which Elsie has had to make for herself since she was a child.

Victoria Brooks was 21 when the Reform Act of 1867 gave voting rights to half a million more men - and not a solitary woman. That was a time of political awakening for Victoria, and many other women of her generation. She was quick to join the National Society for Women's Suffrage as support for the movement soared through the 1870s. But optimism turned to frustration and anger in the 1880s as political parties promised hope and delivered disappointment.

Victoria's daughter, Elsie, took charge of the household they shared, from an early age. Elsie felt she had no other option since she was living with a mother who was both famous and useless.

Politics is the air that Victoria Brooks breathes, protest gives her all the nourishment she needs and locking horns in fiery debates keeps her warm.

But her daughter prefers stoking a fire full of burning coal for warmth, frying up bacon and eggs to fill her empty stomach and knowing exactly how many pennies it takes to cover the household costs. She likes to think that she inherited her pragmatic nature from her father, who was a captain of industry, a wealthy financier, a brilliant inventor - or something like that.

But in reality, she has no idea who her father is. Her mother attended many rallies and political meetings, in her younger days, where untethered emotions often clouded her better judgement.

The passions shared by like-minded suffrage campaigners, of both sexes, could sometimes become more intense than anyone expected. So, even Victoria Brooks is not sure which of those late nights of shared minds and shared bodies had led to the unexpected arrival of her daughter.

Elsie is thinking of the mother she wished she'd had and the daughter she would never be, as she drove her cab out of the churchyard, leaving Sammy lost for words and Arthur holding onto his measuring stick.

She slaps the reins along the horse's back to catch its attention and that is when her brilliant moneymaking notion sparks into life.

A few yards behind Elsie, Kate Johnson is wondering what oddity the stranger she calls Mother will have waiting for her when she gets home.

It turns out to be custard and potatoes. They are bubbling together in a pan on a trivet over the kitchen coal fire at their downstairs flat.

"Not again Mother," Kate says, trying to keep the exasperation out of her voice, and failing miserably. "I've told you before to wait until I get home. It's not safe for you to cook, you could burn yourself."

"But you like custard, and it's easy to make. And potatoes; you've always liked potatoes, haven't you… er… er?"

"Kate. I'm your daughter and I'm called Kate."

"I know that. Of course I know that… um?"

"Kate, mother. I'm Kate."

"Would you like potatoes, Kate? I've got custard as well."

"No mother," Kate says gently. "It's my turn to cook today. I'll make us some sausage and egg, all right?"

"Yes, that would be nice. At least…? Do I like sausage? I forget things sometimes."

That is when Kate has her money-making idea.

Sammy is up early the next day. He has no work to do until the afternoon, but the morning is all he needs to show those two girl cabbies how to make money from nothing.

His first stop is Bishop Auckland Primitive Methodist Chapel where he can see from a message chalked on a notice board that there was a meeting of its mother and baby club last night. He also sees where the new fathers waited to collect their 'precious' wives and 'amazing' newborns. The spot is marked by a circle of cigarette stubs, spent matchsticks and empty matchboxes.

Sammy gathers up what he needs and moves on to the nearest pub, *The Green Tree*, to collect more material before walking a few yards further to the town's railway station, where he finds the rest of the material he seeks.

Time is getting on so Sammy heads towards a public park that Arthur had told him about.

"Nice way for a young lad like you to spend a morning," Arthur said. "All the young nannies and babysitters like to go there and you never know who you might get chatting to. Chatting to them in the morning, then maybe dancing with them at night. What better way to spend the day?"

But Sammy has other things on his mind. He doesn't want to dance or chat; he has a challenge to win.

At the park he finds what he is looking for - a tree with a level low-hanging horizontal branch. On the branch he stands six of the matchboxes he had picked up earlier. Then he unfolds his sling and takes out the first of two dozen broken pegs that he had found in Arthur's shed. Each of the pegs has only one leg.

Sammy takes a matchbox from his sling and pushes out its empty match tray. From a small ball of elastic bands, which had once been part of a bigger ball in Arthur's shed, he takes one rubber band and loops it over the empty tray twice to make it a tight fit, then pushes the tray back into the box and pokes a peg under the loop of elastic at one end.

He takes a spent matchstick from his pocket, tucks it between the peg and matchbox and hooks the other end of the elastic band over the matchstick. The matchstick, bends forward slightly under tension, but stays in place.

With the peg end of the box in the palm of his hand, Sammy hooks his index finger around the other end of the matchbox and squeezes. The peg 'trigger' leans back and the matchstick is launched towards the matchboxes on the branch.

Sammy misses a few times at first, but soon perfects his aim and begins to 'shoot' the matchboxes from the branch.

Children are the first to notice. They soon gather around Sammy, chatting. But Sammy remembers that crafty old crowd manager, Rev Popplewell, and he ignores them.

Then the adults come to see why their charges have stopped running around and shouting. They too, watch as Sammy's skill grows, and he is able to bring down a matchbox with a single shot every time. Still, he stays focused on his game.

Eventually, one of the older and bolder youngsters speaks up.

"Can I have a go at that?"

Sammy turns his head in the direction of the voice and seems to notice the crowd for the first time.

He appears to think for a moment and then says: "Yes you can, come here."

He loads up the matchbox and places it in the youngster's hand.

"Right, aim at the boxes on that branch and slowly squeeze the end of the box and the bottom of the peg together."

The matchstick flies out and flies wild. One of the younger children picks it up and runs back to Sammy.

"Can I try?" he says.

"Yes, of course you can."

But before Sammy can put the matchbox into this youngster's hand there is a chorus of children's voices.

"And me," they all say.

"Yes, but one at a time, so make a queue," Sammy tells them.

They all fire in turn, and miss in turn, until one child, by sheer luck, hits a matchbox and knocks it off the branch. The other youngsters cheer and jump with excitement. Once they see that it can be done they are all determined to do the same and run to the back of the queue for another turn as soon as they loose off their shot.

Then, one of the watching women shouts: "Tommy, come on, that's enough, we need to get back home now."

Tommy bursts into tears.

"But I haven't knocked the matchbox off yet," he sobs.

"Sorry, but it's time to go."

Tommy throws himself on the ground and howls louder.

Sammy smiles because this is what he has been waiting for.

As the woman takes the boy by the arm and lifts him from the ground Sammy intervenes.

"If you like, I can make one for him. I've got what I need here."

"Oh, would you? That's very nice of you, thanks."

Tommy stops howling.

Quickly, Sammy pulls another matchbox and peg from the sling and threads an elastic band around it. He pushes the tray open slightly and puts four spent matchsticks into it.

"There, that's all you need."

"Much obliged. Can I give you something for it?"

"No," says Sammy, loudly enough for the other women gathered around them to hear. "It's just a matchbox, and a broken peg. I couldn't ask anything for that."

The woman, also aware that she is in earshot, says: "But you should have something for your time and kindness."

She takes a penny from her purse and pushes it into Sammy's hand. What Sammy hears next is exactly what he expected to hear.

"I want one." and "Me too."

Two new queues form; one is a line of children, who happily leave with their own matchbox gun, and the other is a line of mothers and carers pushing pennies into Sammy's hands as the others watch.

One woman, who had carefully observed each penny being handed over, ostentatiously places two pennies onto Sammy's palm. Soon the going rate grows to three pence and remains there until all the children have matchbox pistols.

As he leaves the park and walks back to St John's for his date with the deceased, Sammy says a silent 'thank you' to Rev Popplewell for his lesson in crowd manipulation and whoever it was that first showed him how to make a matchbox gun.

Now, who was it that showed me, he wonders, trawling through his memory. *Was it one of the kids at school? No. Was it Dad? No, he hated any kind of gun after coming back from Africa. Wait a minute... yes, I remember now; it was...*

Before Sammy can stop himself and avoid the pain of bringing her back from that far corner of his memory, he remembers...

... it was, Mother.

THE RECKONING

GRIEVING family and friends of Bishop Auckland store manager Albert Woodridge arrive at the churchyard the next morning in four horse-drawn coaches, two with Elsie and Kate at the reins.

Albert was a well-liked figure in his home town and shops along the funeral route are adorned with black bunting as a show of respect. But once the church doors are closed Elsie and Kate hand their reins to two of the funeral director's men and head for Arthur's shed.

They find Sammy inside eating a cheese and apple sandwich. He takes a swig of water from his stone bottle and swallows hard before saying: "Well, how much have you made?"

"Hold on a minute," Arthur's voice comes from behind a bench where he had bent to pick up a big roll of elastic bands from the floor.

"There's no need to rush, no need at all. That's what I say. No need. No."

The other three wait for him to pause for breath and give someone a chance to interject. But they wait in vain. Arthur can, apparently, talk with no need to inhale.

"I want to know how you made this money first, I do. Fair's fair, this money has to be earned from nothing, nothing at all, or it doesn't count, and this young lad has stuck to the rules, I can vouch for him, that I can, so what about you girls, did you stick to the rules too, that's what I want to know, so did you? Because if..."

Kate can wait no longer. "Arthur," she interrupts. "We need to get back to our coaches, so if you can just give us a chance, we will tell you."

She takes a breath. That is a mistake. Arthur sees a chance to own the conversation again and opens his mouth. But Sammy is quicker. He speaks fast and loud drowning out Arthur's words.

"Fine, I'll go first. I made some of these." He holds out a matchbox-peg gun in the palm of his open hand. "And the people who bought them gave me this." He pulls a piece of folded newspaper from his pocket and places it on the shed floor.

Elsie puts a small purse on the floor beside it and says: "That is what I made by selling four of these to bag carriers down at the station."

She places a harness made from thin strips of leather on the floor beside the purse.

"What did that cost you?" Arthur asks, eyeing the leather suspiciously.

"Nothing at all," says Elsie. "I made them from pieces of rein that had snapped and were useless. They had been thrown away, but I fished them out of the rubbish bin."

Sammy and Kate are both intrigued and reach for the harness at the same time.

"What does it do?" Kate asks.

"I took the length of rein and tied a loop at either end, leaving eighteen inches of strap between them. The way it works is that one of the loops is threaded through the handle of a bag or case, then you put your arms through the loops. That way a bag or case can be carried on your back while leaving your hands free to carry other things or open doors.

"The bag carriers and porters down at the station are always complaining about their aching backs, so they were very interested when I showed this to them. I have orders for more, but this is all the money I could make in the time I had."

She points to the purse on the floor but does not offer to open it. Elsie looks at Kate expectantly instead.

Kate puts her purse on the floor and says: "I can't show you what I did, but I can tell you how I made my money."

"Go on then," her friend says.

"Well, after I left you yesterday I went down to the station and had a word with the King of the Beggars."

"Old Joe Thompson?" asks Elsie in a surprised voice.

"That's the one, old 'Buttons' Thompson."

"Why is he called Buttons?" Sammy asks.

"Because that ragged old coat of his has buttons stitched all over it. He says they are jewels."

Elsie sniggers and Kate gives her a sharp look.

"Don't be unkind, Elsie, he's an old man and those buttons might well be treasures to him. Some of them are beautiful in their own way."

She turns to Sammy and explains: "Joe finds button-sized pieces of wood, stone, metal or glass and works on them. He paints beautiful tiny pictures on the stones and wood, he engraves decorations on the pieces of metal and he breaks coloured glass into tiny fragments to make mosaics. Actually, he is very skilled, but won't take money for anything he makes. Joe insists his profession is begging, and that he is King of the Beggars. He's even made himself a glittering crown, which he wears all the time."

Kate sees Arthur open his mouth so she quickly adds: "When I saw him yesterday he had only just finished a fortnight in jail for begging and said he'd spent the entire two weeks arguing with a man in his cell who claimed to be the 'real' King of the Beggars.

"Anyway, I must have caught him at a weak moment and made a deal with him that suited us both."

"What was the deal?" says Sammy.

"And what did you sell?" asks Elsie.

"Well, what I sold was a 'return to' badge. I got the idea from how often my mother loses her walking stick when she goes anywhere. I found a flattened metal canister in the road and took it to our farrier. He loaned me his tin snips, and I cut the canister into small pieces, each piece shaped like a shield. Then I gave them to Joe."

"What did he do with them?" Elsie wants to know.

"He engraved the image of a Bishop's mitre with two lines below it representing a rail track. The images combine to make a symbol for Bishop Auckland railway station.

"If anything with this badge attached to it is lost, it should find its way back to the railway station's lost property office. The badge can be attached to all kinds of bags or cases and, because it is a soft metal, it can also be bent around walking sticks or umbrellas. Joe made twenty of them and I sold the lot at the station this morning."

"And what did Joe get, if he doesn't like 'working' for money?" Sammy asks.

"I made him an offer that he was delighted to accept. I offered to take him in my cab to the police station tomorrow at exactly 12 noon."

"And what is happening at 12 noon?"

"The other 'King of the Beggars' will be released, and when he comes out, he will see a posh cab being paraded up and down the street with Joe inside, wearing his crown and waving regally at him from an open window."

Arthur, Elsie and Sammy laugh so much they almost forget about the contest and who has won it, but eventually Kate says: "Alright, alright, calm down and let's have the count up."

Sammy opens his newspaper first and reveals its contents, all pennies. He counts out 46 of the coins bringing his total to three shillings and tenpence.

"Well done", says Elsie, opening her purse and tipping out her cash. Four silver coins roll onto the floor.

"I sold four of my bag harnesses at one shilling each. There are my four shillings."

Kate tips her coins onto the floor.

"I had twenty badges made and sold them all at twopence each, so that's three shillings and fourpence. Elsie, you win."

"Well done, Elsie," says Sammy. "There's just one thing. The knots in your harness could be better. The way they are now they could, in time, come apart. I can teach you a better knot for them. It's called a taught line hitch and with it the loop knots can be slid up and down the strap, then locked. That will allow the loops' size to be adjusted to make it more comfortable for the person using it."

He picks up the harness, unfastens the existing knots and deftly ties new ones, to show how the knots hold firm, but can be adjusted.

"Now that *is* better," says Elsie. "Do it again, but slowly, so I can follow what you have done."

Sammy repeats the process slowly twice more and then lets Elsie try for herself. She is a quick learner and picks up the knots at her second attempt.

"Of course," says Sammy "if I charge you threepence for that priceless lesson, then I win because I will have earned four shillings and a penny from this contest."

"Oh, but you wouldn't do that, would you?" Elsie tilts her chin down, opens her eyes as wide as she can to look straight into Sammy's.

"Of course not, just joking," he says, almost before he realises that he'd said it.

On their way back to collect the mourners Kate turns to her friend.

"Elsie Brooks, I never knew you could make your eyes so big."

"Well," Elsie answers. "My mother could learn a thing or two from me about getting her own way with men."

Tall and gaunt, Ivan Sinder, the undertaker, scowls at the sight of the two coach drivers laughing as they walk towards him.

"Decorum ladies. Remember where you are."

Together, Elsie and Kate lower their chins and widen their eyes until Mr Sinder tuts and turns on his heels.

That night, Arthur returns to the shed and stands a tin pot on the workbench in front of Sammy.

"The wife thought you might like this broth, she did. Very considerate woman, she is. That's why I married her. Not for the broth, you understand. Oh no, not that, not the broth, nice though it is. She's very considerate, that's why. When we first met, I thought she wouldn't speak because she was shy. But really, she was being considerate. Folk around here used to say I talked too much, but she always stuck up for me. 'There's nothing wrong with Arthur' she used to say. 'He does have an impediment in his shut-up, but he's a nice man and he's *my* nice man'."

"Arthur," Sammy manages to get a word in at last, followed quickly by "that broth will be cold."

"Oh, oh, sorry lad, you're right. Here you are. There's a little wood stove in the corner over there. You can use that to heat it up again. There's kindling and logs beside it. Enjoy your meal."

He turns and leaves quickly knowing if he stays a moment longer, he will have to fill that moment with the sound of his own voice.

Sammy puts some screwed up newspapers into the stove's firebox and lights it before dropping sticks and a log into the flames. As he waits for the stove to reach cooking temperature, he counts all the money he has in the world and discovers it totals five shillings and eleven pence halfpenny. He does some quick reckoning and decides that he needs to make at least a pound before moving on from Bishop Auckland.

After eating half of the reheated broth Sammy thinks it would be wise to keep the other half for tomorrow night. He also decides to sleep tonight in one of the boxes normally used at gravesides for backfill soil. Sammy lines it with some bags of sand and covers them with blankets he'd also found in Arthur's hut. He settles down for the night thinking of tramps sleeping in 'Fourpenny Coffins' and how this backfill box, with its extra space and soft sandbag mattress, must be worth at least sixpence a night. When he wakes the next morning Sammy is surprised to find that he doesn't have a single ache.

Since he now has access to a stove, and half a loaf, Sammy treats himself to a breakfast of toast with the last of his cheese melted over it.

He is munching his way through the final mouthful of the hot, crispy treat, when Arthur lifts the latch on the shed door and starts talking even before he pulls the door open.

"Now then, lad. It's a grand day, so let's get down to it. We've two graves to dig this morning and one this afternoon for Monday's funerals. If you bring the measuring frame and that shovel over there, I'll get the rest of the stuff."

By the end of their workday Sammy has aching arms, an aching back and aching ears. But, at least there is the pay to look forward to.

Stan Pearson arrives just as they finish digging. He has a cloth moneybag dangling from his wrist and from it he pulls out a brown envelope with Arthur's name written on it.

"There you go, Arthur, your normal week's pay, plus half a day for working this afternoon. Sammy, you have dug five graves since yesterday and your remuneration is a shilling a grave, that's digging and backfilling, agreed?"

"Agreed."

Sammy holds out his hand and Stan places into it two half-crown pieces.

"Thanks Mr Pearson, much appreciated. I reckon I can do another couple of days' work like that before I have to move on, if you need me."

"There are funerals on Monday, Tuesday and Wednesday. It gets quieter after that, but the work is there if you want it."

"Oh, I do," says Sammy. "And I enjoy chatting with Arthur."

Stan Pearson turns to leave, then stops and looks back at Sammy with a puzzled expression. He seems about to say something, but instead he shakes his head and walks away.

Sammy stuffs the coins into his trouser pocket absent-mindedly. He is already thinking that while tomorrow is a day of rest for everybody else, he has money to make and he'd better get started right away. His first job is to head for the town's public baths for a good wash. It will cost three of his pennies, but he wants to look tidy and smell clean when he visits shops in the town asking if he can buy a can of Sammyshine.

Once he has the orders, he can spend tomorrow finding raw materials and making up the metal polish.

By the time he returns that night Sammy has visited four of the town's stores with a sample of Sammyshine, and has a collection of 20 empty tins along with commissions to fill them at fourpence a tin. He calculates that will take his total funds up to seventeen shillings and eightpence when he collects the cash on Monday.

Sammy has no 'Sunday best' and feels out of place when people arrive at St John's the next day for the Sunday morning service. He makes himself scarce and goes looking for ashes and candle wax. He already has paraffin in a glass bottle, donated by a shop he visited yesterday.

He takes to the back streets, partly to stay out of sight and partly because that is where he expects to find the discarded items he is looking for.

Sammy is walking down one of the side streets with homes on his left and outhouses on his right when two boys burst through a yard gate followed by a red-faced man in a collarless shirt who is clearly not happy with them.

"I'm sick of you lot clear off and don't come back again. And you can tell that to the rest of your Boy's Brigade pals as well. Bloody kids."

He notices Sammy.

"I can't get a minute's peace with that lot. They're always at my door. 'Can we wash your windows, mister? Can we 'donkey' stone your step, mister, can we chop some wood for you, mister?' Every five minutes one or other of them is banging on my door wanting carnival money."

"Carnival money?" Sammy asks.

"Yes, it's the St Helen's carnival day next week and they'll be after pennies for the rides and sweets. That Boys Brigade lot aren't even marching in the carnival parade, they'll just be there causing bother and expecting the likes of me to pay for it."

"Now, now, Matthew, that's not very charitable, is it?"

The new voice comes from the opposite side of the street. Sammy turns to look in the direction of the voice and blinks hard because he can't believe what he is seeing. It's the same man. He looks back towards the houses and the man at the gate. His short, black hair has a parting on the left and is combed over to the right. Below his left eye he has a distinctive mole, his lips are thin and teeth yellow.

Sammy swings his gaze back to the outhouses and

the man who has apparently just come out of one. He has short, black hair parted on the left and combed over. He also has exactly the same mole under his left eye and thin lips, parted to show yellow teeth. Their round faces have the same lines and wrinkles in the same places.

They differ only in what they are wearing. The man to Sammy's left has a collarless shirt over an undervest and stained dark trousers held up by a wide belt with a double buckle, and clogs on his feet. The man to Sammy's right is wearing a thin, stylish jacket over a linen shirt. His trousers have sharp creases in them and his shoes are polished to a glittering shine.

"Aha," says glitter shoe man, looking at Sammy. "I can see that you have noticed the likeness between myself and my brother. Let me introduce us. This is Matt Bean, overman at Auckland Colliery and defender of this parish against waifs, strays and seekers of charity. I am his older brother Auguste Van-Biene - with a hyphen."

The other man says: "Older by just one minute and we only have the word of the very drunk Dr McKenzie for that, brother."

"Brother?" Sammy looks confused, because he *is* confused. "How can you be brothers if he is Bean and you are Van-Biene - with a hyphen?"

"Good point well made, young critic, and I shall resolve your dilemma with but a single word, and that word is stage."

"Stage?"

"Oh, for goodness' sake, Leo, why do you have to make such a big production out of every blasted thing?" growls the man at the gate.

Matt Bean looks at Sammy with an exasperated expression.

"He means stage as in stage name. It's the one he uses when he is 'August Van-Biene, Master of Memory and Monologue', slapping greasepaint on his face, shouting other folks' words and prancing around in theatreland, while the rest of us have real jobs and real names. His real name, by the way, is Leo Bean and we might look the same as two peas in a pod to you, but we are nothing like each other. He was born with the gift of the gab and I was born with the gift of common sense and I know which I would rather have."

Sammy reckons he has enough 'common sense' to keep out of this sibling row. He suspects that it has been going on for a very long time and may never be resolved; certainly not by an outsider. He decides that the safest option is to disagree with both brothers.

"I was once told that the only thing about common sense is that it is 'common' and not always 'sense', and being able to 'gab' isn't a gift from the gods, it's a curse for the rest of us who have to listen."

The brothers look at each other for a moment then burst into laughter.

"Well, that's us nicely put in our places, brother," says Leo.

"Aye, you couldn't have put it better," says Matt.

Sammy seizes his chance while the twins are conjoined by laughter.

"Mr Bean, either one, can I get some ash from your bin and use your lav?"

"Er? Yes, of course," they say in unison, shaking their heads as they turn and walk together through the yard gate.

As Sammy scoops fine grey ash out of the bin, he can hear more laughter coming from the house they have just entered.

JOINED UP THINKING

THE TINS in Sammy's sling clunk instead of clink because now they are full.

It took an hour to gather the raw materials for Sammyshine from the bins and middens of his back street benefactors, but now Sammy is returning to St John's Church. As he passes the Bean brothers' terraced home, he hears a voice.

"Hello again, dear boy."

He turns and sees the pair at the front door of the property.

The brother in shiny shoes and smart suit says: "I have a question for you if you don't mind answering it?"

"Not at all Mr Bean, but can I call you Leo? It's going to get confusing if I call both of you Mr Bean."

"Of course you can. I'm an actor, so I'll answer to any name you care to throw at me," he replies with a smile.

"Good," says Sammy. "Now, what's your question?"

"Well, my brother and I are curious about the nature of your request to examine our bin and facilities. What are you looking for?"

By way of explanation Sammy unhitches his sling, removes some tins and shows their contents to the brothers.

They share the same confused look until Sammy explains his moneymaking plan, and his need for their ash and melted wax. He also tells them some of his encounters and experiences since leaving Bolton.

"I've met a few people in your line of business, Leo," Sammy continues. "A trumpet player called Harry Rushforth, a Punch and Judy man called The Great Doo-Fell and Wally The Wall-Eyed Hypnotist."

The 'glitter-shoes' brother tells him: "Don't know about the others, but I did once share a bill with Wally. Nice enough chap, but a bit strange to drink with. He orders one pint and gets two."

Sammy smiles at the memory. "That's right. He taught me a bit of hypnosis when I agreed to help him with his act in Preston."

"How exactly, did you help him?" asks the other brother.

Sammy explains how he used his lip-reading skills to help Wally spot the two troublemakers.

"A trouble hunter? Well now, that is interesting. Very interesting, don't you think, Leo?"

The man in the collarless shirt nods.

"Certainly is, Matt," he says.

Now it is Sammy's turn to look puzzled.

"Hang on, I thought you were Matt," he says to the man wearing pit clothes.

"Oh no, dear boy," the man replies. "Whatever made you think such nonsense? Anyone can see that I am the older brother."

"I've told yous afore 'bout that, so shut it Leopold Bean, or I'll chuck yer in thonder midden," says the man in the glitter shoes and sharp trousers.

The brothers glare at each other, then turn towards Sammy and their faces break into twin grins followed by howls of laughter.

They only calm down when they see that Sammy is also laughing.

"How did you like our little performance," says Leo.

"Not bad, eh?" says Matt.

"Better than that," says Leo.

"Showstopper," says Matt.

"Showstopper," Leo agrees.

Sammy nods. "Well, you certainly had me fooled," he concedes. "And I'll take bets that neither of you is really an overman at the pit."

"And why is that?" Leo asks.

"Because neither of you has any blue scars, and every miner I know has at least one pitman's tattoo."

"Oh, Matt, he's got us there."

"He has at that, Leo, but if one of us had a pitman's tattoo then the other would have to have exactly the same one in exactly the same place or we would be out of business."

"Just what business is that?" Sammy asks. "And if neither of you work in the mine what are you doing in a mineworker's cottage?"

"I'll answer your second question first, Sammy," says Matt. "This is our father's place, and he *is* an overman at the pit. We only lodge here when we are passing through."

"We will answer your first question too," Leo says, taking Sammy's arm. "But not out in the street. Come on in for a cuppa. If Wally trusts you enough to take you behind his curtain, then you can come behind ours too and we'll share one of Van-Biene's backstage secrets."

As they walk into the house Sammy notices a pair of rainbow trout hanging from a nail in a small pantry on his left. On his right is the entrance to a combined living and dining room with an open door at the far end. Through the open door Sammy can see a staircase which he presumes leads to an upstairs room or rooms.

A large, solid dining table takes up most of the space in the room they have just entered. It has obviously been varnished many times, to cover up the scuffs and gouges inflicted during the growing years of two boisterous brothers. Repeated coats of industrial varnish now make the table, and the four chairs tucked under it, look black.

A coal fire is burning in a cast iron range that has a set pot for heating water on one side and an oven, with a round drop-down door, on the other. To the right of the range is a built-in cupboard with two doors. One door is as tall as Sammy and the other one, above it, is just over two feet in height.

Curious about it, Sammy asks: "What's that little cupboard for? It will be too hot up there to store food, too small for clothes or towels and too awkward to reach for pots and pans?"

"You've never lived in a colliery house?" Matt asks.

"No, I haven't."

"All miners' houses have one of those, or something like it. That's where miners keep their blasting powder. It's warm and dry, without being too hot, and it's well out of the way of any kids in the house. Dad doesn't do shot-firing at the pit anymore, but he still buys the odd detonator for fishing and keeps it up there."

"Fishing?"

"Yes," says Leo. "Throw a detonator into the river, it

goes boom, and your fish supper floats to the surface."

"Isn't that illegal?"

"'Course it is, but the bailiffs have to catch you first," Matt replies, before explaining: "There's a rule in these parts that as soon as people hear a boom from the river they unlock their front and back doors. If somebody takes too long to lift their catch out of the river and the bailiff gets on their tail, then they can run straight into any front or back door in the street and out the other side. All they have to remember is to drop one of their fish before they run out of the house. If they do that, then the door they came through will be locked again before the bailiff arrives."

"Is that how you caught the trout in the pantry?"

Matt's eyes go wide. "Oh no, not those. I got those from our friend 'Gissie'. He sometimes plays golf with Auguste Van-Biene at Barnard Castle Golf Club. 'Gissie's' is a dreadful golfer, but he does enjoy Auguste's company. Especially when Auguste lets him win."

"So which one of you is the Auguste Van-Biene that plays golf with 'Gissie'?" Sammy asks.

The brothers laugh and Leo replies: "Both of us. It's a neat way for us to play golf at half price. We are both registered as Auguste and, as long as we don't go there at the same time, then nobody is any the wiser."

"Not even your pal 'Gissie'?"

"Oh, no. He thinks us two are one very average golfer, but he seems to enjoy our patter, especially if we are telling him tales about the showgirls and some of their antics.

"To be honest, we like his company too. He's a harmless old buffer who's generous with his pals at the nineteenth hole. He loves fishing as well and often has his man drop off the odd trout or salmon here at Father's place."

"His man?" Sammy directs the question at Leo, but Matt answers.

"His man, yes, that's right, his man."

Leo takes over. "His 'man' is 'Gissie's' chauffeur and 'Gissie' is Lord Guisborough."

"LORD Guisborough!" exclaims Sammy.

"Yes, but we don't hold that against him," Leo replies, with a smile and a wink.

Matt pours milk into three old mugs, each with a transfer image of the late King Edward VII on it. Leo shakes the teapot, puts a tea-leaf strainer over the first mug and pours. He repeats that process for the second mug - and the third.

After a loud slurp Matt bangs his mug onto the table and says: "Right then, our secret. Well, here it is. We rob the rich."

"To give to the poor?" asks Sammy.

"Don't be stupid, lad," Matt laughs.

"To give to us," Leo explains.

"That doesn't seem right," Sammy tells him.

"Not any old rich," says Matt. "Just two."

Leo lowers his mug to the table gently and explains: "One of the two is the tax man and everybody tries to rob him. The other is our robbing, thieving shit of an agent."

Matt leans back in his chair and spits into the fire. It sizzles.

"That bastard steals a quarter of everything we earn - a quarter! Ten percent is bad enough, which is what most of the other agents get. But a quarter is taking our eyes out and coming back for the tears. It's just not right. So we rob him to get back what he owes us."

"How exactly do you rob him?"

The brothers look at each other and smile. Leo speaks first.

"Once a month Matt goes to the agent's office and picks up a list of engagements that he has made for us. He's a real slave driver and tries to have Auguste Van-Biene working every hour that God sends, so that his quarter cut is as big as he can make it."

Matt shakes his head and adds: "I never argue straight away, I just bring the list back and go through it with Leo. We weed out around half of the dates and write back to Mr 25% saying which of the bookings Auguste Van-Biene will attend."

Leo takes up the tale again: "We keep in touch with his secretary and once she confirms a booking was turned down, we contact the theatre and say Van-Biene has had second thoughts and he might be able to squeeze in an extra show for them if they could make it a cash-in-hand deal."

"And that works?" Sammy wonders.

"It has so far. We have to pick and choose our theatre managers carefully, but we have a pretty good idea which ones like to cream off a little cut for themselves. But best of all, Mr Robbing Bastard gets bugger all."

"A quarter does seem to be a big share for him to take. Can't you get out of your contract?" says Sammy.

"We'd love to find a way, but he's got us stitched up. That contract is watertight."

"Who signed it?"

"I did," says Matt. "Leo wasn't part of the deal because we decided not to tell the agent about him, and anyway, on the day I signed the contract, Leo was at a little theatre up in Northumberland. What was it called, Leo?"

"The Miners Theatre," his brother replies.

"Miners Theatre? Does that mean it's in a pit town?" Sammy asks with growing interest.

"Yes, it is. It's in a pit town called Ashington."

Leo grimaces and adds: "Tough town with rough audiences, mostly pitmen."

"Did they give Van-Biene a tough time?" Sammy asks, sympathetically.

"As it happens, no, they didn't. I've worked in plenty of places like that and I've got the measure of their audiences. I walked on stage looking like a posh toff and launched off with some local dialect words and mining phrases. That got them on my side straight away.

"A troupe that had been there the week before me was not so lucky. They were booed off stage."

"Why was that?" Sammy asks.

"Because their comic was Scotch."

"What happened?"

Leo takes a long drink from his cup and puts it back on the table before answering the question.

"I had a long chat with three chorus girls from the troupe who were in the same digs as me. The others had gone back to Manchester, but these girls had decided to stay in Ashington for their own reasons. They didn't care to explain those reasons to me, but I think it might have had something to do with Ashington being a town full of unattached, fit, fast-spending, heavy drinking, young men.

"They told me that the troupe had been on tour in Scotland with a Cinderella panto. A young comedian from Glasgow had joined them for the tour and he was popular with some audiences, but not all. By the end of the tour they hadn't earned as much money as they'd hoped to, so they had a commonwealth week to make more."

"What's a commonwealth week, Leo?"

"It's when a show is arranged by the performers, instead of their agent. The manager of a theatre takes a cut, usually around a third of the takings, and the performers split the other two-thirds between themselves.

"At the end of the Scotland tour they travelled back over the border and came down through Northumberland into Ashington. They arranged a commonwealth show at Miners Theatre. But it was a disaster.

"The Glasgow comic had never been outside of Scotland in his life and his English audience couldn't understand a word he said. They catcalled at first and then threw coins. The comic tried to make a joke of it and thanked the audience for throwing the cost of his lodgings to him, but they couldn't understand what he was saying and the catcalls got worse.

The show was abandoned and the management said they wouldn't pay for an act that hadn't performed, so all the troupe got for their efforts were the coins that had been thrown at them. The next day the leading lady sold some of her costumes and raised £6 to pay for the cost of getting them all back to Manchester.

"The share for the chorus girls who stayed in town was three shillings and twopence each. When I got there, a week later, they still had three shillings and twopence each. As I said, they were three very resourceful young ladies."

Sammy thinks for a moment, but not about resourceful young ladies.

"What about new pits, are there any pits just starting out up that way?" he asks Leo.

"I'm sure that there are new ones, but I'll tell you what, I'll give the names and addresses of anybody I can think of up there who might help you. I've made a few good contacts up that way."

"He means drinking pals," Matt cuts in.

Leo reaches for a lined notepad and a pencil and takes a large diary from a drawer in the table. He flicks through the diary until he finds the page he is looking for.

As Leo copies a list of names onto the sheet, Sammy looks at Matt and says: "I might have a solution."

"A solution to what?"

"A solution to your situation. Sometimes you can be too close to a problem and you can't see the obvious solution. You need an outsider's view, an outsider like me."

Sammy has the brothers' full attention now.

"The obvious thing to do is just walk away from your agent and don't let him make any more bookings for you. That way he doesn't get his 25% cut."

"And we won't get our 75%, that's not much of a solution to the problem," Matt says.

"Oh yes it is, because my idea will get you a 90% share of your earnings. You should ditch the robber and sign for a new agent, one who is fair and reliable. You must know by now who are the good ones and who are the bad."

"If only it was as simple as that." Leo puts his mug back onto the table. "There is the small matter of the contract Matt signed in his moment of madness."

"Not so much of the madness, brother dear. That contract is a huge document full of legalese and Latin. I didn't understand much of it and neither did Agent Robber. The only bit he understood was the line that said he could rake off a quarter of Van-Biene's earnings, and that was so well buried that I didn't spot it."

"Nevertheless, he has a legal contract signed by Auguste Van-Biene," Leo answers.

"And what if that signature is false?" Sammy asks.

"But it isn't false, I signed it," Matt tells him.

Leo leans forward over the table with a grin growing on his face.

"I think I see where the lad is going with this. Yes, you signed it, but I didn't, and with the best will in the world I can't forge Auguste Van-Biene's signature. I have tried and I just can't make a convincing job of it. That's why we never give autographs; because we write so differently."

Matt is still struggling to understand the point that Leo and Sammy are making.

"You want to argue that the signature is a forgery and Leo, as Auguste, couldn't have signed that contract?" he asks in a bemused voice. "But there was a witness to the contract."

"Who was the witness?"

"The Robbing Bastard's wife. She's also his secretary. She was there in the outer office when I signed and he called her in to add her name to the contract as a witness."

Sammy thinks for a moment. "So she wasn't actually in the office when you signed the paper?"

"No, but how does that help us?"

Instead of answering Matt, Sammy asks Leo: "How

many people were in the Miners Theatre when you gave your performance?"

"Around fifty, it was a one-off matinee show."

Sammy nods. "That means you have fifty independent witnesses who can swear that Auguste Van-Biene was on stage entertaining them on the day and at the time the agent will say the contract was signed, and his wife can't say on oath that she saw pen put to paper."

The penny drops for Matt.

"That's right! A false signature and fifty witnesses all saying that the contract is a lie. I believe this lad is onto something, Leo. If you sign as Auguste Van-Biene for a new agent and, truthfully testify that you never signed the other contract that could be a way out. The new agent will also be able to show that his Van-Biene's signature is nothing like the signature on Robbing Bastard's contract."

"He's sure to kick up a fuss, Matt, but could he sue for breach of contract?"

"He might, but I don't think he would," says Sammy. "Remember, he has a reputation as a cheat over this 25% malarkey, he has a contract with a signature you can demonstrate is a fake, and you have fifty independent witnesses against his one witness who depends on him for her income. Who would believe him?"

Both 'Van-Bienes' are nodding now as Sammy tells them: "I don't think it would get as far as court, not if you show him how weak his case is and point out how much it will to cost him to involve solicitors in a case he can only lose. It makes much more sense for him to cut his losses."

Matt looks at his brother.

"Well, well, how fortunate we are to have bumped

into this young man today, I think the curtain is about to go up on a new act for us."

"Amen to that," says Leo. "Would you like another mug of tea, Sammy? And maybe a jam sandwich. I've got a nice Turog loaf, if you like brown bread."

NO ROOM AT THE SHED

BACK in the churchyard shed Sammy rubs his stuffed stomach. The jam sandwich had turned into a banquet as the Bean brothers told Sammy about some of their backstage shenanigans, and he told them about elephants, shorthand, eels and Hellfire Jack.

By the time they finished talking, a chunk of cold ham, a pound of cheese and various home-made chutneys had all gone the same way as the jam and the Turog loaf.

The convivial afternoon turned into early evening before Sammy remembered that he still had 20 cans of Sammyshine to make, so he hurried back to the shed and got straight to work on his orders.

Sammy is halfway through the job when the Sunday evening service finishes and he hears subdued conversation as worshippers leave the church and head for their homes.

He is rhythmically kneading one more lump of candle wax before adding a handful of ash when the shed door is flung open and a sharp voice shouts: "What do you think you are doing?"

Sammy turns in the direction of the voice and sees a stick thin man with a face that looks robbed of flesh.

Its parchment yellow skin seems stretched thin over a skull; lips are thin, cheeks are hollow and eyes sunken.

Around the shrivelled neck below that skeletal face is a white clerical collar.

"Speak up, now. Who are you and what are you doing here?"

Sammy feels he should apologise, but doesn't know why.

"Um, well, I'm here helping the fosser."

"No you're not. He doesn't work on a Sunday, so you can't be helping him."

"Yes I am, or I was yesterday, and I will be tomorrow."

"Then what are you doing in this shed?"

"Ah, well, I have no lodgings and I was told I could spend a couple of nights here, as a sort of watchman."

"We don't need a nightwatchman and your lodgings are not my problem. But this church, and everything in its boundaries, *is* my problem, including this shed, so get out."

Sammy now sees why Arthur wanted him to keep quiet about his presence in the shed. He doesn't want to get the old fosser into any more trouble than he's already in, so Sammy says: "Sorry, I didn't realise it would be a problem. I'll just pick up my things and...."

"Things? What things? What are you doing in here, anyway? What are all those tins for?"

"I was just making some metal polish. It's very good. Better than Brasso."

"Tinkering!" skeleton face yells. "Tinkering in a church shed! How dare you. This shed is on consecrated ground and you defile it with tinker work - and on the Sabbath. Get out! Get out now!"

271

Sammy quickly pushes all of his possessions into his cloth sling, including full and empty tins, along with the raw materials for Sammyshine. He tries once more to apologise, but knows it is a lost cause.

"Sorry again, but I did think I had permission to stay here."

"Well, you don't. I am the only one who can give you permission to stay here, and I don't give it. So please leave the grounds of this church immediately. I can see that you are not one of my parishioners and, if you are a traveller, then you won't be Church of England either."

"I'm not a traveller or a gypsy and I'm not Church of England, or Catholic, or Methodist, or Quaker, or any faith, Reverend. My religion is hard work and honesty."

"No religion? Then you're a pagan and there is no room in that shed for pagans either. Get out."

Sammy pulls the sling over his shoulder and fastens it in front of him as he walks from the churchyard. Stretched along the road ahead of him is the long shadow he casts in the setting sun.

Sammy wonders briefly about finding lodgings for the night, but it now looks as if he won't earn any more money from fossing with Arthur, so he decides not to look for lodgings.

The summer night is warm and dry so he could try to find a quiet alley or doorway in Bishop Auckland, but there are bobbies on the beat in this town and he doesn't fancy being woken by a prod from a truncheon. He decides instead to seek shelter under a hedgerow.

"All I've got to do now is find a nice, quiet country lane" he says aloud.

After walking through the town centre Market Place Sammy comes to an ornate stone-built archway with a clock on top telling him it is 9.37pm. Iron gates below the castellated arch are closed, and a notice tells him that he is standing at the entrance to Bishop Auckland Castle.

Better give that a miss, Sammy thinks.

He follows a bend in the road which leads to a junction and guide posts. One post points the way to Durham City and the other to Shildon village.

Sammy guesses he will have more chance of finding a country lane and a peaceful night's rest on the road towards Shildon, so he heads that way. Tomorrow morning he will return to Bishop Auckland, deliver his Sammyshine orders, and collect the cash for them before making the nine-mile walk to Durham.

At the next junction Sammy again ignores the main road and follows a leafy lane towards the village of South Church where he sees a sign just readable in the day's dying light. The sign says he is headed towards Black Boy coal mine.

In the distance ahead he can see the shadowy outline of a colliery heapstead, with its huge shaft-top winding wheel. In front of it are two short rows of odd-looking houses. Further past the coal mine is open land with a scattering of copses, where he's sure there will also be hedges.

When Sammy reaches the pit houses, they look even odder than they first seemed. The street looks like two terraces of single-storey brick homes, which have had a second storey added to them. But the upper storeys are not made of brick. They comprised a wooden framework covered in thin canvas cladding, giving these homes the appearance of two terraces of bungalows with ramshackle allotment sheds grafted on top of them.   Sammy is appalled and fascinated in equal measure to discover what he thinks must be the cheapest two-storey homes ever built.

He is so taken with the look of these unusual properties that he does not see the front door of the furthest dwelling open. A man wearing a flat cap and a muffler scarf, steps into the dirt track lane outside carrying a paraffin lamp and a tin can in each hand.

"How do young 'un," he says.

"Oh, hello." Sammy replies and points along the street. "I was just looking at these houses, I've never seen ones like this before. Are they miners homes?"

"Aye, that they are. They're all for Black Boys men."

"Black Boys?"

"That's the Black Boys pit thonder and we all work there."

"That's a funny name for a pit; where does it come from?"

"It's not funny at all. We're all white boys when we go down that hole in the ground and black boys when we come up. Black as coal."

"In that case you must be on your way down the pit."

"Not quite. I'm just going down the lane to see the lads coming off the back shift for a game of hoy up."

"Hoy up?"

"You're not a local, are you?

"No I'm not, so what is a hoy up?"

"It's a game that's best played at night with a black face."

"Why is that?"

"Come with me, if you're not busy, and you'll find out."

"I'm not busy; I'm just looking for a soft spot under a

hedge to bed down for the night."

"In that case we'd better get along or we'll miss the lads coming out. By the way, my name is Armstrong, Jonty Armstrong."

"Sammy Kiteland."

"Pleased to meetcha, Sammy, now let's go."

They walk for 15 minutes until they have almost reached the pit. Then they leave the footpath to cross a cornfield which slopes down to a stream. Sammy can't see the stream, but he can hear it. He can also hear Jonty swearing at the paraffin lamp as he struggles to open and light it.

"Hold this for me while I get these damn matches sorted, Sammy."

Sammy sticks out a hand and feels the lamp being pushed into it. Jonty strikes one match which snaps and falls to the ground flaring. He strikes another, which lights, and Jonty puts it to the lamp wick. The wick burns bright, so Sammy looks away from it - and almost drops the lamp. All around him pairs of white eyes seem to be floating in the darkness.

Jonty takes the lamp and lifts it up. "Aye lads, how's it going?"

"Bloody awful," a gruff voice comes from the direction of one set of eyes.

"Fine, fine," says Jonty. "Before we start, this is our watcher for tonight."

He holds the lamp up to Sammy's face.

"Just give me a minute to have a word with him and we'll get the game started."

But Sammy understands already. He knows this game of 'hoy up' by a different name. Back in Bolton the older men at the foundry call this game 'pitch and toss' and occasionally they recruited Sammy to be their police lookout since they were gambling illegally.

It is a simple game to play, requiring just two pennies. Jonty will place each penny on his extended middle fingers and throw them into the air. Players gamble on whether they will land with both heads up or both tails up. If they land with one head and one tail showing, then the stake goes into the pot for the next throw.

It is a highly addictive game for some and Sammy has seen whole wage packets lost in an afternoon. The sight of grown men in tears at the prospect of going home penniless to face their hungry families turned him off ever playing this dangerous game.

"Sammy," says Jonty.

"It's all right, Jonty, I've seen this played often enough; I know what it's all about."

"Then you'll know the only people who can't lose at it are the one who throws the coins and the one who watches for the law. How about two bob and a roof over your head tonight, for being our watcher?"

Sammy thinks, but only for a moment.

"What do you want me to do?"

"Just go back to my place. It's the one on the end and the door is always open. I'm on my own, so you won't frighten anybody when you go in. While you're there, just keep a close watch and tip us the wink if you see any police sneaking past the house."

"And how will I warn you if I'm a fifteen minute walk away?"

"By the front door you'll see a can quarter full of water and beside it a brown paper bag with white powder in it."

"What do I do with them?"

"Nothing at all, if the police don't turn up."

"And if they do turn up?"

"If they do turn up, then you take the can into the field outside my house, pour all the powder from the brown bag into it, screw the lid on tight and throw that can you're able."

"Then what?"

"Then, you run like a whippet back to my place."

"Why, what will happen?"

"What will happen is this. The powder you pour into the can is carbide, which we use to make the gas we burn in bicycle and pit lights. That much powder and water will make a hell of a lot of gas and when the can can't take any more pressure, it will blow with a bang you will hear for miles. I've done this a lot and you can take my word that the can will blow after about a minute, so don't hang around."

Sammy chuckles. "I see now why the lads like to come for their game straight from the pit. If they shut their eyes, they'll just vanish into the dark."

"All except me. I'll just have to play it clever and hope the bobbies don't fan out across the field when they come looking for us. If that happens, and I get lifted, then you've got yourself a bed for the night because I'll be in a cell. But if I do get back, then your bed for the night will be my armchair. Either way, you will be safe and warm for the night."

"You've got yourself a deal then." Sammy holds out his hand and Jonty shakes it.

"Just one thing, Jonty. You are being very trusting letting a stranger stay in your house. I could be a rogue or a thief as far as you know."

Jonty taps his nose. "You're right, but I know something you don't. There's not one solitary thing in that house that is worth a farthing. If you cleared the whole place out, you wouldn't get two pennies for it. So you'd have done your thieving for nothing."

"In that case, I'll settle for the roof over my head and maybe a night in bed."

"For my sake I hope you sleep on the chair tonight," Jonty laughs.

The next morning Sammy wakes up in the chair and Jonty is snoring under the clippy mat that lies over his bed. The canister of water stands by the kitchen door, unused.

After breakfasting on a slice of bread and beef dripping, set sizzling in a frying pan over the open fire, Sammy finishes making up the last few tins of Sammyshine. Jonty hands him the promised two shillings and they part company.

Sammy heads back into Bishop Auckland to make his deliveries and collect the money owed to him. Then he leaves the town once more and follows the sign pointing towards Durham - with eighteen shillings and eightpence in his pocket.

Not quite the one pound I wanted, thinks Sammy. *But it's near enough and I'll not go hungry before I get to Northumberland.*

VINOVIA AND VICUS

THE STONE guide post tells Sammy that Durham City is nine miles away.

To the left of the road he's on is the River Wear, which flows into Durham City and loops around its ancient cathedral and castle, before flowing to the east coast where it will join the North Sea. Sammy reckons that as long as he keeps the river in view he can't fail to find his destination.

But, after a mile, the road ahead divides into two separate routes. The road to his left is empty and has a good view of the river. The one to the right veers away from the river and on that road is a young girl. She is standing beside a bicycle and crying as she stares at a piece of paper in her hand.

Sammy knows he should go left to stay by the river, but he can't resist taking the path to the right.

"Are you all right? Can I help at all?"

She brushes her cheek with the back of her hand and answers: "No, you can't help, nobody can. Not now, it's too late."

"Too late for what?"

"Those stupid, stupid, people. They've ruined it?"

"What have they ruined?"

"The Vicus, that's what. Look at this." She thrusts the paper at Sammy and he takes it from her. He examines the sheet and sees a series of highly detailed pen and ink sketches. The sketches are of ancient block stone walls with earthenware gullies running through them.

"My father made those drawings 30 years ago and buildings he drew are 2,000 years old. He made the drawings so that people could understand what the Romans meant to this place, but he may as well have used a pickaxe as his pen."

"But how does a drawing harm a building?"

"If the building is a secret and the drawing makes it public, that's what harm it can do, and that's what my father did. He was trying to understand what happened here; how the Romans lived and how the locals lived alongside them, but it's all gone wrong."

Sammy doesn't know much about Roman Britain, but tries to ask a sensible question.

"What do you mean by living alongside them? I thought the Romans invaded Britain and fought the locals, or turned them into slaves. That's what I learned at school."

He gets a look of pity from the tearful young woman.

"Then your teachers were wrong. It wasn't all about fighting. The locals from here made a good living for themselves by trading with the Romans. In this place and other Vicus places across the country whole communities built up near forts and military centres to provide food, equipment and other things the soldiers needed. That was what my father and other antiquarians who worked here proved."

She points along the road behind her.

"The Vinovia Roman Fort is just along this path and everybody has known about it for a long time. But Father and the others always believed there was more than just the fort here, and he was right.

"Just outside the fort they found a village, what the Romans called a Vicus. It was a whole range of homes and businesses, built to Roman standards, but occupied by local people, who provided support services for the soldiers.

"Long after the Romans left Britain the Vicus village here kept going, and survived into the Middle Ages."

"That sounds like a good thing, so why are you upset?"

"Because morons and philistines are destroying it, that's why. When the Vinovia fort was first uncovered seventy years ago the antiquarians who did that work published their findings far too quickly and, as a result, people flocked here with shovels and wheelbarrows. They wanted free stone blocks, to build with or carry out repairs, and here they had a supply of them already cut to size and dressed.

"But they didn't stop at dressed stone. They also dug up pots, cups, bowls, and even statues of the old gods; anything they could lay their hands on, to steal or sell.

"Some of that beautiful Roman stonework even ended up as pit props holding up coal seams in a mine near here."

Sammy thinks for a moment about the things he has reclaimed over the past couple of weeks; candle stubs, fire ash, old tins, unwanted newsprint, all of it useless until he gave it a new purpose.

"Where's the harm in using stones that have lain

around unwanted for hundreds of years? Why shouldn't they have a new life? What's wrong with that?"

Sammy only half believes what he is saying, and he regrets his words the moment he utters them.

"Stones?" she hisses. "Stones!" she yells. "They aren't just stones, they are history, our history, and now they are being turned into walls and sheep stells, and even...*pit props!*"

Sammy searches for a different way to calm this angry young woman and asks: "Roman fort? Just down this road? I would love to see it. Would you show me?"

She shakes her head.

"It's that way, but I can't bear to go back. It will just make me cry again."

Without warning Sammy grabs the handlebars of her bicycle and turns it in the direction she has just come from.

"I'll take a chance on that, and if you want to cycle back home, you'd better follow me."

For a moment she stands stunned, then she shouts: "Hey!" and runs after Sammy, who picks up speed, but not so fast that she can't keep up with him.

Vicar's daughter Violet Tindall, was angry before this stranger grabbed her bicycle and now she is livid as she hurries after him.

Sammy keeps just ahead of Violet, hoping the chase will burn off some of her anger. Eventually he slows down, lets her catch up and offers the bike back to her, with a smile.

"How far is this Roman fort? I don't think I have seen one before, has it got high walls and a tower? Is there a moat and a drawbridge? Are there Roman ghosts guarding it?"

Violet snatches the handlebars from him and glares.

"The fort is just there and the answers to your other questions are no, no and no, stupid."

She points towards a hedge on their right and over it Sammy can see a rise in the field beyond.

"I still can't see a fort," he says, noticing how pretty this girl looks without her scarlet, angry face. The face she wears now just looks sad as she stares across the field.

"It was there," she points. "And, like I said, there was a huge Vicus beside it, just as big as the fort, and filled with local people. Long after the soldiers left, the Vicus thrived as a community of its own for hundreds more years. That's what fascinated Father and the others who worked with him.

"They already knew a lot about the soldiers stationed in the fort because of the stuff they left behind. The altars, statues and other things unearthed during the earlier digs showed that although they were Rome's soldiers they were not Roman; most of the ones based here were probably from Spain. But much less was known about Vicus and the local people who lived there."

As she speaks Sammy notices that this girl seems to see something different to what he is looking at. She is seeing this place as it was and not how it is.

Sammy sees an empty field with broken, weatherworn stones scattered across it, but Violet sees shouting, marching, laughing, living soldiers and busy villagers working alongside them.

She tells him in a subdued voice: "Vinovia was once part of a line of forts along Dere Street. That's the Roman road that went from York up to Scotland. In its day Vinovia was Rome's biggest northern fort and thousands of soldiers were based here.

"All of them needed food, drink, and other stuff to make life bearable in a cold, hostile foreign land. So the Vicus grew up next to the fort. That place, and the people who lived there, are what fascinated Father, and why he has spent the best part of his life trying to understand its story."

As she talks to Sammy, she looks over his shoulder towards grassed land beside the fort's visible remains. Sammy guesses that this is a story she has told, or heard, many times before.

"The Roman army finally left England more than 300 years after they first came here, but the locals, and soldiers who'd put down roots in this place, stayed on. The Vicus was eventually abandoned in the Middle Ages and a new village, called Binchester, was developed a couple of miles away and, of course, the blocks of dressed stone at Vinovia and its Vicus were taken for buildings and walls in Binchester. In time, almost everything above ground level here vanished and the rest was covered under a layer of earth."

Sammy nods slowly. "So the work that your father and the others did was to make sure that while Vinovia and Vicus are gone, their place in history will not be forgotten?"

Violet looks into Sammy's eyes and sees he is beginning to understand.

"That is what he was trying to do. He loved to explain the past by drawing and writing about what he found. But it broke his heart when people used his work to steal and destroy that history."

"How can you *steal* history? Surely the past is the

past and once something has happened it can't be made to unhappen? History is always there."

Violet sighs and delivers a message she has heard her father deliver more times than she can remember. "We can't change the past, but we can change history because they are two different things. The past is what happened, and that doesn't change, history is how much we know about the past and that changes every time we dig into the ground and find stuff. So when that stuff is stolen it's our history that is being stolen along with it."

Sammy is silent and the vicar's daughter is not sure that she has completely convinced him.

"I'll give you an example. Some of the work that Father did here was with Rev Robert Hooppell, from one of our neighbouring rectories, and once, while they were working, a servant from Rev Hooppell's rectory came out with lunch for them. As she was handing it around, she lost a hairpin and didn't notice. The hairpin was made from bone and not at all valuable, but it came from a dig Rev Hooppell was involved with in Norway and had been carved in the Scandinavian style.

"Luckily, because Father and Rev Hooppell were so meticulous about not contaminating any site where they were digging, they spotted the hairpin beside one of the Vicus walls and returned it to the servant. But if they hadn't seen that hairpin it would have been buried when they had the site backfilled.

"Just imagine what would happen if, a hundred years later, somebody else carries out a dig here and finds the old Scandinavian hairpin among Roman remains?

"If they are stupid, they might think it proved that the Roman Empire must have had links with Scandinavia.

"If they are stupid and they have lots of fancy letters after their name, then people might be convinced that what they say must be true and that will become accepted as 'historical fact', but it will be a lie."

"I see your point," says Sammy. "I really do. But has that been much of a problem here at this site?"

Violet doesn't reply, she just walks away from Sammy. He follows her across the field towards a patch of uneven ground where she says: "Look again at Father's drawings."

He does as she asks.

"See how he has drawn those small walls with the earthenware channels in them? What you are looking at in the drawings is what he unearthed all those years ago and then reburied. Now, look over there."

She points to hollows of bare earth peppering the grassed field. Some are shallow, but one is a good four feet deep and at the bottom of it Sammy can see part of a stone wall exposed, with fragments of broken earthenware around it.

"Most of that wall, a wall which has stood for more than eighteen centuries, is gone, and Father thinks it is his fault."

"Why does he think that?"

"Because it *is* his fault, that's why. It looks the way does is now because he showed the philistines exactly where to look for the Vicus, when he made these drawings.

"He thought he had been too clever for the thieves, but he hadn't.

"The antiquarians who carried out the 1878 dig went into print with their findings just a year later and people came here from all over the country to see what they had found. Some did come in search of knowledge, but others came looking for souvenirs, or even profit. Who knows what treasures were dug up and now stand on somebody's mantelpiece, or some illicit collector's private museum?

"So Father and Rev Hooppell were more cautious with the Vicus when they excavated that. Once all their measurements were made and their drawings done, the site was backfilled and the surface restored.

"The turf over the remains had been cut carefully, and each sod marked so that the site could be restored exactly as it had been when it was cut. Everyone involved was sworn to secrecy until the findings were eventually published, and even that was delayed.

"Rev Hooppell didn't publish their findings about the Vicus until 1891, just four years before he died. But everything Father did to protect this place was still a waste of time."

"Why, what happened?"

"Dandelions happened, that's what. Come here and I will show you."

She takes him to a part of the field where the grass seems to be greener than the rest.

"The people who backfilled this place knew a lot about antiquary, but very little about agriculture. They didn't account for the fact that digging up soil encourages plants that grow more vigorously in disturbed soil, like dandelions. So the land above the archaeology Father was trying to hide and protect has, in time, changed. It is greener and has more wild plants on it than the areas that were not dug up.

"He might as well have stuck a notice in the ground

saying 'Dig here'."

"And has any treasure been dug up this time?"

"Who knows? Father never found gold or jewellery, when he did the original excavation work, although one or two Roman coins were dug up. But there is more than one kind of 'treasure'."

She points to part of the original excavation area.

"This is where they found the hypocaust of a Roman building which somehow had survived undamaged. They also found carvings and inscriptions as well as fragments of pottery, some of it a beautiful red colour with a yellow glaze inside. Now that is what antiquarians call real treasure."

"What's a hypocaust?"

"It's for warming a building. The Romans had a system where water and air were heated by a furnace. The water was used in the bathing area and heated air was channelled under the floors of rooms."

Sammy smiles and tells her: "Those Romans certainly were clever people, weren't they?"

The vicar's daughter nods.

"Cleverer than us in some ways, but their time here came to an end, for whatever reason, and now it is up to us to take what we can learn from them and use it to make our own lives better."

"Instead of digging up or misusing what they left and not learning from it?" Sammy says.

Violet smiles for the first time since their encounter began.

They met with tears and harsh words, but now they part with a shared respect. Violet climbs back onto her bicycle and heads for home in Shadforth on the outskirts of Durham City where she will report her unwelcome news to her aged and infirm father.

Sammy walks back to the road taking him deeper into the area that locals refer to as 'The Bishopric' but what everyone else calls 'County Durham'.

THE BISHOPRIC

IT IS the strangest-looking building that Sammy has ever seen. The roof looks as if it was created by a careless child. Crooked slates cover its three separated sections, none of which is at the same height or pitch as the others.

The building below the cock-eyed roof looks as if it is being ruthlessly squeezed by the two larger properties that stand on either side. Barely twelve feet wide, the shop has a tiny bay window crammed with sun-bleached dummies of the goods on sale inside. The low, grubby entrance door seems designed to repel customers rather than attract them, and over the shop window a giant metal kettle dangles from rusting chains.

As Sammy walks the road through Gilesgate that will take him down into the centre of Durham City, he can't work out why a giant kettle is hanging over a large hand-painted sign that says 'POST OFFICE'. Then he gets within smelling distance of the shop.

First it is the aroma of fresh-baked bread that fills his nostrils, then the smells of frying bacon and hot, buttered toast reach him.

He looks up at a small sign fastened to the brickwork over the shop's low entrance door. In black letters the sign says 'Dorkins' and below that are the words 'Post Office, Bakery, Cafe, Sea Shells.'

Sammy can master the pangs of thirst and hunger

when he has to, but the pull of curiosity is a tougher temptation, so he ducks under the lintel over the doorway and walks into this place of wonders.

"Yes?"

The voice is clear and young. But the lady it comes from is bent and old. Taken aback, Sammy only manages to mumble: "Um?"

She speaks again.

"Tea? Tea and toast? Tea and toast and egg? Tea and toast and egg and bacon? Unless it is stamps you are after?"

Sammy rediscovers his voice.

"Um, well, I was really interested in the shells," he says.

"Shells are upstairs and are free to look at while you are having tea, tea and toast, tea and toast and egg or tea and toast and egg and bacon."

Sammy now knows there's little chance of leaving this place with the same amount of money as he walked in with, so he does a quick calculation.

"A cup of tea and a slice of toast, thank you," he tells the lady.

"I'll bring them up to you," she replies, pointing a hazelwood walking stick at the staircase.

Sammy climbs the narrow stairway and enters a world of undersea wonders. He sees two tables, each with four chairs tucked under it, but it is creatures of another world which fill the rest of this room.

Shells of all sizes, colours and articulations occupy every inch of wall space. Hanging from the ceiling are even more maritime treasures. They include a five-foot narwhal tusk and a slightly longer sawfish nose, which has a row of long, vicious teeth, along either side a flat blade of nose bone. In another part of the room is the biggest starfish that Sammy has ever seen and a strangely comical puffer fish fully and forever inflated in death.

At the far end of this extraordinary place is a huge mahogany display table, covered in smaller shells and dried sea creatures.

As he looks at it, Sammy notices that a ball-shaped object, coated in wispy, white tendrils appears to be hovering over the table. It hangs in a pool of light from a gas mantle just above the table. Then, suddenly, the object shoots vertically upwards into the darkness beyond the pool of light.

It takes a moment for Sammy's eyes to adjust as he looks away from the light, but, when they do, he sees that the object is not a sea creature covered in white tendrils. It is a man whose pink face is topped by a mass of fine, white hair and encased in a huge and shaggy, white beard. One of his eyes appears at first to be much bigger than the other until Sammy realises that this man has a watchmaker's magnifying lens gripped in one of his eye sockets.

"Male, definitely male," the man shouts in delight.

"What is?" says Sammy, stretching to look over the table.

The man notices Sammy for the first time, but doesn't seem surprised by his presence.

"Hippocampus zosterae, or to you, a Dwarf Sea-horse," the man replies. "It's male, and it's full of eggs."

"Full of eggs? Shouldn't that mean it is female?"

"Oh no. Take this."

The man hands Sammy the magnifying lens.

"Look closely, it's an aplanatic lens, so there is no

distortion. That is definitely a swollen belly you are looking at and that means it is male. Only the male sea-horse has a brood pouch. The female puts all of her eggs into that brood pouch and he carries them around for about ten days until they hatch. From the look of this one they must have been just about to hatch when they caught him."

Sammy peers through the magnifying lens at the tiny dried out creature with the distended pouch.

"Then it's a shame for him, and his babies."

"Oh no, there's plenty more where he came from," the man says, shaking his head. He makes a sweeping gesture that takes in the whole shell-stocked room.

"The sea is full of these things - and always will be."

Sammy's tea arrives in a bone china cup, with the image of a blue sea shell on it. The steaming slice of toast on a plate beside it also has a thick layer of rapidly melting butter.

As he sips tea through butter coated lips and bites into butter soaked toast, Sammy is treated to a bonus lecture about shellfish that includes a host of Latin names, a list of the far flung places they came from, and tales of this odd man's many fishing contacts who send him these colourful and exotic dead things.

The tea and toast cost just one one penny, which strikes Sammy as excellent value. Yet, as he leaves this weird shop, he can't quite come to terms with the strange unease that this parade of sea creature remains stirs in him.

After spending so much time in open country, the centre of Durham feels uncomfortably crowded to Sammy. City shoppers converge on the crowded Market Place from a network of streets around it. Horse-drawn traps and coaches compete for road space with chugging motor vehicles. Women, carrying bags, bundles and babies, bustle through the streets in long skirts, while men in smart suits purposefully thread their way through shoals of window shoppers.

The one thing that they have in common is that they all look clean. At least, that's how they seem to Sammy, and the more people he passes, the more self-conscious he becomes about his own appearance. He has not bathed for a week and he feels that people are giving him a wide berth as they pass.

Sammy wonders if it is just his imagination and sniffs his shoulder. He can smell nothing, but maybe he has just become accustomed to his own odour. He decides he needs some advice and walks over to a small man carrying a huge and dirty canvas bag. The bag is full of newspapers; the man is full of chat.

"Hello there, now how would you be doing?" he says as Sammy approaches. The man's accent does not belong to this city. Sammy's untutored ear can't tell which part of Ireland this man would call home, but Irish he certainly is.

"Could you help me?" Sammy asks.

"Well now, here's the thing. I won't know if I can help you until you've asked your question. But if I can, I will, for sure," he says with a half-moon grin on his unshaven face.

Sammy smiles and asks: "Is there is a public washing or bathing place in the city?"

As Sammy moves nearer to the newspaper seller, he discovers that there is nothing wrong with his own sense of smell, since there is a definite musk hanging around the little man. Sammy thinks if only he had more experience with alcohol, he would know whether that musk is Irish whiskey or Scottish whisky.

"That way." The seller raises his right arm and points down Saddler Street. "There's a one by Elvet Bridge, you'll find it no trouble."

"Thanks very much, um?"

"Casey, John Henry Casey, at your service."

"John Henry. Right. Thank you, John Henry."

The public bathing building has a swimming pool, but Sammy decides not to use it. The pool takes its water from the River Wear and the layer of peat which normally lies at the bottom of the pool is currently being churned up by over-excited swimmers from nearby Durham Boys' Grammar school. A greasy slick is also floating on the surface of the muddied water.

In a cubicle with no door Sammy changes into the old patched trousers and threadbare shirt he wore when he first left Bolton, then he hands the clothes from Kirkby Lonsdale police station to a washer-woman at the baths.

"You're lucky," she tells him. "The hot air drying room is empty, so your stuff should be ready in no time."

In the showers area Sammy undresses and gratefully steps into a stall where he stands for a full fifteen minutes under a deluge of warm water as he lathers up with carbolic soap.

Later, when the city is in darkness and Sammy is cleaner, but nine pence poorer, he goes in search of lodgings for the night.

The Market Place shops are all shut and in darkness, but lit gas lamp-posts throw pools of light onto city centre pavements. At the far end of Market Place

Sammy can see a lamp lighter. He is using a long pole to hook an S-shaped switch at the top of each lamp-post. A quick tug turns on the gas supply, and he lights the hissing mantle.

Sammy's attention is so focused on the line of lights leading down to Framwellgate Bridge that he doesn't see two figures at the foot of one lamp-post in the Market Square, until one of them begins to shout.

"Help, help, murder, somebody help me!"

Sammy runs across the street towards the Market Tavern pub where a small figure is slumped outside the alehouse, in the arms of the other man. The small man is bleeding heavily from a terrible wound to his forehead. Blood runs into the man's thick eyebrows and trickles down both sides of his pale, unshaven face - a face that Sammy recognises.

"Mr Casey," he says. "John Henry, what happened?"

John Henry mutters something, but Sammy can't make out what he is saying. He looks at the man cradling the ageing Irishman, for an answer.

The worried-looking man says: "John Henry told me a tall thin man attacked him. The trouble is that when you are as small as John Henry everybody seems to be tall so that's not much help."

The man holding John Henry is middle-aged, chubby and has thinning hair.

"Help me carry him into my office, would you?" he asks.

"Of course, where is it?"

"Just there." He jerks his head to one side indicating the blue-painted doorway to the offices of the Durham Chronicle.

John Henry is thin, as well as short, so they have

no difficulty lifting him from the pavement and up the two stone steps into the office, where they sit him on a large, wooden chair with armrests. John Henry looks lost in it.

His friend says: "Keep a watch on him while I go upstairs to the reporter's room. There is a telephone in there and I'll call for an ambulance."

John Henry stirs while Sammy is alone with him.

"Don't worry, you'll be all right, John Henry, somebody is upstairs calling for an ambulance."

"Jimmy, is it Jimmy?"

"I don't know his name, but he's balding, chubby and worried about you."

"That's him, that's Jimmy. He's a good boy, he looks after all his sellers, so he does."

"Is Jimmy the boss here?"

"That he is. Circulation manager. He sorts out the papers and we sell 'em."

"Do you know what happened, John Henry? Did you see who did this to you?"

"Tall fellow. Skinny. Hit me before I could see his face in the dark. I'd just stepped out of the Market Tavern when I get bang, right in the face. But he didn't get away with it. I gave him what for before he got the better of me. Nobody lays a hand on a Casey and gets away with it. I sticks one on him, maybe two, or even three, but he was too much for me, he just wouldn't go down.

"Next thing I remember is being on the pavement and Jimmy holding me. Looks after his sellers, he does. Did I tell you that?"

Sammy hears footsteps on the office staircase and the man coming down them says: "The ambulance will be here in five minutes, the infirmary is not far away.

Has he said any more about what happened?"

"No, just what he told you. Oh, there is one thing, he said that he went down fighting, so his attacker might be injured too."

"Yes, that's our John Henry for you. He might be little, but he's a real Irish terrier with a proper temper on him, especially when he's in drink.

"Wait a minute, did you say the other fellow is injured? That means we know he is tall, thin, injured and could still be about, because the blood on John Henry's face is fresh; it hasn't started to congeal yet."

He thinks for a moment, then says: "Right, this is what we will do. You stay with John Henry and make sure he gets into the ambulance. I'm going to look for the swine who did this to him."

Sammy nods and Jim rushes from the office.

He looks back at John Henry and sees a smile on his face.

"See, I told you Jimmy was a good boy, didn't I?"

The horse ambulance, with John Henry in it, has been gone for five minutes and the office door bangs against the office wall as Jim storms in.

"Where is he? Where is that little Irish git? I'll kill him!"

"He left in the ambulance five minutes ago. Why, what's wrong?"

"What's wrong? I'll tell you what's wrong, come with me."

He leads Sammy from the office across Market Place to the Market Tavern.

"I went in there first to see if anybody had seen John Henry being attacked, or knew about a tall thin man. But nobody did. They remembered seeing John Henry leave, but heard nothing of a fight. What they do remember is that he had been knocking back Banns whiskey all night and was in a right state when he left."

"What did you do then?" Sammy asks.

"I went back outside and looked around. I saw blood beside one of the lamp-posts and thought that if the attacker had stood in it, he might have left footprints, but I couldn't find any, so I went back to the blood and then I did find something."

"What did you find?"

"I found more blood, but this blood wasn't on the path, it was part way up the lamp-post. Just about at John Henry's head height."

"How do you think it got there?"

"I don't think. I *know* how it got there, and I will kill him for it. I've got the early editions coming to the office in five hours and no newspaper seller for the Market Place, the biggest sales spot in the city."

Sammy is still puzzled. "But how was John Henry hurt?"

"Isn't it obvious? It's obvious to me. Our John Henry was on a bender. He comes out of the Tavern, blind drunk, and walks straight into the lamp-post. Bang! Only the little bugger doesn't go down, he starts to fight. He tries to stick the nut on that lamp-post and he keeps going until he's knocked himself out."

"Ah, right, I see now, but would John Henry really do that?"

"Oh yes. Fight first, think later. That's our John Henry, and when he gets out of hospital, I'll give him something to think about. That I will, as he would say."

"Jimmy, sorry, I don't know your other name, I can help, if you like?"

"Peary, Jim Peary, and how can you help?"

"I could stand in the Market Place and sell John Henry's papers until he comes back."

"The papers get here at 6am and you would have to be up by 5am to help me get everything ready for them. When they arrive, the papers must be counted, sorted and tied in bundles for each of the newsagents. You'd have to help me with that before you went into the Market Place at seven.

Sammy nods and Jimmy adds: "The pay is a shilling for the work in the office and a farthing for every five newspapers you sell. Would you do that?"

"Yes, I will. But it's late and I do need to find somewhere to sleep for a few hours first."

"That's easy," Jim laughs. "You can have the battling leprechaun's bed. When he is doing an early shift, he sleeps in the storage room at the top of the stairs. We call it the Blue Room, because that is the colour of the walls, the floor, the doors and the ceiling. I think the painter had only one colour left when he did it.

"John Henry has a few bundles of old newspapers made up into a bed, but I'm not sure you'd want to use his blanket, it stinks of drink."

"I've slept in worse places," Sammy tells him, thinking of hedges and stables. But once he is in the Blue Room, he thinks the derelict stable was probably cleaner and healthier.

Sammy resolves to take his mind to somewhere far nicer than the place his body will rest in for the next four hours. *Thank goodness for hypnosis,* he tells himself, *and warm newsprint.*

He lies on the newspaper bundle bed, covered in broadsheet pages full of sales and tales - and relaxes.

Sammy blinks, five hours pass and, from somewhere below, somebody is shouting.

MAKING NEWS

"HEY, hey, up there. Time for work," Jim Peary yells up the office staircase.

Sammy shrugs off his blanket of old newspapers and heads for the blue door of the Blue Room. On the other side of the door is a flight of stairs which takes him down to a passageway with two doors at its far end. One door is marked 'EDITORIAL' and the one next to it opens onto a second staircase which takes him to the ground floor and the circulation office, where Jim Peary is waiting.

"Right, Jimmy, what would you like me to do first?"

"First thing is to make us a cup of tea. The stove is over there and it needs to be lit. There are papers, sticks and coal in the scuttle next to it. Rake the ash out first and get a fire going. The papers will be here in half an hour."

Fifteen minutes later a kettle is boiling on the stove's hotplate and Sammy lifts it to fill a brown, glazed teapot.

"While that is mashing you can give me a hand with the posters," Jim tells him. "Bring that jar over from the windowsill, would you?"

Sammy grasps the jet black jar and discovers it is coated in a glutinous material which sticks the jar to his hand. He tries to put the jar onto a table covered in gouge marks, but has difficulty letting go. When he eventually prises his fingers free, he sees that his right hand is ink black. He looks at the circulation manager and sees a huge grin on Jim's face.

Sammy sighs and shakes his head.

"That was some sort of initiation, wasn't it?"

Jim chuckles softly and nods.

"Sorry, but it has to be done. It's a tradition."

"What is that stuff?"

"Printer's ink, but it's also used for writing posters."

Jim dunks a poster brush into the jar and picks up a poster headed 'Durham Chronicle'. In one-inch thick strokes Jim writes in capital letters 'COUNCIL CHAL-LENGER HERE TONIGHT'.

"This is your poster, Sammy. I'll fasten it to that standing board over there and you can put it on your pitch in the Market Place."

Sammy nods and Jim starts the next poster. He writes 'MARKET PLACE CHALLENGE TONIGHT'.

"These will go to shops around the city; there'll be a good sale today. The man trying to get onto Durham Corporation is John Murphy, and he's a real character is our Mr Murphy. He drinks, he fights, he shouts, he doesn't care who he upsets, and he's got as many enemies as friends. Luckily for us, they all want to read about his latest escapades."

A loud thump at the front door of the office interrupts their conversation, and four more thumps follow.

Jim walks to the door and draws a bolt before heaving it open. A bundle of newspapers tumbles in. Other bundles lie in the doorway and Sammy can see a delivery van already being driven away across Market Place.

"Help me in with these," says Jim.

After dumping the packs of paper onto the office

table, Jim produces a razor-sharp clasp knife and slashes through the string around each pack.

He picks up the first bundle, raps it edgewise on the table and slaps it back onto the table with each newspaper neatly in line with the one above it. Jim does that same with the rest of the bundles, then riffles through each ordered pile counting its contents in seconds.

"All present and correct," he announces after scanning his list of orders from the city's newsagents and street sellers. "These papers are yours. I'll give you a hundred to start with and you can come back for more if you sell them all. It's nearly seven o'clock, and it pays to be an early bird in this business, so off you go."

He stuffs the newspapers into John Henry's canvas bag and hands it to Sammy.

In the Market Place the city is already waking up. Delivery wagons roll through the square loaded with bread, beer, vegetables, milk, meat, furniture and finery, all headed for Durham's thriving commercial outlets. Shop girls and salesmen thread their way through the city centre.

Some people stop and read the poster beside Sammy then buy a newspaper to read more. Others think they already know what they are about to read and offer Sammy their opinions.

"About time that council got what for, and Murphy's the man to give it to them," says one.

"Oh, no, not that gin-swiller," says another, who immediately corrected by his companion.

"He never touches gin, he's a Bann's Irish whiskey man, and I should know; I empty his bins."

An immaculately dressed assistant from one of the city's fashion shops pitches in with: "He's a fighter and he'll fight my corner. That's all I want."

"He should be knighted," says one joker.

"More like beheaded," says another.

Later, back in the Chronicle office with an empty newspaper bag, Sammy asks Jim Peary: "What time is this man speaking in the Market Place? He sounds like an interesting character; I think I will go along."

"Eight o'clock," Jim replies. "He's standing for a seat in the St Nicholas' Ward. He's up against a chap called Penny, Tom Penny."

That night, Sammy is among more than a thousand people who fill Durham Market Place. He finds himself a vantage point on steps below a statue of the Third Marquess of Londonderry. From there he can see a flat-cart in the centre of the market square. On the flatcart are a table and two chairs, and in red and gold lettering along the side of it is the message 'Property of J.J. Murphy, wine, spirit, ale and porter merchant, Durham City'.

From his vantage point, Sammy can also look back to the Chronicle office, where he sees Jim in the doorway with another man. Jim is pointing at Sammy and the other man, portly, grey-haired and wearing spectacles, elbows his way through the crowd towards him. When he gets to the statue plinth, the man is breathing heavily from the effort of just crossing the street.

"Are you Sammy?" he asks.

Sammy nods.

"I am Bob Gudron, the Chronicle's City reporter. I need your help."

"What can I do for you?"

"I've never seen such a crowd in the Market Place and given who is speaking here tonight, things could get very confusing, would you be a second pair of eyes for me?"

"Well, yes, but what do you want me to do?"

"Here," he thrusts a notebook and pencil into Sammy's hands. "When it is all over we can put our heads together in the office and compare notes."

"I don't know about that. I can't report a speech. I don't have shorthand."

"Don't worry about the speech. I do have shorthand and I can take care of that. You just write down anything you see and hear from the crowd. Can you do that much?"

"I'll try."

Two hours later, Sammy and Bob are back in the Chronicle's editorial office. Sammy is breathing hard, and Bob is on the verge of collapse.

"Get me some water lad, would you?" he says, and Sammy hurries downstairs.

On his way back he hears the rapid clicking of a typewriter with just one sheet of copy paper in it. Lying on the desk beside Bob is his open notebook, and Sammy is amazed that he can actually read some of the symbols in it. Bob's shorthand is so neatly written it looks exactly the same as the printed outlines in the Pitman's Phonographic Reporter book he gave to PC Leighton.

"I'll read what was said and you tell me what you remember, or wrote down, about the crowd's reactions to it," the reporter says, after drinking some water and regaining his composure.

After half an hour of typing and talking, Sammy marvels at how fast the older man's fingers have tapped a story into existence.

"All I have to do now is read the story into that

thing," he says, pointing at a wooden box on the wall. It has a handle on one side, two bells on top, and a handset hanging from a metal hook

"It has a direct connection to our printworks in Darlington and the girl there will put me through to one of our telephone reporters. Once I'm connected, I'll just read over my - our - story and he will type out exactly what I say. Marvellous, isn't it? What will they come up with next?"

He doesn't wait for an answer and instead gives the handle three rapid turns and speaks into the mouthpiece.

"Hello? Hello, yes, put me through to the telephone reporter please. Hello? Is that Arnold? No? Who is it? Bernard. Hello Bernard, It's Gudron of Durham here."

He dictates the story that Sammy watched taking shape on the copy paper in Bob's typewriter, including the asides and heckles that Sammy had contributed. Sammy sits on a spare seat and listens to tomorrow's news a day before the Chronicle's customers will read it.

What Bob Gudron says is accurate, comprehensive and explosive. So he knows it will either wreck Murphy's political ambitions or bring him a massive populist victory. But which outcome wins does not interest Bob as much as the future stories it will generate.

Speaking slowly and deliberately, Bob reads his story into the telephone mouthpiece, saying "full point" at the end of each sentence and "full point, new paragraph" at the end of each paragraph.

He says:

> *"Turmoil and confusion filled Durham Market Place and the sur-*

rounding streets last night when wine and spirit merchant JJ Murphy tried to persuade electors to make him the newest member of Durham Municipal Corporation.

Ten minutes after the appointed starting time of eight o'clock Murphy appeared with Durham City fish and chip merchant William Lightley.

Together they approached a rolley positioned in the Market Place and climbed onto it. Murphy raised his hands in the air, displaying two glasses in one and a decanter of Banns Irish whiskey in the other.

'Murphy's best', he announced, and filled both glasses before surveying the surrounding crowd.

He gestured towards his companion and told the crowd: 'I have very great pleasure in asking my good friend William Lightley to speak. He is no stranger to platforms like this, but, like me, he has also been a fool. We are all fools who seek to do any good in this world'.

Lightley took the chair amid loud cheers from the crowd and a glass of whiskey from Murphy's decanter.

He made an exaggerated display

of putting his glass down on the table before saying: 'I go with Murphy on many points. If we are going to eradicate the evils we have to put up with from the Corporation and other bodies, I think it is time there was some agitation'.

The smile on Murphy's face vanished when Lightley went on to say: 'Where I disagree with him is in the amalgamation of the city police force with the county and I hope you will have the goodness to alter that point in your address.'

Murphy, who seemed displeased, told him: 'Under certain restrictions, Chips, if you don't mind'.

But Lightley was not at all happy that his compatriot had interrupted him, and even more put out that Murphy had used his nickname of 'Chips'.

'We'll have no restrictions', he insisted. 'Not a one. At this moment in time we have one of the finest establishments of police in the country'.

Murphy's face turned the colour of a boiled lobster and he shouted: 'Oh, shut up. Chips.' But Lightley snapped back at him: 'Wait till I'm done, and then you can reply'.

Murphy rose to his feet and

*pointed at Lightley. 'Shut up, man,"
he yelled. 'It's me they want to hear
speak'. Lightley yelled back: 'Don't
you interrupt me, sir, I will not be
bullied by you or anybody else here.
I will have my say."*

The election candidate poured
the last of the decanter's contents
into a glass and offered it to Lightley, who pushed it away, spilling
the contents over the table.

'You are going on like a fool,' he
told Murphy. 'But we could do with
a good clown in the Council.'

He shouted at the crowd: 'If you
want to return a clown to the Municipal Board then send Murphy.
There's nothing like a good clown in
a circus. So my advice to the rate-
payers is return Murphy to that
circus we call Durham Municipal
Council'.

He finally sat down to make
way for Murphy, who climbed onto
his chair, with a fresh decanter
of whiskey in one hand and his
glass in the other. After filling his
glass again he downed the contents
in one swallow and said: 'Durham
lads and Durham lasses.' But then
he seemed to lose the thread of
his address and stamped hard on
the chair before declaring: 'That's

the chair and I'm the chairman. So just remember that'. He became unsteady on the chair and jumped from it onto the rolley. Some people in the crowd shouted: 'Shame' while others called out: 'Drunk! He's drunk!'

In response to the angry shouts from the crowd, Murphy raised both hands in the air and jumped off the rolley, followed by Lightley.

Murphy offered a glass of his whiskey to a woman in the crowd, but she refused and yelled at him angrily.

Murphy then threw the contents of the glass into her face and a man charged from the crowd towards Murphy with his fists raised.

There was the sound of glass and a bloody cut opened up on the man's face before he dropped to his knees in front of Murphy.

Strong-armed supporters of Murphy immediately heaved him back onto the rolley. Some also climbed up to guard him while others hauled the rolley through the hooting crowd and out of the Market Place.

As it progressed through Clay-path, past the city police station, there was loud jeering from elem-

ents of the crowd. The rolley was hauled into Providence Row where Murphy lives. Once there, the election candidate was dragged from the rolley by his supporters and carried shoulder high for a distance. When he was eventually set down, he sprinted towards his house, followed by the crowd.

Murphy reached his doorway ahead of the crowd and went inside. Moments later, he threw open an upstairs window and, in full view of those below, pulled off his shirt to display his well-developed biceps.

Murphy treated his supporters and opponents alike by giving them a demonstration of his shadow boxing before swigging another glass of whiskey.

He flexed his muscles again, pointed across the crowd and declared: 'You are free-born citizens of Durham and I am a free-born citizen of Durham and I will fight any man in Durham who says otherwise, the police force in particular - Chief Constable Smith and all. Now I will have a drop of whiskey'.

Before the glass reached his lips the first egg burst against the wall of his house, quickly followed by more. Only one egg got anywhere near its intended target, but Murphy decided to make a strategic withdrawal by closing the window and drawing the blinds behind it.

Police then attended the scene and quickly dispersed the crowd, leaving Durham's famous windmill tilter to consider his next adventure without, presumably, his 'Chips' Sancho Panza."

Bob Gudron looks towards Sammy and says into the telephone mouthpiece: "Full point, end story."

After putting the handset back on its hook, Bob asks: "Well? Did I report the bits you told me accurately?"

"Yes, Mr Gudron. But you said nothing about Mr Murphy's men chasing us all the way back to the office, shouting 'Bloody Press'."

Bob Gudron smiles. "Ah, well, lad. That's not news, you see. That is just part of the job."

THE RAGGED
TROUSERED
PHILOSOPHER

THE NEXT morning Sammy wakes early. He is eager to see how much of Bob Gudron's story is used and to spot his own contributions, even if they were just hurrahs and crowd catcalls.

As he waits impatiently for that day's newspapers to arrive, Sammy watches Jim Peary write the posters for them. The poster that will stand in the Market Place has 'Market Place Mayhem' written on it. Others say 'Durham Rally Chaos'.

"I've ordered a hundred extra for you, Sammy," says Jim Pearce. "You'll sell those no trouble today. Last night's rally got quite interesting, I hear?"

Sammy nods and says: "There was blood, drunken fighting, threats, arguments, treachery, and lots of whiskey."

"Mmm?" says Jim, "Sounds to me like every other corporation meeting. Maybe I'll just give you fifty extras."

Thumps at the office front door tell them that the newspapers have arrived, and Sammy helps Jim to carry them in. Jim slices the binding string on one bundle and hands the first paper from it to Sammy.

The front page is full of classified advertisements, so he opens the newspaper and finds the story he is looking for on page three.

The headline reads "Scene in Durham Market Place" and Bob Gudron's story runs for almost a full column.

"It's funny seeing it in print like this," Sammy tells Jim. "I was standing beside Mr Gudron when he spoke the story into the telephone, so I know that this is exactly what he said, but seeing it in print seems to make it more real."

Jim carries on stacking the papers into pre-ordered piles and doesn't look at Sammy.

"That's the power of the Press, lad. They turn what is here and gone in the blink of an eye into something else, something solid, something permanent. You'll soon forget bits of what happened last night, but in a hundred years from now somebody will be able to pick up this newspaper and know exactly what you saw and heard in the Market Place last night."

Then a huge grin fills his face.

"Listen to me, philosophising. I'm getting as bad as that lad down on Framwellgate Bridge."

"Which lad?"

"Well, he used to be a lad once, but he is one of the university lecturers now - who does some clever begging on the side."

"A lecturer begging?"

"Oh, I forgot, you're new to Durham, aren't you. This is a university town and all university towns have more than their fair share of strange types like him. Most days he sits on Framwellgate Bridge, barefoot, with a notice beside him saying 'Freelance Philosopher - no money please, just conversation wanted'.

"He spends the rest of his time at Palace Green, giving lectures in Natural Philosophy to university students."

"And he doesn't wear shoes?"

"No, he reckons his feet are healthier if they aren't covered, but that's not unusual, quite a few of the more eccentric lecturers do that.

I said that we have more than our fair share of strange types here in Durham, didn't I?"

"If the man on the bridge is begging won't the police arrest him, or move him on?"

Jim shakes his head and replies: "He may be strange, but he is also smart. The police can't touch him because that notice beside him says he doesn't want money, only conversation, and there's no law against talking in the street, at least, not yet. But, people being what they are, if they do learn something new from him they feel obliged to pay for the education."

"I get it now," says Sammy. "He's a philosopher being paid for giving lectures, whether that happens to be on a bridge or in a classroom, so he can't be a beggar, as far as the police are concerned."

"And not just that," Jim stuffs papers into the canvas bag for Sammy. "He also makes more money on Framwellgate Bridge than he does at Palace Green."

"So, some of Durham's lecturers are quite intelligent?" Sammy says as he picks up the full bag.

"Yes." Jim ushers him to the office door. "Some of them."

Three hours later Sammy wishes he'd had enough intelligence to see the punch coming.

A swift jab to the kidneys left him doubled over

gasping for breath. He felt the bag, with half a dozen newspapers still in it, being yanked from his shoulder and was about to snatch it back when he saw the face of his attacker. The face was twisted in anger with everything above the nose swathed in bandages, but Sammy still recognised it.

"John Henry! What did you do that for?" he gasps.

"Thief," John Henry snaps back. "You've stolen my bag, stolen my papers and stolen my pitch. Thief!"

Sammy is too winded to say any more, so he shakes his head and gestures for John Henry to follow him to the Chronicle office.

Inside the office John Henry looks at Jim and points at Sammy. "Thief. He stole my bag, my papers, my pitch."

Jim tries to placate John Henry with a broad grin and says: "Calm down John Henry. He didn't steal your bag. I gave it to him."

The little Irishman walks purposefully across the office floor, dragging his canvas bag after him and looks straight up at Jim.

"THIEF!" he yells.

It takes two cups of tea, a crumbly oat biscuit and two squares of Bob Gudron's Suchard Swiss chocolate, to get John Henry as near as he ever gets to being calm and back on the street to sell the papers that remained in his bag.

"Sorry about that," Jim tells Sammy. "But at least you've made yourself some cash."

Sammy holds out his hand and Jim hands over two half-crowns along with a two-shilling piece, a penny and a halfpenny.

"Just over seven bob there. Not bad for a couple

of days' work," Jim says, and Sammy agrees. His funds now add up to one pound four shillings and threepence ha'penny.

"Where are you headed now?" Jim wants to know.

"I'm on my way to Northumberland. New pits are being sunk up there, and there'll be plenty of chances for me to make something of myself."

"In that case, walk out of the city along North Road and you will pass the Durham Miners' Association headquarters. Call in there and ask for Tom Fenton. He's a pal of mine and he will know people in Northumberland who might help you."

"I'll do that, Jim. Thanks."

From the Market Place it is a short walk down Silver Street, to Framwellgate Bridge and on the other side of the bridge is North Road.

As Sammy approaches the bridge, he sees a crowd of about half a dozen people in animated conversation. He can't hear them yet, but can see that two of them are bare-footed and a third seems to have spent the night sleeping under a hedge, judging from the twigs still in his matted hair.

'Twigman' is shouting and, as Sammy gets nearer, his words become clearer.

"No, no, no! Thucydides was wrong. I'm telling you. He knew nothing."

The crowd parts slightly and Sammy can now see that 'Twigman' is arguing with someone in trousers that are even more tatty than the ones in Sammy's sling. Ragged trouser man is sitting on the ground with his back against a bridge parapet, and next to him is a notice with 'Freelance Philosopher' painted on it.

He nods sagely and says to 'Twigman': "I understand

your point of view Professor, and perhaps there is some merit in it. But surely we can agree that your sources may be flawed. Thucydides, however, was there at the time and able to exercise his intellectual rigour and critical capacity to assess and evaluate information gathered from living people and current events. He was not forced to rely upon so-called facts filtered and distilled by generations of historians, all with their own passions and agendas."

"Rubbish," Professor 'Twigman' snaps back. "All that Greek fraud did was pick up and repeat the gossip and hearsay that everybody was talking about. He didn't conduct any research of significance; he just spent his time eavesdropping in bars and brothels."

A fragment of withered leaf drops from his hair and stays on the professor's shoulder as he moves smoothly from argument to lecture mode.

"After all, Thucydides spent twenty years in exile. So how could he have spoken from personal knowledge? His opinions could only have come from information that was second-hand, possibly even third-hand."

The ragged-trousered philosopher smiles benignly.

"Information can be second-hand, yet still valid if it has been tested honestly and thoroughly. Thucydides himself did warn that 'Most people, in fact, will not take the trouble in finding out the truth, but are much more inclined to accept the first story they hear' so he was certainly aware of the pervasive lure of gossip."

Professor 'Twigman' shakes his head, but before he can say anything more a young girl approaches and tugs his sleeve.

"Professor, could you settle an argument we have

been having in class at St Hild's Training College?" she says.

His manner changes instantly.

"In class? St Hild's? Of course I will, my dear, what is it?"

"It's concerning the Sarissa."

"The Macedonian battle pike?"

"Yes, that's it."

"What do you want to know about it?"

"Well, we were having a debate about it and some of us don't believe it could have ever been used in battle. It is twenty feet long after all. Surely it would only have been used for intimidation, or for ceremony?"

The professor flinches defensively.

"Oh, no, no. It was definitely a weapon of war and you can take it from me that the Sarissa is surprisingly easy to deploy."

"You've used one?"

"Of course, I have one in the college staff room."

"But how do you actually use it? Do you thrust, or swipe, or throw it?"

"It requires a particular action which is difficult to describe, but easy to demonstrate. Go with your classmates to the woods behind St Margaret's Church and I will see you there in fifteen minutes, once I have retrieved my Sarissa and the Macedonian battle tunic that must always be worn when it is in use."

"I thought we were going to debate Thucydides?" says the philosopher on the pavement.

"A plague on Thucydides, I'm off to battle," Professor 'Twigman' tells him.

Sammy wants neither plagues, battles, nor philosophy, so he leaves too. He continues over the bridge to

North Road and sees the domed building ahead where he hopes to find conversations, even arguments, that he can understand.

Sammy gets what he wants. The conversation is clear, simple and brooks no argument.

"Who are you?" he hears as he walks into the Miners' Association office.

"I'm looking for Mr Fenton."

The man tips a shovel full of coal into a tiny stove.

"Are you deaf?"

"No."

"Then *who are you*?"

"My name is Sammy Kiteland, and I'm looking for Mr Fenton."

"Which lodge are you in?"

"Lodge? I don't have one. I have been staying at the Chronicle office while I worked there, so I didn't need lodgings."

"Lodge, not lodgings. Are you sure you're not deaf?"

"No, but what do you mean?"

"I mean *lodge*, or, if you're from Northumberland, I mean branch, which *branch* are you from?"

"Oh, I see. I'm not from any Association branch or lodge, I'm just looking for Mr Fenton, Tom Fenton."

The man points his shovel at Sammy and tells him: "We're only here to help our members. If you're not a member, then clear off."

Sammy can see that he is fighting a losing battle, so he tries one last tactic.

"What about if...?"

The man leans the shovel against the stove and points his forefingers at his ears.

"Sorry, I'm deaf."

Sammy knows when he is beat. He turns and leaves the office to walk further up North Road. The road takes him under a railway viaduct towards a fingerpost that reads 'Pity Me 2 miles.'

When he reaches the hamlet of Pity Me, Sammy finds that he is at one end of a long terrace of red brick houses. The far end of the terrace is also the end of Pity Me where another fingerpost says he is just 13 miles from Newcastle.

After walking for five of those miles Sammy's stomach decides it is time for a late lunch. His route has taken him into the town of Chester-le-Street, through streets of domestic homes and along roads lined with shops and stone buildings housing municipal services, hotels and a variety of religions, but, apparently, nowhere suitable to sit and eat.

Then, as he passes the end of Hopgarth Gardens, he looks down the street and in the distance can see the tops of trees. He heads towards them, hoping they might be part of a park.

At the bottom of Hopgarth Gardens an unattended pony and trap stand on the edge of a large area of grass and woodland. Sammy walks onto the grass and heads for the woodland. As he does so, the sounds of the town recede until all he can hear is the pony munching grass. When he gets closer to the trees he can hear the sounds of a nearby river, the rustling of leaves and birds calling from the undergrowth. Then, there are more sounds. From high in the sky above him comes the trilling of a skylark - and the screaming of a woman.

The skylark drops to the ground like a stone with just a flutter of its tiny wings at the last moment, to give it a soft landing before it disappears into the long grass by the river.

The screaming woman falls more slowly, since cords and a harness attach her to a huge silk canopy. She drifts in the sky, sinking earthward and eventually lands close to Sammy. Her legs buckle and she rolls in the grass as the canopy collapses beside her.

Sammy runs over to the woman. "Are you all right? Do you need an ambulance?" he asks anxiously.

"No, I'm fine. How was my screaming? Did it scare you?"

"Yes, it did. I thought you were in trouble. Is this a parachute? I've heard about them but never seen one before."

"Yes, it is a parachute and I've mastered that, but I'm still working hard on the scream that goes with it. I need to have that scream just right before Saturday."

"Why? What's happening on Saturday?"

The woman reaches into the leather jacket she is wearing and pulls out a piece of folded paper which she hands to Sammy. He unfolds it and reads slowly and with growing fascination.

Chester-le-Street Riverside Park

Saturday June 25 at 2pm

Balloon Ascent and parachute descent.

After dropping from the clouds Slaydene the parachutist will perform on the high trapeze.

Also

Tamamoto. Real Native Japanese Artist direct from the Japanese Exhibition in London

Frank Hope, the well known Royal trick cyclist

Mons Chiyo the slack wire walker and equilibrist

Messrs Relph and Pedley's Modern Amusements

St Hilda Prize band, winner of the Grand Shield Contest Crystal Palace 1909

"Are you Slaydene?" Sammy asks.

"That I am, the one and only. Help me gather up the parachute, would you?"

"Certainly."

Under her direction, they untangle the cords and straighten the canopy before folding it lengthwise and then rolling it into a bundle small enough to tuck under her arm.

"How long have you been doing this?" Sammy asks as they walk across the park.

"The high wire stuff since I was little, but I started parachuting just a few months ago. I read about a woman in Germany called Kathchen Paulus who has been parachuting for the last fifteen years and I thought that I would give it a go."

"Is it hard?"

"It might be if you have a fear of heights, but after growing up as part of a high-wire family, heights don't frighten me."

"Then what was the screaming about?"

"Oh, that's part of the act. I start screaming before I jump, to get the attention of the audience, then, once I have their attention, I jump out of the balloon basket and scream even louder.

"People can't take their eyes off a screaming woman. It's a fact of life. They think they are watching my last moments when I go out of the balloon. Then I let go of the parachute and they have to keep watching to see if it saves me. But if I don't get that scream just right I will be on the ground before they notice me."

"Well, you certainly got my attention."

"Good. Now, could you hold that pony while I pack the trap?"

Sammy holds the reins of Slaydene's pony, which is the one he had noticed as he was walking into the Riverside Park. He watches this slightly built woman haul a trunk from the back of the trap and pack her parachute into it.

"Need a hand putting that back into the trap?" he asks.

"What do you think?" she replies, grabbing the handles at each end of the full trunk and easily lifting it into the trap's luggage space. "And, yes, I am a lot stronger than I look."

Sammy has to laugh at himself because that is exactly what he was thinking.

"What about the balloon you jumped from, what is happening with that?"

"The boys are taking care of that. They have a flat-cart further along the park. We came out together, but I brought the pony and trap because I need to get back to Newcastle quickly while they bring the balloon down and pack it away."

"Are you doing your show there?"

"Yes, we're part of the Temperance Festival on Newcastle Town Moor."

"Temperance Festival? What's that?"

"It's just the biggest travelling fair in the world, and this year, it's bigger than ever. Last year's festival was a disaster, It poured with rain all day and was a total washout, so this year it was a toss-up between scrapping the fair altogether, or making it a three-day event, hoping that the weather would be good on at least one of those days.

"They also made it more exciting this year by bringing in a lot of new attractions, including my balloon parachute jump."

"Then why are you in Chester-le-Street, if the show is in Newcastle?"

"We leave Newcastle tomorrow and travel down here in time for our next show, this weekend. I've come here today to check out the area for any landing hazards - and to get my scream right," she laughs. "Do you live in

Chester-le-Street?"

"No, I'm just passing through. I'm on my way to Northumberland."

"Are you? Well then, if you like, I can give you a lift as far as Newcastle."

"Oh, yes, thanks," Sammy says. "Not that I couldn't walk to Newcastle, you understand, it's only eight miles away. But I want to hear more about parachutes and what it feels like to fly in the sky."

"I can talk all the way to Northumberland about the ups and downs of parachuting, but my lodgings are in Spital Tongues, next to Newcastle Town Moor, so that's as far as I am going. You'll have to make do with that."

It is dark when they arrive in Newcastle. Slaydene and Sammy part company on Claremont Road, close to Durham University's Armstrong College of Physical Sciences building.

From here Sammy can see Newcastle Town Moor and the grazing cattle on it. The hour is late, but it is warm and Sammy looks for a hedge on the Town Moor rather than wander the streets of this unfamiliar city in search of lodgings. He sees a patch of woodland on the moor and heads towards it.

Resting against a tree in the thicket, Sammy unrolls his sling and fishes from it the crumbling pie he had intended to eat before a screaming woman in the sky distracted him.

He swallows the last mouthful of pie with a swig of water from his almost empty stone bottle and settles down for the night with his usual routine of relaxing body and mind.

But then there is a sound.

Voices nearby.

"Dobson?"

"Yes sir."

"You do have a good grip of this, don't you?"

"Yes I do, sir. Don't worry, I won't drop it."

"That is just as well Dobson, because those flasks inside are hand blown and expensive. I used to be able to make them myself when I was younger and still had every finger, but now I have to buy them. Apart from the expense of breaking those flasks their contents will also kill you if they are accidentally combined."

"I know that, sir. I won't break them."

"And if the contents of the blue bottles combine with the contents of the green bottles, they will kill you horribly."

"I understand, sir, I really do, but what I don't understand is why we had to put both kinds of bottles in the same box; surely it's less dangerous to put explosives ingredients in separate boxes?"

"Maybe so, but this is the only box I had in the laboratory which is not labelled "Hazardous Materials" and therefore the only one I could get past the porter's lodge without arousing unwanted attention."

"I see sir, but that does make this box quite heavy. Couldn't we have asked some of your other students to lend a hand as well?"

"Certainly not; I am the oldest professor at Armstrong College of Physical Science and you are its most incompetent student, so who better to get rid of this material than its two most dispensable members."

They are almost on top of Sammy, so he decides to make himself known.

"Can I help at all?" he says.

The young man pivots quickly, startled, and loses

his grip on the crate which has the words 'Jaffa Oranges' stencilled in blue ink on it.

The old man gasps "Oh!" as the younger man struggles to regain his hold.

Sammy reaches out and grabs a corner of the tipping crate and together the three of them steady and level it.

"Thank you" says the old man. "We don't have far to go and possibly an extra pair of hands would be advisable."

He points to a pathway through the woods and says to Sammy: "That is where we are going, but we have to negotiate our way through the undergrowth carefully to reach it. By the way, I am Professor Desmond Arkle and this is one of my students, Dobson."

Sammy notices that the two middle fingers are missing from the professor's left hand.

Dobson says: "I thought you didn't want to involve anyone else Professor Arkle?"

"No Dobson, what I said was that I did not want to involve any of the other students. Some of them have fine minds, others an absolute determination to succeed and the rest have money, or at least, generous parents. Whereas you? Well, you have none of that, do you?

"So I don't think the world will miss an aged academic who ran out of steam years ago, or the dullest student he has ever come across, or even a young tramp."

Annoyed, Sammy says: "I'm not a t...".

The older man cuts him off before he can protest any further, with a raised hand and a stern stare.

"Well, if you're not a tramp, then you should sack your tailor, your chef and your valet. Would you be happier if I said hobo, or maybe gypsy, traveller, wanderer, a man of the road?

"Oh, never mind. Whatever you are, just give us some help with this.

"It may be the last useful thing you do - or possibly the first."

DOBSON

SAMMY feels like dropping the box there and then, but its deadly contents would fall at his feet, so he swallows his pride and just shakes his head with a discontented grunt.

Dobson nods at Sammy sympathetically and the professor points to a large chestnut tree with a thick bush in front.

"That is where we are going, but walk carefully."

When they reach the bush, he directs them to lower the crate to the ground gently.

"Dobson, see where the bush's branches make two loops?"

"Yes, sir."

"Well, take hold of them and tell me what you detect."

Dobson grabs the loops and says to the professor: "They aren't wood sir, they are metal."

"That's right, I had a very clever blacksmith forge the metal to look like twisted branches."

To Sammy he says: "You grab the two loops opposite Dobson and both of you try to lift them."

When Sammy and Dobson straighten up they find they are holding a wooden box which contains the entire bush. At the bottom of the hole where the box had been is a metal hatch held shut by a padlocked hasp.

Professor Arkle produces a key from his waistcoat

pocket which he inserts into the padlock and turns. The padlock clicks open and the professor lifts the hinged hatch.

"Dobson, you go first," he says. "Feel with your feet for the first rung of the ladder and go down. At the bottom you will find two ropes. Bring them both up."

He hands Sammy a carbide lamp and a box of matches and tells him: "Light this while we are waiting for Dobson."

Moments later, Dobson returns with two ropes, and the professor takes the lamp from Sammy's hands.

"Dobson, take one end of each rope and you, what's your name?"

"Sammy."

"You, Sammy, take the other ends, then pull tight so that both ropes make a bridge over the hatch."

Professor Arkle places the orange box carefully onto the 'bridge', with a warning to "keep them tight", then he says: "Gently, very gently, and both of you together, lower it down the shaft."

Watching each other's hands in the flickering carbide lamplight, the two younger men synchronise their actions to keep the box level as they slowly lower it out of sight. Both make sounds of relief when the ropes eventually go slack and they know it has reached the bottom.

"Wait until I call you," says the professor as he grips the first rung of the metal ladder and feels with his feet for the others.

Five minutes later, when Sammy and Dobson are at the bottom of the shaft, they see the professor has edged the box close to a flatcart sitting on a rail track. The flatcart is made from of the undercarriage of a coal chaldron with a piece of wood the size and shape of a door attached to it by four sets of leaf springs.

"Lift the crate up here," says Professor Arkle, positioning the carbide lamp at one end of the rail cart.

They carefully place the crate on the cart's 'door' floor, which sinks two inches under the weight of it. Sammy discovers that even a gentle press of his hand can make it sink even lower.

"Yes," the professor tells him. "That will absorb any bumps or shocks on the way down. I had it made especially for this track."

"On the way down? Down where?" Sammy wants to know.

"Down to the river. That's where we are going."

"And how far is that?"

"Two and a half miles."

"What! Two and a half miles in a pitch-black tunnel with something that will kill me if it gets broken?"

"Yes, that's right, but it's not a problem," Sammy hears Professor Arkle say in his flat, matter-of-fact voice.

"The cart is on a rail track, so it won't bump any walls, and the springs it uses are engineered to my own precise specifications to absorb all vibrations. This track is downhill all the way, which means that gravity will transport the cart to its destination. Speaking of which, do keep a good grip on the cart. It would not be a good thing if it rolled away from us."

Sammy feels the cart begin to move forward as Professor Arkle releases its handbrake. The carbide lamp throws a travelling arc of light onto the tunnel's mould-coated brick walls as it glides past them.

Ahead of and behind that arc of light is an infinity

of darkness. Sammy chooses to stay with these two people and their light rather than try to find his way back to the entrance shaft somewhere in that blackness.

"What is this tunnel?" he asks Dobson as they hold on to the trundling railcart.

Before Dobson can answer, the professor says: "This is the Victoria Tunnel. It opened in 1842 providing a subterranean wagon way to the River Tyne for coal from Leazes Main Colliery in Spital Tongues. It had to be built underground because the city fathers wouldn't allow an overland wagon way through the city centre."

There is no stopping the professor now. He takes the brakes off his tongue and trundles into full lecture mode.

"It took two hundred men just three years to dig and brick this tunnel, and when they finished, it proved to be a huge success for the pit's owners, Mr Porter and Mr Latner. Their coal transportation costs alone were slashed by 88%. Coal wagons specially designed for the tunnel made their own way down to the riverside using gravity to get there and were hauled back by a stationery steam engine at the pit. The end of the tunnel is 220feet lower than the start and the whole tunnel route is on a gentle decline down to the staithes where collier ships were waiting."

"Is it still in use?" Sammy asks in a worried voice.

"No, not for 44 years. Leazes Main pit ran out of coal in 1866 and there was no further use for the tunnel. The end closest to the pit was filled in and the end near the River Tyne was demolished in 1878 to make way for the Glass House Bridge."

"Then how do we get out when we arrive at the

other end?" Sammy asks.

Professor Arkle taps the side of his nose.

"Don't worry, that's taken care of. There's another access shaft, like the one we came down. Once we are there, we will carefully raise the box up the shaft in the same way we lowered it."

"And then what?"

"Then we will carry the box to a small boat I have on the River Ouse. From there we can row into the Tyne estuary and reach the North Sea which will, 'drown', to put it simply, the materials contained in the flasks."

"What are those materials?"

"I won't go into the chemistry, but you can take it from me that the people of Newcastle are most fortunate that the Victoria Tunnel is as far below the city streets as it is. It is also most fortunate that the coal mining industry gave Durham University half the money it needed to create its School of Physical Sciences here in Newcastle.

"That close relationship has allowed university and industry to work together for their mutual benefit in many ways, including supporting my experiments to find new mining explosives and giving me access to this old tunnel to dispose safely and unnoticed of those experiments that prove less than successful."

"The professor doesn't have failures," Dobson chips in.

"Quite so," his tutor agrees. "There is no such thing as a failure in science. Any experiment is only ever a success or a source of useful information."

"What valuable lesson was learned from the experiment you are having to 'drown' in the North Sea?" Sammy wants to know.

"The valuable lesson from this particular experiment is I must take a trip to Sweden."

"Why Sweden?"

"Because that is where Carl Lamm has his Bellite factory."

"What is Bellite?"

"It is an explosive that is every bit as powerful as dynamite, but vastly safer to use. Bellite is comprised mostly of ammonia and dinitrobenzole. However, the real secret to its success lies not so much in the ingredients, but how they are combined, using some kind of steam engine process."

"Professor," Dobson interrupts. "We have just passed the third ventilator."

"Good, that means we will be right under St Thomas' graveyard."

Sammy inhales quickly as he has two flashback memories. One is of stythe gas drifting up a tunnel to suffocate two unsuspecting brothers and their dog. The other is of corpses incinerated in a smoldering churchyard.

"St Thomas' graveyard? Was it built on an old colliery spoil heap?" he asks.

Professor Arkle gently applies the handbrake until the railcart slows and stops without a jolt.

"Spoil heap? No, it used to be meadowland. Why do you ask?"

"No reason, just curious. What about gas? Have there been any reports of gas, or stythe in this tunnel?"

The professor appears to ponder for a moment.

"Dobson?"

"Yes sir?"

"Did you remember to bring the canary?"

"Canary? No sir. I didn't think we needed one."

"Then I suppose we will have to make do with the carbide lamp."

He lifts the lamp towards Sammy.

"See its naked flame? As well as providing illumination that flame is also a gas detector. If the flame goes out, we will have detected stythe. If it turns into a ball of flame that incinerates the three of us, then we have detected some form of incendiary gas."

Sammy and Dobson look at each other, neither of them able to work out whether the professor is having a joke at their expense or making another of his matter-of-fact statements.

"Do you have you a reason for asking your question?" the professor asks Sammy.

"No, none, professor. It's not only mushrooms that grow in the dark. Idle thoughts do much the same."

Professor Arkle sniffs and clears his throat loudly before releasing the handbrake. Sammy and Dobson feel the cart moving away from them and quickly follow.

As they take hold of the cart, another idle thought grows in Sammy's mind.

"Professor? Why do you need to go to Sweden? Isn't Bellite made in England?"

"No, it isn't. Carl Lamm tried hard to set up a manufacturing plant here, but the Explosive Act of 1815 stopped him. That Act is full of restrictions and provisions designed principally to protect against the hazards in dynamite manufacturing plants, but it was also applied in full force to Bellite.

"Lamm's explosive is much more difficult to detonate than dynamite and, a few years ago, he did try to argue that point in the High Court over here. He told the court that, since neither impact, nor fire will make Bellite explode, the heavy restrictions required by the Act should not apply.

"He lost that argument, so he tried to set up a Bellite plant in the Cornaah Valley on the Isle of Mann. The Explosives Act doesn't apply over there so he thought he'd found a way around it. But then the locals kicked up such a fuss that he was forced to abandon work on the Cornaah factory and scuttle back to Sweden."

"Do you think you'll have better luck than him?"

"I do and I will tell you why. I've already mentioned that our mining industry provided half the cost of setting up Durham University School of Physical Science here in Newcastle. Then, six years ago, the school's name was changed to Armstrong College. That was because of the financial support it has had from Lord Armstrong, Britain's most influential arms manufacturer.

"So, it doesn't take much imagination to work out that if an explosive as effective and as safe as Lamm's is developed in Newcastle, with the support of the British mining industry and Lord Armstrong, with his political influence and industrial muscle, a way will be found to set up a manufacturing base for it in this country."

"That's an enormous word," says Sammy.

"Which word," asks the professor?

"If," Sammy tells him. "It is only two letters long, but sometimes it can still be a very big 'IF'."

Professor Arkle gives another exaggerated sniff and clears his throat loudly before releasing the cart's handbrake a further notch.

Dobson and Sammy have to pull even harder to slow

the cart's descent as it rolls closer to its destination.

Secrets have a way of leaking out in the dark, and it is not long before they begin to slip from lips in the Victoria Tunnel.

"Where are you from, Sammy," says Dobson.

"Bolton, in Lancashire. I used to live in a place called Darcy Lever."

"Darcy Lever?" Dobson sounds puzzled. "I've heard that name before, but where? Isn't there somebody called Darcy Lever? Somebody connected with chemistry?"

The voice of Professor Arkle comes out of the darkness: "James Darcy Lever and his brother William Lever bought a soap business in Warrington and went into partnership with a chemist from Bolton called William Watson. I met Watson at a conference earlier this year. It was a Chemistry Society conference, and he was there to talk about how he invented the soap that made all of them a fortune. Basically, he used glycerin and palm oil instead of tallow and it made a lot more lather. Since soap bubbles are just iridescent liquid shells, you could say that Watson and the Levers made masses of money by packaging and selling fresh air.

"Watson called it Honey Soap at first, but the name was dropped and it became much better known as Sunlight Soap. Very apt, don't you think, to put fresh air into a bubble of rainbow colours and sell it as Sunlight, especially when they kept the formula in the dark for so long. I only got it out of Watson earlier this year when he bragged that he had just come back from a holiday in the Belgian Congo and the Solomon Islands. Such a schoolboy error, don't you think, Dobson?"

Dobson looks as puzzled as Sammy feels, which

seems to please Professor Arkle.

"Strange places to go for a holiday," I told Watson. "The only things they have in common are sunshine and palm trees. Would that be what you put in your Sunshine soap - palm oil? He didn't answer, but he didn't need to, his face went white and he made a little choking noise in his throat."

Sammy smiles in the dark. Maybe this stuffy professor has a sense of humour after all, even if it does only revolve around chemistry.

The joke, if that's what it was, is lost on Dobson and he continues from the point he had reached when the professor interrupted.

"If you lived at Darcy Lever and this man is called Darcy Lever, could you be related to him?" he asks.

Sammy replies: "No, I don't think so. One of my mother's distant relations was called Lever, but if I am related at all, then it is a family secret."

Dobson nods slowly as if he is thinking partly about what Sammy said, and partly about family secrets.

"What about your parents, what do they do?"

Sammy shrugs his shoulders and says: "My mother died a couple of years ago and my dad did a bunk a few weeks back, which is why I am here in this tunnel talking to you."

Over the next hour Sammy tells Dobson and the professor why he left Bolton and all that has happened to him over the past two weeks. They listen, but say nothing, and as Sammy reaches the end of his tale Professor Arkle says: "Stop. We go no further."

He raises the carbide lamp towards the curved ceiling and Sammy can see a wooden hatch-cover secured by a padlock above them. Professor Arkle unlocks the hatch cover, and it drops open. The cover has two hand grips on it which the professor uses to haul himself into the shaft above it.

"Wait there while I open the top cover and send down the cradle," he tells them.

Sammy and Dobson wait in absolute darkness because the professor has taken the lamp with him. Sammy holds his hands in front of his eyes. He knows they are there, just two inches from his eyeballs, yet he sees nothing. It is a new and disorientating experience for him, so he seeks a distraction.

"Dobson?"

"Yes."

"I've just realised something."

"What?"

"I don't know your first name."

"You do. It's Dobson."

"Your first name is Dobson?"

"Yes."

"Then what is your last name?"

There is no instant reply, but after a few seconds Dobson says: "Arkle."

"*Arkle?* Are you telling me that…?"

"Yes, I am. That is my father up there."

"DOBSON!" Professor Arkle's voice booms down the shaft. "I'm coming down, so keep away from the hatch - if you can manage such a complicated task."

Sammy can't see Dobson in the dark, but makes an accurate guess about the expression that will be on the young son's face at this moment.

The carbide lamp, which once seemed so dim, now glares and both young men avert their eyes from it. When they look back, they see a wooden cradle which has short lengths of rope attached to each corner. All four lengths are fastened to a steel ring which hangs from a longer length of thick rope.

"Help me get the crate onto this cradle and then go up to the top and I will follow," Professor Arkle tells them.

Dobson Arkle goes up first and is standing at the side of the shaft top when Sammy emerges. Sammy expects to climb out into a field or woodland, but he is mistaken; he is inside some sort of building. In the light of a kerosene lamp standing on a wooden bench, Sammy sees two curving walls on either side of him. They meet overhead where a thick spar of wood stretches ahead of him before it too curves gradually down to the floor. Behind him is a flat wall with a small door in it. The walls are made from pitched planking and every few feet a length of wood curves across the planking from one side to the other as if this building had ribs.

Sammy puzzles about the odd architecture of this place, which is unlike anything he has seen before. More than anything else it reminds him of an upside down...

"Dobson? Are we in an upside down boat?"

"Yes," Dobson replies. "We are in what used to be a seine-netter, or at least half of it. The boat was rotting and abandoned and the professor had it cut in half and turned over to make a shed. Quite a few old boats end up this way in these parts. They make very useful storage and potting sheds."

The professor emerges from the hole and takes over the conversation.

"This particular shed is in the garden of number fourteen Ouse Street. I pay the man who owns that address a fair stipend to have this seine netter shed stand here. It stands over what used to be a ventilation shaft for the Victoria Tunnel, and is now an access shaft."

The hole that Sammy and the two Arkles have just emerged from has a winch positioned over it. The winch barrel has a handle attached to each side.

"You two grab a handle each and turn gently," says the professor. "I will hold the rope and guide the cradle away from the edges."

When it reaches the top, and the cradle winch is secure, they carefully lift the crate from the cradle into a wheelbarrow which has four pneumatic tyres and shock absorbing springs.

Professor Arkle unlocks the shed door and says: "This way."

As they leave the shed Sammy can see that the unkempt garden around it is lit by a gas lamp in the street outside. In the light of that lamp he can also see he has just left the bow half of an overturned boat.

They leave through a garden gate and emerge onto an unmade street. As they haul the wheelbarrow over the rough roadway Sammy is grateful for its soft tyres and forgiving springs.

On the opposite side of the street is a small wall and beyond that the River Ouse.

Professor Arkle points to a gap in the wall half-way down the street and says: "That's where we are going, but take it slowly."

Once they are through the gap, a concrete ramp leads down to the water and a small, flat-bottomed, keel boat tied to a jetty post.

Just beyond the boat is the Glass House Bridge, and on the other side of the bridge the River Ouse flows into the River Tyne.

"Dobson. You hold the boat steady while we lift the crate into it," the professor says to his son before turning to Sammy.

"Young man, I have no money with me, but you do have my sincere thanks for your assistance tonight."

"You are welcome Professor Arkle and don't worry about the money. I can see why you would think there was no need to bring any with you. We didn't pass many shops, pubs or beggars on our way here, after all? But there is something you can do for me."

"What is that?"

"You work closely with some important people in the mining industry, so how about giving me some names that might be helpful when I get to Northumberland."

Sammy sees Professor Arkle smile for the first time and, judging from the expression on Dobson's face, it is also the first time that he has seen that grin.

"I may not carry cash, but I never travel without a pencil and paper. Give me a moment and I will write a note that may help an ambitious young man such as yourself."

As Professor Arkle scribbles, his son asks Sammy: "Where will you go now?"

"Well, I'm headed for Northumberland and the biggest mining town that I can find."

"Ashington," says Dobson. "Head for Ashington. It calls itself a village, but the population there was nearly thirty thousand last time I heard, and ten thousand of those are coal miners. The rest are mostly their wives and children."

Sammy sees the young man's eyes widen as inspiration strikes.

"Wait a minute. I've just had a thought," says Dobson Arkle. "We're taking this boat to the mouth of the Tyne, past North Shields Quay. There's always lots of working boats at the quay, everything from cobles and clinkers to seine-netters and steam trawlers. There'll be part-timers in small boats as well. I bet that at least one of them will be going north up the coast and could drop you off near where you want to be."

Sammy considers the choice of reaching his destination by walking along dark roads with uncertain surfaces, or sitting in a gently rocking boat? He doesn't think for long.

"A boat trip sounds like a good idea."

"It sounds like a good idea to me too," says Dobson. "Because you can row us down the Tyne as far as North Shields and I will only have to row on the way back."

Sammy laughs and puts a hand on his shoulder.

"I'll tell you something, Dobson Arkle. You are definitely your father's son."

Dobson is not amused by the backhanded compliment.

"On the other hand, we could row out to sea and drop you off there instead," he says.

The professor gives Sammy the note he has just written and settles himself onto his boat's bow seat next to the box. He unhitches the mooring rope while Dobson lowers himself onto the stern seat before helping Sammy to fish a pair of oars from under the mid-seat.

"Use one of the oars to push us away from the bankside then attach them both to the rowlocks before you sit down," says the professor.

Sammy's first few strokes are awkward and ineffective, but once he becomes accustomed to the feel of the water against the oar blades, he quickly gets the measure of them and draws the small boat down the river with long, smooth strokes.

The little rowboat leaves the Ouse and glides into the noisy, busy, dirty, smelly River Tyne, where the current flows fast and money flows faster.

WATER WAYS

HUGE sprawling shipyards dominate the banks of the River Tyne, commanding jobs, lives and the area's economy. Those with their own blast furnaces and rolling mills turn raw iron ore into floating titans of steam and steel, destined to transport goods and people on oceans across the world.

But before any of the new builds take to the high seas they must first be tenderly towed from the Tyne by fleets of support vessels.

Barges, lighters and tugs, manned by highly skilled crews, work day and night to coax them along the waterway on their way to the North Sea. Alongside them on this river of industry are working colliers, coasters, steamboats, sailboats, fishing boats and all manner of rowing craft - including one with Sammy Kiteland hauling on the oars.

Sammy feels as if he is racing along this big river at an incredible speed as he dips and drags the keelboat oars. Coal staithes, cranes, dry docks and harbour yards slide past swiftly, while welding torches and white-hot rivets pepper the shoreline with pinprick lights, all dancing to the machine-gun rap of hammers on iron.

They glide by so quickly that Sammy is impressed by how quickly he has mastered the art of oarsmanship - until he tells his fellow travellers.

"You're not that good," says the professor with a wry

smile. "We're riding the ebb tide, that's all. We *are* going fast, but it is the river that is doing the work, not you."

He taps the side of his nose and smiles.

"That was always my plan. The ebb tide will take us quickly to where we want to be and once we are a mile offshore, I will tip the contents of the flasks into the sea where they will be dispersed in the crosscurrents. Dobson will row us back into the river mouth at slack water and then the inflowing tide will take us swiftly back to Ouseburn."

From the stern of the keel boat his son says, with a smug smile: "We do know how to read tide tables and make the river do the work for us."

As they near the mouth of the Tyne, North Shields is on one side of them and South Shields on the opposite bank.

At North Shields a mass of boats cluster around the fish quay.

"Now that's a sight I wasn't expecting," says the professor.

"What is?" Sammy asks him.

"All the boats moored up cheek by jowl like that. You could walk a good fifty yards across them and never get your feet wet."

He points to the oar in Sammy's right hand and says: "Pull hard on your that oar, Sammy, and we will try to drop you off at the fish quay. You shouldn't have any trouble finding someone there who is heading north."

Sammy heaves on the oar until the keelboat is broadside to the current and discovers that landing will be much harder than he expected.

He spots a gap between two small fishing boats and pulls hard, but the fast-flowing river sweeps him past it.

Only when Sammy turns the boat to head directly into the current does he realise just how powerful an opponent he is up against. He pulls on the oars with all his strength, but it is just not enough.

Dobson shouts encouragement, but that is all he can do, and the professor is too engrossed in protecting the box at his feet to care much about Sammy's difficulties.

Then a rope slaps onto the deck, just inches from the box and the professor gives an involuntary gasp.

Sammy hears a voice from beyond the keel boat shouting: "Grab it, son. Tie the line."

There are mooring rings fore and aft on this little boat, but Sammy doesn't want to risk scrambling over the box at the professor's feet to reach the ring in the bow. He grabs the rope and hands it to Dobson, who ties it to the stern ring. The mooring line goes tight and the current swings their boat through 180 degrees, since it is now attached to a small fishing boat with a lowered lug-sail.

A small man with a weathered face shouts from the fishing boat: "What's up, lads?"

Sammy shouts back: "We are trying to land."

"You've no chance of that," the man replies. "The fish market's on and this lot will be here until they've got their cash and drunk it. There aren't any moorings left."

"We don't want to moor," the professor interrupts. "I'm just dropping this young man off and then going to the river mouth."

"If that's the case then pull up closer and he can make his way from here to the quayside."

Sammy unties the line and, with help from Dobson,

hauls the rope through the mooring ring, pulling the two boats together.

With his sling tied securely around him, Sammy scrambles on board the fishing boat. Dobson releases the mooring rope and the two boats part company.

Sammy watches Dobson and the professor being carried on the current towards the river mouth for longer than he intends, anxious in case the keelboat turns from a black dot in the distance, to a grey cloud of detonated explosive.

The man who threw Sammy the line pulls it from the water and winds it in large loops into a storage box before speaking.

"Where are you going to, lad?"

"Northumberland. I'm headed for a place called Ashington. I had hoped to get a lift on one of these boats."

"Well, you won't get a lift from any of this lot, but I'm going up that way now and you can come with me if you like. You'll be company for me."

"That's very generous of you, Mr...?"

"Robinson, Twizel Robinson."

"Thank you Mr Robinson, and if there's anything I can do to help I'll earn my way."

"That sounds to me like a fair deal, er?"

"Sammy, my name is Sammy."

"Right, Sammy, we'll have to get going before this tide turns, but first I need some grub, I'm famished. Here's half a dollar. See that shop on the quayside with the blue frontage? That's the chandlers. Nip in there and get me some cold ham, pease pudding, bread, butter and a bottle of milk."

Sammy has to scramble over three other boats to reach the quayside. He hurries to the shop, but once inside it he comes to a full stop and gazes around.

This place is an Aladdin's cave. There are pots, pans, plates, cutlery, ropes, flags, pumps, hats, coats, wellingtons, maps, gaffs, nets, hooks, stoves, flares, food, drinks, and so much more. Sammy could spend the rest of the day here just browsing through all the fascinating and mysterious artefacts surrounding him.

"What can I get you?"

Sammy can hear the voice, but can't locate its owner. He peers into a dark corner and sees crab pots piled high, looks along a line of white oilskin capes, stares at a set of shelves filled with every brand of tobacco he has heard of, and a good few more besides, but still he can not locate the voice.

Then Sammy sees a movement. One of the oilskin capes turns and Sammy sees a parchment yellow face sticking from its neck hole.

"Oh, sorry. I didn't see you standing there. I thought you were one of the, um, well, it's dark in here, isn't it?"

"It's darker at sea, young man. Which is why fishermen need a pair of sharp eyes, or waterproofs like this."

Sammy sees that the oilskin draped over the shopkeeper is made of whitened sailcloth.

"Just in today and just the job for fishing at night. What size are you?"

Sammy holds up his hands to ward off the sales pitch.

"I don't work at sea, I'm just after some food. Butter, I want a pound of butter, and that loaf to go with it. I need ham, pease pudding and milk too."

The shopkeeper makes up Sammy's order, but does not remove the oilskin. As he hands the order to Sammy he asks: "If you don't work at sea, where do you work? On the land? You'll need oilskins if you work in the rain."

Sammy shakes his head and backs away.

"I'm not working anywhere at the minute, but when I am, it will be down a pit, and it doesn't rain much underground."

The chandlery man rubs his chin in thought and, as Sammy backs through the shop doorway, he exclaims: "Wet! You might have to work wet in the pit."

Back on the quayside, and still laughing at the idea of being dressed for fishing in a coal mine, Sammy takes off his sling and repacks it ready for a sea trip. He wraps his old clothes and clogs in the waterproofed sling cloth as tightly as he can, to protect them from sea spray. He had intended to refill his water bottle, but forgot, so the empty bottle is just pushed into the sling with the other stuff before he twists the sling cloth into a tight tube, which he fastens in front of his chest.

After scrambling his way back to Twizel Robinson's boat, Sammy hands over the food and his change.

"Thanks" says Twizel, unhitching his mooring rope.

The ebbing river takes them quickly into the North Sea where Twizel tells Sammy: "Take the tiller while I sort the lug sail."

He yanks on a rope and a canvas sail slides up the boat's single mast. As it catches the wind, the boat leans to one side.

"See that lighthouse?" he asks Sammy, who nods. "Just stay well to the right of it while I sort my crab pots."

Sammy makes slight adjustments to the tiller as the boat pitches and rolls through the sea swells. But mostly he watches, fascinated, as this fisherman works in deep and silent concentration to prepare the dozen crab pots stacked at the bow of the boat.

Sammy watches him prepare three pots before he asks Twizel to explain the complicated process he is carrying out with such ease.

In response, Twizel unfastens part of the net around the pot's bentwood frame and sticks his hand inside to grab a loop of string at the core of the pot.

"They call this part of the pot the keep and the loop is where I put the bait. When I haul the pots, I'll unfasten this part again to lift the lobster or crab out."

Twizel reaches into a foul-smelling bucket and pulls out the head of a cod, which he puts into the loop of string and locks the head in place with the tug of a slip knot. He points to part of the pot where the netting is in the shape of a funnel

"The crab or lobster crawls onto this to reach the bait. They call this part the monk. Like a monk's hood it gets narrower the further you go into it. The lobster or crab keeps going forward until it gets to the end where the bait is, and as they reach for it, they drop off the monk into the keep where they stay until I come for them."

Alongside the pots are two flags on sticks poking from large blocks of cork.

"What are these for?" asks Sammy.

"Those are called danns. They're attached to each end of a flight of pots and, while the pots sit on the seabed, the danns float on the surface to show me where the pots are.

"I use them for a baited fishing line as well. See those danns with the red flags over there?"

He points to the horizon, and it takes Sammy's untrained eyes a while to spot them, but eventually he does.

"That's my line, I set it last night and we'll take a look at it once I've dropped the pots."

Under Twizel's instructions Sammy holds the tiller steady while a dann is thrown into the sea, followed by the first of the weighted pots. He steers a straight course while the fisherman throws the rest of the pots overboard to lie on the seabed until hungry shellfish find them.

Twizel takes the tiller from Sammy and steers for the other set of danns. When they arrive, he drops the sail and hauls in a thin fishing line with around 100 barbed hooks attached to it. On some hooks are thrashing mackerel, whose bodies seem to shimmer with all the colours of the rainbow. They are dropped into a box on the bottom of the boat where they are soon joined by half a dozen cod and one huge skate.

"Not a bad supper for somebody," says Twizel.

"Somebody?" Sammy asks the fisherman. "What about supper for you?"

"Fish? For me? No thanks, I can't stand fish. It's ham and pease pudding for me."

As they travel along the Northumberland coastline Twizel points out the towns they are passing.

"After Whitley Bay and St Mary's lighthouse, that's Seaton Sluice and beyond it is Blyth. Just after Blyth is Cambois where I'll take the tiller and turn us in to go up the River Wansbeck.

"What's up there? Sammy asks.

"That's where I have my boathouse and harbour, so I will drop you off there. It's just a short walk from the river, through North Seaton Colliery village, and on to

Ashington."

"Thanks for the lift, Twizel, and thanks for the fishing lessons."

"Don't thank me just yet, Sammy. Wait until we are back on dry land. Don't count your chickens until they are hatched as they say."

"It will be a long time before I have chickens to hatch, Twizel. Probably around the same time that pigs will fly."

Sammy grins, but Twizel doesn't. Instead, he reaches into the stern space, below the tiller and grabs a smooth black rock hanging from a piece of string.

"You shouldn't have said that, son. It's the worst luck to mention the Queer Fellow's name at sea."

"What? The Queer Fellow? Who's that? Do you mean the p—?"

"STOP! Don't ever say that word. You'll never hear any fisherman in these parts saying it, especially when they are at sea or on a Friday. You might laugh, you might call it stupid superstition, but when you are out here, you need all the luck there is, just to keep afloat, so you don't tempt fate. The North Sea is called the Old Grey Widowmaker for good reason and it never pays to take chances with her."

"In that case, sorry Mr Porker, I won't mention you again, at sea, or tomorrow. It *is* Friday tomorrow, isn't it?"

The fisherman nods, slowly, but before he can answer Sammy asks: "What's that stone in your hand, Twizel?"

When he holds it up Sammy sees that the stone is smooth, jet black and fits perfectly into Twizel's palm.

"This is a Hag stone. It's for good luck."

"What is it? It looks like coal."

"No, it's not coal, it's black limestone."

"You made a nice job of drilling that hole in it, the edges are really smoothly chamfered."

"I didn't drill it. That was done by an angelwing."

"What's an angelwing?"

"It's a shellfish, with a very boring job."

Twizel smiles at Sammy's baffled expression then explains: "One end of its shell has a series of ridges, like fine teeth and when it attaches itself to a stone it continually rotates on the same spot. Gradually, the angelwing bores its way through the rock leaving a nice smooth hole like this one."

"Why is that thing called a Hag stone?"

"They're supposed to keep nightmares and witches' curses away. A lot of people put a string through them and hang them from a bed or a front door. I like to have mine in the boat with me."

"So will the Hag stone put things right with the p-p-porker?"

Twizel Robinson gives Sammy a long questioning look and turns his attention back to steering the boat towards Cambois.

An hour later they are off the mouth of the river.

"The tide has turned and the current should take us upriver," says Twizel. "We've just got to negotiate the sandbar at the river mouth. It's always shifting because of the currents and the currents here are very strong. There can even be whirlpools, so just do what I say when I say it and we'll be all right."

But five minutes later they are not all right. Twizel rolls helplessly in the shore surf bleeding from a deep gash in his forehead and Sammy hangs onto his last breath as he is tumbles and turns under water, and the icy North Sea takes him in a paralysing embrace of death.

WATERPROOF

FIVE minutes ago:-

Twizel said: "We've just got to negotiate the sand-bar at the river mouth. It's always shifting because of the currents and the currents here are very strong. There can even be whirlpools, so just do what I say, when I say it, and we'll be fine."

Sammy stares hard at the river mouth and even he can see there is something strange and menacing about it.

The waves behind Twizel's boat look as if they are in an orderly queue patiently waiting to roll ashore and meet the beach in a steady surge of surf and sand.

But the waters at the river mouth are different. They turn and curl in a confusion of flow and undertow.

"We just need to catch the right wave and she will take us over the bar, through the deeper water, and into the river sweet as a nut," Twizel says, never taking his eyes off the sea.

"If we hit a wrong 'un, she will shove us onto the bar where salt and fresh water mix and currents go all ways. That could mean trouble."

Twizel passes Sammy an oar, keeping a tight grip on the tiller with his free hand.

When Sammy takes the oar from him, Twizel points to the water.

"Keep a watch over that side for the bar. If you see it, shove the oar in and push us away as hard as you can. I'll steer us to where it's deeper."

Twizel leans hard on the tiller and turns the boat towards the middle of the river mouth. But that means he is also broadside to the waves and the mast lurches from side to side in wide arcs each time a wave impacts. He alters the boat's course slightly, trying to make it run diagonally to the direction of the waves and harness some of their energy.

His plan seems to be working, and the boat picks up speed as it rides a cresting wave. Twizel smiles, but the smile is short lived. The boat skims into shallow water on the bar and Sammy can see sand. He does as Twizel told him and thrusts the oar into the water.

In the split second that follows three things happen. The breaking wave shoves the boat hard against the oar that Sammy is gripping as tightly as he can. The oar flips and catapults Sammy away from the boat, over the shallows, and towards deeper water.

The boat's keel judders along the sandbar as the wave it was riding heaves against its stern, forcing the boat to spin around.

Twizel is pitched into the air and only lands back in the boat because he has two hands locked tight around the tiller. But his luck runs out when he lands on his knees with his head at the same height as the lugsail's wildly swinging boom. It cracks hard against Twizel's skull and throws him out of the boat unconscious.

Sammy still has his arms wrapped around the oar when he becomes aware of a muffled bubbling roar all around him. Time seems to slow to a crawl. He vaguely wonders why the boat, the sea and the sky have suddenly become a galaxy of glittering bubbles, and what is that taste in his mouth. Salt? Is that salt? And who is this he is holding in his arms, all stiff and wooden?

Sammy's senses return in a flash of awareness and he lets go of the oar. He can't tell whether he is up or down. He is spinning and weightless. Then the cold hits. It hits the back of his neck first and travels down his spine like an electric shock. Next, his face feels that same numbing North Sea grip, followed by his legs and arms. But, strangely, it has not yet reached his torso.

With the shock of awareness comes ice cold clarity. He now knows he is not just in the sea, but under it and in the grip of a rip current dragging him into even deeper water. He also understands that what he does in the next few seconds will mean life or death.

He uses those vital seconds to work out why his chest is not as cold as the rest of his body.

Everything is out of focus underwater, so he can't see what it is, but something is definitely clinging to his chest. His sling! His waterproofed sling, with an empty bottle, wooden clogs and old clothes, full of air pockets; all of them reaching for the surface. But Sammy is in the way, which can only mean that the surface is behind him.

As Sammy rolls once more in the water, the sling slides around him and tugs to be free. Now Sammy knows which way to go. He kicks towards the rising bag and breaks the surface. He gasps in a lungful of air and a mouthful of seawater, coughs, spits, and breathes again. Instinctively, he holds in that lungful of air and it helps to keep him afloat.

The rip current has pulled Sammy away from the turbulent estuary waters and rapidly loses strength, allowing Sammy to strike out for the beach he can now see ahead of him.

He swims in a way he has never swum before.

When Sammy learnt to swim at Bolton's Municipal Baths he was taught to take a breath with every second stroke. But here in the North Sea he is swimming for survival. Sammy snatches a breath only when he absolutely needs to. That keeps his lungs fully inflated and gives him maximum natural buoyancy. As long as his lungs are full of air he can't sink, especially with the additional buoyancy from his floating sling and its contents.

One more push from a shore-bound wave and his feet touch the sandy bottom. Sammy wades through the waves.

When he reaches dry land, he drops to his knees and bows his head.

Thank you beeswax. Thank you mutton fat. Thank you, Winnie Wilding.

Now that he no longer needs his lungs for flotation his breathing returns to normal and after a few deep, steady breaths he turns his head to look along the beach. He sees the wallowing boat and, in the surf beside it, a still, prone, figure.

"Twizel!"

Sammy's legs feel like lead as he tries to force them into action. He wants to run, but all he can manage is an ungainly stagger.

Twizel is lying on his back in shallow water when Sammy reaches him. The water nearest the fisherman's head is coloured by the blood running from a gash in his forehead, but he is breathing.

Sammy pulls him away from the water's edge and, as

he turns him onto his side, Twizel throws up a mix of pease pudding and seawater. He coughs and groans.

"Where's Maureen?" he asks without opening his eyes.

"Maureen? There's no Maureen here, Twizel, just us. Who's Maureen anyway? Your wife?

"WIFE! Certainly not." He pushes himself up with one hand and points with the other towards his boat.

"That's Maureen over there. That's my bonnie lass. Is she all right?"

"I don't think she is damaged, but she has lost an oar," Sammy tells him.

"Never mind, I've got another. Besides, the sea will give it back in time. She always gives back what she takes."

He tries to struggle to his feet and fails.

"Do me a favour and fetch her anchor before she drifts off."

Sammy nods and wades through the shallows to reach the beached boat. He finds the anchor under the stern seat. A length of rope attaches it to a rusted metal ring bolted to the sternpost.

"Bring it here," shouts Twizel. "I'll sit with Maureen while you fetch help."

"Where will I find help?" Sammy asks.

"Just over the dunes behind us. That's North Seaton Low Quay and there's a pub there called the Ship Inn. Ask for Geordie Fenwick and tell him what has happened. He'll get somebody to come and lend a hand."

When Sammy sees the Ship Inn, he wonders who is most in need of help, Twizel, Maureen or the pub. The old stone-built ale house has seen better days and is now in need of a lot of care and attention.

The inside of the building is just as careworn as the outside. Its bar is an oak bench standing on two barrels and its tables are more benches on more barrels. There are a dozen customers, all clutching pint glasses or bottles of beer. But Sammy can't see their faces because of the fug of pipe smoke, which doesn't seem to move as he walks through it.

"Mr Fenwick?" Sammy asks as he approaches the figure at the bar.

The hairs on Sammy's neck stand up as he feels a dozen pairs of eyes trained on him, and with each step he takes towards the bar the squelching sound his boots make seems to grow louder.

The man behind the bar with a towel over his shoulder waits until Sammy can come no closer.

"Mr Fenwick? Mmm? Now, I think that might just be..? Well, it could be.. No, no? Yes. Definitely. That's definitely, me. What can I do for you?"

Annoyed, Sammy snaps: "This is no laughing matter, Mr Fenwick. Twizel Robinson is in trouble. His boat has beached at the river mouth and he is hurt."

Sammy hears a scraping sound behind him, but continues to stare at the man with the towel.

"Can you get help for him? He needs help, and he needs it now."

"He's got it," says the man with the towel.

"No, he hasn't. I've just left him. There's nobody but him on the beach; just him and his boat."

The publican doesn't reply. He stares over Sammy's shoulder.

Sammy turns around and peers into the fug. He blinks hard, because the place now looks empty.

He turns back to a smiling George Fenwick.

"They'll take care of him, son. We always take care of our own here. But *you* can come with me and we'll get those wet things of yours dried. It looks like Twizel isn't the only one who's been in the drink today."

The shivering has, at last, stopped and now Sammy sits in front of the pub snug's blazing sea coal fire with steam curling up from him like the wraiths from St John's churchyard in Stainbridge.

George Fenwick had placed a patchwork blanket over Sammy's shoulders before guiding him into the snug and throwing a shovelful of coal onto the glowing embers of its fire. He jammed a flat sheet of metal, with a handle in the middle, over the open fireplace. Sammy knows it as a 'blazer', but the landlord's dialect makes the word sound like 'bleezer'.

"The bleezer will soon suck some life into that fire," he says.

The 'bleezer' does its job of forcing a strong draft to be sucked up through the burning coals turning them white hot and setting the fresh coal ablaze.

Under the blanket Sammy shuffles his way out of his soggy clothes and George Fenwick takes them from him before removing the 'bleezer' in a blast of heat.

"I'll have to rinse the salt out of these before I can dry them off," he says, and leaves the room. He returns a few minutes later with fresh water dripping from the clothes in his hands. Sammy watches in silence as he hangs them over a brass rail above the fireplace.

The publican says: "They won't take long. There's a pan of hot leek broth on the range, would you like a bowl?

"Thank you," says Sammy. "I would."

When the publican leaves, Sammy unrolls his

tightly wrapped sling and fishes from it his old work pants and shirt. They were rolled into tightest bundles that Sammy could manage when he repacked the waxed sling at North Shields Fish Quay.

There is the odd patch of damp on both items, but essentially they are dry, so he pulls them on. In a box beside the coal fire he finds an old newspaper and tears off a sheet. Onto it Sammy tips the coins he'd fished from his trouser pocket before handing his clothes over to George Fenwick. He folds and folds again until the money is once again at the heart of a dry, paper bundle.

"There you are, lad. Wrap yourself around that," the publican says when he returns. He plants a steaming bowl of broth and a chunk of brown bread on the table in front of Sammy, who starts to unfold the newspaper to get some coins.

"No, no, son, put that away," the landlord tells him. "We don't have many rules here, but one of them is that anybody who rescues somebody from the sea or the river gets a drink and a bowl of hot broth on the house. Would you like a nice cup of tea after the broth?"

Sammy nods and asks: "What's happening with Twizel, will he come here as well?"

"He would normally, but, if that head injury is too bad, the boys will put him back into Maureen and take him up to the stake ford, a mile upriver. The tide is still coming in, so the current will take Maureen there in twenty minutes."

"Then what?"

"Then they'll take him to Dr Evers' house. His place is hardly a hundred yards from the stake ford. You can't miss it. It's a big white building half way up Black Close Bank, on this side of the river. The doctor will soon have Twizel patched up."

"Good. He seemed to be recovering when I left him, but that was a nasty cut on his head."

"It's just as well you were there to get help for him. The currents around the river mouth are ruthless."

Sammy scoops a spoonful of the steaming green meal into his mouth and feels it slide down his gullet into his stomach. It radiates welcome warmth and chases the North Sea chill from his core. He spoons again and keeps going until the bowl is empty and colour has returned to his face.

George Fenwick waits patiently for the young rescuer in the threadbare clothes to finish before he asks: "I can hear you are not from these parts. Where do you call home?"

Sammy wonders whether to 'pitch the fork', and earn his meal with a glorified yarn, or curtail his story so as not to bore this man who has shown him kindness and consideration. He decides to do neither and tell the story just as it happened.

Half an hour later George Fenwick says: "Now that is what I call a tale and a half."

Sammy smiles at him.

"And it's just getting started," he says.

They talk more and Sammy discovers that the Ship Inn is about a mile from the mining village of North Seaton Colliery, which lies upriver from it. Another road goes north from the pub and that leads to a handful of rustic cottages and a mansion, also a mile away, which go by the name of North Seaton village.

"Inns are usually at the heart of a community, so why is this one out on the edge of both North Seatons?" Sammy asks George.

"Well, for one thing, this pub was here long before the pit village, and for another, take a look out of that window."

Sammy goes to the window George Fenwick is pointing at and sees the river and a collection of small boats on the other side. A chain stretches from the boats to the North Seaton side.

"That's where Wheatley has his chain ferry and if you don't have a boat, it's the only way to get across the river mouth. It also means that anyone who uses the ferry has to walk past the Ship Inn's doorstep. This place might not be at the heart of the community, but it is bang on target for travelling customers.

"All the same, a few years ago, I did have plans for a new place not far from here."

"What happened?"

"Morpeth County Petty Sessions, that's what happened. I was all set to close this place and transfer its licence to a brand new hotel beside Woodhorn Pit, at a place called Hirst Castle. But the toffs who run the sessions wouldn't let me.

"They wanted me to hand over one thousand two hundred and fifty pounds, as if they were granting a brand new license, and not just moving it from one pub to another. So I said they could shove their licence where the sun doesn't shine, and I don't mean down the pit."

Sammy smiles sympathetically.

"You won't have made any friends at the Brewster Sessions, then?"

"Oh, it's not just me they don't like; they aren't too fond of Ashington Coal Company either. Look here."

He points to a map on the snug wall. It shows the

Ship Inn, at the mouth of the Wansbeck, all 17 streets in North Seaton Colliery and the rail line linked to the pit.

"Just a mile along that line is North Seaton railway station, and somebody else tried to build another hotel just five hundred yards from it. The 'toffs' tried to block that one too, although everybody wanted it, including Ashington Coal Company.

"The plan would have put a beautiful new hotel in a place where it was needed, create two brand new roads, and build nine hundred desperately-needed homes for miners.

"The Duke of Portland, who owns all the land around here, had no objection to the plan, Ashington Coal Company, which leases the mining rights from him, was happy with it, Cowpen Coal Company, which owns North Seaton Pit, supported the idea, and Tom Lorribond, boss of Newcastle Breweries, was so keen to see the hotel built he was going to pay for it from his own money.

"Other people went to the Brewster Sessions to say what a good thing it was, including locals and regular visitors to the area. Everybody was in favour of the idea. Well, everybody but one, that is."

"And who was that one person against it?" Sammy asks.

"Gillender, John Gillender."

"Who's he?"

"He owns the Grand Hotel, almost a mile from where the new hotel was going to be built."

"Is there not room in the area for two hotels?"

"That's exactly what all the others said, but it seems Gillender was in a right state about it, probably because he had spent so much money on the Grand.

"He'd tried for years to get permission for his hotel and was always turned down. Then he came up with a deal which cost him an absolute fortune, but it got him the permission he wanted and he had the Grand Hotel built in 1894."

"What was the deal?"

"For a start, he had to pay five thousand pounds for the land, then he spent ten thousand pounds on the building, and he had to promise to build fifty cottages for Ashington Coal Company's miners."

Sammy whistles and says: "That is an absolute fortune. How was he ever going to get that money back?"

"Black gold. That's how. There's so much coal under Ashington, it will take thousands of men and hundreds of years to get it all out. Mr Gillender thought he couldn't lose once he made his special deal with Ashington Coal Company's directors."

"What was special about it?"

"Well, in return for all the money Gillender pumped into his plan, the coal company gave him an absolute guarantee that they wouldn't allow anyone to build another hotel on coal company land.

"But just a year after the Grand opened, along came the plan to build this new hotel near North Seaton Railway station and he was not at all happy about that."

"I bet he wasn't. But didn't that breach his deal with Ashington Coal Company?" Sammy asks.

"Not at all; the coal company didn't own the land where the new hotel was to be built."

"Who did own it?"

George Fenwick gives Sammy a knowing wink and says: "Mr William Milburn, one of Ashington Coal Company's directors."

Sammy looks puzzled. "Wait a minute. His coal company says it won't allow another hotel on its land, but he buys land next to it with his own private money and says a hotel can be built there?"

"That's the way Gillender put it at the Brewster Sessions and the Bench came down on his side. They refused to allow the new hotel to be built and said Ashington Coal Company should have kept its nose out of the application. They implied that the only reason the coal company was supporting the plan for the new hotel was because of those 900 pit houses that would also be built as part of the deal."

"It sounds as if Ashington Coal Company has some shrewd people running it," says Sammy.

"Very shrewd, because six years, and a lot of quiet negotiating, later, a hotel *was* built exactly where Lorribond wanted it, five hundred yards from North Seaton Railway Station. It's a very nice place too, with lots of fancy carved stonework outside. On the inside it has sitting, dining and smoking rooms. There is a bar and assembly area downstairs as well as a private dining room and bedrooms upstairs. Yet, although it has been in business for nine years, the place is still not making decent money."

"Why is that?" Sammy asks.

"There are just a handful of houses around it and an awful lot of wide open space. They called that place The North Seaton Hotel, but to my mind, and everybody else's around here, that place is, and always will be, a White Elephant."

Sammy and George turn and look towards the snug door when they hear a noise from the next room.

"Geordie! Where are you? There's four thirsty men

here."

George walks towards the door followed by Sammy.

In the main bar four men, all wearing flat caps and dark jackets walk across the room towards a table.

Sammy notices that all four have blue scars on their faces and all four are limping.

"Aha," says George Fenwick. "It's the Glenton Clan."

THE GLENTON CLAN

"FOUR pints and make it sharp," snaps one of the Glenton Clan.

"You'll win no prizes for friendly chitchat, Fred," their host responds.

"Aye well, it's like this, George, chitchat eats up drinking time," Fred Glenton answers as he slumps into a chair and leans back until it is teetering on two of its four legs. "Now where's that pint?"

Another member of the Glenton Clan gang heaves a Hessian sack onto the bar and smiles at the man now pulling a pint.

"Hello George, how are you doin'," says Tom Glenton. "I've been to the allotment and fetched you these."

Sammy has never seen a moving pictures star in real life, but this man could have been one. He has black hair in soft waves, his jaw is square, his eyes are blue and, apart from a horseshoe-shaped miner's 'tattoo' on his cheek, his clean-shaven face is unblemished, taut and tanned. As he lifts the sack onto the Ship Inn bar, honed arm and shoulder muscles also stretch the cotton work shirt he is wearing.

"Thanks Tommy. What have you got in here?"

Tom Glenton answers: "Tetties, snaggies and beets."

The answer leaves Sammy baffled until the landlord places a foaming pint of beer on the bar and opens the sack. Sammy looks inside and sees potatoes, turnips and beetroots.

"They'll be grand for the broth pot, Tommy, thanks," says George, as he slides the beer towards him. Tom Glenton smiles back with a white-toothed grin.

"Hey George, just a minute, I ordered first," Fred Glenton shouts, almost overbalancing his precarious perch.

"No, you didn't," says a voice behind Fred. "You didn't order four pints, you demanded them, and that always puts you to the back of the queue, so sit yourself down properly and shut up."

The speaker is smaller than the others, but John Glenton is the oldest of the brothers and, in this clan, his word is law.

"This one is yours, John," says the man behind the bar as he hands over the next pint.

John takes it with a nod and looks at the fourth brother who sits at Fred's table, smiling and saying nothing.

John tells him: "The next one is yours Ron, and then it is Fred's pint. Isn't that right, Fred?"

Even Sammy can see that it's not a question, it's an order.

Fred grunts.

"Never mind grunting Fred, don't forget that if it wasn't for our Ron, you wouldn't even be here to sup that pint, would you?"

Fred grunts again, but he also nods.

George hands the third pint to Ron Glenton, but before he releases his grip on it he says: "Tell us the tale again Ron."

There is a chorus of "NO!" from the brothers.

George sweeps his free hand expansively towards Sammy and adopts a serious expression.

"Gentlemen, we have before us the only person in North Seaton, nay, the only person in the North East, possibly the only person in the country, who has not yet heard the tale of how hero Ronald Glenton saved his little brother Frederick from upside down drowning."

Ron and Fred both roll their eyes upwards, but George ignores them.

"Tommy, come on, set the scene for us? Twentysix years ago, was it not? A beautiful summer day? You were ten years old, Ron was twelve, John was fourteen and little Frederick was just five."

Tom puts down his pint, looks at Sammy and, with a resigned voice, takes up the story.

"We were having a kickabout in our backyard with a ball we'd made from newspapers and string, and we were making lots of noise."

John chips in: "We didn't notice Fred go out through the backyard gate."

Fred takes up the story: "They were all too big and rough for me, so I went next door to see Mrs Chapman's rabbit."

Ron speaks for the first time since walking into the pub.

"I scored and Tom said I hadn't, then John shoved me and we were all shouting and shoving until we were too knackered to argue or play anymore, so we just sat throwing stones at the cockroaches in the yard. Then our John said 'Where's Freddie?' I said he'd probably gone next door to see Mrs Chapman's mangy rabbit again, and he told me to go look for him."

John takes a mouthful of beer from his glass and says: "Ron whinged, but he went. I was older than him and, in those days, bigger as well."

Fred says: "It was a scorching day, and I thought that the rabbit would be thirsty, since it was wearing a fur coat. I checked the water bowl in the rabbit hutch and it was empty, so I went to fill it from the rain barrel. I was only small and couldn't see inside so I got the cracket."

"What's a cracket?" Sammy interrupts.

"One of those," says Tom, pointing to a small stool near the bar room fireplace.

Fred continues: "I climbed onto the cracket and leaned into the barrel. There hadn't been much rain that summer and the water at the bottom was only about eighteen inches deep. I had to stretch for it and the next thing I knew I was upside down in the barrel. I couldn't get my head out of the water and there wasn't enough room for me to turn around."

Ron takes up the tale.

"I walked into Mrs Chapman's yard, but I couldn't see Fred. I thought he must have gone somewhere else and was turning to go back to the gate when, out of the corner of my eye, I saw something move. I looked towards the barrel and there was nothing at first, but then I saw a pair of bare feet flicking around the rim. I knew it had to be my stupid little brother, so I got onto the cracket and looked inside."

Fred says: "I could feel hands around my ankles, pulling, and I came out of the water coughing and spitting. Ron wasn't strong enough to pull me all the way out, but once he had lifted me so far, I balanced on the rim of the barrel and wriggled out."

"Then the two of you went home and told your mother what had happened," George Fenwick says, choking back laughter. "And this is the best bit, Sammy. Tell them what she said to you, Ronnie, after you had saved your little brother's life."

Ron Glenton is also smiling at the memory of that day when he went home expecting a hero's welcome.

"She said nothing at first. Then she looked at Fred, all wet and snivelling and me with my chest puffed out and she said..."

The brothers slam their pint glasses onto the table and together they chorus: "She said 'Should've let the stupid little bastard drown'."

All four brothers are helpless with laughter by now, as is George Fenwick, and then Sammy.

More laughter, more stories and more pints follow as the brothers argue and remorselessly tease each other, while, in the room next door, moisture evaporates from Sammy's soaked clothes.

Others come into the bar, including some who had taken Twizel Robinson to the doctor at Black Close. They tell Sammy that the doctor inserted four stitches in Twizel's head wound. Later, Twizel walked back to his home in Middle Double Row, at North Seaton Colliery, where verbal wounds were inflicted by the sharp tongue of his worried wife.

As they drink their beers and sympathise with Twizel, each of the Glenton brothers limps to the bar to buy their round.

Sammy is curious about their limps and, since the brothers were happy enough to share their family tales with him, he is emboldened to ask the question on his mind.

"Why are you are all limping?" he says as lightly as he can, and immediately regrets the question.

The Glenton brothers stop smiling and the bar goes quiet.

John Glenton eventually breaks the silence.

"Six months ago, we could all run and kick a ball, and now we don't know whether we ever will again. But at least we can still draw breath."

Sammy wishes he had not spoken, but having started this conversation he needs to see it through.

"What happened?"

Tom speaks now.

"The four of us were coming off the backshift, six months ago. We were riding outbye in a tub, when its 'hambone' clip snapped and we came off the haulage rope. The tub rolled back down the track - fast."

He pauses, shakes his head slowly and continues: "The tubs don't have brakes on them, but there was a piece of wood beside my feet. I picked it up and raked it along the roof, a foot above us, to slow the tub. That didn't work, so I pushed it against the side of the roadway, but that was no good either. Then I tried to shove it into the spokes of the tub wheels. The spokes shredded the wood, and the tub slowed a bit. But I was paying so much attention to the wheel I didn't see one of the roadway supports coming up. I couldn't see past the light of my pit lamp anyway, so it came out of the dark and whacked me. I was out of the tub in a crack."

Ron Glenton takes up the story.

"Tom was out, and the wood was gone. The three of us still in the tub knew it was only a matter of time before it skipped the track and tipped over. All we could do was jump out, but it was black dark and there was no way to get clear of the tub. There's enough space between the roadway wall for a man to stand with his back pressed against the wall, but no way to drop out of a tub and roll clear, especially when there might be more runaway tubs coming behind ours.

"All we could be sure of was that we had to jump and when we jumped we would be damaged. How much damage would be done was down to Lady Luck. Damaged or dead, it had to be one or the other. So we all jumped," John says, looking at Sammy.

"What happened?" Sammy asks, uncomfortably aware that, apart from his voice, the only other noise in the room is the sound of awkwardly shuffling feet.

"I got off the lightest," Tom tells him. "The roof support lifted me clean out of the tub and I dropped onto the track. I smashed my foot, but, like I say, I got off the lightest.

"Fred had his thigh broken and lost the ends from a couple of fingers, Ron had two of his ribs broken and his shin snapped and John, well, we nearly lost John.

"He hit the wall when he jumped and got tossed back against the tub. His shirt caught on the coupling and he was dragged along the track for a good way before the shirt ripped and he was left lying across the line. By that time he had broken more bones than the rest of us put together."

"Yes, but, the bones have mended and one day soon I'll be back down there, with you lot," says John. "I've got to, there's no other way I can make a decent living in these parts."

"You could go fishing, like Twizel," says Fred. "That way, if you doze off, you'll be out at sea and your sleep screams won't wake up the whole of North Seaton anymore."

John slams his glass onto the table so hard that Sammy thinks it will break, but it doesn't. John's chair is raked noisily across the stone floor and, without another word, he storms out of the Ship Inn.

Ron says: "Well done, Fred", shaking his head as he heads for the bar door.

Tom looks at George Fenwick, shrugs his shoulders and sighs: "Foot in mouth Fred strikes again."

Tom's fist closes around Fred's coat collar and he is yanked to his feet before being pushed protesting out of the pub.

George tuts sadly and, as he gathers in the part-drunk pints, he says: "I think your clothes will be dry by now, Sammy, I'll stand by the snug door and make sure that you're not disturbed while you put them on."

THE PRICE OF FISH

SAMMY is deep in dreamless sleep; the best sleep he has had since leaving Bolton. This bed is so soft, but so supportive. With each twitch and turn through the night it moved with him, constantly reshaping itself to mould to his flesh and bone, without triggering cramps or myoclonic jerks.

Dawn light leaks slowly into his consciousness floating Sammy up from the depths of sleep. As he squirms, eyes shut tight, his hand slides through the softness under him.

Sammy has never known sand like this. It feels as fine as caster sugar and he could happily stay here in the dunes at North Seaton all day.

But.

"And there is always a 'but'," he says to no-one in particular as he opens his eyes.

Sammy looks up into a cloudless sky. He stretches, but makes no effort to rise just yet. He needs to think, and this is a very comfortable place in which to think. At least it will be once he has scratched his itchy ear. He scratches his right ear, then rubs his nose and slaps a tickle on his cheek.

Sammy looks at his hand and sees the remains of something small and black. He turns his head to the right and sees a line of ants marching over the sand towards him. He wonders how many have already reached him, but has no way to tell, because he is already itching at just the thought of ants in his pants.

He scans the Low Quay area to be sure that he is alone, then removes his clothes, carefully shaking and slapping each item.

Although he is now naked Sammy can still feel a tickling sensation in the middle of his shoulders, right where he can't reach.

"There's nothing else for it," he says, and walks towards the water ahead.

It is high tide and sea water has flowed through the narrow river inlet to fill the estuary bay at Low Quay. The water is only about 18 inches deep and, because the sand was warm when the incoming tide spread over it, the water has lost its icy bite.

Sammy lowers himself into the tidal pool to get rid of any lingering crawling things. He had planned a quick plunge and then a sprint back to his clothes. But the water feels warmer than he expected, so he stays, floating on his back first, then rolling onto his stomach to swim in the knee-deep shallows. Eventually, he kneels on the sandy bottom for a moment before getting to his feet and wading back to his clothes.

He takes his old work shirt from the sling and uses that to rub himself dry before dressing and heading for a footpath through the dunes.

George Fenwick had told Sammy about the footpath last night when the two of them parted company. He also gave Sammy two of Tom Glenton's potatoes, a peeled and chopped turnip and a boiled beetroot cut into quarters.

After placing them in Sammy's hands, he'd said: "Take the path at the end of the dunes and follow it as far as North Seaton Hall. That's where the path connects with a main road and a lonnen.

"If you turn left on the main road that will lead you to the 'White Elephant' and somebody there will give you more directions. If you turn right on the main road, you'll end up in Newbiggin, but be careful there. Newbiggin is full of rough pitmen, tough fishermen, and stubborn women who take no shit from any of them.

"Straight across the main road is the entrance to Summerhouse Lonnen. That lane leads to Woodhorn Colliery and a narrow path which runs alongside it. Follow that path west and it will take you to the Hirst area of Ashington."

When Sammy reaches the crossroads, he turns right.

Newbiggin sounds like a rough, tough, stubborn - interesting - place, he thinks.

Bessie Dent is making her morning trudge to North Seaton Colliery with Sarah, her grey-muzzled donkey. Together they will spend the next couple of hours walking through the pit rows while Bessie shouts her street cry of 'Caalla Herrin'. Sarah is a good listener, which is just as well, since Bessie does like the sound of her own voice.

As they plod along the road to the pit village, Bessie says: "Howay Sarah, bonny lass, I know your feet are sore, but so are mine. We'll have a rest at North Seaton and I'll get you a drink at the standpipe."

Sarah just keeps her head down and plods along the rough road. The loaded baskets that hang from each side of her back rock to the rhythm of each step that she takes.

Bessie squints towards the hamlet of North Seaton, just ahead of them and says: "Is that somebody coming towards us, Sarah? They're up early, and maybe they haven't had breakfast yet. Let's see if we can make your load lighter, hinny."

The figure on the road ahead becomes clearer as woman and donkey near the hamlet. Bessie can now see it is a young man. He is wearing crumpled clothes, scuffed and dirty boots and is carrying something in a sling which hangs diagonally across his chest.

Bessie smiles at the young man and gestures towards the baskets on Sarah's back, filled with fresh fish and shellfish of all kinds.

"Do you want something?" she asks.

The young man stops and looks at her with a puzzled expression.

"Pardon?" he replies.

Moments earlier, Sammy had spotted two square shapes on the road ahead of him. As they got closer, he could see that the shape on the right was a donkey which looked square because of two baskets hung either side of it. The shape on the left was a woman of some sort, but that took longer to work out. Her shoulders were almost as wide as she was tall and the rolling swells of her substantial upper body were contained in a buttoned garment oiled and shiny from years of contact with herring, salmon and mackerel. From below that garment emerged an equally stained flannel skirt with a flood of folds and creases. The skirt hung straight down from her hips, which were as wide as her shoulders and her overall shape would have been square were it not for a perfectly circular, neckless face that emerged from those shoulders. The face was crowned with a pyramid of battered, skate-green oilskin that may once have been a sou'wester.

"Willicks? What are they?"

The woman reaches a fat, red, hand into the nearest basket on the donkey and pulls out a newspaper rolled into a cone. It is brim full of tiny shells, which Sammy recognises.

"Winkles," he says with satisfaction. "They're winkles. How much are they?"

"Ha'penny," the woman says.

Sammy has not yet had breakfast, and he remembers a day long ago when he ate, and enjoyed, winkles at the seafront in Blackpool. He'd gone there on the train from Bolton with his mother and Cilla while his dad was away fighting the Boers.

"Are they boiled?" he asks.

The woman nods and when she hands them over, Sammy can feel that the shells are still warm from the boiling pan.

He gives Bessie a halfpenny, and she hands him a pin.

As Sarah and Bessie plod away, Sammy picks up the first shell and flicks off the black cap that was once the creature's foot, before poking the pin inside and fishing out a curled slug of cooked flesh. It's slightly sweet, liver-tinged flavour takes him back to the seaside smells of Blackpool, the feel of the warm summer rain, and the sound of Cilla's laughter.

He is eating his fourth winkle before he starts to walk again. By then he has made a decision. He does have some good memories of home and family, which nobody and nothing should be allowed to spoil, certainly not his damaged dad. So he decides that he will entertain himself with some of those good memories for as long as this cone of 'willicks' lasts, and then he will move on to make some new good memories.

By the time he fishes out the last shell he has reached the seafront and is looking across the large crescent of sand that makes up Newbiggin beach.

At the south end of the bay is a natural archway in the cliff. The archway is a wall of rock jutting into the North Sea where centuries of wave power has worn through it like a giant 'angelwing', forming the arch known locally as the 'Needle's Eye'.

On rocks close to the Needle's Eye are two huge cast-iron boilers ringed by the rusting wreckage of the steamship Anglia, which came to grief in a raging storm here six years earlier.

Perched dramatically on the headland at the north end of the bay is ancient St Bartholomew's Church and littered along the beach between the church and the Needle's Eye are dozens of small boats. Some of them are the fat-bellied craft with no keels that Sammy learnt from Twizel Robinson are called cobles.

On the ill-fated journey to the Wansbeck Twizel had talked to Sammy about cobles with a passion that most men reserve for the love of their life, and just like some loves, these boats were also out of his reach.

"They're too expensive and too much for one man to handle on his own," he had told Sammy. "I would need to be a full-time fisherman to even think about having a coble, but they are lovely boats and perfect for Northumberland's beaches."

"How so?" Sammy asked.

"They've got a broad bow, just like the old Viking longboats, and no keel, so they are perfect for coming ashore on Northumberland's big, flat, beaches," Twizel had told him.

Standing in front of a terrace of red-brick houses

overlooking the bay, Sammy can now see what Twizel meant. He can see how the shallow draughts of these beautiful boats will be a big advantage on Newbiggin's gently shelving sandy beach.

Empty wheeled trailers are scattered along the length of the bay and Sammy guesses that they are there to help transport fishing boats from the water and over the sand. He watches other, bigger, boats going about their business offshore. They include colliers, coasters, trawlers, keelboats and the occasional steam-powered paddle-boat.

But one vessel stands apart from the rest. Sammy has never seen the like of this ship before. It is huge, three-masted, and has two large, circular platforms attached to either side of its bow. His young eyes are sharp, but this ship is too far out to sea for him to make out its name.

Further along the beach he sees a group of fishermen unloading one coble. They may have been fishing close to the ship with the platforms, so he decides to ask if they know anything about it.

The oldest man in the group has the most wrinkles that Sammy has ever seen on a single face. Each wrinkle seems to slope upwards from his eyes, brow, nose and mouth making it look as if his whole face is smiling. He wears a flat cap and has a brown-stained clay pipe poking from his toothless mouth.

"Excuse me," says Sammy. "Do you know anything about that funny-looking ship out there? The one with the platforms."

The old man studies Sammy carefully before answering. He takes a long draw from his pipe before tugging it out with a pop.

"That over there is the CS Faraday, and she is the future. Three months from now that ship will lay an electric cable four hundred miles long, from here to Arendal in Norway and, when it is done, people on either side of the North Sea will be able to talk to each other by telegraph. That is what she is, and that is what she does. Now, young Sammy, have you any more questions?"

Sammy is baffled and, for a moment, lost for words.

"Um, well, yes, there is something else that you can tell me. You can tell me how you know my name. Have we met?"

"Nope," says the man with a face full of grins. "But you are in Newbiggin now and in Newbiggin if a rat farts on the moor, we all get to hear of it."

The other fishermen burst out laughing and one of them says: "Tell him Jack, go on. Put him out of his misery."

"Well, it's like this," says the old man, fumbling in his jacket pocket and fishing out an ancient tobacco pouch.

"Oh no, Granddad," says the youngest of the fishermen. "Don't load your pipe, we haven't got all day. Just tell him the short version."

The old man looks annoyed and shoves the pouch back into his pocket.

He says to Sammy: "You helped Twizel yesterday when he had his bit of bother on the Wansbeck bar, didn't you?"

Sammy nods.

"Twizel told his missus what had happened when he got home, and his missus told the Mouth of the Wansbeck."

"Mouth of the Wansbeck?"

"That's what everybody calls her, the woman next door to Twizel and his lass. Davison is her name and gossip is her game."

"Oh."

"Anyway, Mrs Davison was at the Co-op getting her groceries last night, and that's all it takes. Everybody knew by this morning that a young lad called Sammy, from Bolton, who was wearing what you are wearing and carrying a sling over his chest, had been with Twizel when he hit the sandbar, and that lad got help for him."

The younger fisherman says: "I heard about it when I called for a pint at the Ship Inn. George Fenwick told me."

"And I was told about you by Tom and Ronnie Glenton, down at the allotment gardens," one of the other fishermen tells him.

Old Jack pokes Sammy in the chest with the bitten-down stem of his tatty pipe and says: "See what I mean about the rat's fart."

Sammy grins, nods and says: "In that case there can't be much crime in Newbiggin if everybody knows what everybody else is doing?"

"Oh, we do have crime sometimes," says one of the other fishermen. "You can find the young and the stupid even here. Last week one young lad snatched a woman's purse as she was leaving the post office. It took about ten minutes to find out who he was and half an hour to find him. He gave the money back and he won't be doing that again."

"How do you know?"

"The sea convinced him."

"What do you mean?"

"We left him at low water wearing anchor shoes. By the time the sea had reached his shirt he'd given up thievery - in Newbiggin at least."

Sammy nods, but can't work out whether this man is telling him the truth or a popular myth designed for outsiders with crime in mind.

He changes the subject instead.

"I'm feeling peckish, is there a food shop around here?"

The old man points his pipe towards the main street.

"Try the Co-op store around the corner. They'll sell you anything you want."

Three minutes later, Sammy is outside the store and sees it is a huge new building, designed to impress and attract customers. The same can be said for its staff, who also seem polished to a sparkling shine.

Sammy walks to the meat counter where he finds a man with blood on his hands and a straw boater on his head. He is wearing a blue and white striped apron and is squeezing meat into a hand-turned mincer. He looks up at Sammy.

"Mornin' young man. What can I do you for?"

"I don't know. I was just having a look around."

"Look around all you like and let me know when you've decided."

He stares at Sammy.

"I've not seen your face before, are you a blow in?

"A blow in?" Sammy says with a puzzled expression.

"Yes, somebody who's just blown in. A newcomer. Are you a newcomer?"

"Oh, I see what you mean. I'm more of a blow

through than a blow in. I'm going straight out again. I'm on my way to Ashington and I've just called in here to buy something to eat. This is a nice store, it looks brand new."

"We opened eight years ago and I'm not bragging when I say we've got the best store in these parts. See all the things on sale?"

Sammy nods.

"Well, you can see them because we have Belliwell's brilliant electric lights on the walls and ceiling. Out back we have a covered butchery department with hunger houses, pigsties, warehouses and storage units. Upstairs there's stabling for a dozen horses."

"Horses? Upstairs?" Sammy asks. "But what about the, er, the… Isn't there a smell?"

"That's the clever part. Just sniff, go on, sniff. Can you smell anything?"

Sammy shakes his head.

"That's because the floor above us is solid concrete. There's a ramp outside for the horses to walk up to their stables and a hopper system where their manure comes down, and all of it with no smells down here. Marvellous, don't you think?"

Sammy sniffs again and says: "That concrete floor isn't just keeping the smell out, it's keeping the sound out too. I can't hear anything of the horses up there."

A smile spreads across the butcher's face, but freezes when there is a loud 'crack' from above them. Shoppers in the store all stop what they are doing and become like the mannequins in the store's display windows.

Then, there is a second loud bang and suddenly the store is alive again. Shoppers dump their bags and baskets on the floor or counters and sprint for the entrance. Two of the young female assistants hitch up their skirts and slide over the counter to drop onto the other side and run with the rest of the women.

Puzzled, Sammy looks at the butcher for an explanation.

He says: "Cannons. It's the lifeboat cannons. Somebody's in trouble."

Sammy doesn't know what to do, but in case one more pair of hands can help, he hurries to the street outside. There, he sees women of all ages and sizes disappearing into alleyways that lead down to the beach.

He follows them and finds that many are running towards a building above a ramp leading down to the sand. As he nears the building, he reads a sign over its doors. The sign says 'Newbiggin Lifeboat Est. 1851'.

The building's double doors have already been pulled open and Sammy can see the lifeboat inside.

A handful of men in oilskins are scrambling into the 37ft long lifeboat Ada Lewis, which stands on a wheeled cradle. Those wheels are already turning as women at the back of the boat push it towards the open doors. Others, at the side and front of the Ada Lewis, lift ropes attached to the cradle and hoist them over their shoulders. Some women haul on the forward ropes as others grab ropes behind the boat and pull to stop it from rolling out of control down the steep ramp.

When it reaches the bottom of the slope and hits sand, all the haul ropes are taken to the bow of the lifeboat where the women bend forward in unison to take the strain. Their feet sink deep into the sand and the three-ton vessel inches forward as the rescue crew already on board begin preparations for the mission ahead.

It amazes Sammy to see that some of the women pulling with all their strength are quite elderly.

Progress over the beach to the water's edge is painfully slow, but every inch of the ropes has a woman's hand around it. All that the latecomers can do is put their shoulders to the boat cradle wheels, which are as tall as any of the women.

Sammy doesn't know what to do to help, but he feels he should do something, so he runs to the oldest woman he can find on the hauling rope and says: "I'll take that."

Her grip tightens and her eyes flash in anger.

"No you bloody won't. You're not a wife, you're not a mother, you're certainly not a daughter," she snaps. "It's *our* men out there and this is where *we* should be. Just get out of my way."

Other eyes flicker over Sammy and he knows their owners will all tell him the same.

Two men standing together on the beach look at Sammy and shake their heads, so he joins them to watch the women haul the lifeboat over the sand. When they reach the water's edge, they keep going.

Some women are now chest deep in the sea and the lifeboat is only just floating from its cradle.

Not all the women are in the water. A few have their backs to the sea and are staring up the beach towards the lifeboat house.

Sammy follows the direction of their gaze and sees two men running from inside the building. Both are pulling on cork-filled buoyancy aids as they run. They are carrying long, black sea boots and wearing thick socks.

When they reach the water's edge, two of the

women turn and the men jump onto their backs. The women carry them into the water and when they reach the stern of the lifeboat, the men are hauled on board by other crewmen. Moments later a deep-throated engine throbs into life and the rescue boat ploughs through the waves into deeper water.

Sammy turns to the man beside him.

"I don't understand. Why did they jump on those women's backs like that, and why did they carry the men to the boat? Couldn't they have just pulled on the sea boots they were carrying and waded out?"

"You are a stranger here, aren't you?" the man replies. "You must be, or you wouldn't ask a question like that."

Sammy nods.

"The women carry their men to the boat to keep them dry. Those women are wet, but as soon as they get home they can change and dry off. If their man gets wet wading out to the boat, he stays that way for the whole of the time he is at sea and who knows how long a rescue or a search is going to take."

"I see. Do you know which one this is, a rescue or a search?"

"It's a search, but I doubt that they will find anything. I was talking to Hunter Brown, over there. He raised the alarm, but he says there's not much chance they'll find anything."

"Why, what happened?"

"Nobody knows. They found Fair Lass, old Jack Carling's coble, a mile-and-a-half offshore. She was empty, with half a flight of pots in the water and half still in the boat. There was no sign of Jack or his son Phillip.

"Hunter and some others out there, searched for half

an hour before he came back in to get the lifeboat."

"What do you think happened to them?" Sammy asks him.

"Who knows? Jack and Phillip went out at early light to haul their pots. That's all we know for sure, apart from the fact that they are somewhere out there - drowned."

"How can you be sure they're drowned?"

"Because that's the only thing we can know for sure. Jack may have had a heart attack, fallen overboard and Phillip went in trying to reach him or Phillip could have stood on a pot rope and been dragged into the water, with the old man trying to hold on to him. They could have drowned in lots of ways, but drowned they surely are."

Sammy thinks back to his own recent experience of the North Sea and wonders: "If they both went overboard and couldn't get back into the boat, couldn't they swim back to land?"

The man shakes his head sympathetically at Sammy's ignorance of fishing life - and death.

"None of those lads swim," he explains. "They wear sea boots, oilskins, heavy clothes; they've got to, or they'll freeze. Even when the weather is nice, it's still cold at sea and they are out there for a long time.

"So if you're wearing all that gear and you go over the side, then what chance have you got? You can't kick the boots off and get out of all the other stuff. You don't have time for that. Even if you did, you'd last maybe ten minutes in the North Sea before the cold kills you. All of that means there's no point in learning to swim.

"If you go overboard, then you're a drowned man and that's a just fact of life on this coast. Everybody here knows it, and now so do you, lad. So do you."

He puts a hand on Sammy's shoulder briefly and turns to walk back towards the lifeboat house.

Sammy doesn't move. He continues looking over the flat, grey water of Newbiggin Bay and thinks back to the days when he was a toddler, crying over one upset or another. His mother would cuddle him and say: "There, there, Sammy, never mind. Worse things happen at sea."

I know what you mean now, Mother. I know what you mean.

STRANGER TOWN

TWO hours ago Sammy had sauntered into Newbiggin, pin-picking his way through a cone of shellfish with a strange local name.

He knew no-one, but didn't feel like a stranger. That was partly because some people already knew his name and others welcomed, even teased, him.

But that was before a father and son, woven into the living fabric of this place, were torn from it by the Old Grey Widowmaker and the day's catch is a haul of salt tears.

Sammy walks from the beach back to the main street. It is still full of people, but laughter and chatter are missing. Subdued shoppers go about their business with grave faces, or gather in small groups to talk quietly.

Now, Sammy feels like the stranger he is; adrift in this sea place without the anchor of its history or the safe berth of friends and family. He feels uncomfortably detached from the pain and loss all around him. All he can offer is sympathy, but sympathy seems such a small thing to weigh against the burden of grief.

He remembers the boy in the cave near Kirkby Stephen, the tortured screams of the poor lad's parents, his own sense of utter helplessness, and the shame of feeling a guilty relief that down in the darkness of the shake hole he was separated and shielded from their raw torment.

That same sense settles on Sammy now. He can do nothing to help or comfort anyone in Newbiggin, and his need to be anywhere but this bay of death is compelling.

Sammy finds his trail of discarded 'willick' shells and follows it back towards North Seaton Village. As he walks, his thoughts turn to Twizel Robinson - and gansies.

Before they had reached the mouth of the River Wansbeck Sammy wanted to know why, despite of all their exertions, Twizel still wore a thick, blue jumper.

"Aren't you hot in that jumper?" he asked.

"It's not a jumper, it's a gansey," Twizel told him.

"I've never heard that word before. What's a gansey?"

"Some people call them Jerseys, but we call them fishermen's gansies."

"Are they only worn by fishermen?"

"Yes."

"Why?"

"Two reasons. The first is that they turn water. They're made with such a tight knit that sea spray just bounces off them. The other reason is the pattern. See these?"

He pointed to his gansey and Sammy saw that its pattern looked like four vertical lengths of twisted rope, each an inch wide and two inches apart, with zig-zags filling the spaces between them.

"Every fishing village has its own gansey pattern, and this one says that I belong to Newbiggin. See the bottom of this 'rope' on the right? The other 'ropes' all look as if they have four strands, but this one ends in three strands. I always have my gansies knitted that way and what it means is that inside this gansey is Twizel Robinson."

Sammy opened his mouth to ask a question, but couldn't find the right words to phrase it delicately.

Twizel knew what was on Sammy's mind and answered the question without it being asked.

"Yes, lad, it's so that when they fish my drowned body out of the sea, whoever finds it will know I belong to Newbiggin, and when they bring me back, the people here will know who's door to knock on with the bad news. Sometimes it's the fish that make a meal of us instead of the other way around, so the gansey might be the only way to know who I am and where I belong."

When Sammy reaches the crossroads at North Seaton, he looks back towards Newbiggin and wonders how long it will be before the North Sea gives back the two fishermen - and their tell-tale gansies.

A fingerpost at the crossroads points Sammy towards Summerhouse Lonnen and he begins a mile-long walk along the tree-lined lane.

Twenty minutes later the trees, field hedges and fresh air give way to smoke, slag, noise, acrid smells, and the cause of them all - Woodhorn Colliery.

A steam train labours past a range of buildings made from locally fired yellow bricks. A huge spoil heap towers over the pit heapstead, where winding wheels turn slowly as men and materials travel between surface and shaft bottom.

Something is happening everywhere that Sammy looks. Chaldrons loaded with coal are moving in convoy along steel tracks, men are shovelling, shouting and swinging picks, ponies are being led into a low building, and through the wide-open doors of the pit forge Sammy sees sparks fly as hammers batter white hot metal into all kinds of pit tools.

Work, and plenty of it, he thinks with satisfaction.

But Sammy does not stop as he follows the path alongside the railway line. He wants to be at the heart of this industry and, from what he discovered in Durham and from Dobson Arkle, that heart lies in Ashington, a further two miles away. He keeps walking.

George Fenwick had not stretched the truth when he talked about how extravagant Ashington's Grand Hotel was. Now that Sammy is looking at the Grand, he can see for himself that Mr Gillender had spared no expense in creating the first public building for the town's flourishing Hirst area, 16 years ago.

Sammy gives up counting the hotel's windows when he gets to 50. He can see at least four doors giving access to different parts of the building and observes that the corner towers of this extravagant edifice are each embellished with a tall, spired roof.

As he walks towards the Grand Hotel, Sammy passes a construction site on the opposite side of the road. A chalkboard hanging from wooden scaffolding proudly announces, 'Coming next year - The Wallaw, a brand new Walter Lawther picture palace for Ashington'.

The name rings a bell with Sammy and he fishes a piece of paper from his sling. It is the note handed to him in Barnard Castle by the Bean twins, Leopold and Matthew.

He'd glanced through the list of names on the note when it was handed to him, but now he reads it more carefully. The first name on the list of people who might help him is Walter Lawther. Leo told Sammy that Walter Lawther is an ambitious entertainment entrepreneur, well connected in the town.

Other names on the list include two landladies who don't overcharge their lodgers, and the final entry on the list says: 'Also try Ashington Miners Hall. Too many names to mention here, just ask anyone at the hall and they will help'.

Further along the road from the Wallaw site is a group of men, all wearing dark clothes and flat caps. Most are crammed onto a wooden bench. Others lean on a wooden fence beside it, and one man is propped against a street gas lamp.

Sammy approaches him and asks: "Excuse me. I'm looking for Ashington Miners Hall. Is it this way?"

The man turns his head, but continues leaning against the lamp-post.

"The Miners Theatre?" he says.

"No, the Miners Hall," Sammy answers.

"You don't look like a miner to me, you're too tall for a start," says lamp-post man. He turns to the others and asks: "Singer or juggler?"

"Not a singer," says one man on the seat. "Not with a pinched chest like that."

"Not a juggler either. Look at the way he moves," says a man leaning against the fence. "It's all he can do to keep himself up, never mind half a dozen balls."

"A comic?" says a third.

"Nah. Look at that face, who would laugh at that?" says the lamp-post man.

Sammy is about to say he can think of a clown with an even more morbid face than his own when one of the others on the seat says: "Healer! That's it. You'll be that curative magnetism bloke, aren't you?"

Sammy has never heard of curative magnetism and is about to say so when he has a better idea.

"Nearly right. He's my father and I'm taking his stuff to the Miners Hall. So the first one to tell me where it is can have a free treatment."

There is a moment of silence, and then three raised arms point along the street.

"Over the Station Bridge," says one man.

"Past the Harmonic Hall," says another.

"Miners Theatre is next to the Catholic Church," says the third.

Sammy resists the urge to say again that he is looking for a meeting hall, not a theatre and says, instead: "Enough, three of you are all I can manage, I don't have magnets to do any more than three, so it will have to be you three on the bench."

Sammy takes off his sling and lays it along their legs.

"I keep the curative magnets in here, but they work just as well through the cloth as they do when I take them out."

The three laugh and look at each other as Sammy crouches down to look hard at the sling, then into their eyes.

"You will feel a weight on your legs," he says, glad that he had filled the water jug from a standpipe on his way past Woodhorn Colliery, before returning it to the sling.

"The magnetism will slowly relax your leg muscles so that the magnet bag will feel as if it is getting heavier. It won't really get heavier, but because your muscles are relaxing, it will feel that way. Can you feel your legs relaxing yet?"

The three shake their heads, but their smiles are less

self-assured than they were a moment ago.

"You will shortly. Just wait."

"I can," says one. "I think. Not much, but yes, it's definitely getting heavier."

"I think I can too," says the second, and the third nods silently.

"That's good," says Sammy. "If your muscles are relaxing, then the next thing you will feel is that your legs are getting slightly warmer."

"Yes, my legs are definitely warmer where the magnets are lying."

"Mine too."

"And mine."

Sammy offers a silent *thank you* to Wally The Wall-Eyed Hypnotist for his tips on manipulating an audience and continues.

"What happens next is that the magnetism will travel through your body in waves, find your weak spots and energise them. If you have no weak spots, then it will just make you feel generally better."

All three are now being watched expectantly by the rest of the group. With all eyes focused on them each of the three nods slowly as they look at Sammy.

"You shouldn't keep the magnets on for too long when you use them for the first time, so I will to take them off now," he says. "When I do that, your legs will feel cooler than they are now, but that's normal."

He retrieves his sling and backs away as the rest of the group crowds around the three with a barrage of questions.

There is no doubt about it; this place is definitely bustling, Sammy thinks as he walks along Ashington's unmade main street.

Women push prams in and out of shops, street hawkers shout their wares, coal trucks and delivery wagons pass by. All kinds of horse-drawn carts vie with pedestrians, cyclists and the odd motor vehicle, for road space. The smaller vehicles weave around gently steaming heaps of horse-droppings. Others behave as if they aren't even there and plough on through them.

Over the railway bridge that separates the Hirst area from the older part of town, known as Ashington Colliery, Sammy sees ahead of him a long street of shops. Above each shop is a flat and at the end of the street there is an ornate stone construction of some sort.

When he reaches it Sammy discovers the stone structure is a Boer War Memorial, erected eight years earlier, outside a building called 'Harmonic Hall'. At its base is a water fountain and above that are four stone columns supporting a square stone block with a clock built into it. Sammy can see that the time is just approaching 3pm.

He takes a drink from the water fountain before crossing the main road and walking towards a red-brick police station, built 13 years ago, according to the date carved below its roofline pediment. The police station stands on a corner with the side entrance to its magistrates' court facing a huge, buttressed building made from the same red bricks as the police station.

When Sammy crosses the road that separates the two buildings he sees a large, wooden notice board. The bold, gold letters on the notice tell him he is standing outside St Aidan's Roman Catholic Church.

Next to the church is a building with two names. One of the names curving across the top of the three-storey building, reads 'ASHINGTON MINERS HALL'. At ground level there is an entrance with four wide steps leading up to three double doors. Above these doors, in large letters is the second name.

This one says 'MINERS THEATRE'.

Eoin Cafferty has just launched into one of his interminable tales about his beloved Ireland when Sammy walks into the Miners Hall, and Eoin is not a man to interrupt.

"So, there we were, out Lough Caragh way and I was wanting some news," he tells two bored-looking men standing either side of Eoin's roll-top desk. Eoin tilts back on two legs of his chair and, against all odds, keeps his balance with the help of outstretched arms.

"You know how I like the newspapers, and not just for the horses either," he continues. "Anyway, I hadn't seen a newspaper for five days and I was feeling the need. So when I saw this post office I thought, oho, they will have the papers here, so I asked the lady behind the counter.

"Have you the papers, Missus? I says. 'Yes', she says. Good I says. Have you got the Irish Times? 'That I do,' she says. 'Would you like yesterday's Irish Times or today's?' I'll have today's, thank you, I says, and with an absolutely straight face, she tells me 'Well now, you'll have to come back tomorrow for that'."

Sammy is the only one to laugh, and the Irishman seems to notice him for the first time.

"You like my story, do you?"

"I did. Is it true?"

Eoin Cafferty looks genuinely shocked and his chair drops back onto all four of its legs.

"Yes, of course it's true. Every word of it, with not the slightest embellishment. I am Irish, I'll have you know, and who has ever heard of an Irishman blarney-ing?"

Now the other two men in the room laugh. Sammy opens his mouth, then snaps it shut.

Eoin smiles and points at Sammy.

"It's a clever lad that knows when to open and when to shut his mouth and a cleverer one who can do both at once, so you're in my good books already. What can I do for you young fellow?"

"I'm looking for work in the pits and this seems like a sensible place to start. I know that you don't do the recruiting here, but you might point me in the right direction."

Eoin shrugs his shoulders and turns both hands palm up.

"Maybe so, but what kind of work are you looking for? Have you any experience of mine work?"

"No, but I am young and I am fit and I can turn my hand to anything."

The Irishman rubs his chin thoughtfully.

"That's as may be, but what have you done most recently, say in the last month?"

Sammy rubs his own chin as if he is thinking too and then takes a deep breath.

"Well, in the last month I have worked as an apprentice flying shuttle maker at a foundry, I've invented metal polish, learnt shorthand, shovelled shit, helped a stage hypnotist, searched underground for a dead boy, dug graves, invented a game, been a gamblers' look-out, sold newspapers, transported explosives, fished for lobsters and nearly drowned."

Now it is Eoin's turn to laugh, which he does loud and long.

"You'll do boy, that you will," he says, wiping tears from his eyes with his shirt cuff. "If I was you I'd have a word with one of the under-managers first. I'll give you a couple of names to try. Ask for them at the pit offices."

"Where will I find the pit offices?" Sammy asks, still smiling.

Eoin hands him the note and says: "When you leave here turn left and keep walking until you come to the Portland Hotel. Once you get there, turn right. That road will take you straight to the pit."

As he scribbles names on a piece of paper Sammy asks another question.

"I'm not from around here and I don't know anyone at the pit. Will that be a problem? Is this a place where who you know is more important than what you know?"

"I wouldn't worry about that, young fellow. This is a stranger town."

"What do you mean?"

"I mean that we are all incomers here. Just over fifty years ago there were no pits in Ashington. Only a handful of people lived here, and they worked the land, mostly for the Duke of Portland, who owns it. Then railways, steamships and factories came along and they all needed coal.

"People have known for a long time that the land here is full of coal, but there was no big demand for it until steam machines arrived. Coal suddenly became black gold and people like the Duke had a brand new way to get richer, by letting coal companies dig down into their land. But to do that, the coal companies needed people to do the digging for them.

"The hope of work and money drew people from

everywhere to Ashington, and some of the first were from Ireland. That's why Murphys, Gallaghers, O'Kanes, and, of course, Caffreys, are among the oldest names in this young town.

"People from tin mine towns in the south-west joined them. New names, like Penhaligan, Trevithick, Cadwallender and Tremayne, arrived in Ashington. As the need for more workers grew, more people came down from the Border country and across from Cumberland so we got even more new names, like Grahams, Bells, Dixons, Charltons and Robsons. And, of course, they came from Scotland, so we've got McThis and Macthat, by the dozen. God alone knows what the people of Ashington will sound like in a hundred years, when all those accents have melted together."

Eoin stretches his arms expansively and gazes around his domain.

"So, here they came, and they are still coming, from all corners of this country. They may be looking for work, they may be looking for hope, they may be looking for a home and they are all strangers when they get here."

He leans closer to Sammy and lowers his voice conspiratorially.

"But I will tell you this, my friend, they are not strangers for long. Pits have a way of weeding out people who can't get on with each other. That type never lasts long here and those who remain are the sort who can work together, drink together, play together and settle arguments and upsets between themselves."

Sammy is so used to making his own decisions, going his own way, and not working in a team, that he wonders whether he has made the right decision to come to this place. But there is only one way to find out.

He walks as far as the Portland Hotel and turns right into an avenue leading to the colliery.

A coal-blackened man with stark white eyes, points to a grubby building when Sammy asks for directions to the colliery office.

When he opens the office door, Sammy finds he is in a queue. Three women are ahead of him, all wearing floral aprons and with thin, knotted scarves on their heads.

The women are talking quietly.

"They'll not be long now. The buzzer has gone," says one.

"That clock over there says it is half-past three. He should be out by now," her worried-looking friend replies.

"That's pit time," says the third woman. "It's always ten minutes ahead of real time to make sure the men get in early enough."

The worried woman is not reassured. "I wonder if they'll be all right?" she asks the others. "They do say the first day is always the hardest."

"They'll be fine Missus," says a man's voice from an open window in an office wall.

"The deputy's looking after them and I have told him that you are waiting here to collect your boys."

"Here they are," the first woman waves through a window that looks onto the pit yard.

The office door opens, and a man enters, followed by three coal-coated children. The boys are about 12 or 13 years old. All three are weary-eyed and dragging behind them bags meant for their shoulders.

Tears leave a trail in the dirt on one youngster's cheek.

"I'm tired Mam," he sobs.

"He's soft as clarts," says one of the other boys.

The third is silent, his eyes white and wide.

Two of the women crouch down and two of the boys climb onto their backs.

The third pushes her son ahead of her and says: "You're a man now Johnny, so you can walk back home."

As they leave, Sammy turns to the open hatch and asks for the under-manager by name.

From the other side of the hatch a gravel voice says: "Wait there."

PIT WORK

"JOB?" the big man shouts, and Sammy thinks he's going to be thrown out of the office for having the temerity to seek work at this pit. But he is wrong.

"Of course you can have a job. Anybody can have a job here. You can have one if you are bright, you can have one if you are dim. You can be fit or lame, big or small, loud or quiet, none of that matters."

He lifts his left thumb in front of Sammy's face and extends the forefinger next to it.

"There are only two things you can't be; one is late, and the other is a lass. We stopped letting lasses down pits nearly seventy years ago. Mind you, women will soon be counting cash and keeping records in the pit offices, if they get their way - and then where will we be? No more keeping back our beer money if it's wives and daughters who put the cash into our pay packets."

Sammy thinks of a certain redhead who would give this old fossil a run for *his* money if she was here, but he entertains that thought for too long.

Frank Mason sees the glazed look in the lad's eyes and tells him: "Yes, we've even got a place for those whose minds are adrift. We usually put them in the stables where they can spend their shifts talking to the pit ponies."

Sammy forces his mind back into focus.

"Sorry Mr Mason, I was trying to think where I

would fit in best."

"That depends on whether you like digging, drilling, blasting, pumping, sorting stones, plotting, planning, managing materials, managing men, running a pit or being the boss of your own coal company. It's all possible, and it's up to you how far you go."

"I plan to go as far as my body and my brain will take me, so when can I start?"

Frank Mason laughs. "Well, the back shift has just gone down, so you're too late to go with them. Come back tomorrow. Be here at eight in the morning and you can go down with the dayshift men."

He lifts a piece of paper and a pen from his desk and says: "What's your name, son?"

"Sammy Kiteland."

"And what is your address?"

"I don't have one. I've just arrived."

"Arrived from where?"

"I started out in Bolton more than three weeks ago and it's taken that long for me to walk here."

"WALK! You've walked here?" Frank shakes his head. "You must be keen."

"No, just desperate."

Frank stops writing for a moment and looks at Sammy for an explanation.

"I had no home, no money, no prospects so, yes, I was desperate, but something has changed over the last three weeks. I still don't have a home or money, but I don't feel desperate anymore, I've seen too much on my way up here to feel sorry for myself, and I've learned that whatever I come across I can cope with it."

Frank keeps his gaze on Sammy's face for a moment, but says nothing. He looks back down at the paper and signs it with a flourish before handing it to Sammy.

"This has two names and addresses on it. The first is Tom Mavin, who's a tailor for the Co-op. You'll need work clothes and he keeps some ready-made stuff at home. You'll find him at Portland Terrace, beside the Portland Hotel. When you get there show him that note. I've signed it so he knows the money you owe will be taken from your wages at the end of the week.

"The other name is Selina Dawson. Selina lives in Albert Street and she's a widow woman who takes in boarders. I've known her for a while, so tell her that I have sent you. Her son works at Woodhorn Pit and so did her husband until just over a year ago when a stone fell on him underground. His mates lifted the stone and brought him out. But he didn't live long enough to see daylight again."

"Where is Albert Street?" Sammy asks.

"Go into town and when you find the railway bridge walk down its steps to the path beside the track. Follow that path south and when you get to North Seaton Station ask anybody for directions. Victoria Terrace and Albert Street are just beside the railway crossing."

When Tom Mavin answers the knock at his door in Portland Terrace he sees a worn, but usable, navy jacket, a pair of sorry-looking mismatched navy trousers, and a collarless cotton shirt that has seen better days. Then he notices that the young man inside them is holding out a piece of paper. Tom takes it and reads the message from Frank Mason.

He turns and walks back into his house without comment, but leaves the front door open. Sammy waits and a few minutes later Tom returns with a paper package in his hands.

"It's all there, work jacket, flannel shirt, fustian pants and pit socks. Do you want a midge as well?"

"A what?"

He holds up a tin device which Sammy recognises as a carbide gas lamp.

"Yes, thanks, I'll need one."

He puts the 'midge' on top of the package and hands it to Sammy.

"Make sure that you're back here on payday with the cash."

The door closes on Sammy, who stands unmoving for a few seconds before it occurs to him that the transaction is over.

A passenger train pulls into North Seaton Station and a dozen people disembark. Sammy reaches the level crossing next to the station at the same time and asks a man pushing a bicycle from the station platform for directions.

"Albert Street?" the man says. "See that cut?" He points to the other side of the road. "Go down there, towards the isolation hospital and you'll see Victoria Terrace and Albert Street on your left."

Many of the houses in the long terrace that is Albert Street have wooden boards attached to their walls and chalked on most of them are numbers. Some have the number seven and others the number three. But one board is different. This one has letters as well as numbers, and the letters above the numbers seven and three, spell the words 'BOARDING ROOMS'.

As he opens the backyard gate Sammy briefly wonders whether this landlady will be loud, or small, theatrical, or full of eel tales. He is wrong on all counts.

The lady who opens the door to him is only an inch

or two shorter than Sammy, has raven-black hair and a face still waiting for its first wrinkle. She looks as if she is in her late-20s, but has to be older. Her eyes are friendly, but have a weary look to them.

"I'm looking for a room and Frank Mason sent me here," says Sammy.

"Fetch yourself in then," she says with an accent that has a hint of the Scottish Highlands about it.

"I'll show you the room in a minute, but would you like a cup of tea first?"

As they drink the tea, Mrs Dawson listens to Sammy's tale, then tells him hers.

In a soft, sad voice she says she lost her husband, Jim, 15 months ago.

"Jim used to be a fisherman at Newbiggin. He worked a coble with his brothers, but they thought there was more money in pit work and wanted to sell the boat. Jim decided that fishing was a fine enough way for a bachelor to make money, but too unreliable for a man with a wife and a son to look after, so he followed his brothers into the mines. Eighteen months later he was dead. His brothers dug him out and our son, Edward, helped them to carry his dad's body away from the coal face.

"Edward still works at Woodhorn Pit. He's got to; he's the man of the house now. He's only fourteen and on a boy's pay, but I help as much as I can by taking in boarders, so we manage - just."

The kitchen door bursts open and two young men tumble in, laughing and tussling for possession of a newspaper rolled into a ball.

"GOAL", yells the younger of the two. "My goal!"

"Never," laughs his rival. "That was offside by a

mile."

"Offside? How can you have offside when there's just one man on each team?"

"Them's the rules," says the older youth.

"What rules?"

His rival appears to be thinking.

"Queensbury, the Marquis of Queensbury's rules," he says with confidence.

"That's boxing," says the other.

"Well, you were fighting for possession, weren't you?"

The younger boy looks at Sammy, rolls his eyes and shrugs his shoulders.

"Sammy," says Mrs Dawson. "This is my son Edward, and this is John, who is boarding here."

Sammy smiles and nods at the other two. John nods back, but Edward seems more interested in his mother.

"What are we eating tonight, Mam?"

"I thought I'd boil up a pan of mussels," she answers.

"Great," her son says. "I love mussels."

"All you have to do is fetch them from the river."

She grins and Sammy notices that this lady doesn't even have crow's feet when she smiles.

Her son looks as if he is about to protest, but thinks better of it.

"I'll get the stuff," he says.

Mrs Dawson turns to Sammy. "Why don't you go too? You're going to be living under the same roof, so the sooner you three get to know each other the better."

A few minutes later all three walk from Albert Street towards the rail crossing and a path on the other side of it which leads down a bank to the River Wansbeck.

When they get to the water's edge they walk towards a huge timber trestle bridge that carries the Blyth and Tyne Railway line over the Wansbeck.

Further upriver, beyond the bridge, Sammy can see a road leading to a shallow crossing point where a series of tall wooden stakes are driven into the river bed.

"Is that the stake ford?" he asks.

"Yes it is," Edward replies. "I thought you said you haven't been here before?"

"I haven't, but I can read minds, and when you looked at that crossing you thought 'stake ford'.

"Guess," says Edward. "Just a lucky guess."

"Okay then, let's try something else," says Sammy. Now that he knows where he is, he decides to have some fun with his new companions.

"Look around us and find something to concentrate on. What about the house we've just walked past?" Edward looks back along the path that they have just walked down. A large, white house stands alone at the top of the road.

"Don't speak. Just look at that house and think about it," Sammy tells him, placing a finger on Edward's forehead.

"Aha, you're thinking about medicine bottles and a man with a stethoscope. Could it be a doctor?"

Edward's eyes widen and his mouth opens.

"Say nothing," Sammy orders, as he recalls the Ship Inn and being told that Twizel Robinson had been stitched by a doctor in a white house beside the stake ford. "Just think. I want to go deeper. Let me see if I can find a name. Ah. There it is. Evers, Dr Evers. You were thinking about Dr Evers, who lives in that house."

"You're right. I was," Edward tells him, amazed. "How did you do that?"

"I'll tell you one day, but not just now, you've got supper to catch."

Edward hesitates for a moment then shakes his head and bends to open the sack they had carried to the river bank. He pulls out a battered old canister with the name Castrol in worn lettering on it.

"What are you going to do with that," Sammy asks.

"Dad made this years ago. I need it to get the mussels. Come on, I'll show you."

Edward carries the canister, and the Hessian sack it had been inside, to the water's edge where he and John both remove their boots and trousers.

For a moment, Sammy is puzzled, but as they both wade into the water he understands and does the same.

When they are waist deep in the water Edward points towards the bridge footings.

"There are some old bedsteads and bicycles in there and that's what we are looking for. That's why I need this."

He holds up the oil can. Its base has been cut away and replaced with a sheet of glass, held in place with putty.

Edward pokes the can into the water, unscrews the cap over its pouring hole and peers into it. He sweeps the can from side to side as he walks towards the bridge and soon shouts: "Here!"

Sammy and John wade towards Edward who passes the viewing can to John.

"There's a good few around the bicycle handlebars," John says, handing the can to Sammy.

Peering into the pour hole is like being under the

water. Sammy can see everything so clearly. There are his feet, looking pale, with clouds of silt rising between his toes. There's a flash of something white, but whatever it is moves so quickly that Sammy can't tell whether he has just seen a fish or an eel.

He sweeps the can from side to side and eventually sees something poking out of the silt. It may be part of a bicycle or bedstead, but he can't tell because a mass of mussel shells cover it, looking like leaves on an ossified plant.

Sammy wants to look longer at this fascinating underwater world, but Edward takes the viewing can from him and pushes the sack into his hands.

"Hold this open while we collect the mussels," he tells Sammy.

By the time they have finished, the bag is bulging and, once they are wearing their trousers and boots again, they take turns to carry it back to the boarding house.

A huge pan of water is already boiling on the range when they arrive, and Mrs Dawson takes charge of the sack.

"I'll pour them onto the newspaper on the floor and you lot can sort them. Sammy, have you done this before?"

Sammy shakes his head.

"Well, you simply drop them into the water once you have sorted them. The main thing to remember is that if any of the shells are open, they can't go in the pan; they have to be thrown away. If they're open that means the mussel is already dead and eating it could give you the gut ache."

Sammy turns back to the shells, carefully picking

out the few that are already open. He wants to be absolutely sure that he doesn't turn up for his first day of pit work with 'the gut ache'.

PUMPED UP

SAMMY leaps out of his bed ready to tackle the burglar, but can't find him. He scans the room slowly, observing a marble wash stand on cast iron legs, the bed he has just jumped from, and the still-sleeping figure of his fellow boarder, John. But no burglar.

Yet something definitely startled Sammy awake. A noise? Yes, that's it. He'd heard a loud rapping from the direction of the window. Sammy hurries to the window and sees that it is not cracked or broken. But, just beyond the pane, something is moving and it looks menacing.

"John," Sammy shouts. "Wake up. Somebody is trying to break the window with a long pole."

John does not open his eyes.

"It's the caller," he mumbles.

"Who's the caller?" Sammy wants to know.

"Did you see the chalk boards outside the houses in this street?"

"Yes."

"What numbers were on the one outside here?"

"Seven and three."

"Right, that means you and Edward are on the day shift, so the caller comes and knocks on the window at seven. I am on the back shift today, so he'll come back at three o'clock and knock on the door for me. Now let me get back to sleep."

Sammy and Edward are about to leave for work when Mrs Dawson says: "Aren't those the same boots you came here in, Sammy? Don't you have any pit boots?"

Sammy shakes his head.

She reaches into a wooden box beside the fireplace and pulls out a pair of polished pit boots.

"You can borrow these until you get some of your own. They look to be about your size. They're my husband's, so look after them. Here, you might as well take his pit hat too."

She hands Sammy a leather helmet.

"You'd best put that straight on," says Edward. "It'll keep you safe if the Bait Bandit tries to crack your skull."

"I've told you before, Edward. There's no such thing as the Bait Bandit," his mother says with a sigh. "It's just the old miners telling tall tales to scare the younger ones."

Edward shakes his head defiantly and insists: "Yes there is a Bait Bandit. Tommy Bell told me. He said Will Farnham's brother's friend was hit over the head and had his bait bag pinched while he was waiting for the bus, and he had nothing to eat or drink for his whole shift."

"Don't worry, Mrs Dawson," Sammy tells her with a wink. "We'll stick together until we get to the town centre. The Bait Bandit wouldn't dare tackle two of us, and once we are on the main street there'll be plenty of others for Edward to walk with to Woodhorn."

Sammy quickly slides off his 'dead hero' boots and pulls on the dead Mr Dawson's pit boots. They are a better fit than he expected. They also have lines of metal studs in the soles and segs in the heels.

For part of the route Sammy and Edward take to work their feet clatter in unison on paving stones. It is a strange and unfamiliar sound to Sammy at first, but then they reach the main street and join hordes of other workmen, all rapping the same pavement tattoo with their studded boots. Sammy turns left to head for Ashington Pit and Edward turns right to go to Woodhorn.

The clattering from all the pit boots heralds the start of the working day for Sammy's shift of pit workers. Some of the younger pit lads run to a part of the street where the paving slabs incorporate fragments of flint and they skid across the surface to send showers of sparks flying from their feet.

At the pit, Sammy walks through the office doorway just as Frank Mason emerges from a side room.

"Right lad; I'm starting you out on datal work. That means you'll work wherever you are needed and be paid one shilling and sixpence at the end of each day. You'll have every Sunday off and one other day every fortnight. Once you prove to me that you're a good worker you'll get a chance to move to better paid jobs. I've put you under Alex Jobson today, he's a master shifter and he'll tell you what he wants you to do."

The under-manager opens the office door and shouts at a man passing by.

"Arthur. Come here a minute."

A small, bald man walks to the door and is told: "This lad is just starting today. Take him to Alex Jobson, would you?"

The man doesn't reply. He just looks at Sammy and jerks his head as an invitation to follow him.

When they reach a group of shuffling miners, Arthur

walks into the middle of them and looks at a man carrying a safety lamp.

"Yours," he says, and jerks his head towards Sammy before walking away.

"Are you Mr Jobson?" Sammy asks.

"It's Alex, son, and you must be Sammy."

"I am."

"Right, we're all here now, so let's get down."

The trip in the cage to the shaft bottom is like nothing Sammy has known before. It starts with a stomach churning jerk and he soon feels as if he is falling to the bottom of this pit rather than being lowered.

Then he starts to feel heavier and realises that the sensation is an illusion brought on by the cage slowing its rate of descent. It reaches the bottom of the 600ft deep shaft with a clunk and the wire mesh cage door clanks open.

The other miners, who all know where they are going and what to do, disappear into the darkness of a tunnel to their right, leaving Sammy, Alex and another man outside the cage.

The master shifter points towards some machinery in a low tunnel to their left.

"Right Sammy, this is what I want you to do. See that tunnel over there?"

Sammy nods.

"The pump house is about a hundred yards down there. I want you to go with John here. He's the fitter in charge of keeping the roadway and the coalface dry. Do exactly what John tells you to do, but remember that he lads don't like working wet and the boss doesn't like paying them extra for working wet. It's is up to you and John to keep everybody dry and happy."

When they reach the pumping station John lifts his carbide lamp towards a lever.

"See that?"

"Yes, what is it?"

"That's the pump switch. Turn it on and the pump sucks water away from the work way and dumps it in the standage area over there."

He points towards an area to their left beyond the reach of light from their lamps.

"Switch the pump on for five minutes in every 30. Got that?"

"Yes, but..?"

"But what?"

"How will I know when the time is up?"

"You can count, can't you? Just count the seconds until five minutes have passed, then switch it off. I've got my watch and I'll be back before the 30 minutes are up."

"Where are you going?"

"The most important part of this job is to make sure that the pipe doesn't block or come out of the standage hole, so that's what I'll be doing. Throw the switch now - and start counting."

Sammy watches the fitter walk into the darkness. The flicker from John's carbide lamp dances in the velvet blackness and vanishes completely when he turns a corner.

With only the throb of the pump to keep him company Sammy counts aloud: "One second, two seconds, three seconds..."

He reaches 60 seconds, picks up a stone from the ground and counts from one second again. Eventually, he has four stones in his hand.

"…57 seconds, 58 seconds, 59 seconds, 60 seconds."
He drops the stones and turns the pump off.

The silence that follows takes him by surprise. He feels as if he has been suddenly struck deaf, so he taps his lamp against the pump. The dull 'clunk' that follows is strangely reassuring, but other sounds from the darkness all around him are not.

There is a faint scuffling, followed by a squeak. Sammy can see that John's tool bag, made from a piece of rubber conveyor belt held together with pit rivets, is hanging from a nail over the pump. He decides that is a good idea and lifts his own sling from the ground, away from things that squeak. He hooks it on the nail alongside John's bag.

The scrabbling of small creatures is bad enough, but the other sounds are worse. Creaks, clicks and groans all around him tell of coal and stones shifting, wooden supports bending and pit props straining. Then the noises that don't exist creep into Sammy's imagination. Is that the sound of a child's voice? Are those footsteps nearby? Is that the faint roar of the North Sea overhead?

It could be the roll of waves on a shore, Sammy thinks. There is a definite rhythm to it, and that is not his imagination. But it isn't coming from above him. It is coming from the direction of the standage where John had gone.

Sammy shouts: "John" and is answered with a snort and a cough and the 'sea surge' rhythm of John's snoring stops.

"Aye, lad. Everything's fine at my end. How's it at yours?"

"Fine here, John, but is the 30 minutes up yet?"

"Just a minute while I check. Aye, time's just about done, so you can fire her up again."

Sammy throws the switch and discovers he is grateful to hear the sound of something that is real and mechanical."

By the end of the shift the late afternoon sky is pumped full of gloomy clouds, yet Sammy still has to shade his eyes as he steps from the cage into daylight and heads for the office to collect his day's pay.

On the office wall is a noticeboard with an assortment of papers pinned to it. Some notices are handwritten and offer items for sale, others are invitations to social events at halls and workingmen's clubs in the town.

Sammy still has the night ahead of him and doesn't care to spend it waist deep in the Wansbeck again or staring at a bedroom wall, so he inspects the contents of the noticeboard carefully.

One notice advertises a talk at the town's Weslyan Reform Church by temperance firebrand Rev Ironside Seabrook, and he has called it 'Drinking in Satan's Citadel - Are Ashington's Workingmen's Clubs Its Road To Ruin?'

Think I'll give that one a miss, Sammy decides.

Another notice informs him that The Great Doo-Fell, 'Seaside entertainer extraordinaire' and 'Fresh from Blackpool' will be at Newbiggin Sea Front on Saturday 30th July from 2pm.

But the one that really catches his interest is an invitation to an event taking place tonight at Ashington's Grand Street Workingman's Club.

The note says: 'Literary and Debating Society meeting. Subject - The Truth About Coal Miners'.

GRAND STREET

IT IS ONLY eight years since the first pints were pulled from the Grand Street Workingmen's Club's beer pumps. But the tobacco smoked by its coughing customers has already redecorated every public room in the building to precisely the same shade of nicotine brown.

A thick, blue haze fills the club's upstairs meeting room when Sammy walks into it. At the far end of the room is a table, which faces five rows of chairs, most of them occupied. Sammy spots one of the few that are empty and quickly sits on it.

Seated beside him is an old man holding a clasp knife. The blade of the knife looks lethal after being worn into the shape of a miniature scimitar by years of sharpening on an oilstone.

The old man ignores Sammy as he sits down. His attention is focussed totally on his hands as he expertly shaves strands from a plug of tobacco in an 'Uncle Jeff Twist' wrapper. The shavings drop into the man's palm until he has all that he needs. He folds the knife and pokes it into his shabby waistcoat pocket, along with the remaining tobacco in the wrapper.

The man's attention returns to his hands as they follow a familiar ritual. The edge of his right hand slides up between each finger of his left hand to displace any crumbs of tobacco lodged there. Then, he places right hand over left and rubs, gently, rhythmically. When the hands eventually part, the strands of tobacco have been rolled into the shape of a rugby ball.

Satisfied with the look of what he sees, the man fishes a pipe from his waistcoat pocket, sticks it between his lips and gives two quick puffs to clear out any old ash. Holding the pipe between his teeth he pokes the fresh plug of tobacco into the scorched bowl and tamps it down with his dark-brown forefinger.

From another pocket he fishes out a box of Swan Vestas matches, strikes one and holds it over the pipe bowl. He sucks so hard on the pipe stem that the match flame turns upside down setting alight the tobacco in the bowl. The flame flips twice more between exhaled clouds of thick, sweet-smelling smoke.

The expanding cloud around this man brings tears to Sammy's eyes before it floats up to the room's high ceiling to play its part in the gradual process of nicotine redecoration. Only then does the man turn to Sammy.

"Oh, sorry son, I didn't see you there. Did my smoke get in your eyes?"

Sammy tries to say "yes", but can only cough.

"Never mind, you'll get used to it," says the pipe man.

Other people in the room are also coughing, but from a different irritation.

Two of the three seats behind the speaker's table are empty and in the third is an embarrassed-looking man.

He gets to his feet.

"Gentlemen."

A disgruntled murmur ripples through the room.

"As you know, we had booked Professor Harold

Abramski from Ruskin Hall, at Oxford University, to give us the talk he calls 'The Truth About Coal Miners'. He should have arrived half an hour ago, but there is no sign of him yet and no explanation for his absence, so we have a choice. We can go downstairs and have a few pints or, given that this is a literary and debating society, we could talk about books and philosophy while we wait for Professor Abramski."

"Pint for me," says one man, getting up. Three others follow him, but the rest remain seated, including Sammy.

"Fine," says the man at the table. "What shall we talk about then? Remember, the theme for tonight is the truth about coal miners."

People in the audience turn and look at each other, but no-one speaks.

"How about this," says the man at the table. "When I was younger, we often played a game at home where we had to take something out of our pocket and talk about it for five minutes. We are all coal miners here, so why don't we each pull one thing from a pocket and tell the truth about why it is there? Would that do?"

The old man next to Sammy reaches into his coat pocket and holds up his clasp knife. Others follow and raise into the air objects ranging from books to hip flasks, photographs to coloured handkerchiefs. Sammy finds in his pocket the note that Professor Arkle wrote for him on the banks of the Tyne. He unfolds the note and reads the pencilled message.

It says:

> To whom it may concern, the bearer of this note, Sammy Kiteland, has helped me unselfishly

with a task requiring resourceful-
ness, courage and determination.
Should you be in need of someone
who possesses these qualities, he
comes with my full endorsement.
Desmond Arkle, Professor of
Chemistry, Armstrong College of
Physical Science.
23rd June 1910.

Sammy raises his hand, with the note in it, and looks around. He can only see one man whose arm is not raised, but there may be more.

"Tommy," the chairman says to a man in a tweed coat. "What's that you've got?"

"It's my membership card for this club."

"And what truth does that tell us about coal miners?"

"The truth it tells is nobody gets between a miner and his beer. Not even old Ironside Seabrook and his temperance gang"

Some in the room laugh, but Tommy doesn't smile.

"It's no joke," he says. "Remember before the work-ingmen's clubs started up? We had to pay through the nose for our ale from the Portland Hotel at first and then the Grand when that opened. As for the White Ele-phant, well, we were stone cold sober by the time we trekked all the way home from there.

"Worse still was the swankey beer the gypsies sold by the bucket. We had to be really desperate to buy that stuff.

"We didn't have the money to build our own pub or to pay for lawyers to fight for a drinks license, so we were stuffed. At least, we were stuffed, until one of us came up with the idea of key clubs."

This is all new to Sammy, so he pays close attention as Tommy tells his tale, with the help of others in the audience who support or contradict what he says. What Sammy learns is that groups of miners had banded together to raise enough money to rent several properties in Ashington. Every person who contributed to the rental was given a key to 'their' property. Each 'key club' was furnished with chairs, tables - and beer.

No laws were broken, because the beer was not being sold, it was being 'supplied' to the property's lawful occupants to consume in their own, locked, premises.

"So we found a way around the profiteers and the lawmakers," says Tommy. "That's what happens when you get between a miner and his beer."

He sits down to laughter and applause from the rest of the audience.

The chairman holds up his hands, and the noise abates.

"Who is next? Dick Thompson, how about you? What's that in your hand?"

"It's today's North Mail."

"And how does that bosses' rag tell us the truth about miners?"

"By going on fire," Dick tells him. "When we had the last strike and coal was running low, I worked out how to turn these into paper logs."

"How did you manage that, Dick?" a voice shouts from the back of the room.

"Well, I'll tell you," he says. "I found that if I put a load of papers into a bucket full of water and left them overnight, it turned them into a wet mush. I got a drain-pipe, packed the mush into it and used a ramrod to squeeze the water out of it. Then I pushed the paper out of the drainpipe and left it to dry. When all that was done I had a rock-hard block which burned as slow, and nearly as hot, as coal. I might even seek a patent for it if I can get the money together."

"Take a tip from me," says the chairman. "Try to find somebody who will back your idea with their cash. It's always better to lose somebody else's money than your own."

Dick nods in agreement and sits down.

"Right then, let's have something literary now. Isaac Wright, what's that book you are holding up?"

A man in his thirties stands and holds aloft a pocket-sized book in a brown cover.

"You all know me, and you all know I love my books. I take a different one with me down the pit every day just so that some of you can joke that I'll be blind by the time I'm forty because I read by carbide light.

"But since we are telling the truth about miners, I'll tell you a truth about me. I'm not married, and I can't see that I ever will be because, for one thing, I don't have the spare time, and for another, what woman would put up with a man who spends all of his money on books and all of his time reading them.

"In fact, I'm like Odysseus, because Naussica is the only woman for me and, like Odysseus, I'll only ever be able to dream about her."

The other men in the room look puzzled, but say nothing.

Isaac continues: "I counted up the other day and in the room I use at my parents' place there are exactly one thousand eight hundred and seventy four books."

A gravel voice from the audience shouts: "Get on with it Isaac, what's that one in your hand?"

"It is a translation of Thucydides' 'History of the Peloponnesian War'. I'm doing a Workers Educational Society night class on it."

The puzzled looks remain for all but Sammy. He is thinking of Durham's Framwellgate Bridge and a philosopher in ragged trousers waiting for a debate.

Maybe it is time this debating society got to know about Sammy Kiteland, he thinks.

"Thucydides knew nothing," Sammy ventures.

Eyes in the room turn on this young stranger.

Isaac feels a literary, and possibly a philosophical, debate coming on.

"I beg to differ," he says. "'History of the Peloponnesian War' is a masterpiece."

"Go on son, you tell him," gravel voice urges Sammy, with a laugh.

"Come on then," Isaac says with a smile. "This is a debating society so let's have a debate. I said Thucydides' account is widely accepted a masterpiece. So tell us why do you think it isn't?"

Sammy is confident that although his knowledge is limited, his memory is sharp.

"Well, for a start, what are his sources?"

"What do you mean? His sources were his own eyes and ears. He wrote about a time as he was living through it. What better sources could he have had?"

In his mind, Sammy is replaying the debate he witnessed on Framwellgate Bridge and he repeats Professor 'Twigman's' riposte word for word.

"But he didn't see it all with his own eyes. He was

in exile for twenty years. At the very least, his information had to be second hand, possibly third hand."

Isaac makes a move to open the book in his hand and check his facts, but thinks better of it in case he looks unsure of his argument.

"He's on the ropes. Go for it lad," gravel voice chips in.

"Not at all," says Isaac. "Thucydides was the first great historian; his work results from meticulous research, combining personal experience and pedantic questioning of other eyewitnesses."

Isaac is proud of that word 'pedantic', since he rarely gets a chance to use it down Ashington pit.

But Sammy grabs the chance to deliver his punch line.

"This so-called history is second-hand, at best, and maybe even third-hand, because Thucydides picked up all his information by listening to gossip in bars and brothels."

Sammy says it with a straight face, but the rest of the room explodes into laughter at the mention of bars and brothels.

Isaac tries to speak, but can't make himself heard among the hoots and jeers.

Sammy waits for Isaac's response, knowing he has fired his best shot and depleted his stock of quips. Professor 'Twigman' had left his argument with the ragged-trousered philosopher hanging in the air when he marched off to show the students his Macedonian battle pike.

But before either Isaac or Sammy can say another word, a man walks to the table at the front of the meeting room. Sammy recognises him as the person who made no attempt to take anything from his pocket at the start of the debate.

The chairman raises his hands again and slowly lowers them.

"Gentlemen, gentlemen, let's have best order if you please and allow me to introduce Professor Harold Abramski, of Oxford University."

There is an instant hush as the professor smiles and says: "I'd like to thank you all for coming to my exposition on the truth about miners. I hope you all enjoyed it."

The men in the audience are looking bemused, so the professor continues: "What we have seen tonight is that miners are resourceful when they need to outflank authority, inventive when they are up against a challenge and, finally, that they always stand up for what they believe in.

"Your chairman and I arranged this little experiment to demonstrate in a practical way what I would otherwise have told you in my usual bone dry academic fashion. I hope that you will forgive us and let me thank all of you who engaged in this demonstration, particularly our erudite combatants in the Peloponnesian War."

He looks at Sammy.

"By the way, young man, I see that you plucked a piece of notepaper from your pocket at the start of this evening's event. Satisfy my curiosity about it, would you? Is it, by chance, a billet doux from a girlfriend? Were you about to tell us about a true romance?"

"No," Sammy replies. "It's a note from an important man. I thought at first it was to tell an employer about me. But, after reading it again, I think he was actually trying to tell *me* something about myself."

"Did he say you were resourceful?"

"Yes."

"Determined?"

"Yes."

"Inventive?"

"Yes."

"What is your name?"

"Sammy Kiteland."

"Well then, I would say your note has introduced you to the real Sammy Kiteland, the Sammy Kiteland who is in the right place, at the right time, with the right qualities.

"This young town still has a long way to go. As, I suspect, do you, young Mr Kiteland."

The clapping begins slowly and builds into solid applause.

EPILOGUE

THREE years ago, in that hot month of June 1910, Sammy Kiteland discovered he had endurance and determination when he made the walk from Lancashire to Northumberland. Since then, he has built up a bank of skills and experience working underground, and also found that, in this town of strangers, he is a stranger no more.

It is November 30, 1913, and Bart Goonan says: "Pass me that shot box, Sammy. I need to load up for tomorrow."

Sammy reaches under the table in Bart's front room and places a solid metal box in front of the old man. He attends closely to Bart's every move, because Sammy's future - and, some day, maybe his life - could depend upon what he sees now.

Although Sammy has learnt much about mining since he arrived from Bolton, he has yet to be shown how to handle and deploy explosives. But now he is looking for a better paid job at the Betty Pit in Ellington village, two miles north of Ashington, and working with blasting powder will be part of that job.

The race to dig down to Betty's rich, untapped coal seams began a year before Sammy arrived in Ashington and now, four years later, the first of the pit's huge reserves of high quality coal are being brought to the surface.

For men with determination, and the right skills, Betty Pit offers the promise of opportunity and reward. Sammy wants to be one of those men.

Bart Goonan is the longest surviving, and therefore the best, shot-firer at Ashington's Duke Pit, so it is to Bart that Sammy has turned to discover the art and science of blowing up without being blown up.

Bart takes a page from yesterday's Daily Mirror newspaper and cuts it into a triangle with a pair of razor sharp scissors.

"I want half a dozen exactly like that," he tells Sammy, pushing the scissors towards him.

Sammy watches Bart walk to a cupboard beside the fireplace at his colliery house in Seventh Row.

Above the cupboard door is a smaller door which he opens. Bart reaches inside and pulls out a wooden box which he carries to the table. Stencilled on the box in white lettering is the word EXPLOSIVES and when he lifts its lid Sammy can see that the box is half-full of black, loose-grained blasting powder.

"Pass me the broomshank now," Bart tells Sammy. After putting the broomshank into Bart's hands, Sammy watches him wrap a triangle of newspaper around the top, leaving an inch of paper loose at the end.

Bart doubles over the loose end of the newspaper triangle, then flips the shank upside down and beats it hard on the cement floor. When he slides the newspaper tube off the broomshank one end is sealed tight.

Bart carefully spoons loose gunpowder from the box into the open end of the tube and compacts it before picking up a wooden rule and checking the height of the powder - or at least, trying to.

"What does that say Sammy? The numbers on this ruler look like they are dancing around to these old eyes of mine."

Sammy checks and says: "Three-and-one-quarter inch."

"Put another spoonful in. It should be three-and-a-half exactly."

Sammy spoons the precise amount into the tube and Bart seals the open end before laying the finished shot carefully against three others in the metal shot box on his kitchen table.

He picks up another triangle of Daily Mirror, but instead of wrapping it around the broomshank he squints at it.

"I didn't know that!" Bart exclaims.

"Know what?"

"That our Duke of Portland has shot an Austrian prince - Archduke Franz Ferdinand, it says here."

"No? Is that right, Bart?"

"Yes, it's here in the paper, look."

Sammy reads the story and shakes his head.

"That's not what it says, Bart. It says the Archduke was almost shot by one of Portland's men."

"Well, that's what I said, apart from the 'almost' bit."

Sammy shakes his head and says: "Leave your powder for a minute, Bart, and listen to me. I'll tell you what this article actually says."

Bart smiles and waits.

"What it says here is that William Cavendish Bentinck, the Sixth Duke of Portland, invited Archduke Ferdinand and his wife, Sophie, Duchess of Hohenberg, to his place at Welbeck Abbey, near Worksop, for a week of pheasant shooting."

Bart nods and Sammy continues: "They were out on the last day, to a covert called Gleadthorpe, when a loader slipped in the snow after loading a gun and both barrels were discharged in the direction of the Archduke and the Duke of Portland.

"Now, this is the important bit, Bart. The Daily Mirror says here, in black and white, that the shots passed within a few inches of the Archduke and the Duke, but missed both men. It was a close thing, I'll grant you that much, Bart, but I'll say it again. Both shots missed."

"So what," says the old shot-firer, with a shrug of his shoulders?

"What do you mean by 'So what'?"

"Well, there's no shortage of European aristocrats is there? They breed like rabbits over there. Europe has all kinds of royals and titled toffs. So what difference would it make if the world had one archduke less tomorrow than it does today?"

Bart taps Sammy's chest with his powder blackened pointing finger.

"I'll tell you this for nothing, Sammy, and mark my words. It wouldn't make a scrap of difference to your life, or to mine, if that Archduke Franz Whatshisname had been killed in Worksop, or anywhere else, for that matter. Not a scrap. That's what.

"Not a scrap."

****

ACKNOWLEDGEMENTS

My wife, Hazel, for her encouragement and support in bringing this story to life Also my daughter Lisa, for her advice and expertise in helping me to deliver this tale, and my son David for his impeccable memory for events that I had long forgotten.

I also had invaluable help from supportive friends, Lillian, Sexton, Mark Dixon, Pam Ingoe, Mary McDowell, Ian McDowell, Morag Hindson, Peter Taylor, Will Hawley and Tony Strudwick.

My gratitude goes to Pat Farnham and Michael Craigs, who happily shared their tales of North Seaton and knowledge of pit work.

But most of all, thanks to my grandfather Sammy Gledhill who sat down with me and my brand new Phillips cassette tape recorder in the late 1960s and told me his story.

He explained how he was deserted by his dad and left homeless on the day of his sister's wedding, and of watching Revered Popplewell from the steps of Bolton Town Hall, two weeks later, before deciding to walk to Northumberland and find work in a coal mine.

His tale gave me the bones of this story.

Imagination and the British Newspaper Library provided the flesh for those bones.

Vince Gledhill 2019

SOURCES

BOOKS

Bentinck, William Cavendish, 6th Duke of Portland, **Men, Women and Things**

Charlton, Cissie, with Vince Gledhill, **Cissie**

Kell, Bill, **Best Scotch or Ordinary**

Kirkup, Mike, **The Biggest Mining Village in the World**

Leslie, Jack, **Opening Time, The Origins of Clubs and Pubs in Ashington**

Neville, David, **To Make Their Mark**

Pitman, Isaac, **Phonographic Reporter**

NEWSPAPERS

Birmingham Gazette and Express
Bradford Daily Telegraph
Brighton Gazette
Durham County Advertiser
Lincolnshire Echo
Morpeth Herald and Reporter
Northern Daily Mail
Northern Daily Telegraph
Northern Echo
Somerset and West of England Advertiser
Sunderland Daily Echo
The Athletic News
The Berwick Advertiser
The Derby Daily Telegraph
The Derby Journal
The Evening Telegraph

The Huddersfield Chronicle
The Illustrated Police News
The Isle of Man Times and General Advertiser
The Lancashire Daily Post
The Leeds Times
The Manchester Courier
The Mercury
The North Eastern Daily Gazette
The Scotsman
The Shields Daily News
The Stage
The Walsall Advertiser
The Wigan Observer and District Advertiser
The Yorkshire Evening Post
The Yorkshire Post and Leeds Examiner
West of England Advertiser
Yorkshire Gazette

HOME OFFICE REPORT

Circumstances attending an Explosion which occurred at Washington "Glebe" Colliery, in the County of Durham, on the 20th February, 1908.

ARTICLE

Hooppell, R. E. (1887). "Vinovia". Journal of the British Archaeological Association.

Printed in Poland
by Amazon Fulfillment
Poland Sp. z o.o., Wrocław

52384387R00263